1·2·16

KT-558-368

Books should be returned or renewed by the last
date above. Renew by phone **03000 41 31 31** or
online *www.kent.gov.uk/libs*

Libraries Registration & Archives

CUSTOMER
SERVICE
EXCELLENCE

CSE

Kent
County
Council
kent.gov.uk

LAUREN CHILD

YOUR POISON

HarperCollins *Children's Books*

First published in hardback in Great Britain by HarperCollins Children's Books 2015
HarperCollins Children's Books is a division of HarperCollins Publishers Ltd
1 London Bridge Street, London SE1 9GF

For Ruby Redfort games, puzzles, videos and more, visit:
www.rubyredfort.com

*Visit Lauren Child at **www.milkmonitor.com***

1

Copyright © Lauren Child 2015

Series design by David Mackintosh
Illustrations © David Mackintosh 2015

ISBN: 978-0-00-733426-1

Printed and bound in the UK by
Clays Ltd, St Ives Plc

For **Louis**

The queen looked out from her window and down upon Snow White.

Gazing at the girl's raven-black hair and flawless skin made the queen sad.

"How good she is, how well loved," she hissed, plucking up a rosy red apple. Turning it in her hand, the queen caught sight of her image in its perfect polished skin. "Is there a person who loathes her other than I?" Letting out a cry of rage she brought the apple to her lips, opened her mouth and sank her teeth into its white flesh.

A perfect storm

WAY OUT TO THE NORTHEAST OF THE CITY WERE THE
FLATLANDS, acre upon acre of prairie grass that waved in the
warm winds blowing in from the ocean.

The girl was taking the long road to her grandmother's ranch
house. She imagined it would take her no more than an hour, so
she would still be in good time; she had promised to be there by
noon. The weather station had warned of an electrical storm and
dark clouds were already forming in the great skies above her.

The girl had tried to coax her dog, a young husky pup, to
travel with her in her bicycle basket, but the dog had looked up at
the sky and howled when she tried to carry him from the house,
his fur standing right on end.

It was as if he knew what was coming. There had been talk
of a tornado looking to bear down and she had a mind to see
it begin to pick up before it whirled in. Timing, she knew, was
everything when it came to tornadoes. They could whip up
quick and vanish in minutes, the average for these parts being
around twenty. You had to be careful – you mistime it and you

might be snatched up inside that wind funnel, for you could not outrun a tornado, only sidestep it; this her nine-year-old self knew for a certainty.

She hadn't travelled more than halfway there when she realised she had left it too late. Turn back, keep going, it didn't matter – she was never going to make it to the ranch before the storm struck. A lone tree grew out from the only raised piece of land in more than a hundred miles, a tree bent sideways by the relentless west wind and the only landmark on the whole horizon other than the marching telegraph poles.

But it was a good landmark. She remembered how the tree grew out of rock, not a cave exactly but a pile of stones so heavy that they looked like they hadn't moved in more than ten thousand years. The girl saw at once that if she could make it to those rocks and climb between them then she would escape the tornado's hold.

She let go of her bike and abandoned it right there, where it fell, on the tarmac road. She began to run across the open grassland, feeling the whipping wind as she fled. She ran, ran like the devil himself were chasing her, ran like all hell was biting at her ankles. The coarse grass was slurring her movement, wrapping about her legs, but she wouldn't let it pull her down. There were the rocks and the half cave. She threw herself in just as the whirling funnel picked up over her head, and through the crack in the stone she saw her little green bicycle hooked up by the finger of wind and pulled high into its centre.

She didn't notice the hissing thing: the wind drowned out its sound. Nor did she notice it raise its head and open its jaws wide, exposing those perfectly sharp prongs of teeth. She felt it though: a sharp pain followed by a sickening ache. A strange sensation.

She turned to look it in the eyes. Black eyes set in an arrow-shaped head, dark diamonds running down its brown back. She looked at it, unblinking, as it slowly wound itself back into the shadows.

Suddenly everything became hyper real, the strange crag of the rocks, one jutting stone looking almost like a dog's head – she thought of her husky and wished he was at her side. She tried to steady her breathing and reached for the notebook and pencil she had tucked inside her pocket. She drew the head shape and the markings, making a note of the colours, and once she was sure she had all the information, she removed the sneaker from her left foot followed by her striped sock, cutting away the toe part with her penknife. Then she pushed her arm into the tube of knitted cotton and slipped it over the wound, not too tight but enough to support her deadening limb.

Slowly she began to move herself towards the road, keeping her arm down so that the bite wound was below her heart.

Looking behind her she saw the tree was gone, carried away by the tornado.

The farmer who drove by in his truck an hour later was surprised to see this young girl stumbling down the road on her own.

The doctor on duty in the local hospital was astonished when upon arrival she produced a notebook containing a perfect drawing of a Western Rattlesnake.

'That's... what... bit me,' she said, her arm badly swollen by now and her voice losing its strength.

'Smart of you, noting everything down like that,' he said as he injected the antivenom. 'Rattler venom can kill in two hours. If we'd wasted any time trying to identify the species, well...'

Which was why from that day on Ruby Redfort resolved to know every snake by the pattern of its skin – such knowledge might just save your life.

An ordinary kid

WHEN RUBY WAS TEN her father was due to take part in a tasting for the Olivarian Society, so called because in order to become a member of this esteemed club one had to blind taste twelve different types of olive, identifying the variety and the region in which they grew.

For reasons to do with bad weather in Boston, Sabina Redfort had failed to make her Twinford flight and was stranded at the east coast airport. Mrs Digby the housekeeper was on annual leave, Brant Redfort refused to leave his daughter home alone and his daughter refused to have a sitter. Therefore it was decided that Ruby would have to accompany her father to the club on Fuldecker Avenue, a grand old-fashioned building with plenty of carved wood and marble. It being highly irregular to bring a child to the club, Ruby was taken to the small club office, where she might read and wait out the two hours until her father was ready to go home.

Brant Redfort was blindfolded and led to a table on which twelve olive dishes were then placed. There were three olives that Brant Redfort found very difficult to place, but he filled in what he could and, once finished, his completed papers along with the olives were returned to the club office.

Ruby, who was fond of olives, had been his home-study partner and now had a very keen palette and a wide appreciation of olives from all regions. She decided therefore to take the test herself and, finding her father's answers to be good but not great (considering the time he had given to this pursuit he should really have excelled), she amended his test sheet accordingly.

She detected every herb and every spice, and almost every variety of olive: young, old, barrelled in oak, pickled in sea brine, from the western slopes of Mount Etna and from the northern coast of Corfu.

Brant Redfort was declared a worthy Olivarian and was sworn into the club with a hearty cheer, and Ruby was able to get back to her book.

Some several years later...

Chapter 1.
Wrong place wrong time

WHEN RUBY REDFORT AROSE THAT MORNING, she could not have foreseen what kind of day it was going to turn out to be.

She certainly hadn't meant to find herself running for all she was worth down the Amster back alleys, nor had she pictured how grateful she would be to see that dumpster in front of the Five Aces Poker Bar. It just happened that way. Sometimes things unfold in a way you could never predict.

RULE 1: YOU CAN NEVER BE COMPLETELY SURE WHAT MIGHT HAPPEN NEXT.

Actually, at the moment when she left the house, Ruby was expecting her Saturday to be entirely peaceful. Expecting and hoping. She hadn't been sleeping well recently, and she wasn't exactly feeling sharp. She was planning to nod hello to Ray Penny as she entered his secondhand bookshop; if the mood grabbed her she might even ask after his dog, Jake, who was recovering at the vets having poisoned himself by eating an entire bar of chocolate. Then she would browse the shelves for a good thriller and sit down to read. She didn't feel like too much human interaction today.

True to the weather report, the wind was really beginning to take a hold, and as she headed down Cedarwood Drive her usually tidy dark hair was yanked free from its barrette and was now wildly wrapping across her face and over her glasses, making it very hard to see.

The 'gusters', as Twinford folk referred to them, had been blowing for the past fortnight, ever since the night of the Scarlet Pagoda Film Festival, an evening Ruby would never forget, for although it was not the first time she had fallen from a tall building, it was the first time she had been pushed from the top of one.

The building in question had been the Hotel Circus Grande and the pusher had been thief and psychopath Lorelei von Leyden. Ruby had not been the target, she had just been in the wrong place at the wrong time and, now Lorelei was incarcerated in a maximum security jail awaiting trial, Ruby could sleep more easily. Ruby felt Lorelei was one of those people who just might bear a grudge.

As she turned the corner into Main, Ruby spotted Del Lasco striding out of the recently opened Slush Store, her left hand gripping a blue ice drink, her right hand, newly sprained, in a sling and her face wearing a sour expression. Ordinarily Ruby would have been pretty pleased to see Del but on this particular afternoon she sensed something was brewing. Eleven seconds later and this feeling of foreboding was confirmed as Del and

Ruby's Junior High nemesis, Vapona Begwell, marched out of the store followed by several of her cronies. It was obvious to even the casual observer that Vapona wasn't about to ask Del the time of day.

'You wanna say that again, Lasco?' Vapona shouted. 'I didn't quite catch it.'

'You heard me, Bugwart,' said Del.

'So say it to my face, if you dare.'

'If you'd point me in the direction of your face, I'd be glad to,' replied Del.

Vapona didn't wait for another insult, nor did she try and extract an apology, she just clenched her fist and aimed to sock Del right slam in the mouth, only Del, who was used to kids taking a swing at her, ducked and Vapona found her fist making contact with friend and sidekick Gemma Melamare, and it was Gemma's dainty little snub nose that took the hit.

The sound that came out of Melamare's mouth made everyone freeze in their tracks; everyone but Ruby. She took the opportunity to yank Del by the hood of her sweatshirt and propel her right across the road towards the back alleys off Amster. Vapona's gang, spellbound by what had just happened, took a minute to realise Del Lasco had left the scene.

'Hey! Come back here Lasco, you chicken liver.'

'Run!' shouted Ruby.

Del let go of the blue slushy and she ran. They both did.

They fled down the back of the minimart and along the alley

that joined Maize, over the street (car brakes screeching and horns honking) and on through the next two alleyways, across Maple, across Larch, across Fortune, and beyond, heading east to the busy road that was Crocker with all its countless seedy bars and secondhand shops filled with nothing you would ever want to buy.

They could hear Bugwart and her pals not so far behind, their voices yelling out across the fenced passageways. They kept running; only trouble was, there was nowhere to hide, no more back alleys on Crocker, just a long wide strip of flat road and bars, pawnbrokers and gambling outlets, nowhere for a kid to blend. When they reached the Five Aces Poker Bar, Ruby realised they were in trouble. Bugwart wasn't giving up and though Ruby, using the parkour skills that Hitch had taught her, could now easily climb a low-rise and sprint across the roofs, Del with her sprained hand and lack of parkour skills could not.

Which was how come they ended up scrambling into the Five Aces dumpster and pulling down the lid.

Undignified for sure, but as the old saying went, beggars really can't be so choosy and (if you wanted another one) any port in a storm.

Or, as Ruby's **RULE 73** had it: **SOMETIMES YOU JUST HAVE TO WORK WITH WHAT YOU'VE GOT**.

Unsurprisingly, it wasn't a nice place to hang out, and Ruby was at that moment regretting her decision to leave the tranquility of her bedroom and venture out into the big bad world.

They could hear Vapona talking to her gang.

'Where did they go?'

'Beats me.'

'They just disappeared!'

Thump.

Vapona slammed her fist on the dumpster.

'We lost em.' She sounded pretty angry about it. 'When I find Lasco, I'm gonna pulp her!' To illustrate this intention, Vapona thumped the dumpster again, this time so hard that Ruby felt the thud vibrate through her.

The two of them listened to Vapona's gang's footsteps as they receded back towards Amster, their dread threats becoming less and less audible until only the thrum of passing cars could be heard.

Twenty minutes later – Ruby wasn't taking any chances – they struggled out like earwigs emerging from debris.

They brushed themselves down, Del picking a fish head out from Ruby's hooded top, Ruby peeling chewing gum from Del's jeans, then they shook hands.

'Congratulations Lasco, you're alive,' said Ruby.

'But I smell like I died,' said Del, sniffing the air. She looked at Ruby. 'Your glasses look wonky.'

'That's the least of my problems,' said Ruby. 'Listen, nice bumping into you and all but I think I gotta take a shower,' she called as she strode off towards home. The garbage smell was making her nauseous and she needed to clean up before the stench knocked her out.

'Thanks for your assistance anyway,' called Del.

'No problem,' shouted Ruby, breaking into a run. She felt this day could surely only get better, that was until the wind blew her hair over her eyes and – vision impaired – she collided with a parking meter.

Winded, she sat down for a moment on the sidewalk.

A banana skin fell from her sleeve.

It had to be said, this was not the kind of day she'd expected.

Chapter 2.
News travels fast

AS RUBY STUMBLED IN THROUGH THE KITCHEN DOOR, Greg Whitney's voice jingled out of the radio:

'SO THOSE WINDS LOOK LIKE THEY REALLY MIGHT HIT HARD.'

'YOU GOT THAT RIGHT,' replied Shelly the weather girl. **'THEY ARE REALLY BEGINNING TO WHIP UP AND IT WON'T BE LONG BEFORE TWINFORD CITY EXPERIENCES SOME VIOLENT STORMS.'**

'RAIN TOO, SHELLY?'

'YOU CAN COUNT ON IT, GREG!'

Mrs Digby put down her apple peeler and planted her hands on her hips. The dishevelled state of Ruby was one thing; the smell of her a whole lot worse.

'Child, have you been crouching in a garbage can by any chance?'

Ruby opened her mouth to explain but the housekeeper put up her hands.

'Before you make up a whole bundle of untruths, I might as

well tell you that Mr Chester saw you climbing out of a dumpster and he didn't wait more than a minute before dialling up my number and spreading the good news.'

Ruby rolled her eyes.

'The man is a virtual loudhailer of other people's business,' said Mrs Digby, 'if you can call crouching in a garbage can "business".' She tutted. 'Not that it would have escaped my keen eye that you look like something the cat dragged in but, that said, whatever you have been up to, and for whatever reason you thought it necessary, one thing's not up for discussion: you need to take a bath.'

Ruby sniffed the air. 'Yeah, it was sorta rancid in there.'

'I thought you were lying low today?' said the housekeeper.

'I was trying to, and then I bumped into Del Lasco.'

'Say no more,' said Mrs Digby. 'That child will have you banged up in the Big House before you can say, "call my lawyer".'

Ruby went upstairs to her room, set the shower running and scrubbed the dumpster dirt out of her pores. She sprayed herself with a large waft of Wild Rose scent and put on some clean clothes – a pair of jeans, striped socks and a T-shirt. Like most of her T-shirts, it said something, this one bearing the words: *I've heard it all before*. She put on her glasses and could immediately see that there was a problem. The fall into the dumpster had bent them out of shape and the left arm no longer made contact with her left ear, so the glasses now sat at a strange angle. Since right at that moment she had no idea where she had put her spares, she would have to resort to her contact lenses: without either option, life was a total blur.

Once that was taken care of, she took a book from the bookcase and sat down to read.

Ruby owned a lot of books, ranging across all subjects. She read for every reason: inspiration, information and escape. If she valued any of her books above the others, perhaps the ones she would single out would be her code books. After all, it was her interest in codes that had landed her a job at Spectrum, an organisation so secret it was hard to know who actually controlled it, and who it was actually working for. All Ruby really understood was that the agency was on the side of good, a fact she had taken at face value when LB, her boss and head of Spectrum 8, had told her so.

Along with the job came her own personal minder and protector, a field agent who went by the name of Hitch and who disguised his true purpose by acting as the Redfort family household manager (or *butler*, as Ruby's mother preferred it). He could have fooled anyone, and *did* fool *everyone*. To the outside world Hitch was one of those enviable assets – a manager who ensured one's domestic life was pressed and ironed, and anything *you* forgot *he* was sure to remember.

Yet he *also* possessed skills most domestic managers lacked. These included scaling buildings, leaping from rooftops and the odd karate chop when required. He wasn't bad in a crisis either: should you need to board a plane when it was already taxiing down the runway, Hitch was your man. To Ruby's mom he was the best darned butler this side of the hemisphere; to Ruby he was a mentor, bodyguard, loyal ally and at times royal pain in the derrière.

The volume Ruby was engrossed in today, however, was neither codebook, textbook, nor true-life story. Today she was reading to relax her brain, a totally necessary pursuit if one wanted to find the answer to something one just couldn't grasp.

RULE 6: SOMETIMES NOT THINKING ABOUT A PROBLEM IS THE BEST WAY TO FIND THE SOLUTION.

And there was a pretty big question that needed answering: what in tarnation was going on in Twinford? Ruby had worked four cases now for Spectrum, and all of them had been resolved, more or less.

But there was something still nagging at her. A sense that those cases were *connected* somehow, in some way she couldn't grasp.

She hadn't got a long way through *Kung Fu Martians* when one of her many phones began to ring. She had a good collection of telephones by now, having become interested in them when she was just five years old: every shape, every design, from a bar of soap to a squirrel in a tuxedo.

She reached for the donut and flipped it open.

'Twinford Garbage Disposal, we depend on your trash.'

'Ruby?'

'Oh, hey Del.'

'Look, thanks a load Rube, I owe you one, man.'

'Don't mention it,' said Ruby. 'I mean, who hasn't jumped into a dumpster to prevent a friend being socked in the kisser?'

'Most people,' said Del. 'Anyway, the thing is, all I'm saying is I appreciate it.'

'Any time,' said Ruby. 'Don't think me rude, but I oughta get back to reading my comic book; I'm trying to figure something out here.'

'Go figure,' said Del.

Del hung up and Ruby went back to her reading until the next interruption, which came from the ACA Insurance Company.

'Hello ma'am, how are you today, my name's Doris, I'm calling from the ACA Insurance Company and I would like to invite you to take out an ACA life insurance policy with ACA Life Insurance at half the cost of our usual policy and if you join us today right now over the phone I can throw in an alarm clock radio and a free watch, worth a grand total of fifteen dollars and ninety-nine cents.'

'Well, thank you for the offer Doris,' said Ruby, 'and as good as that sounds, I regret to say I am only thirteen years old and have no dependents depending on my income and no income to speak of, a perfectly good alarm clock radio and a better than ordinary wristwatch, besides which I do not plan to die just yet.'

'Oh, sorry dear, might I speak to your mother?'

'She too has a wristwatch and no plans to die.'

'None of us *plan* to die, dear.'

'Believe me, my mom's not dying, she looks half her age and eats muesli for breakfast – thank you for your call.'

Ruby replaced the phone and resumed her reading, but three minutes later she was interrupted again. This time by Mrs Lemon.

'Oh Ruby, I'm so glad I caught you, I was just wondering, I mean *hoping to goodness*, that you might be able to watch baby Archie tomorrow?'

This was not a call Ruby wanted to take, and just how Elaine Lemon had got hold of her private number was a mystery and something she would be taking up with her mother when she came back from wherever she was.

'Well, jeez Elaine, it's good of you to think of me but I am up to my eyeballs right now.'

'Up to your eyeballs in what?' asked Elaine.

'This and that,' said Ruby. 'I got the girl scouts and band practice and cheerleading, not to mention the Christmas pageant.'

'Really? Aren't you a little old for Christmas pageants?'

'Never too old to join in, Elaine, and I'm a joiner.'

'It would seem so. My, they do begin these Christmas rehearsals early these days, it's not even October,' said Mrs Lemon. 'Well, Ruby, if you are too busy then I won't press you and I must applaud your get-involved spirit.'

'I appreciate that Elaine, I really do,' said Ruby. Then she hung up and once again went back to her comic. By the time the fourth phone call came in Ruby was a little strung out.

'What!' she yelled into the receiver.

'You OK Ruby? You sound a little tense.'

'Oh, it's you Clance, sorry about that,' said Ruby, relieved to hear the voice of her closest friend and most loyal ally, Clancy Crew, coming back down the line.

'Yeah, well I've had a kinda tense few hours,' she explained, 'not what I had planned.'

'Yeah, I ran into Del, she told me what happened. She was concerned that you might be mad at her,' said Clancy.

'Well, I'm not,' said Ruby.

'I told her you wouldn't be,' said Clancy.

No one knew Ruby like Clancy did, not even Mrs Digby, and she knew Ruby back to front and inside out.

'So are you worried that Mrs Digby will tell your mom and dad?'

'What makes you think Mrs Digby knows?'

'You think she doesn't?'

'She knows,' sighed Ruby. 'She always knows. Mr Chester rang her, but she has no interest in getting my folks involved. You can imagine how they would react, right?'

Clancy sucked air through his teeth; he knew all right.

'So what have you been doing?' asked Ruby.

He let out a weary sigh. 'I've been trying to make this petition to oppose Mrs Bexenheath's suggestion that the school lockers be moved from the main corridor to somewhere totally inconvenient.'

'Yeah, well that's Mrs Bexenheath all over. Just so long as things are nice and tidy for her then she's not interested in whether it works for any of us,' said Ruby.

'She doesn't get it. The lockers are more than a place to keep your tennis shoes,' said Clancy, 'they are integral to social interaction.'

'You're preaching to the choir Clance, it's Principal Levine you gotta persuade.'

'I know,' said Clancy, 'but I have no idea how.'

'You'll think of something,' said Ruby. 'I have total faith.'

Pause.

'So you watching *The Ex Detective*?' asked Clancy.

'I totally forgot it was on this afternoon. What's the deal?' asked Ruby.

'Larry's got his mom in town, but she's just been kidnapped.'

'I didn't know that Larry had a mom.'

'*No one* did,' said Clancy, 'but now she's been kidnapped Larry realises how much he's been missing her and wishes he hadn't let the grass grow under their relationship.'

'It's always the way,' sighed Ruby.

'Yeah,' agreed Clancy, 'you just don't know what you got until it's gone.'

'Talking of gone, when exactly are you flying to Washington?'

asked Ruby.

'In about three weeks,' said Clancy. 'My dad's planning on bringing along the whole pack of us.'

'So what's the point of this trip – pleasure or pain?'

Clancy sighed. 'He won't tell us, but he said this time we'll enjoy it. Unlikely, I think. I'll bet he just wants us to be there looking like a super-happy family. It's good for politics.' Clancy's father was *Ambassador* Crew and he liked his family to fall in behind him in a nice straight line and generally make him look good. The Crew children struggled with this, partly because they weren't suited to a life of smiling and waving but mainly because Ambassador Crew was much more focused on himself than he was on them.

'Jeepers Clance, just how much smiling time has he got you down for?'

'Forty-eight hours at least,' said Clancy. 'I don't think my jaw will stand it.'

'You're pretty resilient, Clance,' she yawned, 'you'll think of something to smile about.'

'I doubt it,' said Clancy. 'Anyway, have you spoken to Hitch since the whole, you know, *thing*?' he asked.

Ruby glanced around her as if somewhere in this Twinford teenager's bedroom something lurked and listened. She was right to be concerned – it wasn't prudent to talk on an unsecured line. She had learned this the hard way a few months back. Spectrum was not some sort of employment agency, it was a spy agency, and as anyone knew, spy agencies should not be blabbed about. In fact, blab and you could pack up your spy kit and head on home. It was Spectrum **RULE 1: KEEP IT ZIPPED**. Talking to your best pal Clancy Crew about Spectrum would also bring about a termination of your contract, but then Spectrum weren't going to know about that since when it came to secrets, Clancy Crew was a vault and though Hitch knew that Clancy knew, *he* was *also* a vault.

So you could be pretty certain this secret was well and truly secret.

'No,' said Ruby, 'Hitch hasn't been around here. He told my folks he's in the Bahamas with his mother.'

'I didn't know he had a mother.'

'I'm not sure he does.'

'You think he just made her up?'

'When it comes to Hitch, I think it's hard to know *what's* true. You *think* you know him but, look at it this way, what do I really have as hard evidence? Do I know anything?'

'You know he likes coffee,' suggested Clancy.

'What I know Clance,' corrected Ruby, 'is that Hitch *drinks* coffee and a lot of it, but does he drink it because he likes the taste of it or because he needs to keep from falling asleep? Well, it's anybody's guess.'

'So you wanna meet?' asked Clancy.

Ruby paused, for a moment torn between the pleasure of chatting to her friend and the pleasure that was reading *Kung*

Fu Martians. She sighed. 'Sure, why not, my day is ruined anyway.'

'Oh, thanks a bunch, buster.'

'I didn't mean it like it sounded,' said Ruby. 'Just meant I was planning on a little downtime, but I guess your company might restore my mood.'

'I'm beginning to think yours might have the entirely opposite effect,' said Clancy.

'See you in ten,' said Ruby.

Chapter 3.
Leaf peepers

THEY MET WHERE THEY USUALLY MET when they didn't want to bump into anyone else – the old oak tree on Amster Green. It was a good spot for hiding coded notes when there were secrets to be passed, and it was also a pretty perfect spot to sit and observe the comings and goings on Amster. The leafy branches provided good cover from passers-by, even this late in the year. October was almost here and most of the leaves still clung to the branches, the colours vivid and varied. It was an exceptional fall due to the late summer and sudden cold snap, the old oak's leaves turning a whole host of colours.

'Ideal for leaf peepers,' said Ruby.

'What?' said Clancy.

'Leaf peepers,' repeated Ruby, 'folks who like to spend their free time looking at leaves turning.'

'There's a *name* for people who do that?' said Clancy. 'Looking at leaves changing colour has an actual *name*?'

'Everything has a name,' said Ruby. 'And this is an especially good fall for leaf peeping. It's due to that Indian summer we had; I mean, until a few weeks ago the days were pretty sunny, unusually so. We've also had some cool evenings and no rain to speak of – as I said, ideal conditions for leaf peepers. It all has to do with sunlight, sugar and sap.'

'What?' said Clancy.

'The green in a leaf is chlorophyll, right? Well, chlorophyll disappears more quickly when the sunlight is bright and the evenings are cool. And dry weather makes more sugar in the cell sap, which accelerates production of red compounds. So: bright days, cool nights and no rain means the green goes fast and lots of red is made to replace it. A leaf peeper's idea of heaven.'

'Jeepers, you really retain all this stuff in your actual brain?'

'You never know when it might come in handy,' said Ruby.

'Apart from a biology test, I don't see this info coming in super handy,' said Clancy. 'It's not knowledge you need to have at your fingertips.'

'How do you know?' said Ruby. 'You never know when a piece of information might prove vital for your future survival.'

'I think you can be fairly sure this leaf thing isn't going to help you in a life-or-death situation.'

Ruby knew a lot of facts like this – she spent an awful lot of time looking them up in books. She sometimes even attended lectures on subjects which interested her, slipping in unseen to the Twinford University seminars. The more you know, the more you know was a motto of Ruby's, and she knew a lot.

Clancy and Ruby were sitting high in the oak's branches and

looking up at the sky and the dark clouds that were beginning to gather. Was the wind picking up or was there rain coming in?

'You reckon you could outrun a tornado?' mused Clancy.

'No,' said Ruby.

'You say that, but I mean could you? I mean, has anyone tried?'

'I'm sure plenty have tried, but unless they can run at two hundred miles an hour then no, they haven't succeeded.'

'Even on a bike?' asked Clancy.

'Who can ride a bike at two hundred miles an hour? Who does anything at two hundred miles an hour?' said Ruby.

Clancy changed the subject. 'So how are you going to explain climbing into a garbage can?' he asked.

'To whom?'

'Your folks?'

'How are they gonna find out? Mrs Digby's sure as darn it not gonna tell 'em.'

'Yeah, but Mr Chester might.'

'Oh, so he's been broadcasting in your neighbourhood as well?'

'Well, my sister Lulu knew about it. She overheard Mr Chester telling Mr Nori when she walked past the bus stop.'

'Why doesn't Mr Chester just get himself a radio station? It would give him wider coverage.'

'I'm not sure it would,' said Clancy.

As parents went, Sabina and Brant Redfort were two very

easy-going people, but bad manners and lack of social graces turned them very uptight indeed – especially if these failings were their daughter's. And getting spotted by the town busybody as you climbed out of a dumpster in front of a poker bar was *not* socially graceful.

'Let Mr Chester gossip all he likes,' said Ruby. She wasn't concerned; she would figure out exactly what to say. 'So what was the exciting thing you wanted to tell me?'

'What do you mean, what exciting thing?' said Clancy.

'Come on Clance, it is written all over your face, practically oozing out of the corners of your mouth. I can tell you've been dying to tell me something since you got here.'

'No fooling you, huh?' said Clancy.

'I can read you like a book, baby.'

Clancy frowned. 'Let's hope a more interesting book than the one about how leaves turn red.'

'So what's the news?'

'I'm going to the Environmental Explorer Awards,' said Clancy, smiling the smile that he would be wearing on the night.

'You're *going* to that?' Ruby felt like she might fall off her branch.

Clancy nodded. 'Yes, I am.'

'Since when?' said Ruby.

'Since my dad had this extra invitation.'

'How did he manage *that*?' asked Ruby.

'My mom's not keen on some of the live exhibits.'

'I guess you got lucky,' said Ruby.

'I know,' said Clancy, 'it's this year's big money-can't-buy ticket. It must be one of the few perks of being the Ambassador's favourite son.' (Clancy was also the ambassador's *only* son.)

'What about your sisters? They not wanna go?' asked Ruby.

'Minny's banned due to some misdemeanour or other, Lulu's not into that kinda thing, and since I'm the third oldest the others don't actually get a look in.'

'I must say, for once I envy you my ambassadorial pal,' said Ruby.

'Are your mom and dad going?' said Clancy.

'Need you ask?' said Ruby. The Twinford Environmental Explorer Awards was a three-yearly event held in the Twinford Geographical Institute, a grand modernist building near the Twinford City Museum. A large cheque was presented by a local dignitary to the environmentalist deemed to have made the biggest impact on some area of world ecology. It was a big deal event. Of course the Redfort's were going. Ruby's parents were Twinford's premiere socialites, attending on average two major functions per week along with a sprinkling of private parties, launches and fundraisers.

'You couldn't, like, wrestle a ticket?' asked Clancy.

'It's a sell out,' said Ruby, 'everyone wants to be there. I guess I will be left watching it on TV.'

'It's because of the exhibits,' said Clancy, 'that's what makes it so popular. They said there's going to be moon rock there and probably one or two astronauts floating around.'

'If you get to speak to one of them you gotta ask, which is the more comfortable space suit: the G4C, or the A7L?' Ruby thought for a moment and then added, 'Also, does the moon really smell like wet gunpowder?'

Clancy said, 'I'm going to ask them how they can sit in a rotating spacecraft without getting dizzy? I mean my sister Nancy would puke all the way to the moon.'

'Which isn't saying a lot since your sister Nancy looks like she's about to puke every time she climbs aboard the school bus. No, the real question to ask is – *"Aren't you concerned about all that space junk you're littering the galaxy with? Sooner or later someone's going to bump into a lump of it..."* – that's what I wanna know,' said Ruby. 'That and what Virgil Hipkip does in his spare time.'

'Can you even imagine?' mused Clancy. 'I mean how does a guy like that relax?'

'Ah, he probably knits,' said Ruby.

Virgil Hipkip was a survivalist and explorer of hostile terrain, and known for many hair-raising feats, but the most notorious was when he swam beneath the Arctic ice with a polar bear.

'He's the reason my mom doesn't want to go,' said Clancy. 'She thinks he may have insisted that jungle grubs be served as canapés.'

'A not entirely unreasonable worry,' said Ruby.

'I'm hoping to meet him,' said Clancy. 'As they say, he hangs out with *the rare and dangerous*, or is it the dangerously rare?'

'Well, talking of dangerously rare, if you get a chance, ask him if he's run into the Blue Alaskan wolf recently – I'll betcha he hasn't.'

'Yep, we must be the only two kids alive today who have seen that old wolf,' said Clancy. They were talking about a creature thought to be extinct until August that year. Ruby and Clancy had cut it loose. Had they left it caged up there on Wolf Paw Mountain where Lorelei von Leyden and the mysterious Australian woman she was working for had trapped it, then its fate might very well have been the same as that of the dodo.

'So who do you figure is going to get the big cheque?' asked Ruby.

'My money's on the woman who discovered that new snake species.'

'Why's that?'

'I don't know, just a hunch,' said Clancy. 'I just got a good feeling about her. It's the sort of discovery that takes a hold on people's imaginations.'

'That's because people are scared of snakes,' said Ruby. 'People like to be thrilled.'

'True, but more than that, this snake has an amazing yellow skin, I mean, fluorescent yellow,' said Clancy. 'On top of that, it has a really weird venom, interesting weird.'

'What does it do?' said Ruby.

'Well, it doesn't kill you,' said Clancy. 'At least, not immediately. First of all you sweat, like *a lot*. I mean you basically sweat to death unless you drink about a gallon of water; if you don't, you end up like a raisin. The worst of it is, you find you can't close your eyes – they are sort of pinned open, which is very unattractive and unrelaxing.'

'You think you would be able to relax with symptoms like those?' asked Ruby.

'It also gives you really bad breath,' added Clancy.

'Gross. How come you know all these reptile facts?' asked Ruby.

'My dad was given the literature on account of him being on the award's committee. I read up on it. It's top secret though; I shouldn't even be telling you,' said Clancy. 'I hope you're not going to blab.'

Ruby rolled her eyes. 'Give me a break.' Hearing about the snake made her wish more than ever that she could make it to the Explorer Awards; snakes were of particular interest to her.

She had spent an awful lot of her time watching the nature channel and had seen more than a few programmes about deadly snakes and their habitats. It was a subject that fascinated both her and Clancy, and one that they had often argued about.

They were always trying to figure out which was the most deadly snake of all. Clancy would usually argue: 'It has to be the hook-nosed sea krait because it requires the least venom to kill.'

'Come on, it has got to be the Russell's viper,' Ruby would answer. 'I mean, it has to be considered the more dangerous on account of it being a more aggressive reptile and it packs more venom. You also have to consider that you are much more likely to cross paths with a Russell's viper than our hook-nosed friend.'

Clancy refused to accept this argument and merely countered that this was not the point – if one happened to meet the *Enhydrina schistosa* then the chances of making it back to the beach to enjoy a little more sunbathing activity were pretty much non-existent. This argument had been going on for the past five and a quarter years and a compromise had yet to be found. What they both did agree on was: 'Whichever one you meet, just be sure you don't upset it.'

'This snake lady,' said Ruby, 'what's her name?'

Amarjargel Oidov? Or as they say in Outer Mongolia, Oidov Amarjargel.'

'That's where the snake's from? Outer Mongolia?'

'No, that's where *she's* from. I don't know where the snake's from,' said Clancy. 'It sounds cool, doesn't it?'

'What, the snake?'

'Outer Mongolia. I mean, how many countries are called 'outer' whatever?'

'You mean like outer space?'

'Yeah sorta, just makes it sound exciting, kinda wild,' said Clancy.

'Speaking of outer space, my money's on the Mars exploration,' said Ruby. 'I mean, what could be more exciting than the big question... is anyone out there?'

'...And will they infiltrate human society?'

'Well, if they *are* and they *do* then please let them be on the side of wholesome good-citizen-like behaviour because we already have more than enough bad guys mooching around, most of them in Twinford, as far as I can tell.'

The face of the Count loomed up in her mind's eye – she could see him laughing, his dark eyes unfathomable. He'd been involved in more than one of the cases Ruby had worked on. Did he have further plans to bring his deadly ambitions to town? She had a bad feeling that all of the cases she'd solved so far were only building up to something bigger. Something infinitely deeper and darker than her worst nightmares could conjure.

She shook her head, trying to dislodge the image, and said, 'Boy, if I could just get my hands on one of those Explorer tickets.'

'You'd be lucky,' said Clancy. 'My dad said people are ready to commit murder for them.'

And Ruby could almost hear the Count laugh.

Chapter 4.
Brainless bivalves

WHEN RUBY OPENED THE FRONT DOOR she could hear her mother's voice. Sabina Redfort was on the phone and speaking in a vaguely hushed tone. Ruby paused on the stairs, trying to figure out who her mother was talking to. She sounded serious, very serious.

'*You know, I'm just at a loss, what am I going to do? It will be a total disaster if I don't find them... I can't tell him...*' Silence. '*Oh my gosh, are you sure?... You really mean it? I mean, I can see the sense, they are practically identical... I don't know how I can ever thank you!*' She sounded beyond grateful. '*That would just about save my life... What's that? No, I hadn't heard... Today you say?*'

Ruby froze, waiting for the next words. Was someone about to tell her mother about the dumpster incident?

'*Sure thing, yes, I'm dying to go to the Melrose Dorff sale but it will have to be tomorrow, I have a party tonight... Meet you at the perfume counter, sounds perfect, tomorrow it is. I'll see you in town, bye, bye, bye.*'

Marjorie Humbert! thought Ruby. *Has to be.* She recognised the sign off: *'bye, bye, bye'* was what her mother and Marjorie always ended their conversations with.

She exhaled; she was getting paranoid, seeing trouble where there was none. Nothing serious had happened. Her mom no doubt was worrying about her outfit for the Explorer Awards and Marjorie was lending her a pair of shoes or earrings, something her mother had mislaid.

As it happened, Ruby was on the money.

'Hey Mom, how's it going?' she said as she walked into the living room.

'A whole lot better since two minutes ago. Marjorie has saved my life!'

'Literally?' asked Ruby.

'Sort of literally but not exactly,' said Sabina.

'How did she manage that over the phone?'

'By lending me her ruby-eyed snake earrings. Don't tell your father,' said her mother, adopting a conspiratorial whisper. 'He'll never spot the difference, even though Marjorie's are cobras and mine are sea serpents, but he'd be so mad if he knew I'd lost them. You see, I clean forgot to put them on the insurance.'

'When did you last have them?' asked Ruby.

'During my stay in New York City.'

'So they could be at Grandma's place?'

'She's looked and looked but they haven't shown up,' sighed Sabina, 'not on the night stand, not in the bathroom or anywhere obvious.'

'So I take it Dad's not home?' said Ruby.

'Not yet honey. He was called in for an emergency meeting about the Explorer Awards. The caterers stepped out at the last minute – the chef apparently has a considerable fear of snakes. Brant offered to find a replacement... He is late though,' she said, looking at her watch. 'I hope everything's OK. I have a bad feeling about this whole function.'

It was most unlike Sabina to have a bad feeling about anything – losing her jewellery had clearly rattled her.

Ruby sank down on the sofa opposite her mother.

'You're sitting on the menu,' said Sabina.

'What?'

'The menu,' said Sabina. 'You happen to be sitting on it.'

'Oh.' Ruby pulled the card from under her. 'So is this what they're serving on the night?'

'It was going to be,' said Sabina, 'but who knows now, it might just be crackers.'

Ruby began reading from the card. 'Looks fancy. Caviar, oysters...'

SABINA: *'I do love oysters, but I feel very uncomfortable eating them now it turns out they have a brain.'*

RUBY: *'I think you are getting mixed up here. They don't have brains, they are brain food, i.e. meant to be food for the brain.'*

SABINA: *'Whose brain?'*

RUBY: *'Your brain – anyone's brain.'*

SABINA: *'You sure?'*

RUBY: *'Yes. By the way, you eat plenty of other things with brains.'*

SABINA: *'I know, but I've been eating oysters all this time and thinking they don't have brains.'*

RUBY: *'Well, you can relax 'cause they don't.'*

SABINA: *'You're sure about this?'*

RUBY: *'Where do you think they would keep them?'*

SABINA: *'In their shells, of course.'*

RUBY: *'Where in the "body"? I mean, you've shucked enough oysters to know.'*

Her mother mulled this for half a minute.

SABINA: *'Now I come to think of it, no, I have never noticed an oyster with even a face.'*

RUBY: *'There you go.'*

SABINA: *'What gets me is how do they think?'*

RUBY: *'They don't need to think. They're bivalves, they are pretty much gills and a mouth. They catch plankton in their mucus and—'*

SABINA: *'OK, mucus does it – that's it for me and oysters.'*

Ruby was saved from any more oyster talk by the sound of a key in the front door.

'That'll be your father, don't blab about the earrings,' hissed her mother.

'When do I ever blab?' said Ruby.

'Brant?' called Sabina.

'Sorry I'm late,' he called back.

'We'll be late to the Feldman's party,' said Sabina.

'Sorry honey, I got held up, but guess who I have in tow?'

'Hola, Mrs Redfort.'

'Consuela?' cried Sabina. 'Is it really you?' And in walked Consuela Cruz, large as life and in six-inch scarlet heels.

'Meet my new caterer,' announced Brant. 'She has agreed to save the day.'

'Bravo!' cried Sabina.

For a very short time Consuela Cruz, a dietician and talented chef from Seville, had been in the Redforts' employ, hired by Mrs Redfort to bring health and wellbeing to the family, though what had actually happened was the cause of a certain amount of indigestion.

Mrs Digby and Consuela Cruz had not hit it off and had disagreed about most things. Plates had been thrown and tomato juice flung. Mrs Digby had felt very much discarded, her cooking somehow relegated to second best – all in all it had been a less than satisfactory arrangement. It was a mercy Mrs Digby had already departed the house for poker night.

'Great seeing you again,' said Ruby.

Consuela gave her a hard stare. 'Have you been eating your kale, Ruby Redfort?'

'Course I have, never miss it,' lied Ruby.

'Don't try and pull wool over me, chica. I can see just by looking into your eyes, no kale has passed your lips.'

'Oh, honey,' fretted Sabina, 'is this true?'

'I'll go fix her a kale juice once we have debated the menu,' said Consuela.

Jeepers, thought Ruby, *one minute in the door and she's ruining my life.* 'Really nice to see you again Consuela,' she said, 'but if you would excuse me I just need to go and tidy my sock drawer.'

Ruby grabbed some banana milk from the refrigerator while her parents and Consuela Cruz talked oysters. Consuela wanted to serve them on seaweed.

'I'm not sure we should serve oysters on anything,' said Brant, 'because of the green pearl discovery. The marine explorer – what's his name? – might be offended.'

'More likely to be offended that you can't remember what he's called,' said Ruby.

'He wouldn't have discovered a green pearl if someone had not been trying to eat it,' said Consuela.

The logic of this statement didn't register with Brant Redfort.

'We can't eat anything endangered,' he insisted.

'Oysters aren't in danger,' said Consuela. 'No way José.'

'Were you aware they don't have brains?' said Sabina. 'Not even faces.'

Ruby decided it might be time to retire to her room.

Chapter 5.
Loose ends

RUBY PULLED THE BLOCK OF WOOD FROM THE DOORJAMB and took notebook 625 from its hiding place. The previous 624, all varying shades of the same colour, were hidden under the floorboards. She had been writing things down in yellow notebooks since she was no more than four years old, when it had struck her that the smallest detail was what made up the whole big picture. **RULE 16: EVEN THE MUNDANE CAN TELL A STORY**. No one knew about the yellow notebooks, not even Ruby's closest friend, Clancy. She wasn't sure why she hadn't told him; she just hadn't.

She flipped back to see what she had written over the last few weeks. There was a lot there, most of it still fresh in her mind, but she was hoping that there might be some detail that once re-read might mean more than perhaps it had when first jotted down. Some detail that made everything fit together, that revealed the pattern she couldn't see. She sank back into her outsized beanbag and began to read.

Her life as a Spectrum code breaker had begun in March,

getting on for seven months ago now, and it had been no easy ride.

Ruby, who was an ambitious kid, was determined to do more than crack codes: her lifelong dream was to be a field agent. That dream – and her life – had been almost snuffed out by various murdering thieves and kidnappers, but that only served to make her more determined. She had made it this far, she wasn't dead, why give up now?

It was the Cyan Wolf case that had led her to the blue-eyed Australian, and it was the conversation with her on Wolf Paw Mountain that kept circling her mind. She turned back several pages and read her notes on the case. It was up there on the mountain where things had taken an almost fatal turn, though in recent months things had had a habit of taking near fatal turns.

Sometimes she thought she could still smell the fire that had burned around her, the forest catching light as she had dared the woman to explain her dark motives.

'All this so you can make some money out of some stupid fragrance.'

How the woman had laughed at that.

'Is that what you think this is about? No sweetie, this is not about some high-end perfume counter cluttered up with rich folk wanting to waste their money. This is about something important, more important than you could ever imagine.'

The woman had been talking about the Cyan scent, the scent of the Blue Alaskan wolf. A scent so rare that just a few drops were worth unimaginable riches, a scent with an irresistible pull – breathe it in and you fell under its spell. But the Australian had made it clear that she was not interested in it for its value as a perfume – she had far bigger ambitions.

Ruby was chewing on a pencil and looking down at a blank page.

She had been recruited by Spectrum in March to crack a code, just one. Her first (and supposedly last) assignment was to figure out what code-breaker, Lopez, had discovered before she mysteriously died. It turned out to be a plot to steal the priceless Buddha of Khotan. Thanks to Ruby's work, the Buddha had been saved and the criminals identified. One incarcerated – Baby Face Marshall; one dead – Valerie Capaldi, aka Nine Lives; and one at large – Count von Viscount.

It had all seemed to tie up quite neatly, everyone at Spectrum was satisfied, but Ruby was no longer feeling so complacent. Though the Buddha was now safely back in Yoktan (formerly the ancient city of Khotan), might it be that something *had* after all been stolen?

Ruby wrote:

```
Was something stolen from the Jade Buddha
itself?
```

She leafed back to the note she had made about the case when it had all been deemed over, done and dusted, put to bed.

She had seen him take out a small torch-like device and shine it into the eyes of the Buddha. What had he seen there? What secret might be held in the eyes of the Jade Buddha of Khotan?

The case of the Jade Buddha was supposed to be her one and only code-breaking exercise, but Spectrum had kept her on, despite her age and despite LB's reluctance to take on a mouthy school kid (the Spectrum 8 boss had been clear about that). Perhaps she hadn't had much choice – even she could see that, had Ruby *not* been there, things would have ended very differently.

Ruby turned to a fresh page and wrote:

LOOSE END ONE: the jade.

The second case had been a confusing one. The death of a Spectrum diver had turned out to be accidental, and some worrying pirate activity that had seen Ruby's own parents taken hostage was in fact a cover to allow Count von Viscount to recover the lost treasure of the Sibling Isles. But on reflection this too turned out to be a bluff, a distraction – something much more sinister was going on. Clancy had told her just how pale the Count had turned when he discovered the vials of indigo he was carrying were smashed and his relief when he had found one, just one glass vessel, still intact. The indigo was the ink obtained from the cephalopod – a giant octopus sea creature – the stuff of legend and a legend no one (until then) had believed in. This indigo ink worked exactly like a truth serum – once ingested, you couldn't help but tell the truth. Ruby had first-hand experience of it's powers and could see just why any master criminal would want to have it sitting in his or her cupboard of villainy, but Ruby had a strange feeling that the Count had some bigger purpose for it.

The pirates and their leader had been captured and marched to jail. The Count's henchman, Mr Darling, had died in the strangulating grip of the octopus. But the Count himself, as always, had sailed away into the sunset, or in this instance into the dawn.

```
LOOSE END TWO: the indigo. Was it acquired
for some specific purpose?
```

The third case was the Blue Alaskan wolf: rescued, but not before some of its valuable cyan scent had been extracted and stolen.

This time it was the mysterious Australian who had been running the show, and no one had seen her since she made Ruby take a long walk off a cliff edge. Her co-conspirators had been less lucky: Eduardo had wound up dead, his own boss had seen to that, the bulk of the gang had fled the scene only to be captured by Spectrum agents, and as for Lorelei von Leyden, new villain on the block, well she, like smoke, had disappeared into the atmosphere before the mountain was engulfed in flames.

There had been no sign of the Count in the cyan case, but had he been lurking behind the scenes? Had he been the one pulling the strings?

LOOSE END THREE: the Cyan.

Which just left Ruby's most recent case – the one that had begun with a pair of missing canary-yellow shoes. It was the shoes that had led them to uncover the whole plot, and eventually locate the invisibility skin, stolen to order by a cat burglar named Claude Fontaine, hired by their old friend Lorelei von Leyden. Ruby had recovered the skin and returned it to the Department of Defence, but she had known as she crouched on the rooftop that night that the invisibility skin was not the whole story. With hindsight, it was clear that the skin had been stolen in order to perpetrate another crime.

The *real* trophy had been the 8 key. A coder key belonging to Spectrum boss LB, which became useless to anyone as soon as it was known to be missing, since all it took was the press of a button to deactivate its functions. The only part of it that seemed to be in any way interesting was the Lucite tag attached to it, and this was only of interest to LB since it had once belonged to

Bradley Baker, legendary Spectrum agent and LB's long-dead sweetheart.

So why had the Count strived so hard to obtain it? Why risk incarceration for a key that would be deactivated as soon as it was discovered missing? A key therefore that would never unlock one single Spectrum door, not one file, not one secret?

And the bigger question: since the key had been locked away inside a DOD safe room, protected by LB's own code, how had Claude got to it? Had someone from the DOD or even Spectrum given him inside information? Investigations were of course being conducted – Ruby didn't have to be told this to know it was so. She thought that was probably why no new code-breaking cases had been landing on her desk; activity had been suspended pending security clearance. So was Hitch likely to be 'on vacation' with his 'mother' at this time of high alert? Answer: not a chance.

```
LOOSE END FOUR: the key.
What's the link?
```

She paused before writing,

```
Beats me.
```

She didn't know what else to write, except for the one thing she didn't want to write: *has a bad apple found its way into*

Spectrum, or is someone in Spectrum rotten to the core? Someone I know? Someone I trust?

She sat back and exhaled a weary breath. 'Where the Sam Hill are you Hitch, and why can I never find you when I need you?' The question, muttered aloud, roused her trusty husky dog and he ambled over and licked her hand, a display of loyal affection Ruby was grateful for.

'Come on Bug, let's you and me go get a snack, how about that, huh?'

The dog began to wag his tail. Ruby wriggled out of the beanbag and the two of them exited the room and went quietly on downstairs.

When she arrived down in the kitchen she fetched a dog treat from the pantry and fed it to Bug. Then she opened the refrigerator to see a large glass of green with a note pinned to it written in Spanish:

SI QUIERES MEJORAR TU MALA VISTA, DEBES TOMAR ESTO!*

It was undoubtedly from Consuela.

If I wanted to wind up with dog breath – no offence Bug – then I would. She wasted no time in pouring it down the sink, trying not to breathe in the kale smell.

Mrs Digby had made her a small fish pie. Ordinarily Ruby would have been pleased (Mrs Digby made a good fish pie), but due to her earlier encounter with fish heads she decided she might give it a miss. Instead she sliced some bread, dropped it in the toaster and waited in silence for it to toast. She thought about Hitch again and where he might be – was he part of some investigation into the 8 key or had he been kept out of it too? How did people so good at keeping secrets investigate other people who were equally good at keeping secrets?

Her thoughts were interrupted by the pop of the toaster and just like that one of her questions was answered.

Meet me at the Dime a Dozen.
Aisle 17. 8pm. DON'T BE LATE.

Chapter 6.
Canned goods

THE MESSAGE WAS GRILLED INTO THE TOAST, the words clear but edible, an advantage to any hungry spy looking to cover her tracks. The fax toaster was Spectrum issue and, while useful, some might feel it had its downsides – not everyone wanted to be contacted about work assignments at 8pm when they had just popped into the kitchen for a snack. But then Ruby Redfort wasn't everyone.

She spread the toast with mayonnaise (the Redforts were out of butter), stuck it between her teeth and pulled on her waterproof coat. Rain was due anytime soon – that's what they kept saying, though it was the wind that had the city in its grip.

Then she headed out into the dark to Greenstreet subway station. The train journey wasn't a long one, but even so Ruby was frustrated with herself for forgetting to bring her book. So instead of reading she stared at her reflection in the dark window. Someone had stuck a sticker to the glass. It was of a boss-eyed cartoon kid licking its chops – on the tongue were the words: **It's On the Tip of Your Tongue.**

There was also part of a newspaper discarded on the ledge behind the seat, its headline mirrored in the glass:

MAYOR ANNOUNCES HALLOWEEN FUN.

She picked it up and continued to read:

THIS YEAR'S HALLOWEEN PARADE BIGGER THAN EVER!

Mayor Abrahams, keen to make himself popular before the mayoral elections, had decided that there should be a special televised Twinford Halloween parade in Harker Square. The meteorological service thought this unwise due to the recent violent gales and predicted torrential rain, but Mayor Abrahams was not to be deterred:

"No little rain shower is going to dampen Twinford's spirits!"

Ruby's friends, Red in particular, were keen to make a big impression, costume-wise. There had been a lot of talk but so far no decision on what ghoulish theme they would all be adopting.

She resurfaced at Crossways, the subway stop just northeast of the Village and not so far from the Twinford River. On Broker

Avenue traffic was heavy no matter what time of day or night, and to traverse meant dodging cars. The Dime a Dozen 24-hour supermarket was her destination: brightly lit with fluorescent tubes, the aisles signed with giant cardboard numbers suspended from the ceiling.

Aisle 17 held canned vegetables and jarred baby food on one side, chilled goods in tall refrigerators on the other. She didn't immediately spot Hitch. He was browsing chickpeas: a tall, good-looking man, wearing an elegant raincoat over a dark suit.

In his hand – only slightly marring the look – was a Dime a Dozen paper bag.

'Been doing some shopping?' she said.

'You're only three minutes and forty seconds late, good going kid,' he said.

'Isn't this a bit inconvenient?' said Ruby. 'I mean, having to walk through a store every time you want to reach Spectrum?'

'On the contrary,' he said. 'It's a convenience store.'

She rolled her eyes. 'You know what I mean.'

'For those in the know, there are always other ways in, I just thought this one would appeal to your sense of mystery,' said Hitch. 'Besides, we were out of butter.'

'I know,' said Ruby, 'but how do you know?'

'Lucky guess,' said Hitch.

Boy, thought Ruby, *that's some butler*.

'So I've managed to restock the dairy goodness *and* get to work on time,' said Hitch, shaking the bag.

'Where's the door then?' she asked.

'Right here,' said Hitch, pointing to a section of shelving bearing all kinds of fly sprays, fly papers and fly swatters. He reached behind a can of Fly-Be-Gone and the shelf swung open and they walked through into a very white, very cold space. Nothing was in it at all but for a tiny image of a white fly on the white wall in front of them, almost invisible but not quite. Hitch pressed his thumbprint onto it and the wall slid back and stairs were revealed.

At the bottom of the staircase – an industrial refrigerator door; on the other side – Spectrum. A hive of spies all secretly going about their business.

Hitch went over to check in with Buzz. She looked the same as always, bland and beige and looking sort of like a mushroom sitting there in the middle of her round desk surrounded by telephones. Ruby watched her as she phoned through to LB's office.

'Agent Hitch and Agent Redfort,' she said.

This time there was no waiting and Ruby and Hitch were told to just go right on in to the boss's office.

If LB had been looking tired and twitchy last month, then she seemed doubly so today. And if the dark circles around her eyes were anything to go by, perhaps her head had not been hitting the pillow as often as it should. Next to her was a man Ruby recognised as Agent Trent-Kobie, head of Spectrum 5, aka Sea Division. He was someone LB had a lot of time for and clearly trusted.

Everyone shook hands.

Ruby noticed LB's face slightly brighten when she saw Hitch. 'Sorry to bring you back from your vacation, Hitch, I appreciate your returning at short notice.'

'Don't mention it,' said Hitch. 'To be honest I'm not a big fan of sand in my shoes.' Ruby couldn't swear to it, but she thought she saw a flicker of a wink as Hitch spoke – no doubt because he and LB knew the vacation was bogus.

LB turned to Ruby, no smile. 'Sit down, Redfort.'

Ruby sat.

LB dropped an aspirin in a glass of water before saying, 'Oh, and Redfort, please don't irritate me today; I'm a little out of sorts and you may find me less than my usual affable self.'

'I'll keep it, you know...' Ruby mimed turning a key in a lock.

'Would you?' said LB. 'I have a lot on my mind and a rather bad headache to contend with, so please try not to act your age, Redfort... just pretend you're someone more reasonable.'

Ruby resisted the impulse to roll her eyes. 'Got it,' she said. 'So you have something for me?'

LB shook her head. 'As you are probably aware, we are not assigning cases to field agents in training at this time,' she said.

There was a knock at the door and Blacker entered with a Styrofoam cup and a brown paper bag.

LB looked only a touch alarmed. 'Lose the baked goods

would you Blacker.'

'Oh, sure,' said Blacker, exiting the room and returning without the bag.

'Actually, would you mind relinquishing the coffee too? You know how it is with white carpets... every little mark.'

'No problem,' said Blacker, popping out once again and returning empty handed. He winked at Ruby and sat down.

'I requested that Agent Blacker join us since this is as much about coding as it is security,' said LB. Blacker was a more senior code expert and had collaborated with Ruby on most of her cases.

There was a buzz from LB's intercom. 'Yes,' she said.

'*Agent Delaware has arrived,*' said Buzz.

'Send him in,' said LB.

The door opened and in walked a very short man with not too much hair. His blue-black suit was perfectly pressed, he held a shiny briefcase under his arm, had neat glasses on his nose and looked like he got things done.

'This is Agent Delaware from Spectrum 1,' said LB. She nodded at him. 'Good to see you, Stanley.'

Agent Delaware shook everyone by the hand, opened his briefcase, took out a leather-bound notebook and an expensive-looking fountain pen, closed the briefcase, placed it next to his chair, opened the notebook, unscrewed the lid of the fountain pen and held it poised above the blank page.

'Agent Delaware will be spending some time with us here

in Spectrum 8,' said LB. And that was clearly as far as she was going to go with her explanation as to what this man was doing sitting there with his smart little notebook.

LB looked at Ruby. 'Redfort, it would be helpful if you could walk us through the events that took place on the night of the 15th of September.'

'You want me to say it all over again?' Ruby asked, looking from one agent to another.

'I am aware that you have been through the debriefing process already, Redfort, but for the sake of our visiting agents, Agent Trent-Kobie and Agent Delaware, could you tell us exactly what occurred up there on the roof of the Circus Grande Hotel and the events leading up to it?'

Ruby took a deep breath and said, 'OK, this is how it breaks down.' She tore a piece of paper from the notepad on the desk.

'You might want to use the board, Redfort,' said LB.

'What board?' said Ruby looking around the room.

LB pointed to the huge expanse of glossy white wall on the right-hand side, which Ruby realised as she looked at it was more than just a wall. It doubled as a very sophisticated blackboard: instead of chalk there was an electronic pen device. Ruby picked it up, unsure what to do next.

'Just write,' said Hitch. 'It will translate your handwriting into typeface.'

'Oh, cool,' said Ruby. She picked up the pen and began writing out what she knew. 'Can I draw with this thing too?'

'If you really feel the need,' said LB.

'OK, so this is Claude Fontaine, our acrobatic cat burglar. He steals the invisibility skin from the Department of Defence and uses it to break in unseen to the DOD safe room and steal the 8 key, your key.' She looked at LB. 'What we are in the dark about is how Claude knew it would be there, and how he knew the code to your safe locker. But what we can be sure of is he had some help, probably from the woman who had hired him to do the job, Lorelei von Leyden. How she came by this information we really don't know.' Ruby paused briefly before adding, 'I should mention that Lorelei was disguised as Nine Lives Capaldi and that threw me for a while, after all Nine Lives was confirmed dead back in April, which of course she was...'

Ruby caught the look on LB's face which suggested she might want to stop rambling.

'I say this only because Lorelei, it seems, is a master of disguise, which makes her pretty tricky to trace. Fortunately she is now incarcerated in a maximum security government facility, pending her trial – a long way from here, at least I think.'

'Could you move it along Redfort?' growled her boss. '*Where* this woman is living out her days is not pertinent to this discussion.'

'This is a discussion?' said Ruby. *Boy you could have fooled me*, she thought, but didn't say. 'Getting back to the question of who might have accessed the safe code...'

She drew three military stars.

'Maybe someone in the DOD leaked it.'

She drew a fly to symbolise Spectrum.

'Or it could have been someone here in Spectrum.'

She drew a figure to represent Lorelei von Leyden.

'Maybe Lorelei hacked into our security system, or the DOD's security system.'

'Claude was meant to pass both the skin and the 8 key onto Lorelei von Leyden in return for a sizeable chunk of cash. Lorelei in turn was to pass the key and, maybe I'm guessing, the skin also onto the Count, but she was planning to double-cross him.'

'You're sure about that?' asked Blacker.

'I'm sure she was meant to deliver them to someone because I overheard her saying so and I'm sure it had to be him because the Count was waiting for her.'

'Why would he wait for her on the roof? If he'd employed von Leyden then why not wait for the items to be delivered?' asked Agent Trent-Kobie.

'Because,' said Ruby, 'I'm *also* kinda sure he was expecting Lorelei to betray him; either he knows her pretty well or he's not much of a truster. What Lorelei was not expecting was for him to second-guess her actions.'

'So coming back to Claude, what did he say before he disappeared?' asked Agent Delaware.

Ruby remembered this very well. 'He said, "Let the girl go Capaldi, or your treasures will be lost forever." Then he held up the key in one hand, and the invisibility skin – which of course

I couldn't see – in the other, and then he said, "You want this? *And* this?" and then he threw them both into the air. And then he just vanished.'

'So you have no idea where he might have gone?' asked Agent Delaware.

'Why would I?' asked Ruby. 'We never exchanged addresses.'

'Would you regard him as a risk to Spectrum?' asked the agent, his voice so steady that it unnerved her.

'I don't see why he would be,' said Ruby. 'His criminal motivation was highly personal – he was stealing items to avenge his wronged mother and the chances are we will never hear from him again.'

'You are very quick to dismiss him as a threat,' said Agent Delaware, without a hint of accusation.

'You asked me if I felt he was a risk and I said no,' said Ruby.

'Why no?' asked Agent Delaware. He had stopped writing, his eyes trained on her every blink, her every twitch.

Ruby tried to keep her voice even and not betray her irritation. 'He used the skin to steal a pair of yellow tap shoes, a paperweight, a tie-clip and a poetry book, all things once belonging to his mother, and all stolen for sentimental reasons that had *nothing* to do with the core plan, which was to steal the 8 key, and *everything* to do with a personal vendetta against Margo Bardem.'

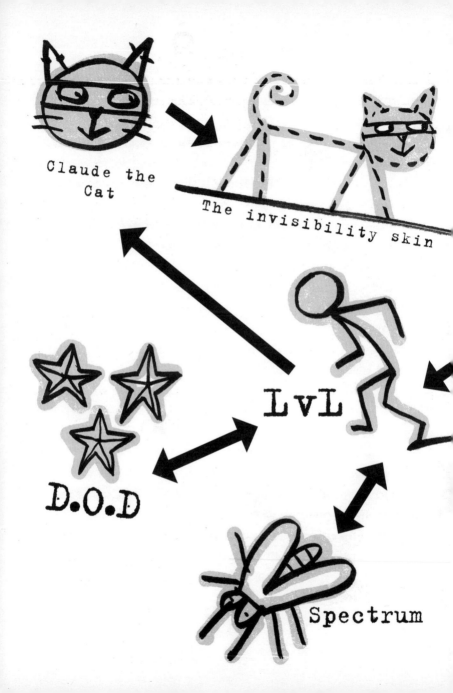

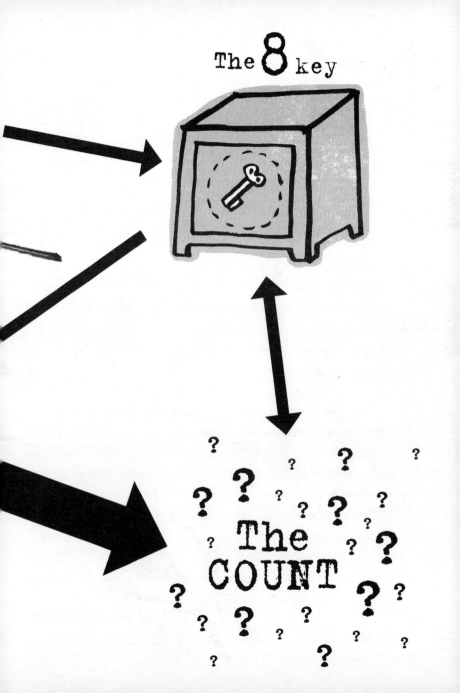

'You sound like you have a degree of sympathy for him, Agent Redfort.' An observation or an accusation? It was hard to tell.

'He seemed like a pretty broken man. I felt sorry for him, if that's what you mean.'

Agent Delaware's eyes were firmly fixed on hers, not a blink, not a twitch. 'Didn't he save your life?'

'Yes,' replied Ruby.

'Twice?' said Delaware.

Ruby nodded. 'I guess.'

'Why would he do that?' asked the agent.

'How should I know?' said Ruby. 'Perhaps he hates to see kids go splat.'

'As far as he was concerned you were the enemy,' said Delaware, 'wouldn't you say?'

'I'm not sure he saw it that way,' said Ruby.

Agent Delaware cocked his head very slightly to one side.

'Look, I was just someone who might get between him and his goal. I think he wanted to keep me at bay until he had done what he needed to do. He wasn't what I would term a "danger to society".'

'This man somehow obtains a highly classified code and breaks into a top security safe room, and you don't think he is a danger to society?' said Delaware.

'I was talking about his personal motivation,' said Ruby. 'In my opinion, he is not one bit interested in bringing about world destruction. What *should* concern us though is the man who is.'

'And who is this man?' asked Delaware.

'The Count,' said Ruby, looking around the room. 'He took the key, and given that it was deactivated even before he took possession of it, what I'm struggling to understand is – why? Why would he want it?'

'Wasn't it you who let him take it?' said Agent Delaware.

'You think I had a choice?' said Ruby, aware that there was an edge to her voice. *Keep cool Redfort.*

'But you *did* see him take it?' said Delaware.

There were a whole bunch of sarcastic replies coming to mind, but in the end Ruby opted for silence. Sometimes silence was the only option, or as Ruby's **RULE 4** had it: **IF IN DOUBT, SAY NOTHING.**

Agent Delaware gently tapped his pen on the page of his notebook and asked, 'So what do you think is going on here?'

'I think we have to assume that there is something much bigger at stake,' said Ruby, 'that this – everything I mean: the cyan scent, the truth serum, the Jade Buddha, the 8 key – is not the end of it. But I have no idea where it's leading us.'

Agent Delaware gave her that same look, like he was trying to fathom her mind.

'Do you have a question for me?' he asked.

She did actually, what she really wanted to ask was, '*Why do I feel like I am under suspicion?*' but instead she said, 'Agent Delaware, do you think the threat is coming from within or without?'

'That is the million dollar question, Agent Redfort,' he replied.

'And if you decide it's from within, do you think you'll find the mole?' she asked.

'The difficulty with moles, or double agents as I prefer to call them, is that they are always very smart. I could be staring into the eyes of a traitor right this very moment and not know it,' said Delaware, not shifting his eyes from Ruby's.

'Do you ever consider that when you look in the bathroom mirror?' asked Ruby.

He smiled very slightly. 'I'm pretty sure it's not me, if that's what you're getting at, but to take your question less literally, seeking the truth can lead you to some uncomfortable places and searching for answers often sends you down blind alleys.' He closed his notebook and replaced the lid on his fountain pen.

The interview-stroke-grilling at an end, Ruby stood, shook hands with all present, and with much relief left the room. She took some bubblegum from her pocket and popped it in her mouth. The taste of strawberry reminded her reassuringly of less complicated days. She was looking forward to getting back home – it had been a long Saturday and she was tired.

She blew a bubblegum bubble as she walked to the exit, but leaving wasn't going to be so easy.

'*Agent Redfort.*' The voice of the administrator came across the Spectrum intercom system. '*Agent Redfort, please report to Dr Selgood.*'

Pop went the gum.

'You have to be kidding,' muttered Ruby.

Ruby walked over to Buzz's desk. 'How about we do this some other time?' she suggested.

'The psychiatrist will see you now,' said Buzz.

Chapter 7.
How are we feeling today?

RUBY HAD ALREADY HAD THE DUBIOUS PLEASURE OF MEETING THE SPECTRUM PSYCHIATRIST NOT SO LONG AGO, when she had been suffering from a bad case of fearlessness.

What Ruby thought of as 'doing what it takes' Selgood had called 'the miracle complex' – a syndrome that prevented fear from kicking in since the sufferer could or would not accept that death was even a possibility. The result was that those afflicted put themselves in unnecessary danger. Ruby had seen risk and danger as *all part of the job*.

Interestingly, she had changed her tune since her little encounter with LvL. It still didn't mean she was thrilled to be here.

DR SELGOOD: *'Good to see you in one piece.'*

RUBY: *'How many pieces were you expecting me to be in?'*

DR SELGOOD: *'It says in this report that you fell from a hotel rooftop.'*

RUBY: *'Can I just say that was not down to me.'*

DR SELGOOD: *'You were pushed?'*

RUBY: *'I was dropped, but technically it amounts to the same thing.'*

DR SELGOOD: *'But you climbed up to the top of that building yourself?'*

RUBY: *'It wasn't so hard, I took the stairs most of the way.'*

DR SELGOOD: *'And found yourself on a rooftop with a dangerous and unstable felon.'*

RUBY: *'I wasn't exactly planning on her being up there.'*

DR SELGOOD: *'So what was the plan?'*

RUBY: *'To stop an actress being dropped from a great height.'*

DR SELGOOD: *'You knew this was going to happen?'*

RUBY: *'I was fairly convinced.'*

DR SELGOOD: *'And there was no one else who could have prevented this?'*

RUBY: *'No.'*

DR SELGOOD: *'And did you succeed?'*

RUBY: *'Yes.'*

DR SELGOOD: *'You prevented the actress from being dropped and killed?'*

RUBY: *'No, but yes.'*

DR SELGOOD: *'Meaning?'*

RUBY: *'No, she wasn't killed, but yes, she fell anyway.'*

DR SELGOOD: *'But she didn't die?'*

RUBY: *'No.'*

DR SELGOOD: *'And why was that?'*

RUBY: *'Hitch caught her.'*

DR SELGOOD: *'So did you in fact need to be up there on that roof to prevent her from dying?'*

RUBY: *'Look Doc, I am hearing you, and I do get where we are going with this, but I had to get up there because I had figured out the tightrope walker's intention and there wasn't a whole lotta time to persuade him otherwise.'*

DR SELGOOD: *'So you alone knew what was going to happen to the actress?'*

RUBY: *'No, I managed to contact Hitch and he contacted those other Spectrum guardians of the galaxy, but time was tight.'*

DR SELGOOD: *'So you went ahead alone?'*

RUBY: *'What would you have done, let her go splat because no one else arrived on time?'*

DR SELGOOD: *'Maybe I would; most people don't have your unwavering courage.'*

RUBY: *'Try living with the memory of knowing you might have been able to save someone if only you had possessed the nerve to run up a flight of stairs, climb out of a window and stand on a roof shouting.'*

DR SELGOOD: *'So you are saying that you felt your very presence on that rooftop might save the actress's life?'*

RUBY: *'Now you're making me sound like I have a god complex.'*

DR SELGOOD: *'Do you?'*

RUBY: *'I reckon that's your job to figure, I have far more important things to think about.'*

Dr Selgood nearly smiled at that one. 'I'm going to suggest you take on some psychological training. Meanwhile you might want to read this.' He handed her a book entitled *Six Seconds Could Save Your Life*.

'Sure, thanks Doc. I could use a light read; I left my book at home.'

Hitch, it seemed, could not be contacted, and so Ruby had to return to Cedarwood Drive alone. During the short subway ride, she opened Dr Selgood's book and began reading. Actually it wasn't as irritating as she had imagined and there seemed to be some evidence that this simple technique might actually work.

Basically, the idea was this: if you found yourself in a stressful, frightening or emotionally unsettling situation, you should take six seconds to quietly reflect before making any decisions. It was a simple concept, but there was some science behind it too: as Ruby flicked through the pages she saw that there had been some research showing that this moment of reflection helped the prefrontal cortex to modulate signals from the amygdala – which was where anger, fear and aggression were registered.

She thought she might try and give this technique a go; it was worth a shot.

Not wanting to alert anyone to her late arrival home, Ruby went in the back way through the yard and climbed the tree to her window. She went into the bathroom, took out her lenses, looked in the mirror, debated whether she should have a shower and rejected the idea before falling fully clothed onto her bed.

Meanwhile...

...the prison officer handed prisoner 2185 his package.

It had already been opened and checked by the prison security team.

'It's your lucky day, a surprise gift – home cooked too! Someone on the outside likes you.'

Prisoner 2185 carried the gift over to the table and took it out of its wrapping. Inside was a tin and a note was taped to the back:

Thought these might take you out of yourself. We'll all be waiting for you when you get out.

P.S. Remember there's always light at the end of the tunnel. Your Uncle Ed

The handwriting looked like it might belong to a gorilla.

The man prised open the lid and looked inside: the tin contained muffins. He picked one up. Heavy, he thought.

He slowly bit into it and felt his teeth knock on something hard. He tried another, the same thing.

He smiled.

He would eat these later, much later when everyone had gone to bed. He had a feeling this batch of baked goods might just be his ticket to freedom.

Chapter 8.
Wake up and
smell the banana milk

RUBY WOKE UP TO THE SOUND OF A CHICKEN CLUCKING
INSIDE HER HEAD. Actually it wasn't inside her head, it was
sort of underneath her pillow, and it wasn't an actual chicken,
it was a novelty telephone shaped like an egg. Now the cheerful
cluck of the Chicken Licken ringtone roused her from a series
of forgettable dreams.

'Ruby?'

'Yeah?'

'It's Mouse.'

'Oh, hey Mouse, did I oversleep or something?'

'Yeah.'

'Sorry... where am I meant to be?'

'The Donut.'

'Now?'

'A half hour ago.'

'Sorry.'

Silence.

'Do I *need* to be there?'

'Kinda.'

Ruby was trying to think.

'Halloween costumes!' She finally got it.

'Yeah and I wish you would hurry up, the conversation has been wearing thin. Clancy has this new pen. He says it's a space pen, you know, writes upside down, zero gravity...'

'I know,' said Ruby, 'it's meant to be like the most permanent permanent marker there is. Apparently you can write on a space shuttle and it won't come off.'

'Well, it's causing permanent boredom, the kinda boredom that makes you wish you *were* in space.'

'I'll be there, Mouse, just give me ten minutes.' Then she glanced at herself in the mirror: *brother!* Something weird had happened to her hair. 'OK, better make that fifteen.'

She walked to the bathroom, stepped into the shower, squirted shampoo on her head, rubbed it in, cleaned her teeth, rinsed her hair, combed it through, dried off, pulled on the clothes that happened to be lying on the floor, looked for her lenses, couldn't find them so instead reached for her battered glasses, stepped into her Yellow Stripe sneakers and laced them up. Then she climbed out of the window and down the tree – she didn't need to run into her parents; that would certainly slow things up.

She walked the familiar route to the Donut Diner, feeling almost like a zombie. Man, she needed a waffle to perk her up.

A guy in a baseball cap handed her a flyer as she approached the coffee shop. She barely noticed she had it until it was torn out of her grip by a gust of wind. She watched it whirl away across the street, the image of a kid biting into an apple landing on the windshield of a parked car.

Finally she made it to the Diner, fourteen minutes and eleven seconds after Mouse's call.

'What happened to you?' called Elliot. 'Ever thought of getting a watch?'

'Sorry, man,' said Ruby, 'I had a rough night, must have slept right through the alarm.'

'Yeah, you look... not yourself,' said Red. 'What happened to your glasses? Did you sleep in them or something?'

'Give her a break,' said Del, patting Ruby on the back. 'It doesn't matter Rube, at least you're here now. Have a waffle.' Del passed her a plate and began sliding food onto it.

Ruby looked around. 'Where's Clancy?'

'In the restroom,' said Elliot.

'So you wanna hear the plan?' said Mouse.

'Shouldn't we wait for Clancy?' said Ruby.

'He heard it already,' said Mouse, 'we've been here nearly an hour. So you wanna know?' She was clearly going to pop if she didn't say it.

'Sure,' said Ruby, 'tell me the plan.'

'OK,' said Mouse, 'the idea is that we go as the Rigors of Mortis Square.' Everyone waited for Ruby's reaction.

The Rigors of Mortis Square had first appeared in a comic strip and then as books and finally as a TV show. It was a situation comedy about a bunch of people, or rather dead people: ghosts who lived in a strange apartment block named Mortis Square, situated in New York City. The Rigor family were the main focus of the show, but there were other characters too: Liv Inded for instance, who was always to be found rummaging in the trash, looking for bones, her cat constantly chided for running off with one of her fingers or occasionally hands. It was a very popular show and Ruby for one loved it.

'But that would require pretty elaborate costumes,' said Ruby. 'Where we gonna rustle those up at this late hour?'

They looked at her like she'd dropped a marble or two.

'My mom promised to get us all costumes from the film studio,' said Red. Nothing was registering on Ruby's face so Red continued, 'It's kind of a birthday present to me, don't you remember Ruby, the other night when you guys were all over at my place?'

Ruby was kind of vague on this point; she really didn't remember. Sure, she remembered dinner at Red's place and she remembered Red's mom being there, she even remembered catching the bus home, but beyond that, no. The problem was she just hadn't been getting enough sleep and, as her mother was always telling her, teenagers need their sleep.

'My mom said we could choose *any* six costumes on the lot – it's a big deal because there's gonna be a film crew there filming... you gotta remember that?' said Red. 'It was in the paper, the mayor putting on this big Halloween do?'

No, still nothing was coming back to her, but the way Red was looking at her made her feel uncomfortable. So she said, 'Yeah, sure I do.'

'What have I missed?' asked Clancy, sliding back into the Diner seat.

'Red was just telling me about the Halloween costumes.'

'So what do you think?'

'I would say sounds genius to me.' And it did; she really meant it. 'So who am I going as?'

'*We*, that's you and me,' said Del, 'will be going as Hedda Gabble.' Hedda Gabble was the Rigors' nanny.

Ruby looked at her with unease.

Del continued, 'I will be wearing a floor-length fur-trimmed velvet coat which covers me from head to toe – literally speaking.'

'So what will I be wearing exactly?' asked Ruby.

'You, my friend, will be going as my severed head.'

'Will it hurt?' said Ruby.

'Funny,' said Del. 'You will be under the coat with your head sticking out at the side, sorta tucked under my arm.'

'Sounds *very* uncomfortable,' said Ruby.

'It's not so bad,' said Del. 'Erica Grey did it for years.'

'So why don't you be the severed head and I'll tuck *you* under my arm?' suggested Ruby.

'I'd be delighted but you're way too short to carry off the coat part of the costume. I'd have to practically bend double to tuck my head under your puny little arm.'

Del took a photograph out of her backpack – it was a TV still that showed the actress Erica Grey, her head tucked under the arm of who knew who. Her pretty face was made up to look very pale indeed, huge dark circles around vacant eyes, lips blood red and black hair piled elaborately in some kind of historical do.

'I don't know what you're complaining about,' said Del. 'It's you that gets the glory, I just get to stand about under a coat all night.'

'So choose a different costume, why don't you?' suggested Ruby, biting into the waffles. 'Boy, these are good.'

'That would spoil the whole deal,' said Red. 'We are meant to be going as the Rigors and there are five principle characters.'

She waited for Ruby to click.

'You and Del will be one person, so that works out well with the six of us,' said Red, slowly.

'What about the baby?' asked Ruby.

'We don't have a baby, obviously,' said Mouse.

'But the baby is a big part of the comedy,' argued Ruby.

'Well, it's too bad because we don't have one,' said Red. 'But we can get a headless dog 'cause that can be Bug.'

'Pardon?' said Ruby.

'No, not really,' said Red. 'What's with you? There *isn't* a headless dog in the show.' That was true; the dog in the show was called Toadstool and he floated. That wasn't going to be easy to pull off either.

'Bug will be on skates,' said Del.

'Skates?' said Mouse.

'Maybe a skateboard,' said Del.

'But toadstool is a pug,' said Ruby. 'Bug is a husky.'

'We have to make compromises,' said Red.

'Yeah, 'cause where are we gonna get our hands on a pug?' asked Del.

'I've always wanted a pug,' said Elliot.

'How does that help?' asked Mouse.

There then ensued a long discussion about who might have a pug they could borrow and this led to another discussion about the pros and cons of owning a pug. The overall conclusion was having a pug would be a good thing, the main reason: because it would be very useful if one wanted to dress one's pug up as Toadstool Rigor.

When the noise level had died down, they tuned into another sound: it was coming from Ruby Redfort who had her head on the table, one arm stretched out towards her milkshake. The straw had never made it to her mouth.

'She's sleeping like the dead,' said Mouse.

'Boy, should *she* get to bed earlier,' said Del. She looked at Ruby, sleeping so soundly and then she picked up Clancy's special permanent space pen and wrote on her arm:

REDFORT WAKE UP AND SMELL THE BANANA MILK.

'Del, you do realise that's a permanent marker,' said Red.

'Not just permanent but super permanent,' said Clancy. 'They use these pens in outer space.'

'If you repeat that one more time I'm going to end up outta my mind,' said Mouse.

Del rolled Ruby's sleeve down. 'Maybe she won't notice.'

'What's going on?' said Ruby, scratching her arm. 'I fall asleep or something?'

'I don't know,' said Elliot, 'do you snore when you're awake?'

'Huh?' said Ruby.

'What's with you today?' said Mouse. 'It's like the lights are on but no one's home.'

'She's preparing for the part,' said Elliot, beginning to snicker. 'Her head is somewhere else.'

Chapter 9.
The first drop of rain

MRS DIGBY WAS IN THE KITCHEN trying to manoeuvre a large pumpkin into the pantry when Ruby walked in.

'Child, you shouldn't be out in this weather without a hat, you'll catch your death. I swear this wind will blow your mind away and your good health with it.'

'You're sounding very Halloweeny, Mrs Digby.'

'I just tell it like it is,' said the old lady. 'Your lips are blue and your nose is running and it is a most unattractive combination.'

'Well, thanks for your honesty, it really is refreshing.'

'You won't thank me when you're dead.'

'But I might come back to haunt you,' said Ruby.

'Of that I'm certain,' said the housekeeper. 'You haunt my every waking hour, why give up the habit when you're dead?'

Ruby opened the refrigerator, took out a carton and poured herself a glass of banana milk, then headed up to her room.

Inspired by the breakfast conversation about *The Rigors of Mortis Square*, Ruby flicked on the TV, tuned to channel 17 and waited for the next episode to begin. They were rerunning the entire series to coincide with Halloween fever.

The Rigor family was having trouble with the plumbing and Cordelia Rigor, who had died in a drowning incident, was wading through the kitchen wearing water wings. Toadstool was hovering in swimming goggles and barking a lot.

The telephone rang and Ruby reached out for the receiver.

'You rang?' she said.

'Look Rube, can I come over? My sister Olive is driving me crazy.'

'What's she doing?' asked Ruby.

'The usual,' said Clancy. 'She's eaten all my *Spy Scoundrel* figurines.'

'Actually eaten them?' said Ruby.

'Chewed their heads off,' said Clancy.

It was when Ruby heard things like this that she was relieved that she didn't have a little sister or in fact siblings of any age.

'Sure Clance, come on over, but you better make it quick, the weather guy just said the rain's coming in.'

'I'll bring my galoshes,' said Clancy.

An hour later, Ruby and Clancy were sitting on her rooftop looking at the sky. They were both wearing their parkas, hoods pulled up over woollen hats to protect them from the wind.

'Boy, this is about as stormy as I can remember,' said Clancy. 'When do you suppose the rain's gonna hit?'

They could see the lightning way off over the ocean, but it

was moving their way.

'Maybe ten minutes, maybe fifteen,' said Ruby.

It was like watching a badly dubbed movie, the sound was so far behind the action that it didn't seem to relate to what was going on.

'So what new case have Spectrum given you?' asked Clancy.

'That's the thing,' said Ruby. 'They aren't handing out cases to junior agents right now, at least that's what they're saying, but I wouldn't be surprised if it's just me.'

'That doesn't sound very likely,' said Clancy, 'not after everything you've been through – on Spectrum's behalf, I mean.'

'Well, I had a meeting yesterday and I got a strange feeling like they sort of didn't quite trust that I was telling the truth. If you'd been there, you'd know what I was talking about.'

'So what exactly happened?' said Clancy.

'I was interrogated is what happened. They wanted to know all about Lorelei von Leyden and what occurred on top of that roof,' said Ruby. 'They brought this agent in from Spectrum 1 and he was all busy with his little notebook writing everything down and looking at me with his squirrelly eyes.'

'Don't you think this is actually what spies like to call a debriefing? I mean, it's their way of getting to the bottom of things, right?'

'I told them what happened several times in triplicate. I was the one who got the darned invisibility skin back to the

Department of Defence, so why am I under suspicion?'

'Maybe you're not, or maybe *everyone* is. You gotta see that something is going on here, right? That someone in Spectrum is involved in something they shouldn't be. So they have to clear everyone before they can see what might be the cause of the leak.'

'It might not be someone on the inside,' argued Ruby. 'It could just as easily be a security breakdown caused by a faulty computer program.'

'Exactly my point,' said Clancy, 'but until they know for sure then they can't discount the idea that it's one of you guys.'

'I don't like it,' said Ruby. 'If they don't trust me then how can I trust them?' She stuffed her hands in her pockets and looked out at the approaching storm. Neither of them spoke for a while, until Ruby finally looked at Clancy.

'What?' she said.

'You're taking this too personally,' he said.

'Who wouldn't?'

'A professional agent wouldn't,' said Clancy. 'This is just business to them. Spectrum are there to protect justice and prevent evil doing.'

'This isn't a *Spy Scoundrel* comic,' said Ruby.

'Exactly,' said Clancy, 'which is why they have to conduct an investigation rather than lasso villains and zap people with laser guns – you should see that what the guy from Spectrum 1 is doing is simply his job.'

Ruby sighed. 'I know you're right, OK, I guess it just freaked me out because now Spectrum doesn't feel like the safe place it was. It could be anyone and it might be no one. I look around HQ and think to myself, if there is a double agent in the building then I am 100% sure it isn't me, which means it has to be one of these other people, all of whom I trust, even Froghorn I guess, and it gives me the shivers.'

Just then a fork of lightning split the sky above them, thunder cracked a split second later and the rain began to pour.

'Time to go,' shouted Ruby.

Clancy fumbled with the hatch.

'Jeepers Clancy, would you open it already.'

'It won't budge,' shouted Clancy, 'it's completely jammed.'

'Let me have a try,' said Ruby, and she began sliding the catch back and forth in an effort to get it free of whatever had caught it.

'It's no use, it's totally stuck.'

'I told you,' said Clancy. 'So what are we gonna do now?'

Ruby peered over the top of the roof and into the tree's branches – it looked perilous, but possible. 'We could climb down,' she suggested.

A fork of lightning lit the sky just overhead. She remembered her Dr Selgood conversation and suddenly that didn't seem like the greatest idea.

'How about we shout?' said Clancy.

'Good idea,' said Ruby, and they began to yell at the tops of their voices, which made no impact whatsoever.

Five minutes later, they heard a scratching sound on the underside of the hatch door and a faint yelping.

Ten minutes later, Mrs Digby stuck her head through the hatch.

'What are you, a couple of fools? Get yourselves down here and inside before I lock this hatch closed once and for good.'

Ruby and Clancy bundled down as fast as they could but still a fair amount of rainwater came with them.

'Thanks Mrs Digby,' said Ruby, whose teeth were chattering so much she could barely be understood.

'Don't thank me, thank that hound of yours,' said the housekeeper. 'If that dog hadn't been howling himself hoarse, you might have been up there all night.'

Mrs Digby sent Clancy to the guest bathroom to dry off while Ruby struggled to peel off her drenched clothing.

When she saw the handwriting on her arm she exclaimed: 'Del Lasco, I am going to strangle you!'

Chapter 10.
Geek central

'RUBY!' Her mother's voice came through the house intercom, small, tinny, yet authoritative.

Ruby groped for her glasses and pushed them onto her nose; they sat there unhappily, bent out of shape. She peered at the alarm clock.

'6.32,' she muttered, 'not even breakfast time.' It was unlike her mother to shout through the intercom unless there was a matter of some urgency.

'Is the house sinking, on fire, falling down?' Ruby grumbled.

Ruby fell from her bed, stumbled to her feet, staggered to the intercom and spoke into it. 'Hello caller, please divulge the nature of your query?'

'Have you forgotten about the mathlympics meet?' said her mother.

Yes, she had actually.

'Oh geez!' she moaned. Why did her mom enter her for these lame loser geek-central dork fests? What was the point of it all? Did she want to waste a precious day of her life sitting in a school gym or on a theatre stage with a whole bunch of other kids who were good at math?

No, she did not.

She knew exactly how good at math she was and she didn't need to stand on a box, finger on the buzzer, answering quiz questions to prove it. But this time there didn't seem to be any way out. She was going and that was that. Her mother could be a very determined woman.

While she was brushing her teeth, she peered out of the window. Mrs Beesman was out in what looked to be a dressing gown and pushing her shopping cart down Cedarwood. There was one sneaker sitting in the middle of the road, possibly a man's tennis shoe. She made a note of this in her yellow notebook and wondered how all these stray sneakers came to end up in the middle of roads; it was not by any means an unusual sight.

When she climbed into the car – her mother had already been sitting waiting for her for 'fifteen minutes, for goodness sake' – Sabina Redfort turned to her and said, 'Really? You had to wear *that* T-shirt?'

Ruby's T-shirt choice was one bearing the words: ***dorks beware***.

'And your glasses...?' said Sabina. 'What in the world of Twinford has happened to your glasses?'

Ruby shrugged. 'OK, let's get this over with.'

It was a long and testing day, not because the competition was especially tough, nor because the test questions were especially tricky, but because one of the candidates, one Dakota Lyme, was a royal pain in the butt.

Dakota Lyme was a girl Ruby had met twice before on the mathlympics field. Once when Ruby was four and once when she was eight. Dakota was one year and nine months older than Ruby and behaved like a child of that exact age.

She was a sore loser and what, was worse, she was an even sorer winner. On both previous occasions she had narrowly beaten Ruby in the final round and spent a lot of time afterwards crowing about it. Though what Dakota's parents had not pointed out to their little prodigy was that Dakota had been coached in the advanced math that was at the competition's heart and Ruby had just that day happened upon it.

This time things went a little differently.

They were equally matched right up until the final question, and the tension emanating from the parents could almost be touched.

'OK, you two,' said the compere, 'draw the shape represented by this formula.' Letters and numbers appeared on the screen:

$$\{\, (x_1, x_2, x_3, x_4) \in \mathbb{R}^4 \, ; \, -1 \le x_i \le 1 \,\}$$

Ruby frowned for a moment, then smiled. She glanced over at Dakota, who was looking panicked; it was obvious that nothing was coming to mind.

Ruby drew quickly. She had worked out in seconds that the

formula represented a tesseract, or a 4-dimensional cube – a shape with 24 edges that was to the cube what the cube was to the square. She chose to render it as a kind of fake 3D image that she knew was called a Schlegel diagram:

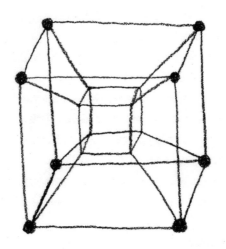

Then Ruby hit her buzzer.

'Redfort, you have the diagram?'

'Yes,' she said.

'Bring it to the podium for checking, please.'

She took her piece of paper over to the desk where the math checkers sat. They in turn checked it over and handed it on to the compere.

'Correct!' declared the compere. 'We have our winner.'

Dakota Lyme glared at Ruby, one eye covered by her long dark hair. Her mouth was pinched like she had just eaten something sour, her arms folded tightly across her chest.

The photographer stepped up to take some pictures and Dakota and Ruby were asked to stand uncomfortably close.

'If I could ask you to hold up your trophy Ruby, and Dakota, your runner-up prize.'

Ruby tried to force a smile, but it was hard because she hated this kind of dorky contest and even more than that she hated the dorky victory photographs. Dakota couldn't force a smile because she was too sore about her defeat. So they stood there looking in some ways remarkably similar. They were the same height, same build, had the same long dark hair, they even sort of dressed alike, though Dakota's T-shirt was pink and said *Party Girl*, and her sneakers had glitter detail and her jeans had a heart patch on the pocket. But their expressions weren't so very different – even if Ruby managed to look coolly aloof and Dakota unattractively bitter.

It was in the parking lot that Dakota became even less attractive. Ruby and Sabina were just driving slowly towards the exit when Dakota Lyme shouted, 'You're a phoney, Redfort. You cheat, I know you cheat, and your clothes are ugly, you dress like a boy.' Dakota stamped her foot.

Sabina Redfort reversed the car, wound down the window and said, 'And you, pipsqueak, are a very unpleasant little

madam who will never be attractive no matter what you wear!'
Then she put her foot down on the pedal and took off at more
speed than was wise.

Ruby winked at her mother and said, 'Nice going, Mom.'

And her mother said, 'I simply can't abide a sore loser.'

Chapter 11.
The talk of the town

TUESDAY MORNING CAME AND RUBY STUMBLED OUT OF
BED. She looked out of the window and there was Mrs Gruber
walking her Siamese cat. Mrs Gruber always walked her cat on
a Tuesday; it was something you could count on.

Ruby got ready for school and went down to the kitchen.
No one was there. She was about to grab a bagel and walk out of
the back door when she caught sight of an envelope lying on the
table. On the front, written in her dad's neat hand, the words:

For Ruby, congrats on the big math win, love Pop

And on the back:

P.S. I had to go through hell and high water to get this

She slit it open and pulled out a leaf-shaped piece of green
card that said:

**YOU ARE CORDIALLY INVITED TO THE
ENVIRONMENTAL EXPLORER AWARDS.**

She smiled. *Nice going, Dad*. There was a further note under
the envelope, this one from her mother:

I've ordered you new glasses, the pair you liked, as opposed to the ones I liked. Love Mom. P.S. Am I a nice mom or what?

Ruby smiled. 'Nice going, *Mom*.'

Ruby climbed aboard the school bus and made her way down to her usual seat and sank into it. Stuck to the window was that same sticker of the cross-eyed kid and someone had scribbled **WAKE UP AND SMELL THE BANANA MILK** underneath.

Del, thought Ruby, pushing back her sleeve to see the still very loud and clear message written on her arm. *That's not gonna disappear any time soon.* Someone else had put a line through Del's words and written, **WAKE UP AND SMELL THE COFFEE**.

Who drinks coffee on a school bus?

She caught sight of Bailey Roach sitting across the aisle – *probably him*, she thought. For just a second they locked eyes, but neither of them said a word. To the casual observer, this was no different from two strangers glancing at each other in the street, but to a person with good observational skills, the boy's awkward running of hands through hair and biting of lower lip told a story.

They were not friends, Ruby Redfort and Bailey Roach: he had blown his chances of friendship when he had picked on Clancy Crew. It wasn't just that Clancy was Ruby's closest friend; it was also a lot to do with the fact that Ruby couldn't stand watching someone get picked on, period. Roach might be a bully, and his previous actions could certainly be deemed cowardly, but he was not a fool. He had figured out that to cross Ruby Redfort was to take on one determined enemy and, to be frank, Bailey Roach always went for the easy target.

That was why Bailey Roach had avoided coming face to face with Clancy ever since the Marty's minimart incident. No one in Bailey Roach's gang, least of all Bailey, had understood how a wimpy-looking boy like Clancy had beaten him in a fight. Word had gone round school that Clancy Crew was not someone to be messed with, that he had some special moves, probably taught to him by some kung fu master. Whatever the reason, Roach certainly didn't want to repeat the experience.

Ruby made it into school in good time. This would give Mrs Drisco no opportunity to comment on Ruby's lack of regard for the school clock (something her form teacher did most days) but she *would* have ample opportunity to comment on the T-shirt Ruby was wearing, which read: ***Have you had a frontal lobotomy or have I?***

The first person she ran into was Del, who said, 'So I saw a picture of you in the paper standing with your little identical twin friend.'

'What?' said Ruby. 'What are you talking about?'

Just then Mouse came running down the corridor. 'Hey, Ruby,' she called, 'who's that kid in the Twinford Mirror, you related or something?'

'She looks nothing like me,' protested Ruby.

Five minutes later Elliot arrived, waving the newspaper

excitedly. 'You have a doppelganger!'

The photograph was black and white and did not show the vivid pink T-shirt or the glittery sneakers, the heart patch on the jeans, or indeed much of Dakota Lyme's mean, pinched face.

Red walked over, and peered at the picture. 'Hey Ruby, congratulations. I didn't know you had won the mathlympics prize!'

'Don't you think that girl looks like Ruby?' said Del.

'Not even slightly,' said Red. 'Dakota Lyme is a total vacuum.'

Ruby thanked Red for her support and went off to find Clancy, who was sitting on a bench reading his *Garbage Girl* comic.

'You're *early*?' said Clancy.

'Maybe I'm turning over a new leaf,' said Ruby.

'I give you one day, possibly two.'

'For what?'

'For your leaf to turn back over.'

'I'm inspired by your confidence.'

'I just *know* you – likelihood is you are going to revert to your old ways.'

'Well, that's kinda depressing.'

'Talking of depressing, look who it is,' said Clancy.

Vapona Begwell walked by with her little gang. Gemma Melamare's nose was encased in a triangle of splint and wadding. Ruby almost felt sorry for her; Gemma was very proud of her nose. It was certainly the cutest thing about her.

When they passed, Vapona gave Ruby the evil eye and hissed, 'Tell Lasco she's a yellow-belly.'

'Jeepers Vapona, tell her yourself,' said Ruby. 'I haven't got time to run little messages between you guys.'

'You're in my sights, Redfort!'

'I'm flattered,' said Ruby as she walked into her form room.

'So what's the real reason for your punctuality?' asked Clancy.

'I got something to tell you,' said Ruby.

'Please don't make me guess,' said Clancy.

'My dad gave me this.' Ruby took out the invitation.

'You must be in his good books,' said Clancy. 'My dad said you either got to know the right people or part with a whole lot of cash.'

The first class of the morning was behavioural science and Mr Cornsworth was excited to announce a project which he hoped all the students would take part in.

'I would like you to explore the idea of social interaction and think about the way human beings form groups and clubs and the various ways they communicate. Perhaps you could explore and investigate the importance and significance of these rituals.'

There was a lot of exaggerated yawning from Vapona Begwell and Gemma Melamare. Bailey Roach, who was sitting at the back of the class, was throwing balled-up pieces of paper across the room. Mr Cornsworth was not a confident teacher and had little clue when it came to controlling a class of thirteen and fourteen-year-olds, but when he went on to mention there would be 'extra credit' suddenly there was a lot of interest.

Vapona, Gemma and Bailey Roach really needed to make up their grades. So did Clancy, as a matter of fact, but he was interested in the project for other reasons. Already he could see the outlines of a way of making a strong challenge to Mrs Bexenheath's proposal that the school lockers be relocated. Not only might he change Principal Levine's mind, but he could also gain a big tick on his grade sheet.

Clancy started planning immediately, chewing on his pen.

Ruby felt she had enough on her plate, psychologically speaking, without having to think about other people's behavioural patterns – and besides, she didn't need the extra credit. She might not be the most punctual, but she was a straight-A student.

The issue more *immediately* facing her was the psychological falling apart of her basketball teammates. She had been thinking about this for much of the morning, already dreading the moment when school would end and she and her team would have to make their way to the Basketball courts, where they would almost certainly lose.

Mouse was sat on the bench just down from the lower Amster stop when Ruby got there, waiting for the bus that would take them to the tournament. Opposite was a large brick wall and newly pasted there was an advertisement for something which showed the massive cartoon head of a kid, eyes crossed, and twisting from the mouth in huge curly letters the words:

Taste Twisters

Weird, thought Ruby. *What's that supposed to—*

'What do you think the likelihood is that we get totally slammed?' said Mouse, interrupting her thoughts.

'You know that's not a great attitude, Mouse.'

'I just hate losing, and with Del on the bench we probably will.'

'I read in this tennis coaching magazine that you're a whole lot more likely to win if you love winning.'

'I do love winning, that's what I said.'

'No, you said you hate losing. You shouldn't be focusing on the losing, just set your sights on winning.'

'Yeah, I guess you're right, but I don't think we're gonna.'

Ruby sighed, knowing this was probably true: most of her teammates did not have the killer instinct.

'What do you reckon Taste Twisters are?' said Ruby, staring at the image of the boss-eyed cartoon kid.

Mouse studied the picture.

She shrugged. 'Some kind of candy – aimed at kids.'

Ruby continued to stare. 'It's odd that they don't tell you what it is, don't you think? I mean, ordinarily they would want you to know.'

'What are you guys looking at?' called Elliot. He was walking towards them along the sidewalk, his gym bag over his shoulder. Del and Red were lagging a little behind.

'We are trying to figure out what a Taste Twister is,' called Mouse.

Elliot joined them on the bench and he too turned his gaze on the poster. After a couple of minutes he said, 'A drink – it's a drink of some kind, most probably a kids' drink.'

'Why a drink?' said Mouse.

'Because of the straw,' said Elliot.

'Where's the straw?' asked Mouse. 'I can't see any straw.'

'The twisting words, they represent a straw.'

'I don't see it myself,' said Mouse. 'But if it *were* a drink then what flavour would it be?'

'Milk,' said Elliot. 'Milk. Has to be.'

'Why?' said Mouse.

'Look at the kid's teeth. If it was for soda or something then they wouldn't emphasise how white the kid's teeth were. They're saying drink milk and have strong white teeth.'

'When do they ever advertise a drink and show the kid with rotten teeth?' said Ruby. 'Doesn't matter if the drink is choc full of sugar and treacle, they would still show the kid smiling a pretty smile. White teeth proves nothing.'

'Who cares what it is,' said Del. 'I'd as soon drink a blue slushy, they're super good.'

'Think like that, my friend, and you'll never taste anything better,' said Red.

'What's better than a slushy?' said Del.

'You'll never know,' said Red.

'I like slushies,' said Del.

'You should broaden your horizons,' said Ruby.

They sat looking for a little longer until Elliot shook his head and said, 'I gotta make tracks.'

The bus came into view and Mouse picked up her bag and waited for it to pull into the stop.

Ruby sat a little longer. *Cross-eyes*, she thought. *If it's a drink then it's a sharp-flavoured drink. It has bite.*

The game itself might only have been forty-eight minutes plus stoppage time, but it was a *long* and *uncomfortable* forty-eight minutes plus stoppage time. Vapona Begwell and her team (the Vaporizers) took every opportunity to step on Ruby's toes, elbow her in the ribs and knock her over.

The Deliverers (Ruby's team) did not make it through to round two, and so as far as Ruby was concerned, there didn't seem like a whole lot of point sticking around until the end of the tournament. She certainly wasn't going to sit there and watch the Vaporizers grab victory.

Vapona's parting words were, 'I'm gonna pulp you Redfort.'

'Yeah, change the record would you, you said that at least forty times.'

Del Lasco didn't have to suffer the insults and general barging because her wrist was still strapped and she was sitting comfortably on the sidelines.

'She's only looking to pulp you because she can't pulp me,' said Del.

'Is that supposed to make me feel better,' said Ruby, 'knowing that just being your friend causes me pain?'

Chapter 12.
Beware of the dog

MOUSE AND RED HAD STUCK AROUND TO WATCH THE REST OF THE GAMES, but Ruby and Del didn't have the heart. They now had time on their hands.

'You wanna go down to Back-Spin and play table tennis?' asked Del.

'Oh, interesting, you can hold a ping-pong bat but you can't dribble a basketball?'

'Table tennis isn't a contact sport,' countered Del, 'basketball can be.'

'You don't need to explain that to me,' said Ruby. 'You wanna see the bruises Bugwart laid on me?'

'I can't wait for my sprain to heal – I'll be only too glad to have her try and land a punch.'

'I'd be happy to point her in your direction,' said Ruby.

'Don't worry about it, I'll get her soon enough.'

'You should give up on the fighting, it doesn't achieve a thing. You think if you punch her she's not gonna punch you back?'

'It's an honour thing,' argued Del. 'If I let her knock me down and I don't retaliate, what will people think?'

'That you're not as dumb as you look.'

In the end they decided to give the table tennis cafe a miss and instead hang out at Ruby's house. Ruby was keen for Del to keep a low profile and, in any case, Mrs Digby had mentioned that she might be baking. Mrs Digby's baking was right up there with sliced bread – her cookies were in a league of their own.

When Del and Ruby made it home to Green-Wood house, they found Mrs Digby peering at a large piece of black and white paper rolled out on the kitchen table. She had a comedy-sized magnifying glass in her hand and was moving it across the paper, back and forth.

There was no sign of any cookies.

'What are you looking at Mrs Digby?'

'A map of old Twinford,' she said without looking up. 'Your father got it for me.'

'Why dya wanna look at an old map?' asked Del.

'I like to see how things once were in this town,' said the housekeeper.

'And how were they Mrs Digby?' said Ruby, her head in the pantry.

'Better,' said the housekeeper. 'Seems every day now they go knocking an old building down or running a road through it. I barely recognise my own neighbourhood, find I get lost in my own city. If it weren't for the place names, you wouldn't have a blind clue what used to be there.'

'So Mrs Digby,' said Ruby, 'we were sort of wondering if there might be any, you know, cookies?'

The housekeeper put her hands on her hips and said, 'Upstairs in your room, and don't ever go about saying I'm not a slave to your every need.'

It was while they were sitting on the roof eating Mrs Digby's cookies that misfortune struck.

Ruby had just popped down to the kitchen to fetch some banana milk and returned to find Del peering over the top into the next-door yard.

'What are you looking at?' asked Ruby.

'Your comic – I just put it down for a second while I put on my sweater...' said Del.

Ruby looked over the roof edge: there was the comic sitting on Mr Parker's lawn.

'It was an accident,' said Del. 'The wind sorta took it.'

'You know, *Kung Fu Martians* is rare – that's a collector's edition, plus I haven't finished reading it.'

'I'm sorry OK,' said Del, getting to her feet. 'Look, I'll go knock on his door and ask for it back.'

'You're kidding. You think you can just go over to Mr Parker's and ask for your comic back? You must be crazy.'

'Sure I do – what's the worst he can do?'

'One – feed it to his dog; two – feed *you* to his dog.'

'You're being a little dramatic, aren't you?'

'No,' said Ruby, 'actually, NO. Remember Red's hat?' Del made a face, she remembered all right. 'Oh, and don't forget Clancy's sweater, Clancy's left sneaker, Clancy's trumpet, my mom's scarf – he apologised for that one, he even returned it, though the whole middle section was missing.'

'OK,' sighed Del, 'I get your point, I'll have to climb over the fence.'

'With your wrist strapped? I don't think so.' Ruby stood up. 'It's me that's gonna have to get it.' Without another word, she stepped off the rooftop and onto the eucalyptus branch that extended towards the house. *Darn it Del*, she thought.

Ruby walked the branch like a tightrope walker might, arms outstretched and feet stepping one in front of the other, until she reached the end. From there she looked out across the yard and the alley that ran between the backs of the houses. She was looking to see where Mr Parker was and, perhaps more crucially, Mr Parker's dog, Bubbles. Mr Parker was a man who rarely had a good word to say about anyone or anything. He just didn't like people and as Mrs Digby so wisely said, 'Steer clear of folks who don't like folks.' Bubbles, meanwhile, was a *dog* who didn't like people, but did enjoy biting them. For these two reasons Ruby rarely trespassed on Mr Parker's land, not if she could possibly help it.

She stood there perfectly still, listening for activity that might warn of her neighbour's presence, but she could only hear the wind and feel its keenness to snatch her from her perch.

She took a deep breath and leapt.

She landed on the branch of the tree next door and she didn't stop, running now, climbing as high as the tree would take her. She moved so quickly that the weaker branches had no time to snap, her weight gone before the branch realised it could not hold her.

As Ruby swayed from limb to limb, reaching out to grab another, stepping lightly from one to the next, she felt almost like she were defying gravity, treading the space between things. Having left the safety of her own yard, she wanted nothing more than to retrieve the comic and get out of there. She couldn't see Bubbles. She waited, she scanned the yard, looking all around, but there was no sign of the Doberman, which meant Mr Parker was out. Below her, a large cat watched, tail twitching, ready to pounce should the strange bird fall.

If Bubbles was here, she reasoned, *then this cat would be running for its life.*

She dropped to the ground, ran to the middle of the lawn and snatched up the comic, then stuffed it down her sweatshirt and began to climb back up the tree.

'What exactly are you doing?'

The voice came from far below.

It wasn't one Ruby recognised and in her confusion she nearly toppled from the branch.

'Relax!' came a different voice. 'It's just me!'

'Jeepers Clance! Is that supposed to be funny? You nearly

'half scared the wits out of me.'

'Sorry Rube.' He was staring up from the alley at the back of the houses, his eyes hidden behind a pair of flower-shaped dark glasses. 'But actually what *are* you doing?'

'Dicing with death.'

'I'll say,' said Clancy. 'You do know that if Mr Parker catches you you'll be skinned alive?'

'That's the kind of thing Mrs Digby would say.'

'Yes, and she happens to be right.'

'And I happen to know he's gotta be out – there's no sign of Bubbles.'

'I wouldn't bet on it.'

'You scared, Crew?'

'Sure I'm scared – and not of the dog. Mr Parker is one mean old man.'

'You don't wanna be scared of Mr Parker,' said Ruby, preparing to jump back towards home. 'Mr Parker is a pussycat.' She leapt.

At that exact moment a voice bellowed and Ruby, losing concentration, failed to catch the branch her outstretched arm was reaching for and tumbled through the leaves, grabbing at any flimsy twigs that might prevent her fall.

'Boy!' the new voice boomed. 'What are you doing peering over my yard fence?'

Clancy twisted around to see the angry beet-coloured face of Mr Parker.

'Oh, me,' stammered Clancy, 'me?'

'Yes, you, idiot. Is there another skinny, good-for-nothing chump looking into my yard?'

'I wouldn't think so Mr Parker, I'll bet I'm the only one.'

'So answer me quick – what's got you so interested in my property?'

'I saw a raccoon,' said Clancy, 'more than one, several, in fact lots of them. I was going to inform you because I thought you would want to, you know, call raccoon control?'

'I don't need raccoon control,' he spat. 'I'll simply set my dog on them just as soon as I find her – she's gone AWOL.' He whistled a command as if to illustrate the point. 'Disappeared into thin air,' said Mr Parker. 'I don't suppose you know something about that, do you?' He trained his beady eyes on Clancy and Clancy stepped back a pace.

'Why would I, Mr Parker? But I'm happy to help you look.'

Unfortunately, Ruby's cluster of twigs parted company with the tree at that moment and she was again tumbling through the branches and this time to the ground.

'Ouch.'

Mr Parker's ears pricked up. 'Was that an *ouch*?' he said, fumbling for his gate key.

'I doubt it,' said Clancy. 'I've never heard a raccoon say ouch.'

'Don't get smart with me boy. It's that Redfort girl, isn't it?'

'I wouldn't think so sir.'

But Mr Parker wasn't listening. 'Girl!' he bellowed. 'You're in trouble so deep you'll need that hound of yours to dig you out.'

'Hey, let me help you with that key,' said Clancy, knocking the key out of the old man's hand. It fell between the bars of a drain cover, clattered into the darkness and that was that for Mr Parker's gate key.

This delaying tactic gave Ruby just enough time to stumble to her feet, then half-run half-limp across the Parker lawn.

Mr Parker whistled again to his dog and this time Ruby thought she did hear something: not a bark, not a yap, but perhaps a whimper. It was the noise an injured dog might make. It was coming from the space underneath the house.

Mr Parker's house was built in the old tradition – a clapboard house on short stilts off the ground. Ruby paused and looked, and what she thought she saw was a tangled reel of rubber hose come to life.

It couldn't be.

So she stepped in closer and stared into the darkened space.

What she saw made her take a sharp breath and hold it.

Yes. It could be.

For under the Parker house was a writhing mass of snakes, and Bubbles, lying on her side, drool around her muzzle.

'Oh jeez, Bubbles,' said Ruby. 'This ain't good.'

Chapter 13.
Never poke a nest of vipers

MR PARKER WAS FURIOUS. Clancy could tell that by the way his nostrils flared – also by his constant repeating of the words, 'Don't be surprised if I don't skin you alive!' and 'What kind of delinquent are you?'

He was very unhappy about the lost gate key. 'Now I've got to go all the way down the street to my sister's house to pick up my spare.'

'You have a sister, Mr Parker, that's nice,' said Clancy.

'Nice? Why is it nice?' demanded Mr Parker. 'Just another drain on me, another individual trying to get their hands on my fortune.' And off he stomped back down the alley. When he was out of sight, Clancy stuck his head over the fence. 'He's gone,' he hissed, 'you can get out of there.'

But Ruby stayed right where she was, crouched on the ground.

'What are you doing? What's happened?' said Clancy.

'You better get over here,' said Ruby.

'Is the dog there?' asked Clancy.

'Yeah, but she's not going to be much interested in trespassers today.'

'OK, if you say so,' said Clancy, scrabbling over the fence. He ran over to where Ruby was kneeling. 'Jeez,' he exclaimed, 'what happened to her?'

'Snakes,' said Ruby. 'Can you wait while I call for help?'

'Sure,' said Clancy, 'but don't be long, she doesn't look good, plus I don't want to be here when Mr Parker comes home.'

'I'll be quick – don't get too near, Clance, you know what they say about injured animals. Not to mention that whole nest of vipers there.'

Ruby leapt the fence into her yard and ran into the house, where she picked up the phone.

Then, for just a moment, she paused. If she did this, she was almost certainly going to blow her cover. They'd know it was a girl who had called – and Mr Parker would find out she was in his yard.

On the other hand, she couldn't just leave Bubbles to die, could she? She didn't like Bubbles a whole lot, but that wasn't Bubbles' fault.

She sighed, and dialled the emergency vet – who, lucky for Bubbles, was available and on her way.

Next she called the emergency services. Ruby wasn't exactly sure which department might deal with a nest of venomous snakes, but she was sure someone would be interested.

'I'm calling to report a dangerous animal situation in my

neighbour's back yard,' she said.

'What nature of dangerous animal?'

'There's a ton of snakes under his house.'

'What kind of snakes?'

'Venomous ones, if you're taking an interest.'

'How do you know that?'

'Because I know a bunch about snakes. They're Mojave Greens if that helps, you can look them up in your encyclopaedia under V for vipers. Why they've left the desert I don't know. Maybe it's this weird weather.'

'Maybe you know about snakes, but how do you know they're in your neighbour's back yard?'

Ruby took a breath. 'Because I was there.'

'You were in your neighbour's back yard and you saw a nest of Mojave Green snakes.' The woman didn't sound convinced.

'Look, I'm not the biggest fan of Mr Parker and, believe me, if he didn't have a dog I might think twice about calling you. I just want to make it clear that I am doing this for Bubbles and I say this as someone who doesn't even like Bubbles.'

The vet arrived within seven minutes, heading straight for the alleyway and the back yard. The snake wrangler turned up not long after – luckily he travelled with a ladder, which cut down on the fence climbing. It was quite a busy scene in Mr Parker's yard and when Ruby heard the latch click on the back-yard gate she ran for all she was worth up the ladder and over the front fence, out onto Cedarwood Drive and up her own front steps and in the front door. She would rather not be Parker-side when her neighbour discovered the drama.

She arrived back in the Green-Wood house kitchen gasping to catch her breath.

Mrs Digby continued slicing potatoes.

'Can I expect a knock at the door?' she said.

Ruby did her best to adopt an innocent expression, though she was unable to puff out a word.

There was a heavy *thud thud* at the door, followed by an angry tirade.

Mrs Digby put down her knife. 'I wonder who that can be,' she said, her eyes fixing on Ruby. She picked up her broom and off she went in the direction of the front door.

Del, by now, had crept down from the roof and joined Ruby in the kitchen and the two of them stood by the door and listened.

'Well, howdy Mr Parker, what can I do for you today?'

'I'm not here to exchange niceties,' snarled Mr Parker.

'Well, blow me down, that is a surprise,' retorted Mrs Digby, sounding not in the least surprised. 'Now state your business or I'll sweep you off my stoop with this broom.'

'My yard is crawling with vets and snake wranglers and it's all that girl's fault.'

'I suppose you mean Ruby?'

'Don't play the innocent with me. Pest Control said a girl called them. She's been in my yard again. Are you saying you're not concerned about that? The girl is a criminal. Property boundaries mean nothing to her.'

Ruby looked at Del, rolled her eyes and shrugged before walking out to face the old man.

'Hello Mr Parker, what can I do for you?' she said.

'You can stop trespassing on my property!' shouted Mr Parker.

Mrs Digby – who was standing between them, arms folded, broom in hand – said, 'What's this about snakes?'

'Mr Parker has a nest of vipers under his house,' said Ruby. 'One of them got Bubbles.'

Mrs Digby shivered. Snakes were one of God's creatures she wished had never made it onto that ark.

'If this is true Mr Parker, and I see no reason in tarnation to doubt that it is, then why are you cluttering my doorstep and wasting my valuable time with your pointless griping?' Mr Parker opened his mouth to continue griping, but Mrs Digby wasn't finished. 'I am sure it is an offence to harbour dangerous reptiles under your property and so it seems to me like you should be shaking this child by the hand and thanking her for not turning you in.'

'She had no right to be on my property in the first place,' snarled Mr Parker.

'Well, that I can't argue with,' said Mrs Digby, 'but that aside, answer me this: where would your dog be now if she hadn't a been?' Mr Parker looked lost for words, but Mrs Digby wasn't. 'Somewhere in dog purgatory, if I know Bubbles.'

'Yes, but trespassing on my property!' said Mr Parker. 'That girl needs to learn to respect her—'

Mrs Digby stepped forward, raising her broom. 'Well this is *Redfort* property,' she said. 'So I suggest you remove your ungrateful behind before I sweep you off it.'

For a moment, Mr Parker eyed the broom. Then he glared at Ruby. 'This isn't over,' he said. 'Trespass is illegal. It's the principle of the thing. You, girl, are a delinquent! A degenerate!'

Ruby had had enough. 'Yeah?' she said. 'Well, you're a small-minded jackass who should stick his principles where the sun don't shine. And you know what else? You can...'

She told him what else and then some. Most of it did not bear repeating.

'Hey Ruby,' called a small lispy voice.

Quent Humbert had appeared on the pathway behind Mr Parker. As the old grouch stormed off, shouting back at Ruby as he went, Quent was almost knocked off his feet and into the bamboo.

'Quent?' she said.

'Hey Ruby, how are you?' said Quent. You could be forgiven for thinking the previous minute's confrontation hadn't happened.

'Oh you know, fine Quent, I was just talking to that nice neighbour of mine about the reptile infestation under his house which is about to poison the entire neighbourhood starting with his own dog.'

Quent nodded. 'I'm glad he's not my neighbour, he's kind of

grouchy.' Then Quent stuck his hand in his jacket pocket and rummaged around for a few seconds before pulling out a small book which had a picture of a mouse on the front. The mouse was holding a camera and in the camera flash was written the word *Autographs*. He handed it to Ruby.

'What, you want my autograph?' she said.

'I already got it,' said Quent, 'but I was hoping you could take my book to the Explorer awards and get as many signatures as possible. My dad told me you were going. I wish I was, but I'm not, I can't, there aren't any more tickets.'

'Look Quent, I'd like to help out but it might be kinda frenzied, you know, trying to get signatures and all.'

Might be kinda dorky too, was what she was thinking.

Quent looked like he was going to have a lower-lip tremble. Plus Mrs Digby gave a meaningful sniff before turning and going back into the house.

Ruby sighed. 'Hey, I tell you what, you hold on to it for now and I promise I'll take it on the night. I'll do my best, OK?'

'Thanks Ruby, it would be unbelievably super if you could.'

'Like I said, I'll do my best.'

'So my mom said you're not coming out tonight?'

'Why would I be coming out tonight?' asked Ruby.

'For a family dinner,' said Quent. 'I hoped you'd be able to come, but your mom said you had a big basketball tournament.'

'That's true, I did have a big basketball tournament.'

'So why are you here?' asked Clancy.

'It was cut short,' explained Ruby.

'What happened?'

'We lost.'

'Great, so now you can come?' said Quent hopefully.

'Sorry to disappoint you know, Quent, but as you can see I'm all tied up with community stuff.'

'Too bad,' said Quent. 'Another time.'

'Not if I see you first,' said Ruby.

He smiled. 'You're funny Ruby.'

Ruby walked back inside.

'Boy, that kid has some issues,' said Del.

'Talking of issues,' said Ruby, 'are you short sighted or something?'

'How do you mean?' asked Del.

'You were supposed to be looking out!'

'I was looking out, but what was I meant to do? Shout "Ruby get the heck outta there, the old trout is on his way"? I mean, that would have been kinda obviously giving the game away, wouldn't it?'

'Have you ever heard of sound signals?' said Ruby. 'A hoot, a whistle?'

'You want me to hoot like an owl?' said Del. 'How suspicious is that in the middle of the day? Owls are night birds.'

'Well, it's no great surprise you're not a secret agent.'

'Yeah, well as far as I heard neither are you,' said Del.

Chapter 14.
Two wrongs make a right

RUBY WASN'T SURE WHAT VIEW HER PARENTS WOULD TAKE ON THE MR PARKER INCIDENT, not after her mom had taken the call from Mrs Boyce informing her about the Five Aces dumpster episode, gossip, which had travelled down from the biggest mouth of them all, Mr Chester. Mrs Digby had warned Ruby that the 'cat was out of the bag' and that Ruby should 'brace herself for a truck of trouble'.

'How do you know?' asked Ruby.

'Your mother phoned me from work – asked me if I was aware.'

'What did you say?' asked Ruby.

'I said I don't waste my time listening to tittle-tattle,' said Mrs Digby.

'She hasn't just heard about what just happened with Mr Parker, has she?' said Ruby.

'One crime at a time,' said Mrs Digby.

'Maybe I'll have an early night,' said Ruby.

'That's why your mother was calling – she wants you to meet

at the restaurant.'

'What restaurant?'

'Cipriani's, you're having a family supper.'

'What?' said Ruby. 'Tell me Quent will not be there...'

'Quent will be there.'

'They're torturing me,' said Ruby.

'Well, for what it's worth,' said Mrs Digby, 'I think you did the right thing. And even if Bubbles is the devil's own dog, she deserves an owner better than Mr Parker. If you hadn't done what you did, Bubbles would be dead and buried, and you would be sitting here feeling worse than wretched.' Mrs Digby looked Ruby square in the eye and said, 'Be true to yourself, Ruby Redfort, and it will steer you right.'

When Ruby arrived at the restaurant, she found her mother sitting waiting for her, a bowl of fat green olives on the table and another dish already a quarter full with olive stones. Not a good sign: her mother only ate fast when she was angry.

'Where *is* everyone?' said Ruby, wishing they would appear.

'I wanted time alone with you,' said Sabina Redfort, popping an olive into her mouth. 'We need to straighten a few things out, young lady.'

'Mom, you sound like Knuckles Lonagon from *Crazy Cops*.'

'It's all around town,' said her mother.

'Are we talking about what I think we are talking about?'

'You have something else to confess?'

'Not right now,' said Ruby.

'Well, no matter, I'm sure Mr Chester will pick up the phone if there is.'

'Mr Chester must lead a very dull life,' said Ruby.

'Yes, he does,' said her mother, depositing the stone in the dish. 'We should pity him for having nothing more interesting to talk about than *you* but, before we do, let's pity the long-suffering mother who is raising a daughter who thinks it's perfectly acceptable to jump into a trash can.'

'It wasn't *planned*,' said Ruby.

'Well, that is a relief,' said Sabina. 'I really would be depressed to discover you had planned to start your day by jumping in garbage.' She reached for another olive. 'Boy are these olives good.'

'Pugliese,' said Ruby.

'Pardon?' said Sabina.

'They're Pugliese – from Puglia in the south of Italy, firm to the bite, creamy texture, not in the least bitter – in my opinion they're the best kind.'

'When did you learn so much about olives?' said her mother.

Ruby shrugged. 'Just picked it up, I guess.'

'Well, getting back to the point...' said Sabina.

'I'm sorry,' said Ruby. 'If it helps then I should say that I have no desire to do it again.'

'It helps a little,' said Sabina.

'Can we please go back to pitying Mr Chester for leading such a futile life?'

'No,' said her mother, 'I haven't finished being mad at *you*.'

'Is there something I can do to make it up to you?'

'Yes, you can rinse out our garbage cans and clean up the trash that is blowing around in front of our house, starting tomorrow.'

Ruby rolled her eyes. '*Now* you're *encouraging* me to engage with garbage, make your mind up.'

The restaurant door opened and Sabina started waving like crazy at Freddie and Marjorie Humbert.

'Over here!' she called.

'Ruby!' shouted Quent. He had a large Band-Aid wrapped over the lobe of his ear. 'I got bitten on the ear by my gerbil, do you want to see the wound?'

'That *just* happened? I mean, you were at my house about an hour ago,' said Ruby.

'I know!' beamed Quent. 'Unlucky, huh? It's really oozing.'

Ruby looked around the restaurant; it felt like everyone was looking.

'Keep your voice down Quent or they'll all want a peek.'

Everyone settled into their seats and chit-chatted for a bit. Ruby attempted to dissuade Quent from revealing his gerbil bite (unsuccessful), the waiter came over, orders were taken, the main course was eaten and things were going pretty smoothly, if a little dully, until Quent piped up.

'So Ruby rescued a dog.'

Ruby kicked Quent under the table.

'You rescued a dog?' said Brant.

'Not really,' said Ruby.

'She did!' said Quent. 'My gerbil's vet told me.'

'I thought it was you that got bitten?' said Sabina, looking confused.

'Boy, word really does get around,' said Ruby.

'It was being attacked by snakes,' said Quent.

'The gerbil or the dog?' said Marjorie.

'The dog,' said Quent, 'it was bitten by snakes.'

'Snakes where?' said Sabina.

'Under the house,' said Quent.

'Whose house?' said Freddie.

'Mr Parker's,' said Quent. 'But Ruby saw it and called for help.'

'What were you doing looking under Mr Parker's house?' said Brant.

'I wasn't. Look, if you must know, I was just retrieving my comic which had blown into Mr Parker's yard and then I heard a dog whimper, saw some snakes, called the vet and the emergency services, end of story,' said Ruby picking up her menu. 'Does anyone feel like dessert?'

'Mr Parker must have been quite relieved,' said Marjorie.

'He was furious,' said Ruby.

'Why?' asked Freddie.

'He doesn't like people trespassing,' explained Brant.

'What, a kid can't occasionally kick a ball into his yard without the cops being called?' said Freddie. 'What kind of person is he?'

'A grouch,' said Sabina.

'I quite agree,' said Brant, agreeing. 'I mean, why shouldn't a kid occasionally drop something in another person's yard and need to retrieve it?'

'And if Ruby hadn't been so careless then the man's dog would be dead as a doormat,' said Sabina.

'Dormouse,' said Marjorie.

'Dodo,' said Ruby.

'She's a hero of dogs,' said Quent.

'You got that right,' said Sabina. She raised her glass. 'Congratulations on saving the life of that awful dog,' she toasted.

'That poor unfortunate awful dog,' said Brant, chinking glasses.

And just like that, Sabina Redfort stopped being mad about the dumpster incident and was beaming with pride about her dog-saving daughter.

**The unpleasant clank of
the wake-up alarm sounded
in the penitentiary...**

...and the prisoners waited to file out of their cells. The usual count began, but this time the numbers did not add up right.

'Marshall? Where in all curses is Marshall?'

There was no reply, just the drip drip sound from the prison-cell faucet.

'Toss the cells!' bellowed the guard. 'Check every darn crevice of this facility!'

Thirty minutes later and all that was recovered was the prison-issue uniform of prisoner 2185.

Five hours later and a tunnel was discovered, beginning to the left of the sink and winding its way through the inside of the building's walls where all the pipes converged, and exiting...

...500 yards beyond the prison fence.

Chapter 15.
In the doghouse

IT WAS ONLY WHEN RUBY TOOK THE STAIRS DOWN TO BREAKFAST THE NEXT MORNING that she realised that although her parents were happy to let the matter drop, Mr Parker was not.

'I want to know what you are going to do about your daughter?' she heard him demand from the front stoop.

'What do you mean? She saved your dog, didn't she?' her mother replied, her tone indicating that she was trying to reason with a most unreasonable man.

'She did no such thing. She trespassed on my land is what she did.'

'And discovered a whole bunch of snakes,' argued her mother.

'Which she had no business discovering,' countered Mr Parker.

'But if she hadn't then Bubbles would be dead, poisoned to death at the hands of one of those vipers.'

'Who's to say what would have happened? Maybe I would

have found Bubbles and saved myself a vet bill too.'

'Look Mr Parker, we are very happy to cover all expenses,' said Sabina, trying to calm things down.

'That isn't the point.'

'Mr Parker, you are one contrary man,' announced Mrs Redfort.

'Now you are sounding like that daughter of yours, I'm sure she gets her foul mouth from somewhere.'

'Well, I beg you pardon Mr Parker!' cried Sabina. 'I do not have a foul mouth and I only ever curse when I feel there is no alternative which happens to be just about n—'

Brant Redfort arrived on the scene.

Brant: 'Now Mr Parker, my wife is only trying to point out that my daughter's actions were well meant. I'm happy to pick up the vet bill if you are happy to let the matter drop.'

'What?' spluttered Mr Parker. 'After what your daughter said to me?'

Brant Redfort swallowed nervously. 'I'm sure Ruby wasn't intending to offend.'

Mr Parker: 'Well if she wasn't intending to offend then why did she call me a small-minded jackass who could stick his petty principles where the sun don't shine?'

Oh dear, thought Ruby, *well at least he stopped there*. But unfortunately for Ruby, Mr Parker hadn't stopped there, he went on to repeat word for word all the other stuff Ruby had enjoyed telling Mr Parker and, as much as Ruby knew her father loathed

Mr Parker, she also knew just how much her father loathed any kind of rudeness. *Don't sink to the level of bottom feeders or you yourself will become a bottom feeder*, was something Brant Redfort regularly trotted out.

Ruby waited until the front door had been closed before coming down to the kitchen.

Her father looked up when she entered the room.

'I'm guessing you're aware that Mr Parker just paid us a visit.'

'Oh is that who it was,' said Ruby. 'Did he have anything nice to say?'

'When does that man ever have anything nice to say?' said her mother.

'I understand this fellow could make a saint swear, Ruby, but I would hope you were above that,' said Brant.

'Well, sorry, I'm no better than a saint,' said Ruby.

'I'm afraid I'm going to have to ground you,' said her father. Ruby's parents rarely, if ever, grounded her. They looked most uncomfortable about it too, it just wasn't their style – she could see how embarrassing they found it and that made it worse somehow.

'Do what you gotta do,' said Ruby, who had never been successfully grounded her entire life, though of course her parents didn't know this. 'I better go ring Red, tell her I won't be meeting up to plan the Halloween costumes.'

'Well...' began Sabina, 'maybe we could make an exception

for that. We could ground you afterwards, that way you wouldn't miss out.'

Brant raised his eyes to heaven. 'The whole point, honey, is that she does miss out, otherwise why ground her?'

'I don't know, Brant, it just seems a bit harsh.'

'Look,' said Ruby, 'don't let's go getting our underwear in a bunch. Dad's right, I'll miss the meet up, that way everyone will feel I'm suffering – I'll suffer, my friends will suffer, you'll suffer...'

'Wait a minute, how will we suffer?' said Sabina.

'You'll have me cluttering up the place. We'll all suffer together for what I said to Mr Parker even if he in fact deserved it,' said Ruby.

'Well, we know he deserved it,' said her mother.

'That's not helpful honey,' said Brant.

'It's fine, I'll do my time,' said Ruby.

'Oh, thanks Rube, that's very good of you,' said Sabina.

'Don't mention it,' said Ruby, 'so are the Explorer Awards off too?'

Her parents looked troubled. 'No, of course you mustn't miss the Explorer event,' said Sabina.

Her father said nothing for a minute and then, 'Look, since you are being such a sport about all this, why don't we all agree to skip this whole grounding thing this time,' he said. 'I mean, I think we are all on the same page here, don't you?'

'Don't swear at the neighbours. Got it,' said Ruby.

❀ ❀ ❀

Clancy was looking pretty happy when Ruby got to school that morning. He was standing by her locker waiting for her.

'What's making you all at one with the world?' she asked.

'I figured how I'm going to tackle my behavioural science project,' said Clancy. Clancy was pleased because he often agonised about these things. When everyone else seemed to have come up with their brilliant idea he was still sitting there chewing his pencil. 'It's good, really good, but I'm going to need a state-of-the-art video camera.'

'What?' said Ruby.

'I wondered if you could maybe borrow one from the Spectrum gadget room?'

'What?' said Ruby.

'A tiny little video camera, nothing too big,' he explained.

'Are you aware of the magnitude of your request?' asked Ruby.

'I know it's a biggy,' said Clancy. 'I'd owe you one.'

'You'd owe me plenty,' said Ruby, 'so you might as well forget about it.'

Mouse and Elliot arrived on the scene.

'So,' said Mouse, 'I heard you had a brilliant idea.'

'Did I not tell you?' asked Clancy.

'No,' said Elliot, 'I guess Mouse is the only living breathing person you forgot to inform.'

'Well,' said Clancy, 'you know how Principal Levine was saying how the lockers might be moved to another part of the building because there was no need for them to be in the main corridor?'

'Uh huh.'

'Well, I'm going to put up a hidden camera and film student activity in the corridor.'

'A hidden camera? Where are you gonna get one of those?' asked Mouse.

'Oh somewhere,' said Clancy.

'Is that really interesting?' said Elliot. 'Watching people opening and closing their lockers?'

'Sure, it's interesting,' said Clancy. 'You get a sense of how important the lockers are, socially I mean, how they are at the heart of student interaction.'

'Sounds thrilling,' said Del, who was busy trying to stuff her sports kit into her over-stuffed locker.

'I think it sounds like a good idea,' said Mouse, meaning it.

'Yeah, right,' said Elliot, 'maybe they could show it on prime-time.' By now he was laughing. 'They could call it, *Look who's Standing by my Locker*, or *Take a Locker at This...*'

'Yeah, OK Elliot, stick a sock in it would you,' said Clancy. 'It's a psychological experiment not a sitcom.'

There was a *thunk* sound followed by a 'sorry' – it was Red Monroe, who had collided with Mr Walford. 'Sorry sir, I didn't see you there.'

'Miss Monroe, it would help considerably if you would actually look where you were going. This is a corridor people walk up and down all the time. Why is it so difficult for you to avoid them?'

'I'm not sure sir,' said Red.

Mr Walford marched off, no doubt to find some other student to reprimand.

'Hey,' said Red, 'I've been looking all over for you guys.'

'Bang goes your social locker theory,' said Elliot.

'I would have come here, but you said yesterday we should meet by the donut van,' said Red.

'Yeah, but it's raining,' said Del.

'Well, I didn't know rain was going to mean you were going to just up and change the plan,' said Red. 'Look at me, I'm drenched.'

'Sorry,' said Mouse, 'it just seemed the obvious thing to do.'

'Not to me,' said Red. 'A plan's a plan.'

Bailey Roach was walking down the corridor towards the lockers, but when he saw Clancy he made out that he had just remembered something and veered off in the other direction. No one saw it except Clancy and Ruby, but that didn't matter – this was Clancy's new super power, scaring Bailey Roach, and it felt good.

The bell sounded and everyone began making their way to class. Clancy looked at Ruby, a sort of pleading and pitiful expression.

'What?' she said.

'Nothing,' he said, 'it's just I have a shot at raising my grade average.'

Ruby rolled her eyes. 'Jeepers,' she said, 'OK, I'll try all right, but I'm not making any promises and I'm definitely not doing it if you keep making that stupid face at me.'

'OK, I'll stop making the face,' said Clancy. 'Thanks Rube.'

'Yeah, well, you might want to save your thank yous because I have no idea how I'm gonna get hold of a tiny surveillance camera from Spectrum, especially when we're on lockdown because of the whole mole thing.'

But it wasn't like she hadn't taken gadgets without permission before. She could give it her best shot and if she got caught, well...

'You're a life saver Ruby, you know that?' said Clancy.

'Yeah,' said Ruby. 'Yeah, I know, but who's gonna save me if I get found out? That's what I wanna know.'

Chapter 16.
Look who's back

WHEN RUBY GOT IN SHE RAN UPSTAIRS AND FLICKED ON THE TV – she had done her homework on the bus ride home and was looking forward to a little downtime. She wasn't sure if it was a reaction to the wind and the feeling of being tugged this way and that that was causing her to feel so unsettled – irritated almost – or if it was something to do with the constant dodging of trouble: Vapona and her gang, Mr Parker, Bubbles. Whatever it was, she just wasn't feeling her regular sociable self. She changed the channel to 23 and waited for the *Crazy Cops* title sequence to begin – she had a few minutes, just enough time to fix a snack.

She grabbed a bagel from the pantry – the news was blaring out from the TV, she had it turned up too loud, Mrs Digby was always telling her so – and began rooting around for something to go with it.

'*SO KIRBY, WHAT MORE DO WE KNOW ABOUT THE IDAHO JAIL BUST?*'

'*WELL, NOT MUCH, BRETT, IT WAS AT 7AM THIS*

MORNING THAT IT BECAME APPARENT THAT A PRISONER WAS MISSING FROM HIS CELL, AT WHICH TIME AN EXTENSIVE SEARCH WAS MADE OF THE PRISON COMPOUND.'

'AND JUST HOW DID HE GET OUT, KIRBY?'

'WELL, BRETT, IT SEEMS HE BROKE THROUGH HIS CELL WALL USING A SMALL AND HIGHLY EFFICIENT, STATE-OF-THE-ART STONE-CUTTING GADGET.'

'SO KIRBY, JUST WHERE WOULD ONE COME BY SUCH A TOOL?'

'WELL, BRETT, THE ANSWER IT SEEMS IS IN A TIN OF MUFFINS. PRISON GUARDS BELIEVE THAT EACH MUFFIN CONTAINED ONE COMPONENT, AND ALL THE INMATE HAD TO DO WAS BREAK OPEN THE MUFFINS AND CONNECT THE PARTS. HE THEN CUT HIS WAY THROUGH THE WALL, CLIMBED INSIDE THE CAVITY, DOWN THE WATER PIPES, AND TRUDGED THROUGH YARDS OF SEWER PIPE TO GET BEYOND THE PERIMETER FENCE.'

'YEEKS, SOUNDS PRETTY DISGUSTING, KIRBY. SO WHAT SHOULD WE CONCLUDE?'

'BRETT, THIS LEADS THE PRISON GUARDS TO THE ONLY CONCLUSION POSSIBLE – THAT THE PRISONER HAS ESCAPED FROM THE PRISON GROUNDS AND IS ALMOST CERTAINLY ON THE WRONG SIDE OF THE PERIMETER FENCE.'

'*SO YOU ARE SAYING HE HAS ABSCONDED?*'

'*YES, I AM BRETT.*'

Jeepers Brett! How many ways does Kirby have to say it, the guy is gone!

'**IN OTHER WORDS, KIRBY, THIS FELLON IS AT LARGE IN THE NORTHWESTERN COMMUNITY?**'

'Well duh, Brett, it would seem likely,' muttered Ruby. 'Now where is that cream cheese?'

'*THE FBI CAN NEITHER CONFIRM NOR DENY THIS, BUT IT WOULD SEEM LIKELY.*'

'**AND, KIRBY, CAN WE PUT A NAME TO THE CONVICT?**'

'YES, HIS NAME HAS JUST BEEN RELEASED AND HE IS ONE BOYD MARSHALL, ALSO KNOWN BY HIS CRIMINAL NICKNAME OF BABY FACE.'

Ruby dropped the cream cheese.

Baby Face Marshall, she mouthed.

She made it back into the living room to see the implausibly innocent face of Boyd Marshall big on the screen.

'EARLIER THIS YEAR HE WAS APPREHENDED, ACCUSED AND CONVICTED OF PLAYING A PART IN THE PLOT TO STEAL THE JADE BUDDHA OF KHOTAN FROM THE TWINFORD CITY MUSEUM. HE WAS ALSO CONVICTED OF ATTEMPTED MURDER.'

'*SO WOULD I BE CORRECT IN ASSUMING THIS GUY IS CONSIDERED DANGEROUS, KIRBY?*'

Ruby looked around the room, appealing to an invisible audience for some kind of sanity check here.

'WELL, BRETT, I WAS ABOUT TO GO ON TO SAY, HE HAS MURDERED MORE THAN ONCE.'

'HE SOUNDS LIKE A THOROUGHLY UNPLEASANT CHARACTER, KIRBY .'

'YOU BETTER BELIEVE IT, BRETT.'

'AND I WOULD IMAGINE HE SMELLS PRETTY BAD TOO, RIGHT?'

{ **LAUGHTER** }.

'I SHOULDN'T WONDER, BRETT, BUT SERIOUSLY, WE WOULD LIKE TO WARN ANYONE WHO THINKS THEY HAVE SEEN HIM NOT TO APPROACH THIS MAN. HE MIGHT LOOK LIKE A NICE GUY BUT HE IS IN FACT DEADLY.'

That was the thing about Baby Face. He really had the cutest face, people just wanted to trust him. Ruby sat down with a thump. She could hear Bug in the kitchen, evidently taking full advantage of the cream cheese accident. She scrabbled to find the remote and switched to the news channel, hoping to find a slightly more in-depth report.

BOYD MARSHALL, KNOWN TO FELLOW CRIMINALS AS BABY FACE, WAS IMPRISONED FOR HIS PART IN THE ATTEMPT TO STEAL THE PRICELESS JADE BUDDHA OF KHOTAN, A PLOT FOILED BY TWINFORD POLICE.

Of course it was actually Spectrum who had foiled the plot,

but the downside of being a secret agency was never getting the credit.

MARSHALL HAS BEEN LINKED TO CRIMES DATING BACK FIFTEEN YEARS, THOUGH UNTIL NOW THE POLICE HAVE NEVER HAD ENOUGH EVIDENCE TO CHARGE HIM. HE FORMERLY WORKED IN A CHEMICALS WAREHOUSE DEALING WITH TOXIC SUBSTANCES AND POISONS – POISONS HE IS BELIEVED TO HAVE USED ON SOME OF HIS CRIMINAL RIVALS. THE POLICE HAVE REASON TO BELIEVE THAT MARSHALL IS ALREADY OUT OF THE COUNTRY. SOMEONE FITTING HIS DESCRIPTION WAS SEEN BOARDING A PLANE TO BRAZIL.

Up popped a very fuzzy-looking black and white CCTV still of a man in a hat.

I guess it could be him, thought Ruby, *but who helped him to get out?*

She didn't have long to wonder about this. Her Spectrum-issue Escape Watch blinked at her and she knew where she needed to be.

She pulled on her parka, zipped up and stepped out into the dark.

Ruby arrived just before the briefing was due to start and sat down in a seat next to Blacker.

'Who helped him break out?' whispered Ruby.

'That's what we're all wondering,' said Blacker.

Their conversation was interrupted by a fake cough. LB was now standing at the front of the auditorium.

'So,' she began, 'the news of Boyd Marshall's prison breakout hit the news stations before it even reached us.'

This sent a wave of muttering through the room. LB gave another impatient cough and the muttering stopped immediately.

'Baby Face Marshall is a very high-profile criminal, even his nickname is a household name, and this of course could be to our advantage. Let's hope so anyway.'

Ruby could see her point. Baby Face really wasn't going to want to stroll up and down advertising his whereabouts. If he had any sense, he would get across the state line and head in the direction of anywhere that wasn't the United States of America.

'I'm going to hand over to Agent Delaware from Spectrum 1 who is better acquainted with the details of the Marshall escape.'

Agent Frank Delaware peered at his audience from over his glasses. He looked a little like a buzzard, a very neat and tidy bald buzzard in a blue suit.

'Doubtless Boyd Marshall is going to want to avoid suffering any more jail time,' said Agent Delaware. 'Some documents were found in his cell, concealed inside the wall. It is clear from these that he was intending to escape across the border to Mexico and then make his way on to Brazil – indeed there is anecdotal evidence to support the theory that he boarded a flight to Brazil yesterday.'

Agent Delaware paused to sip some water. 'We know it was an outside job,' he said. 'Marshall escaped with the help of one of his mob connections – we figure it was a *quid pro quo* arrangement – and though we would all be happy to see him brought in, we will be leaving that to our FBI colleagues and will not be considering this an active Spectrum case. He poses no threat to Spectrum and no threat to our agents.'

'Finally some good news,' muttered Ruby.

'Mr Marshall,'
said the figure standing
at the window...

'...how nice to see you out of your chains.'

'I'm glad to be free of them, believe me.'

'How does it feel to be in Brazil?'

'I have to admit, I wish I was.'

'You will be soon if you keep to the plan – you've done all right so far.'

'That's down to you; they swallowed every clue you planted.'

'People swallow what they want to swallow, Mr Marshall. It suits them to believe you are gone for good and always.'

'So long as they don't look for me here in Twinford.'

'And they won't. Now, are you aware of how things are progressing?'

'Yes, my sources kept me up to speed.'

'Excellent.'

'You've been busy.'

'Oh, you know, the devil makes work for idle hands.'

'So you have work for me?'

'Yes, it's a sort of disposal job, needs to be handled with great delicacy.'

'Of course.'

'The lady in question has a public face so we don't want to arouse suspicion, which is why I felt an event such as this would be the perfect send off.'

'You want it to look like natural causes.'

'Quite so Mr Marshall. By all means be creative, but not so creative that you trip up. What I am looking for is a nice, elegant murder;

you have such skill in that department.'

'Not a problem. Are you looking for something inhaled, ingested or perhaps merely touched?'

'Dealer's choice.'

Chapter 17.
Witness protection

RUBY SLEPT SLIGHTLY MORE SOUNDLY THAT NIGHT and got out of bed feeling better than she had done in a while. To show her appreciation of her parents' large-mindedness concerning the past few days' events, she decided to dress to her mother's satisfaction or at least an approximation of what might satisfy. She wasn't prepared to go the whole nine yards and dolly herself up like child star Shirley Temple, but she could meet her mom halfway.

So Ruby fished out a yellow and black vintage dress that fitted pretty well – the hem wasn't even stuck in place with sticky tape, nor were there any rips or holes in it. Next she pulled on a pair of over-the-knee black and white striped socks and slipped her feet into the red clogs her mother had bought her for the Twinford City Museum do. These clogs had proved strangely lucky on that April night. She had successfully wrong-footed the Count by aiming the left one at his head, and it was this clunk to his dome that had prevented him from stealing the Jade Buddha of Khotan. These clogs were a lucky charm and she hoped that by wearing them for the next few days they might do a good job of keeping the peace.

Ruby was on her way to school when she reached in her pocket for a cube of Hubble-Yum only to discover there was none. She walked into the nearest store, picked up a pack (strawberry flavour) and joined the line at the counter.

The short red-headed kid in front was holding everyone up by turning out his pockets trying to find the right change for a can of soda.

'Here,' said Ruby, handing him a dollar, 'have it on me, I got to be somewhere – don't you?'

The kid paid up and the line moved quick enough until a boy of maybe fifteen asked, 'Can I get one of those Taste Twister things?'

'What Taste Twister things?' asked the woman behind the counter.

'They're advertised all over,' said the boy. 'You must have seen the billboards.'

'Never heard of it,' said the woman. 'What is it? A drink?'

'I don't know,' said the kid.

'You don't know but you want one?'

'Yeah,' said the kid. 'The ads are pretty cool.'

'Well,' said the woman, 'I for one do not know what you're talking about.'

'How can you miss it?' said the boy. 'There's a billboard right on Trip Street.'

'Stan?' called the woman. 'Do you know what a Taste Twister is, 'cause I sure as heck don't.'

Jeepers, thought Ruby.

The storeowner came over. 'I know the Taste Twister advertisements, but we haven't had any sales reps come by trying to sell it to us.'

'So you don't know where I can get it?' said the boy.

'No,' said the man shaking his head. 'You could try Babe's, they stock a lot of new brands, more product ranges than we could ever hold.'

'Already did,' said the boy. 'They never heard of it either.'

The storekeeper shrugged. 'Sorry I can't help.'

'They shouldn't advertise things that aren't for sale,' said the kid.

The storekeeper scratched his head. 'Well, if I see Taste Twisters around, I'll try and get them in.'

'I wouldn't mind,' said the boy, 'but it's them that keep going on about how good it tastes.'

It was a funny thing, Ruby thought as she popped a Hubble-Yum in her mouth and headed for school, because *she* hadn't seen it in any stores either and what sort of manufacturer would bother to advertise a product that wasn't for sale?

When at last Ruby made it into school, she was greeted by a very excitable Clancy Crew.

'So did you hear?' hissed Clancy.

'I heard,' replied Ruby. She knew exactly what he was talking about. Baby Face Marshall, escaped criminal and bogeyman of the moment.

'You think he's at large here in Twinford?' Clancy was on the brink of flapping. 'Do you think he's coming for us?' He had come face to face with Boyd Marshall back in April and he knew only too well what this man was capable of – he was a cold-blooded murderer with a twist of sadistic.

'Clancy, do you really think he has gone to all the trouble of busting out of jail just so he can murder you?' asked Ruby. 'I mean think about it – you must be way down the list of people he wants to murder – I think you can relax for a while.'

'Well that's kind of a relief,' said Clancy. He looked calm for a minute and then not so calm. 'Hey, what do you mean about me being way down his list? You think he has a *list*, you think I'm actually on it?' Now he *was* flapping.

'I'm kidding Clance! Get a grip would you,' said Ruby thumping him lightly on the shoulder. 'He isn't interested in you. To him you're an ant, you're nothing, you're no one.'

'Thanks a bunch.'

'All I'm saying is, sometimes being unimportant and sidelined is not so bad.'

There was a loud clearing of the throat followed by, 'If Ruby Redfort and Clancy Crew seem to think that their conversation is so important that they can interrupt roll call then perhaps we should all hush up and they can come stand at the front and tell us all about it.'

Boy what a cliché line, thought Ruby. *If I was a teacher, I would put that line to bed and come up with something original.*

'Otherwise,' continued Mrs Drisco, 'I can write D for detention and you can both spend your lunch hour writing me a couple of essays on manners.'

Clancy looked at Ruby and Ruby looked at Mrs Drisco and Mrs Drisco put her hands on her hips like she meant business.

'OK, Mrs Drisco, if you really want to know and you really want the whole class to know then I'll tell you,' said Ruby, 'but it isn't pretty.'

'I'll be the judge of that,' said Mrs Drisco.

'You might have heard about this escaped convict. I think he goes by a sort of nickname, Baby Face Marshall or something. Anyway, he is considered armed and dangerous and Clancy here might well be in his sights, if you know what I'm saying.'

'Well, that sounds highly unlikely to me,' said Mrs Drisco.

Ruby gave her the wide-eyed stare – an expression that conveyed not only innocence, but bafflement too. Once fixed with this stare most people crumbled instantly, but Mrs Drisco had been a teacher at Twinford Junior High for more than twenty years now and she did not crumble easily.

'If you want to know what I think, I think you have been watching a tad too much television.'

'I know,' said Ruby, 'it does sound sort of unbelievable, but here, I can prove it,' and out of her satchel she pulled a note.

Warily Mrs Drisco took the piece of paper.

This is what the note said.

DEAR MISS R REDFORT,
AS YOU MAY OR MAY NOT KNOW, A DANGEROUS
CRIMINAL HAS ESCAPED HIS BONDS AND IS
BELIEVED TO BE HEADING TO OUR OWN DEAR
TOWN OF TWINFORD CITY.
THIS VILLAIN IS NO LAUGHING MATTER AND IS
OF EXCEPTIONAL INTEREST TO US, THE POLICE
FORCE AT LARGE. WE HAVE BEEN INFORMED THAT
THIS CRIMINAL MAY BEAR A STRIKING GRUDGE
TO ONE CLOSE TO YOU. I WILL NOT NAME NAMES
BECAUSE THAT WOULD BE UNPROFESSIONAL, BUT
SINCE YOU ARE AN IMPORTANT ACQUAINTANCE OF
ONE CLANCY CREW I FEEL I MUST WARN YOU TO
BE VIGILANT.
YOUR FAMILY FRIEND AND LAW ENFORCEMENT
OFFICER,
SHERIFF BRIDGES.

Mrs Drisco went pale and seemed just a little flustered. Ruby could imagine what she was thinking. She would be turning it over in her mind, unsure if she should take it seriously and embarrass herself if it turned out to be untrue, or *really* humiliate herself by not taking it seriously only to discover she was wrong when Clancy turned up dead.

Finally she handed the note back to Ruby, gave Clancy a sympathetic nod and brushed the matter to one side.

After school Clancy asked, 'So what did it say, that note?'

'I don't want to give you sleepless nights.'

'I think I can handle it.'

She handed her friend the note and Clancy read. Not even a whimper, not a flap, not an intake of breath.

'She fell for *this*?' was what he said.

'It's the element of surprise,' said Ruby. 'She didn't give herself time to think.'

'But it's not even written like a cop would write it – I mean, "an important acquaintance"? What's that supposed to suggest?'

'I know,' agreed Ruby, 'I wrote it years ago when I was just a kid.'

'How did you get hold of the police department paper?'

'I went on a tour of the police station once, managed to grab a few sheets from the sheriff's desk,' said Ruby.

'And the sheriff's signature?' asked Clancy.

'I asked for his autograph, got him to sign right there at the bottom. I'd covered the letter with another piece of paper, of course.'

'Of course,' said Clancy, somewhat sarcastically. 'You're lucky you didn't get arrested – that has to be a crime.'

'I was only five,' said Ruby, 'but it's super lucky I happened to write it – it kept you out of detention and, I mean, what are the odds that there really would be a dangerous criminal on the loose and looking to hunt you down?'

'I thought you said he wasn't interested in me?' said Clancy, looking panicky again.

'Clance, I'm still kidding,' said Ruby.

She slotted the note back into her note file. 'I thought if I left a letter like this lying around I could spook Elliot one Halloween.'

'Too late now,' said Clancy.

'Or not,' said Ruby, pointing towards Elliot who was hurrying their way.

'I just heard,' he said, pulling up a chair.

'What?' said Clancy.

'That you're in the witness protection programme.'

'I'm not,' said Clancy flatly.

'But it's all around the school, there's an escaped convict after you and you are in the witness protection programme.'

'If I was in the witness protection programme then I wouldn't be here, would I?' said Clancy. 'I would be in some other junior high, talking to some other kid called Elliot or not called Elliot.'

Elliot looked at him for a moment, not talking just looking and then getting it.

'Oh yeah,' he said, 'so there isn't a hit man after you?' He almost looked disappointed.

'No,' said Clancy, 'I don't think so anyhow.'

'You sure fooled Mrs Drisco.' Elliot was smiling. 'I mean,

she thinks you're in deep trouble,' he laughed. 'I mean she is *totally* fooled.' He was beginning to lose it.

'I'd like to remind you that you were the one who came running over here asking if it was true,' said Clancy.

'That's different; I always believe this kinda thing – it's exciting.'

'It's exciting to you that someone wants to kill one of your closest and dearest friends?' said Clancy.

'Nah, not *actually*,' said Elliot, giving him a friendly thump. 'The idea of it is exciting, not the reality. Though that said, would you leave me your pogo stick in your will?'

'I don't have a will.'

'So that's a no?'

'You can have it now if you want it so much, it's not exactly the most useful thing I've ever owned.'

'Thanks man,' said Elliot, 'how can I ever repay you?' He clearly meant it as a joke, but Clancy wasn't going to let the offer go so easily.

'There is something actually,' said Clancy. 'Teach me to railslide on my skateboard.'

'Sure,' said Elliot. 'You got elbow pads? You're going to fall a lot.'

'Yeah,' said Clancy.

'Well OK then,' said Elliot.

'By the way,' said Ruby, 'that Taste Twister product we were talking about? A kid was asking for it in the store, but no one seems to be able to find it and no one knows what it is.'

'I told you, it's a drink,' said Elliot.

'So why don't they come out and say it's a drink?' said Ruby.

'They're holding back because they want you to figure it out for yourself,' said Clancy.

'What?' said Ruby. 'Why would they do that? They're an advertising company – they want you to go and buy it, not waste time trying to figure out whether it's a drink or a candy.'

'That's what you think,' said Clancy, 'but I tell you, I once read about this company that made super high-quality jeans using special Japanese denim. They didn't want to simply sell their jeans and just gradually creep into the jeans market, they wanted to become the number one most desired jeans brand out there. So they never did any advertising, didn't have a logo, or anything. And they were never in ordinary stores – a shipment of jeans would just turn up with a sales assistant in an empty lot, like a flash sale. You just had to be in the know. It's called a –' he thought for a second – 'a secret brand, that's it.'

'Where did you even read that?' asked Elliot.

'In this marketing magazine I picked up in the dentist's office,' said Clancy. 'The point is, this jeans company, they didn't want to sell the *most pairs*, they wanted to have everybody *talking* about their brand.'

'What was it called?' asked Elliot.

'I don't remember,' said Clancy.

'So I guess it didn't work,' said Elliot.

'That's not my point, duh brain,' said Clancy, 'my point is...' But Elliot had started laughing, never a good thing if you were halfway through a story or arguing a point – his laughter was infectious.

'My point,' said Clancy trying to make his voice heard, 'is even if it didn't work for those jeans people, it is a kind of marketing strategy – get everyone talking about it and by the time you release the product onto the wider market everyone knows what it is and everyone wants it.'

But no one was listening any more and Elliot was by now gasping for breath, lying on the sidewalk.

'Oh forget it,' said Clancy. 'I'm heading home.'

He started walking off.

'See you tomorrow Clance!' called Ruby.

'I'm not in school tomorrow,' shouted Clancy. 'On the upside, I get to miss French, but on the downside I have to go to this dumb photoshoot with my dad.'

'You win some, you lose some,' said Ruby.

'Hey, you wanna meet after dinner tonight?' shouted Clancy. 'I'll have the low-down on the Explorer Awards line-up.'

'Sure,' shouted Ruby. 'I'll meet you up the tree.'

'Are you likely to be late?' asked Clancy.

'I promise I'll be there by 8pm, not one second later.'

Chapter 18.
A rock and a hard place

RUBY HAD TO STOP OFF ON THE WAY BACK FROM SCHOOL to pick up her new glasses from the optometrist on Longacre. She had been looking forward to trying them – her old pair were more than a little cranky – so rather than wait until she reached home, Ruby took them from their case and put them on.

'Cool,' she said, looking at her reflection in a shop window, 'very cool.' She turned the corner onto Oakwood and immediately wished to goodness that she had taken the bus right to her door.

'Oh, you have to be kidding,' muttered Ruby, for there was Del Lasco standing outside Sunny's Diner, and in the distance walking towards her with her gang of girls was Vapona Begwell.

RUBY: *'You can't be serious.'*

DEL: *'Just go on home Ruby, this is between me and Bugwart.'*

RUBY: *'You have your hand all bandaged up Del, are you nuts?'*

DEL: *'I can take her with or without a left hand. I figure I could punch her lights out if I had both my hands tied behind my back.'*

RUBY: *'Oh really, that I'd like to see.'*

DEL: *'Well, hang around and you will.'*

RUBY: *'No one's going be hanging around, Del, because you're coming with me.'*

Ruby began pushing Del towards the bus stop.

RUBY: *'I'll tell you what's going to happen, we are going to catch the bus to Amster and we are going to grab ourselves a milkshake (you can pay if you insist) and we are going to have a nice little sit down and chat about your strange compulsion to get smacked in the face.'*

DEL: *'Look Rube, I appreciate your concern, but I think you should go home.'*

But it was too late for that. Vapona Begwell and her gang had just crossed the road.

'Jeepers Del,' hissed Ruby.

'Oh that's nice, Lasco,' said Vapona. 'I see you have your little sidekick with you – she can watch me beat the pulp out of you.'

Why do I have to be wearing a stupid dress and a pair of dumb clogs today of all days? was what Ruby was thinking.

'Look at *you* Redfort, dressed up all like a dolly,' jeered Gemma Melamare. 'Off to a children's party?'

'She looks like a bumble bee,' said a heavy-set girl.

'Is that the best insult you got?' said Ruby.

'What do you expect Rube?' said Del. 'Melamare's probably wondering why she wasn't invited.'

'Redfort, you're gonna wish you were at a little tea party playing pass the parcel,' said Vapona.

'You have to be kidding, Bugwart,' jeered Del. 'You're not even gonna get near Redfort, she'll have you flat on your backside before you can cry for Mommy.'

'Is that right?' said Vapona.

'You *know* it is,' said Del. 'Your crew are gonna be so busy begging for mercy that they won't be able to peel you off the floor.'

'Shut your trap would you Del,' hissed Ruby. 'There are four of them, all of them bigger than me, and I'm planning on getting out of here alive.'

But it was too late for running. Vapona lunged at Del and missed, but then the tall girl who seemed to do nothing but chew gum landed a punch square on Del's jaw.

That did it. Del lashed out at the tall girl, socking her one in the arm. 'Ow!' screamed the girl, and Del saw her chance, running at Vapona, knocking her off her feet, and the two of them tumbled into the heavy-set girl with the short hair. Gemma Melamare yanked Ruby's hair and in doing so knocked off Ruby's new glasses – they clattered to the sidewalk.

Ruby dropped to her knees and felt about, looking for her specs, the world now out of focus. All she could see were blurry limbs moving violently this way and that. Uncomfortable noises, biffs, thwacks, squeals and curses.

'Ouch!' shouted Ruby as she felt something, a foot maybe,

colliding with her nose. She staggered to her feet and doubled her efforts to pull her hot-headed friend from a ball of fists. This was not immediately possible, and though Ruby was a lot tougher than her small size suggested, she just couldn't seem to propel Del from the fight. She was aware of being shoved against a trashcan and she was aware of the smell of the garbage as it spilled across the sidewalk. There was a cracking sound as wood split, or was it her head, it could have been her head, it certainly felt like it – though it was in fact a small maple tree.

She half saw a bottle roll across the sidewalk, but where were her glasses? This thought was followed almost immediately by a sound almost exactly like the sound of glasses being crunched underfoot. *Rats*, thought Ruby.

Everything became a blur then, and who knows what would have happened had it not been for the sound of a nearing police siren, which sent the kids running in all directions. Ruby, hampered both by her inability to see clearly *and* her fancy clogs, was the last one standing. There was not a whole lot of sense running at this point, too late for that, and in any case she would have to abandon her footwear and then the cop in question would no doubt track her down using the Cinderella method, which would be humiliating, to say the least. So instead she waited coolly for the car door to open and the cop to brandish his badge.

She would bluff it out.

Chapter 19.
Last one standing

'HEY RUBY, WHAT'S BEEN GOING ON HERE?' said a familiar voice.

Ruby could not believe her dumb luck: the law enforcement officer was Sheriff Bridges, a friendly acquaintance of her parents and a man not easily bluffed.

'Dropped my glasses,' said Ruby.

The sheriff looked at the sidewalk, reached down and picked up the mangled frames of what had been Ruby's new eyewear. 'So how did that happen?' he asked.

'The wind sorta blew 'em right off my face and then this whole crowd of kids stormed out of nowhere, guess they trampled them.'

'From what I could see,' said the sheriff, 'there seemed to be some kinda fist fight going on.'

'Really?' said Ruby. 'Well, that would explain a lot.' She held up her specs. 'These are pretty much goners, I would guess.'

Sheriff Bridges nodded. 'That would be *my* assessment.' He didn't say anything for a moment or two, just let tumbleweed blow through the silence. 'So I guess those kids must have been causing quite a rumpus to break this little maple tree in two?'

Ruby nodded. *He's not going to like that,* she thought.

'Trash everywhere,' he tutted, picking up a glass bottle, on the label a shape. It was blurry to Ruby's eyes, but it seemed to be a face, maybe a face with something curly winding out of it. The sheriff righted the trashcan and dropped the bottle into it. 'Now that's not fair on this fine community, those kids really didn't oughta have done that.'

Ruby was beginning to feel uneasy. Where was he going with this, and if it was somewhere uncomfortable then could he hurry it up?

'So Ruby, you want me to drop you somewhere? The doctors for instance?'

'Why?' asked Ruby. 'Why would I want to go to the doctors?'

'You seem to have a pretty good nosebleed going there, maybe it should be checked out.'

Darn you Melamare, thought Ruby.

The sheriff sighed. 'Come on kid, let me drive you home, get Mrs Digby to ice that for you.'

The Redfort housekeeper merely tutted when she opened the door to find Ruby standing on the front step next to Sheriff Bridges.

'Child,' she said, 'what scrape have you got yourself into and who are you thinking of blaming?' Mrs Digby had taken care of Ruby since she was an hour old and she honestly believed nothing 'the child' did could ever surprise her.

I've seen it all and then some, was the sort of thing Mrs Digby was fond of saying.

'Whatever it is,' said the sheriff, 'this little lady isn't about to spill the beans.'

Mrs Digby looked heavenwards. 'I've told her before Sheriff – save yourself and save everyone else a whole host of trouble.'

The sheriff nodded. 'Whilst I understand the code of honour, I regret to tell you, someone's got to take the fall, and since you are the only visible contender, Ruby, looks like it's you.'

'You arresting me?'

'No, nothing like that. But there's going to be some community service in your future, Ruby, I gotta be clear about that.'

Ruby shrugged. 'I'm not gonna whine about it or anything, but you do know this whole incident had nothing to do with me?'

'I believe you Ruby, but if you aren't prepared to give me names so I can sort this whole thing out fair and square then I got no choice – trees get broke in two, trash gets scattered, it's not fair on folks if something isn't done to put things right. So, you going to name names?'

'Like I said, I didn't see much on account of my glasses getting broke.'

'OK, then.' He wished them both good day, explained that he would be in touch with Brant and Sabina, and then went on his way.

'Just perfect,' said Ruby.

'Only got yourself to blame,' said Mrs Digby. She sat Ruby down at the kitchen table and gave her a dishcloth full of ice to hold against her bloody nose. The bleeding soon stopped but the swelling wasn't going to disappear before her mother and father returned home.

'They're gonna be mad,' said Ruby.

'They're going to be mad,' agreed Mrs Digby, handing Ruby a mug of tea. 'Your parents aren't ones to suffer social disgrace lying down.'

'This is hardly social disgrace,' countered Ruby, 'just a casual disagreement.'

Mrs Digby looked at the note that the sheriff had handed her. 'Destruction of public property, littering of the neighbourhood... I'd say it was the very thing that would send your mother and father into an early grave.'

'Mrs Digby, you're being dramatic.'

Mrs Digby put her hands on her hips. 'You're not one to get in fights, so what got you into this one?' she asked.

Ruby said nothing.

'No doubt it was that Del Lasco,' said the housekeeper.

Ruby said nothing.

'She could make a saint grow horns and sprout a forked tail, that one.'

'It wasn't her fault,' said Ruby, though what she was thinking was, *Del, you're a numbskull.*

'You're the one that's going to get punished,' continued Mrs Digby.

'You win some, you lose some,' said Ruby.

'Well, you're going to be losing out tomorrow night,' said the housekeeper. 'Your father won't be taking you to that explorers thingummyjig, you can be certain of that!'

'I know he'll be mad at first, but he'll come round,' said Ruby.

But she was wrong about that.

Chapter 20.
Throwing in the towel

DINNER THAT EVENING WAS AN UNCOMFORTABLE MEAL.

'Ruby, what were you thinking?' said her mother over and over.

'She *wasn't* thinking,' said her father, 'that's just the problem.'

Ruby was keeping quiet.

'Last month you practically killed yourself on a skateboard, this month you want to get your head knocked off in a senseless fight.'

'Two totally different situations,' said Ruby.

'And your new glasses!' exclaimed her mother.

'Are you looking to kill yourself or kill someone else?' said her father.

'I was just in the wrong place at the wrong time.'

'If you are not responsible then who is?' asked her father.

'I really couldn't say,' said Ruby.

'Will she get community service?' said her mother.

'It seems likely,' said her father.

Sabina suddenly looked alarmed. 'Do you think they'll make her wear one of those orange boilersuits?'

'If they do, they do,' said her father.

'Orange is such an unforgiving colour,' said her mother.

'You know I can't abide fighting, Ruby,' said Brant Redfort.

'I've seen you watch the boxing,' said Ruby.

'That's utterly different,' said her mother. 'There's a referee and there's towels.'

'So if I had had a towel it would have been OK with you?'

Fortunately her father wasn't listening, he was on a roll. 'Fighting and spreading trash all over the place, I mean, really.'

'Yes,' agreed her mother, 'this town is knee-deep in garbage already. I mean, if you must fight then avoid knocking into the garbage cans,' she paused as she let the picture take hold in her mind's eye, 'and the bacteria involved, it just makes me shudder.'

Brant looked at his wife concernedly. 'The point is, honey, she shouldn't fight, period, she's been told. Fighting is not a solution to anything.'

'Exactly,' said Sabina, 'and littering just makes it 150% less of a solution.'

'I don't know what to say,' said her father. 'I mean, after what happened all those years ago... I thought you would have learnt your lesson, I thought we had agreed. You made a promise.'

'And I kept it. I wasn't fighting,' said Ruby, 'I don't fight. I didn't land a single punch, not even a pinch.'

Brant Redfort stood up. 'The Explorer Awards, you can forget them. I mean Ruby... I just don't know,' then he left the room.

She opened her mouth to protest, but thought better of it. Instead, Ruby got up from the table and took her dish into the kitchen. She was surprised to see Hitch there, she hadn't heard him come in, yet there he was polishing a pair of black shoes, shoes so shiny you could use them for a looking glass.

'Do you use those for spy work?' she asked.

'You never do know when you're going to need to have something reflected back at you,' replied Hitch. He paused. 'You OK kid?'

Ruby nodded.

HITCH: *'Your dad sounds pretty mad. I've never heard your folks go off at the deep end like that.'*

RUBY: *'They don't like social embarrassment.'*

HITCH: *'Who does?'*

RUBY: *'Plus a tree got damaged, my dad's a nature lover.'*

Hitch continued to shine the shoes and Ruby stacked her plate in the dishwasher.

HITCH: *'Doesn't sound like he's too keen on fighting either.'*

RUBY: *'He has a thing about it.'*

HITCH: *'You could tell him what really happened.'*

RUBY: *'Oh yeah, and what really happened?'*

HITCH: *'You found yourself between a rock and a hard place – Lasco and Begwell.'*

RUBY: *'How do you know it was between Del and Vapona?'*

HITCH: *'It's obvious.'*

RUBY: *'I was trying to talk some sense into them.'*

HITCH: *'So you're not much of a negotiator.'*

RUBY: *'You ever try reasoning with two people who hate each other?'*

HITCH: *'Actually yes, it's sort of my day job, but I only ever stand in the middle if I know I'm going to come out the winner.'*

RUBY: *'What choice did I have?'*

HITCH: *'Del Lasco can fight her own battles.'*

RUBY: *'She has a hand sprain.'*

HITCH: *'She's got legs, doesn't she? Walking away can work.'*

RUBY: *'Del's more of a fighter.'*

HITCH: *'Pretty dumb to fight when you have a busted hand.'*

RUBY: *'Pretty dumb not to fight when it means you wind up getting socked in the nose.'*

HITCH: *'If you knew how to avoid getting into a fight in the first place, you wouldn't have been socked in the nose.'*

RUBY: *'When Bugwart wants a fight, you don't have a whole lotta choice – you just get pounded.'*

HITCH: *'Or you run real fast. You can run kid, I've seen you.'*

RUBY: *'Yeah, and I'm happy to run, it beats getting smacked in the kisser believe me, but if I had then I would have left Del to face Bugwart's gang alone.'*

HITCH: *'Like I said, seems to me this was Del's fight.'*
RUBY: *'Del's fights have a habit of becoming everyone's fight, if you know what I'm saying.'*
She turned to leave.
HITCH: *'Well, kid, you know what they say – it's your nose.'*

Ruby returned to her room and walked into the bathroom. She peered at herself in the looking glass – her nose didn't look too pretty.

Mirror mirror on the wall, Ruby Redfort, you look awful.

She wasn't sure but she thought that particular blow had come from Gemma Melamare, an eye for an eye, a nose for a nose. She just hoped the swelling would subside by sun up.

The light on her message machine was blinking like crazy and she rightly guessed that was down to Del.

'Rube, you there? You not answering my call because A: you're mad at me? or B: you're not allowed to take calls, or C: you're dead? Look, anyways, whatever, I'm seriously sorry, OK, I'll speak to you tomorrow... if you're not hospitalised, that is.'

The answer machine had just finished replaying Del's message when the phone rang. She took the receiver from the squirrel's paw.

'You're late,' said Clancy, his voice loud in her ear. 'I'm at a phone box on Amster and you are late!'

'It's worse than that,' said Ruby.

'You mean you're not coming.'

'I can't come.'

'Why not?'

'I got into a bunch of trouble.'

'Yeah? Well, it better be the sort of trouble that involves the cops or I'm gonna be mad about it.'

'Actually it is.'

Clancy began flapping his arms; she could hear him doing it. 'You're kidding,' he said. 'You *are* kidding, aren't you?'

'No, as a matter of fact I'm not, Clance.'

'I'm coming over,' he said.

'I wouldn't advise it,' she replied. 'They're kinda furious, my folks, I mean.'

'But your folks are never furious,' said Clancy.

'Well this time they are and I don't think they are going to back down.'

'But you're still coming to the Explorer Awards, right? I mean they're not so mad at you that they would ruin your life?'

'I'm afraid they are,' sighed Ruby. 'Look I'm sorry I forgot to call, probably something to do with being punched on the nose, but I'll see you in school.'

'I'm not in school tomorrow, remember?' said Clancy. 'I got that whole pre-party photo op thing with my dad.'

'Oh yeah,' said Ruby. She'd forgotten about that. 'I'm losing my mind.'

'You're just not sleeping enough,' said Clancy. 'So when am

I going to see you? I mean, if your parents aren't letting you out, I'm not going to see you all weekend.'

'Don't worry, I'll come up with a brilliant plan,' said Ruby, and she hung up.

She changed out of the ill-fated 'keeping the peace' clothes and climbed into bed, then she lay there in the dark, thinking. She could make this all go away, her dad's disappointment in her, her stupid punishment, if only she gave up the names of Del Lasco and Vapona Bugwart. Most people would understand, even Del might understand. But Ruby couldn't square it with herself.

It was like Mrs Digby said: *be true to yourself, Ruby Redfort, and it will steer you right.*

She hoped so.

**No one knew where the
first dollop of mashed potato
came from, but it was
all it took...**

...seconds later and the canteen of the women's high-security correctional facility was a chaos of food ammunition, clattering metal trays and spinning cutlery. It seemed that every single inmate was involved and every single one of them was shouting. By the time the prison officers had taken control, every inch of the place was covered in stewed vegetables and Jell-o.

Remarkably there were no casualties, but for the one prisoner found knocked out and lying face down on the floor covered in mashed potato and vegetable stew inside the walk-in refrigerator. It was also discovered that one of the prison officers, Officer McClaren, was missing. A search was conducted, her car was gone from the warden parking lot and the CCTV footage showed her driving out of the prison grounds during the riot.

'This will be a disciplinary offence,' said the warden. 'She had no right to leave the prison compound during a security breach.' The warden's administrator picked up the phone to call Officer McClaren back in.

There was no answer. Either McClaren was ignoring the call or she had not yet arrived home.

Meanwhile, the unconscious prisoner was taken to the prison sanitorium to be checked out by the medical team. Only after the food and dirt was wiped from the face of the prisoner was it discovered that the prisoner was not a prisoner. The prisoner was Officer McClaren.

The sirens sounded and the manhunt began.

Chapter 21.
Taking it on the chin

RUBY WAS RELIEVED WHEN MRS LEMON CALLED ROUND DURING BREAKFAST. This was not normally a cause for rejoicing, but right then Ruby could use the distraction. The day had got off to a bad start when there was an angry phone call from Consuela Cruz. Apparently she had been told *'just two minutes ago, not even'* that chicken could not be served at the awards due to Mrs Abrahams, the Mayor's wife, suffering from a chicken phobia.

'Who has a phobia against the chicken? This woman is loco, crazy, a fruit cake.' Consuela was set to walk out, resign, tell them to *'stick their stupid awards to the explorers!'* but Brant had talked her down. That crisis had but barely been averted when the Sheriff called to inform Ruby's parents that Ruby was to be assigned six hours of community service.

'I was just wondering if you might want to babysit Archie on Sunday?' said Elaine Lemon. She looked at Ruby as if this were the offer of the century and there might be nothing a thirteen-year-old girl would rather do than spend her weekend looking after a one-year-old boy.

'Sure,' said Ruby, 'be delighted to, but the thing is I'm grounded.'

'That's OK, Ruby,' said her father, 'you will be doing Elaine here a good turn and you won't be having fun, it's a win win. In fact, let's make it a regular arrangement.'

Elaine looked a little perturbed by Brant's assertion that looking after her son would not be fun, but she was so relieved that she had finally pinned down some childcare that she kept her mouth firmly closed.

When Ruby climbed on the school bus she saw Del Lasco waving at her eagerly from a seat near the back. Ruby stumbled down the aisle and sank down next to her.

'Why haven't you called?' said Del.

'I haven't been getting a lot of "me time",' said Ruby.

'How did your folks take it?' asked Del.

'Ah, you know,' replied Ruby, 'a little bit badly.'

'Like on a scale from one to ten?'

'Maybe thirteen.'

'So you're in trouble?' asked Del.

'Well, the Explorer Awards are off,' said Ruby.

Del made a horror-struck face. 'Now I feel really terrible,' she said.

'It's not your fault,' said Ruby.

'I think it is actually.'

'It's not.'

Del gave her friend a good-natured thump on the arm. 'Look, thanks a million for not ratting me out, I really massively appreciate it.'

'Of course,' said Ruby.

'Yeah but I mean, thanks, my mom would have grounded me till Christmas if I had been caught fighting again.'

'It's OK,' said Ruby, 'you would have covered for me.'

'You got that right,' said Del, 'but I feel bad. I didn't mean to leave you there, I mean I never woulda, I thought you were right behind me – I had no idea your glasses had been totalled.'

'My stupid clogs didn't help, but it's not a big deal,' said Ruby, 'don't make a thing of it.'

'Not a big deal?' said Del. 'But you were really stoked about going to that explorer thing tonight.'

'Yeah, well, I'm sure the six hours community service will take my mind off it.'

'Oh jeepers, not that too,' said Del. 'Look, I'll help you out.'

'You won't be allowed,' said Ruby, 'and in any case, if you do, then they'll figure it was you I was covering for.'

By the time they made it to Junior High they were talking about other things.

At least they were up until they ran into Vapona Begwell.

'Hey Lasco, who knew you could run so fast?' jeered Vapona.

'I'm surprised you even noticed given you split the scene before the cops even turned the siren on.'

'I guess I musta been trying to catch *you and Redfort*.'

'Actually Ruby took the fall, she was picked up by the sheriff.'

That silenced her. 'You were arrested?' said Vapona after a pause.

'Of course I wasn't arrested,' said Ruby. 'What, you think having your glasses stomped on, and your nose smooshed makes you responsible for wrecking a tree and kicking over a bunch of trashcans?'

'So I suppose you squealed, Redfort?'

'Are you kidding Bugwart, Ruby doesn't squeal.'

'Which is lucky for you, Lasco.'

'She saved *your* butt too, Bugwart.'

Ruby didn't want to be reminded of the dumb argument that had led to her missing the event of the year so she walked off in search of a more intelligent conversation.

Back home again and Ruby was trying hard to take it on the chin, but it wasn't so easy when the thing you really wanted more than anything had just been taken away from you. She had played it down with Del, the big disappointment about missing the Explorer Awards, because she didn't want Del to feel bad, and though in a way Del was sort of responsible for the whole mess, it was like Hitch said: all Ruby had had to do was walk away. Well, she wasn't going to demean herself by begging; she knew by the look in her father's eye that he would never change his mind. Her mom she reckoned she could break down, but her dad, no chance. She went straight up to her room, did her homework, watched no TV and read a book called *The Four Dimensions of Taste*.

When it was 6pm she came downstairs.

Ruby walked into the living room and found her parents there, her mom looking out of the window, an anxious expression on her face.

'It's just so windy out there,' she said, 'I'm not sure it's even safe to drive.'

'It looks worse than it is honey,' said Brant. 'It's a little blowy is all.'

'Why does Hitch have to be out of town tonight?' sighed Sabina. 'I trust his driving.'

'Bob's a good driver,' said Brant. 'There's no need to be concerned, honey.'

'I know,' said Sabina, 'I like Bob, it's just I feel more secure when Hitch is around, you know what I mean?'

Ruby *did* know what she meant, but then Ruby had witnessed Hitch taking on tougher challenges than driving a car on a windy evening.

As sore as Ruby was to be missing out on the evening, what she wasn't going to do was whine about it, so she made herself a big bowl of popcorn, flicked on the set and settled down to watch the whole thing on TV. Mrs Digby watched with her, up until the snakes appeared.

Then the housekeeper got to her feet. 'Seen enough of those critters to last me a lifetime,' she said, turning to leave the room.

'A rare snake that you have never even seen before has that big an effect on you?' said Ruby. 'You're never gonna meet this snake, Mrs Digby, it lives hundreds of miles away in... actually I have no idea where it's from, but not any place near here.'

'I don't mind if it happens to be from Mars, I don't need to look at the thing,' said the housekeeper. 'I stared enough rattlers in the eye when I was a child to know I don't want to look at one again.'

Ruby shrugged. 'If that's how you feel, that's how you feel,' she said, turning back to the screen.

It was towards the end of the televised event that she spotted Quent Humbert on screen. 'Brother! How did he get to go?' said Ruby out loud. And then the penny dropped.

'*He* got my ticket! That little shrimp got *my ticket!*' Of all the people in the world Quent Humbert was not a deserving case. He wouldn't be a bit interested in the explorers and was no doubt most excited about the chance to be seen on live TV. As if to confirm her suspicion, Quent, suddenly realising he was in shot, began frantically waving into the camera. She could see his little autograph book in his hand.

'Get out of the way you idiot,' Ruby shouted at the television. She was finding it hard to concentrate on what the man from the moon was saying and the camera operator was having difficulty keeping Quent out of shot.

Her shouting was interrupted by a loud crashing sound outside and Ruby sprang to her feet to look out of the window. Bug was barking like crazy, but Ruby couldn't instantly see what had happened.

'What in the Sam Hill is going on?' shouted Mrs Digby from downstairs.

'I don't know!' yelled Ruby.

Mrs Digby joined her in the living room. Bug was still barking his head off and Ruby switched out the lights so it was easier to see into the darkness.

There was a certain amount of debris, a couple of broken pots and a lot of leaves and twigs scattered about the place, but nothing that would cause the kind of cracking sound they had just heard.

'Must be down the street,' said Ruby, 'a tree or something.'

She was keen to go look for damage, but Mrs Digby wasn't having it.

'Child, I am not letting you step a toe outside this house, not while this gale is blowing.'

By the time Ruby gave up arguing and returned to the TV, the Explorer Awards were over.

'So who won? Darn it! Snakes, polar bears or little green men from Mars?'

Chapter 22.
Sick as a dog

RUBY LOOKED UP FROM THE TV HOURS LATER to see her mother tottering into the room, almost tripping over the overly long red gown she was wearing. Her face was not the happy face of a person who loved parties and had just spent the evening in the company of the great and good of Twinford.

'Mom, you look like you ate something bad,' said Ruby.

'My pride is all I ate,' replied her mother. 'I can't remember when I've ever been so humiliated.' Sabina sank onto a chair and tossed her silver clutch bag to the floor miserably.

'What happened, exactly?' asked Ruby.

'I can hardly bear to talk about it,' she said shaking her head as if to shake away the memory of a terrible vision.

'Try,' said Ruby, who knew her mother liked nothing better than to talk things through, no matter what the subject.

Sabina sighed. 'Imagine you are one of two people wearing red evening gowns.'

Ruby scrunkled her brow. 'I'll try,' she said, 'but it may not be easy.' Ruby wasn't in the habit of dressing up, and if she did then it was more likely to be a misshapen secondhand number smelling of mothballs.

'Imagine that these evening gowns are not only exactly the same red but exactly the same gown.'

'Oh, Sabina honey,' interrupted Ruby's father as he walked into the room, 'I don't know why you are making such a big deal about this. You were a complete knock-out in that dress, knocked it out of the park.'

But Sabina put up her hand to silence him. 'And,' she continued, 'imagine if that same dress is being worn by one of the honoured guests,' her voice quavered a little, the force of her emotion making it crack.

Ruby rolled her eyes. 'This is what has you looking like you ate a bad oyster?'

'It's social suicide, it's an honest to goodness cocktail crime scene.'

'Mom, you gotta lighten up with the trivia. You are about to hit the superficial super wall – you are about to head on out into superficial hyper space.'

But Sabina Redfort just groaned and slumped back in her chair. 'To top it all, the store didn't even do the alterations I asked for. I clearly told them I wanted the dress to be ankle length so you might see those diamante mules of mine, but instead I was tripping up over the darned thing all night and I might just as well have been wearing bedroom slippers for all anyone would know, plus they had obviously steamed it to get the wrinkles out but it was still damp, and to top it all the stupid belt kept twisting around 'cause it was too big. I abandoned it in the powder room, which destroyed the look.' She sighed a regretful sigh. 'I feel completely burnt out by it all.' She slumped even further into the chair.

'Maybe you should have eaten more – all those martini cocktails on an empty stomach...' said Brant, 'it's no wonder you have a headache.'

'Oh, I could hardly eat at all,' she said. 'The dress disaster upset me too much.'

'You should have tried the oysters, they were something else,' said Brant.

'What, are you kidding? After Ruby told me about the mucus, no siree Bob, I stuck to the nibbles on sticks.' She sighed. 'Oh, run me a bath would you Brant, I've got to wash away this evening and pretend like it never happened.'

Brant helped his wife to her feet and, putting an arm around her, guided her downstairs. No matter how much Ruby might mock, one thing was clear: the night really had taken a toll on her mom. She looked as fragile as a sick bird.

Ruby climbed the stairs to her room. She got into bed, but something about her mom's defeated appearance niggled her. She picked up her science magazine and read an article exploring the possibility of colonising Mars. From the sound of it, it was entirely possible it would happen, probably many years from today, many decades on from 1973 – perhaps not until 2030 or so – but just because it seemed more than probable didn't necessarily mean it was a very appealing idea or even (in Ruby's opinion) a good one. Mars didn't have a whole lot of oxygen and that seemed a good reason not to climb aboard the spaceship and that was just for starters. Once you factored in lack of food and water it really seemed like a no-brainer.

Jeepers, thought Ruby, *give me Death Valley any time.*

She was just imagining how her mother might cope on the Red Planet – a woman who could be struck down by the embarrassment of a party dress double-up – when she heard a noise that sounded a lot like her father shouting, 'Call the paramedics!'

She jumped out of bed, opened the door and was halfway down the stairs before Mrs Digby made it out of her housekeeper's ground floor apartment.

'What's going on, Dad?'

'It's your mother, she isn't doing so well.'

'It was just a dress, Dad, aren't you all being a little melodramatic?'

'It's not the dress, Rube, something is very wrong. She's sick as anything. She got all uncoordinated and started staggering about. Then she fell over and now she can't stop throwing up.'

'Food poisoning?' asked Ruby. She was trying to keep her voice steady, but she could see the look in her father's eyes – he looked scared. It wasn't like Brant Redfort to be scared. Maybe because life had pretty much always dealt him an even hand, it had never really occurred to him that things could go badly wrong.

'I don't know,' said Brant, 'it could be. She looks terrible Rube, just terrible...' His words tailed off.

It was Mrs Digby who took control. 'Now Mr R, don't you go flapping, she'll be fine. That Sabina's been through more than a lot in the years I've known her. Ruby will call 911, you call the doc and I will attend to Mrs R.' She paused. 'You got that?'

Brant nodded, and the housekeeper disappeared into Sabina's room.

When Ruby entered her mother's bedroom – the ambulance now on its way – she could see there was reason enough to flap. Sabina had not even managed to get out of her evening gown, she was lying on the bed, swaddled in the red silk which was in great contrast to the pallor of her face. Her skin had turned an unfortunate colour, like that of some creature already dead. In fact were it not for the beads of sweat sitting on her forehead, it would be hard to imagine she were alive at all, her breathing was so shallow, and when Ruby felt for her mother's pulse, it was there but barely.

'My hands won't seem to go where I want them to,' murmured Sabina. 'The room is spinning. My head aches so and my mouth tastes like metal.'

The paramedics arrived, lights flashing and sirens sounding.

Sabina was stretchered into the vehicle and Brant held her hand the whole way to the hospital, and stayed there all night.

While Brant was at the hospital, Ruby and Mrs Digby sat up scouring books. If food poisoning was to blame then what exactly was the source of the malady? Her mother claimed to barely have nibbled more than a few canapés.

Though it was past midnight Ruby picked up the phone and dialled Clancy's number.

CLANCY: *'Ruby?'*

RUBY: *'Are you awake?'*

CLANCY: *'Yeah, but why are you?'*

RUBY: *'I was just wondering, are you OK?'*

CLANCY: *'Yeah, why wouldn't I be?'*

RUBY: *'And your dad, how about him?'*

CLANCY: *'Fine.'*

RUBY: *'He's not throwing up or anything? No headaches?'*

CLANCY: *'Ruby, what's this about?'*

RUBY: *'My mom ate something that didn't agree with her.'*

CLANCY: *'Is she OK?'*

RUBY: *'The paramedics took her, my dad's at the hospital.'*

CLANCY: *'How bad is she?'*

RUBY: *'Pretty bad.'*

CLANCY: *'Are you worried?'*

RUBY: *'A little.'*

CLANCY: *'Who's that in the background?'*

RUBY: *'Mrs Digby, we can't sleep.'*

CLANCY: *'I'm coming over, I'll keep you company.'*
RUBY: *'You don't have to Clance.'*
CLANCY: *'I know.'*

Chapter 23.
A rogue bivalve

CLANCY MUST HAVE RIDDEN HIS BIKE AT SOME KIND OF SUPERHUMAN SPEED because he was there before Mrs Digby had even begun to boil the milk for the hot chocolate she was planning on handing him when he walked through the door.

'Boy, you got here fast,' said Ruby.

'The wind was behind me,' said Clancy. 'The storm might have blown through, but it's still kinda gusty. You know a tree's come down on the corner of your street? I had to clamber right over it.' He paused. 'So what do you think made your mom sick?' he said, pulling himself out of his raincoat.

'I wouldn't be surprised if it isn't down to that Consuela Cruz's cooking,' said Mrs Digby. 'People think she's the bee's knees, but the question is: does she keep a clean kitchen?'

'Mrs Digby, I think you're clutching at straws,' said Ruby. 'Just because you're no big fan of Consuela's, it doesn't mean she's going around poisoning everyone.'

'So you're sure that's what it is – definitely food poisoning?' said Clancy.

'It's the logical thing,' replied Ruby, 'but what *kind* of food poisoning, that's the big question.'

'Your dad's OK, my dad's OK, I'm OK,' said Clancy.

'So let's assume it's not "general food poisoning",' said Ruby, 'let's assume there was one bad morsel there and my mom is the unlucky consumer.'

'Sounds like shellfish poisoning,' said Clancy. 'I mean it can't be chicken poisoning, because if the chicken was off then a whole bunch of people would be in the ER right now.'

'Plus Consuela didn't serve chicken,' said Ruby.

'She didn't?' said Clancy. 'I could have sworn I ate chicken.'

'Probably frogs' legs,' said Mrs Digby. 'I hear they taste just like chicken.'

'I thought it was human beings that tasted like chicken,' said Clancy.

'I would imagine it's unlikely Consuela served either,' said Ruby, 'so maybe we should stick to the likely contenders.'

'So a rogue oyster?' suggested Clancy. 'Or a mussel? Or maybe a prawn or shrimp or something? There *were* shellfish there, you know what those are like for stomach cramps.'

'Yeah,' sighed Ruby, 'and she *was* all dizzy and complaining of a terrible headache.'

'Well, what you are describing sounds very much like a wrong oyster to me. My sister Nancy ate one once and I can tell you it wasn't a pretty sight – barf central.'

Clancy really liked to read up on diseases and sickness

generally; if he was going to contract something horrible then he might as well know what he was in for. It helped to be prepared. *I mean put it this way*, he would argue, *if I know it's normal to puke for twelve hours non-stop, then I can tough it out. What I don't want to hear is, "This is highly irregular, we have never seen this kind of reaction in a human being before."*

Clancy liked to be prepared for the worst.

'That's that then, she must have eaten a bad bivalve,' he said.

'Perhaps,' said Ruby, but she didn't sound convinced.

Clancy looked at her. 'You don't think it is oyster poisoning?'

'I don't know, you're probably right and it probably is. The only thing I am surprised about is my mom seemed dead set against eating oysters on account of the mucus.'

'Mucus?'

'Yeah. We had a whole conversation about the structure of an oyster because she thought they had brains and I said— Actually, it doesn't matter. The point is she said afterwards that she wouldn't ever eat another oyster.'

'What colour was she?' asked Clancy.

'What?' said Ruby.

'Pale as the grave,' said Mrs Digby.

'Not puce?' asked Clancy. 'You eat a bad oyster and you usually turn puce.'

'No,' said Mrs Digby firmly, 'ghostly she looked.'

'She also mentioned her mouth tasted of metal.'

'I haven't heard that before,' said Clancy. 'My sister Nancy kept whining that her teeth were falling out, but it turned out that's one of the symptoms.'

The three of them sat up all night discussing food poisoning and the various forms it could take until finally Brant telephoned at 6am to tell them Sabina was out of danger.

'They say she's going to be OK.'

'Do you know what the cause was?' asked Ruby.

'We think it was probably stomach flu,' said Brant. 'The doc said he'll stop by later today and fill me in.'

The conversation didn't last long since Brant didn't seem to have much useful information other than Sabina had suffered no permanent damage.

Ruby replaced the receiver and picked up the *Twinford Echo*, lying on the doormat. The front page was a photograph from last night's Explorer Awards. She turned to page four for the story. There were photographs of some of those who had attended but nothing about Sabina Redfort being taken ill. She guessed her father would have tried to keep this quiet, not wanting to offend the organisers or cast a shadow over Consuela Cruz's catering.

On one page, there was a picture of the winning explorer: Amarjargel Oidov, the woman who had discovered the new snake species. *So that's who won,* thought Ruby. She glanced at the text under the photo:

AMARJARGEL OIDOV was honoured last night at the Explorer Awards for her role in discovering an all-new species of snake in Bhutan. The judges further cited her conservation work, including her tireless efforts to save the snake's natural habitat – a small forest deep in the mountains, and sought after by timber merchants. The snake species itself is notable for…

Ruby skipped the rest. She looked again at the black and white picture – the snake woman, standing next to Ambassador Crew and Mayor Abrahams, all smiling at the camera. Ambassador Crew looking slightly perturbed by the snake that was wound around Ms Oidov's arm. There was something about this photograph that triggered a thought in Ruby's brain. It flickered there for a second, and then was gone.

Clancy and Ruby went down to survey the damage on Cedarwood Drive. Considering a large tree had come down, it wasn't as bad as it might have been, however there was *one* casualty.

'What's she gonna do without her wheels?' said Clancy.

'I don't know,' said Ruby. 'I've never seen her without her vehicle.'

They were staring at Mrs Beesman's shopping cart. It was totally crushed and currently lying under a ton of tree.

The cans of cat food still in the cart were also crushed and the cat food itself was oozing out. Mrs Beesman was finding it hard to keep the cats from trying to get it and in so doing cut themselves on the sharp metal of the torn-open tins. The old lady had rigged up a sort of fence construction, but the cats weren't giving up. Mrs Beesman had a lot of cats, some people said she had around seventy-four of them – whether this was an accurate number or not, really didn't matter. The important thing was: she had a problem and she needed help.

'Don't worry Mrs Beesman, we can handle this,' said Ruby.

Mrs Beesman grunted, the closest she ever got to speaking.

Clancy and Ruby cleared the mess easily enough, but the cart was a goner.

Lunch was interrupted by the chimes of the doorbell.

'That will be the doc,' said Ruby's father, jumping to his feet.

He scooted down to answer the door and returned with the doctor in tow.

'Would you like to join us?' asked Brant.

Dr Shepherd shook his head. 'No, I just dropped by to give you the good news – Sabina's on the mend and she's going to be just fine.'

'So what was it? A bad case of stomach flu?' asked Brant.

'A bad case of shellfish poisoning,' said Dr Shepherd.

'Sabina is pretty adamant that she ate next to nothing last night on account of the dress mix up,' said Brant.

'She probably absent-mindedly popped an oyster and the rest as we say is a nasty case of vomiting and stomach cramps. One rogue oyster is all it takes to have you flat on your back with a few tubes in your arm.'

'Well, thanks Dr Shepherd, I really appreciate you taking a look at her.' Brant shook his head. 'I don't mind admitting it, for a minute there I thought she might not pull through.'

Dr Shepherd put his hand on Brant's shoulder. 'The good thing is that she's going to be OK, AOK, nothing to worry about. She'll be back home tomorrow.'

Brant smiled. 'Well, having her back safe and sound is all I care about.' He looked over at Ruby. 'All *we* care about.'

Ruby nodded, though she didn't feel quite as reassured as her father did. Something was still gnawing at her.

Something about shellfish. And oysters. And her mother's ghostly pale face as she lay in that red dress.

Chapter 24.
Pick your poison

ONCE THE DOCTOR HAD LEFT, Ruby returned to her room and found Clancy asleep on the beanbag. It had been a long, sleepless night, but Ruby was wide awake. She began scanning her bookshelves, running her hands across the spines, trying to locate a very particular volume. The book she was after was one with a cover illustration showing a perfect red apple. The back cover showed the same apple gone bad. The book was called: *Pick Your Poison.*

Actually it was about a whole lot more than poison. It covered venom and toxins too. As the book's introduction said: *'Simply put, poisons are chemical substances which have an impact on the biological functions in other living organisms. A toxin is a poison produced by a living organism. Venoms are toxins, which are injected by way of sting or bite into another living organism. A venom is a toxin, but it does not follow that all toxins are venoms, just as all toxins are poisons but not all poisons are toxins. Any substance if taken in large enough quantity can be a poison and can lead to death. Even water, though essential for life, can be lethal if too much is consumed.'*

The book also had an epigram from Paracelsus, the father of toxicology: *'Everything is poison, there is poison in everything. Only the dose makes a thing not a poison.'*

Interesting, thought Ruby. She turned to the second part of the book, a large glossy picture of a frog announcing the section that covered transdermal poisoning, beginning with a chapter on deadly frogs and toads.

1. Strawberry Poison-dart Frog {Oophaga pumilio}

A tiny vivid red frog native to Central America. Beautiful to look at, but contact with it will cause swelling and a burning sensation, though in comparison to other poison-dart frogs its toxicity is mild.

Ruby didn't make it past the strawberry variety of frog: by the time the clock struck three, she was fast asleep.

When Ruby awoke, she found herself still thinking about frogs. And thinking about frogs led her to think about fairy tales. Frogs were big in fairy tales, and the more she thought about fairy tales, the more she began to think about murder. There was a lot of murder in fairy tales too, or at least a lot of attempted murder.

Take *Snow White*, for instance. Just how many times did that stepmother queen try and kill poor little Snow White? Three times? More if you included her ordering the huntsman to do

it for her. 'Cut her heart from her...' Wasn't that how it went?
Ruby reached for her Brothers Grimm and laid it down next to
the poisons book and began to leaf through, looking for that most
compliant of victims, Snow White.

'I hope you're not planning foul play.'

Ruby nearly jumped out of her socks.

'Mrs Digby! You shouldn't creep up on people like that.'

'I wasn't creeping, it's your guilty conscience that's got you
jumping,' said the housekeeper. 'What are you reading up on?'
She reached for her glasses. 'Plotting a murder, are we?'

'I was reading up on frogs and poison and that made me
think of fairy tales.'

'I don't remember there being a frog in *Snow White*,' said
the housekeeper.

'There isn't, but there is poison,' said Ruby, 'and a lot of it.'

'Yep, that poor old queen,' said Mrs Digby. 'She asks that
huntsman to do one little murder and he lets her down – so she
just thinks to herself, if you want a job doing properly then do
it yourself.'

'You remember what she does next?' asked Ruby.

'Sure I do,' said Mrs Digby. 'As I recall, she tries a poison
comb, and apples, but she's foiled every time by those interfering
dwarves.' She sighed. 'The apple of course would have done the
job had it not been for that sappy prince.'

Ruby tutted. 'You sound like you're on the wicked queen's
side, Mrs Digby.'

'No,' said Mrs Digby shaking her head, 'I'm not in favour of murder, not a bit, but I have sympathy for her plight none the less. She was the best at something, even if it was only the best at being beautiful.'

'Doesn't mean she should go around killing teenagers though,' said Ruby.

'Quite so, I couldn't agree more,' said the housekeeper, 'just saying it can hurt like misery when you lose that number one spot in the beauty parade, don't matter if it's looks or brains.'

'Were you a beauty queen, Mrs Digby?' asked Ruby.

Mrs Digby rolled her eyes. 'Lawks no child, but for a while I was the most talented cake baker in the county until Brenda Hathaway came along.'

'I see your point,' said Ruby, remembering how Dakota Lyme had reacted to coming second in the mathlympics meet.

'That Brenda Hathaway,' said Mrs Digby, 'it might not have been her fault, but it stung like poison oak losing out to her.'

No wonder Mrs Digby had objected so to Consuela Cruz taking over her kitchen.

'Well, I'll leave you to it,' said the housekeeper, shaking her head as she gathered the dirty mugs, glasses and cereal bowls onto her tray and tottered back downstairs.

'I'll holler when supper's done,' she called. 'You'd better wake old sleeping beauty there and ask him if he wants to stick around for nourishment or if he's planning on heading home any time.'

Ruby flicked through the pages of *Pick Your Poison*, leaving the frogs and toads behind her.

CHAPTER 9   DRESSED TO KILL

The first section of this chapter covered Greek myths and legends – like that of Glauce, poisoned by a dress. Ruby knew the story already: when Jason (of Argonauts notoriety) abandoned Medea to marry Glauce instead, Medea took revenge by sending Glauce a wedding dress and a crown as a gift, both soaked in poison. Glauce wore the dress and crown, and she died. *Boy, that Medea was not the sort to bow out gracefully*, thought Ruby. As ancient Greek as all this sounded and a long way from real life, it did make Ruby wonder. She remembered her mother complaining that the altering service at the dress store had returned the dress damp.

What if the dress Mom was wearing was soaked in something toxic? What if that toxin soaked into her skin and poisoned her?

It seemed like a pretty stupid thought until she turned to the next section and there was a story about a young woman who purchased a second-hand wedding dress from a thrift store. Unfortunately the dress had previously been worn by a dead person and was soaked with embalming fluid, unfortunate because the young woman who wore the dress to her wedding very nearly died as the poison began to work its way into her system. It was a far-fetched scenario, no doubt apocryphal, some kind of urban myth, but it did make the whole poison dress idea seem much more possible.

First question to answer was: if her mother's dress was poisoned with some toxic substance then how did it get there?

Had her mother accidentally spilt something on the dress? Had someone else accidentally spilt something on the dress?

What kind of scenario would allow you to spill something dangerously toxic on a dress and not even notice?

She leant over and shook Clancy, who had been sleeping solidly for the past several hours.

'Hey Clance, wake up!'

He murmured but continued to sleep. She shook him more vigorously.

'Wake up!'

'Huh, what, I didn't do anything,' he called out.

'Relax Clancy, it's me.'

'Oh, what is it? Something happen?' he asked.

She looked at him. 'Maybe,' she said.

Ruby pointed to the page illustrated with the drawing of the swooning bride. Clancy read. It took him two reads before he got it.

'You're saying your mom's dress was poisoned? That doesn't seem very likely.'

'I'm saying it could have been, it's a possibility, but just say it was... *then* consider *how*.'

'On purpose?' Clancy was looking at her. 'You think if it happened it would be on purpose, right?'

Ruby paused before saying, 'I know it sounds far-fetched, but on the other hand, how could it happen by accident? I mean, just how do you accidentally poison someone's evening gown?'

'You spill something, knock something over, the cat knocks something over, your mom spills something on it... What something are we talking about here?'

'Could be various things. But based on her symptoms – the dizziness, the paleness, the lack of coordination, the metallic taste in her mouth – I'd put my money on methanol. It's used for embalming and so the question to ask would be: why would it be anywhere near a dress shop or my mom's bedroom for that matter?'

Clancy flicked through the pages of *Pick Your Poison* till he found a section called '**Methanol Poisoning**'.

Methanol is the simplest alcohol compound and is highly toxic. It can enter the system by ingestion, inhalation or absorption through the skin, and its effects can be fatal. Its primary toxic mechanism is a process of formate production: methanol is metabolised in the body into formic acid. This inhibits mitochondrial cytochrome c oxidase, creating hypoxia at the cellular level, which—

'What's hypoxia?' said Clancy.

'Lack of oxygen,' said Ruby. 'It basically suffocates your cells.'

'That doesn't sound nice.'

'You got that right, It would have you looking like the Rigors of Mortis Square given time. '

'So if this poison is so dangerous,' asked Clancy, 'then how come your mom didn't die?'

'She cured herself,' said Ruby.

'How could she?' said Clancy. 'She had no idea what was making her sick.'

'It was just a fortuitous coincidence,' said Ruby. 'One of the cures for methanol poisoning is ethanol, because the body processes that instead and excretes the methanol – and my mom happens to like the odd glass of ethanol.'

Clancy's face suggested a total blank in the brain, so Ruby filled him in.

'Alcohol. Ethanol is the chemical name for alcohol, and my mom drank martini cocktails that night and that's what saved her life – she administered her own antidote.'

Clancy stared at her, eyes huge.

'If I could get hold of the dress then I could prove it,' said Ruby.

'You think?' he asked.

'I could be wrong, it's just a theory,' said Ruby.

'Yeah and a really creepy one,' said Clancy, 'if you don't mind my saying it. I really hope you're wrong.'

'Are you a complete
brainless wonder?'
said the woman...

'...Let me explain,' he replied.

'I'd like that,' she said, 'because the thing is, sweetheart, I just can't seem to square it... Why did we go to all that trouble of springing you from jail when you seem to be a complete and utter waste of space?'

'I thought the plan was foolproof.'

'I thought you were supposed to be some kind of expert, but it seems you're just an idiot.'

'I was off my game, I've been out of action cooped up in a cell six foot by seven foot.'

'You'll be six foot under if he has his way.'

'Has he said anything?'

'I don't think you want to know.'

'What can I do?'

'You better make it right, sweetie – you better get to that hospital and retrieve the dress.'

'You want me to destroy it?'

'That's about right. If anyone cares to take a long hard look, then they'll know the truth and we don't want this coming back to bite us.'

'Consider it done.'

'No, sweetie, I'll consider it done when it's done. Until then you better pray he doesn't decide to terminate your contract, and by terminate I mean...'

'I know what you mean.'

'Good, I hate having to spell things out. Oh, and I wouldn't run if I were you, that'll just make him angry, you know what he's like, and he'll only find you anyway and it won't be pretty when he does.'

Chapter 25.
Dressed to kill

THE NEXT MORNING WHEN SHE OPENED THE FRONT DOOR, Ruby thought her mother looked frailer than she had ever seen her. Sabina stepped unsteadily out of the car, her skin so pale that she could have doubled for the part of Cordelia Rigor, and Ruby hoped her father had a firm grip on her mother's arm because if that wind caught her then she might be snatched up and whirled away.

'That's the last time I eat an oyster,' said Sabina easing herself into a chair like she was a very old lady.

'I didn't think you did,' said Ruby.

'I am beginning to think I must have, everyone says I did, but one thing's for sure – I don't want to look an oyster in the eye ever again.'

'Oysters don't have eyes,' said Ruby, 'or at least not what you would consider to be eyes.'

'Don't they?' said Sabina. 'How do they see?'

'I'll get you a book on the topic,' said Ruby. 'I have one upstairs.'

Sabina thought for a second. 'Oh yes, that's right, they don't have faces... You know, would you mind if we changed the subject?'

'Happily,' said Ruby.

Sabina was silent for a minute as she took in the entire picture that was Ruby. '*I think I'm about to barf*,' she said.

'I'll get you to the bathroom,' said Ruby.

'No, I was just reading your T-shirt,' said Sabina. 'I know the feeling only too well.'

'Oh sorry,' said Ruby, 'I'll just go change into something less descriptive.' She glanced down at her left arm. She could see her mother trying to make out what it said. 'Something with long sleeves,' she added.

Ruby was remembering what the doctor had said: 'Try to make sure your mother avoids stress of any kind.'

Ruby wasn't sure if it was stressful for her mother to look at an arm which said WAKE UP AND SMELL THE BANANA MILK, but she was certain it was kinder not to remind her about how Friday night had been spent.

Sabina had retired to her bed by the time Ruby returned to the kitchen, so she made her a cup of tea and went on down to her mother's room. Brant had gone to the store to get some particular herbal remedy, one Mrs Digby swore by, so Ruby stayed a while, chatting to her mother and generally being thoughtful and, when the moment came, she enquired about the dress.

'So what did you do with your evening wear?' she asked,

faux-casual. She was peering into the small suitcase her father had packed for Sabina and could see no red dress.

'I really don't know,' said Sabina, 'but I have to say, I really don't care either. I don't think I'd wear that dress again to save my life.'

'So what do you think happened to it?' said Ruby.

'I guess it got lost. It should have been in my hospital locker, but that was empty when I checked out.'

It was while she was babysitting later that morning that Ruby put her master plan into action. She figured it would not only get her out of the Lemon house with no objection from either her parents or Elaine, but also save her from momentous boredom.

'Of course, good idea, take Archie out, Ruby, he could use the air.' Elaine Lemon looked like *she* could also use the silence, but Ruby said nothing to that effect and instead packed Archie into his stroller, gathered up the mind-boggling amount of stuff that people seemed to insist a baby needed and left the house.

She wasn't actually headed to the park as she had told Mrs Lemon, but instead to Clancy's house on Ambassador Row.

Clancy was looking down from the upstairs window and when he spotted Ruby he called out.

'What are you doing?'

'I'm babysitting,' said Ruby.

'What?' said Clancy. He couldn't quite believe his ears. 'You are not serious?'

'Totally,' said Ruby.

'What happened? Did you lose your mind finally?'

'It's tactical,' said Ruby.

'How so?'

'I do a little babysitting and my parents regard me in a more sympathetic light, also it makes them feel I am being punished, which in a way I am.'

Clancy was really looking at her now.

'Plus it means I get to leave the house, legit.'

'This is your plan?' said Clancy. 'Your brilliant plan?'

Ruby shrugged. 'The best I could come up with at short notice,' she said.

'Impressive,' said Clancy. 'Where does one pick up a baby at short notice?'

'Elaine Lemon's,' said Ruby. 'Can you come down and open the gate?'

'Sure thing,' said Clancy, and he ran downstairs and buzzed her in.

'He might be needing a drink already, you got any milk?' asked Ruby. 'I tell you, all this kid does is poop and eat.'

They walked into the kitchen where they found five-year-old Olive Crew reading a book, or at least pretending to read a book; most of it she had simply memorised.

'You want me to read him a story?' asked Olive. 'I can read really good.'

'*Well*,' corrected Clancy. 'It's well, not good, and by the way, you can't.'

'I can too,' said Olive and she plonked herself down next to Archie and began the job of pretending to read.

'Once upon a time... you see?' said Olive. 'I'm reading.'

'You're not reading,' said Clancy, 'you're remembering.'

'It's the same,' said Olive.

Ruby and Clancy opened a bag of cookies and Clancy chatted on to her about the Explorer Awards evening.

'I mean those snakes,' said Clancy, 'they were something else. One bite and you start sweating a river.'

And then Ruby told him about how her mother's evening gown had disappeared.

'Someone must have taken it from her hospital locker,' said Ruby.

'Maybe it just got lost in the emergency room,' offered Clancy. 'I mean, it must have been pretty dramatic, a life and death sorta situation.'

'Yeah, maybe,' said Ruby. 'Either way, we got no way of proving my theory.'

Olive's little voice droned on in the background. 'Who is the fairest of them all? ... Clancy what does this word say?'

'Liver,' said Clancy. 'The queen told him to cut out her heart and her liver.'

'Oh,' said Olive. 'The queen told him to cut out her heart and her liver,' she wrinkled her nose. 'What's a liver?'

'It's one of your main internal organs,' said Ruby, 'cleans

your blood.'

'Do you need it?' asked Olive.

'Yeah,' said Ruby, 'you're basically flat-out dead without a liver.'

'So what's Snow White going to do when the man cuts out her liver?' asked Olive.

'She's going to die,' said Clancy. 'What do you think is going to happen?'

Olive ignored him and continued with her story.

'So how long do you think your parents are going to keep this up?' said Clancy.

'The whole grounding deal? I don't know,' said Ruby, 'they'll get bored soon enough, want me to go to some party with them and that will be that.'

'What's a b-o-d-i-c-e?' asked Olive calling out the letters phonetically.

'Like a corset,' said Ruby.

'What's one of them?' said Olive.

'Something you wear, straps you in real tight,' said Ruby.

'Like what?' said Olive.

'It's a piece of clothing. You lace it up and it wraps tight around your middle.'

'Like a belt?' said Olive.

'No, not really, but pretend for the sake of interruption it is.'

'OK,' said Olive.

'And when do you have to do your community service?' asked

Clancy.

'I'm still waiting to hear,' said Ruby.

'So the queen pulled the belt really completely tight and Snow White couldn't breathe and fell over on the floor and was dead, but not quite.'

Ruby stopped talking.

'What is it?' asked Clancy.

'What did you just say, Olive?'

'So the queen pulled the belt really completely tight and Snow White couldn't breathe and fell over on the floor and was dead but not quite.'

'Lost property,' said Ruby.

'What?' said Clancy.

'My mom was wearing a belt the other night at the Explorer Awards.'

'So what?' said Clancy.

'So I need to get to the Geographical Institute and search through the lost property.'

'Because she might have lost her belt?'

'She left it in the powder room, and it might be evidence of my poison theory – I have to get down there, right now!' She caught sight of baby Archie. 'Only I can't because I gotta get the Lemon home. Darn it!'

'Simple,' said Clancy, 'I'll get the belt, you lose the Lemon!'

'Clancy, you're a genius.'

'No,' said Clancy. 'I'm just thinking straight.'

They had just barely made it to the bus stop when it seemed the baby was trying to tell them something.

'Is it food you're after?' asked Ruby. The baby may have smiled, it was hard to be sure with babies; one infant's smile was another's gas.

'Oh brother,' Ruby said as she pulled out one more jar of mush. She began to look for a spooning device.

'Here,' said Clancy, 'I always keep one with me.'

'Thanks,' said Ruby. 'Weird, but thanks. That kid's doing my head in.'

'He's a lot better than Olive,' said Clancy.

'No, I don't mean the Lemon, I mean that kid.' Ruby pointed ahead of her. 'The cartoon kid.'

Ruby and Clancy were sitting on the bus stop bench and there was a flyer stuck to a lamppost. The drawing was of that same cartoon kid, the words winding out of its mouth.

'Oh, yeah,' said Ruby. 'In all the drama I forgot to tell you – Elliot was right, it *is* a drink, at least I think so. I saw the bottle the other day when I was getting socked in the nose by Gemma Melamare. It fell out of the trashcan. I can't be sure because I couldn't see too well on account of my glasses being broken, but I could swear it was the same image.'

'Well that's good, so it was all worth it, getting arrested by the sheriff then.'

'I wasn't arrested, Clancy.'

'You went in the car.'

'Yeah but that's not being arrested; going in the car doesn't mean arrested.'

'Did he put the lights on?' asked Clancy.

'Why would he put the lights on, Clance? What possible reason would there be to put the lights on?'

'I thought you said you had a nosebleed?'

'What, are you outta your skull?' said Ruby. 'No one puts flashing lights on for a nosebleed.'

'So what did the bottle look like anyway?'

'Just a glass soda bottle with a sort of twisty glass shape and that cartoon kid.'

'Did you keep it?' asked Clancy.

'Why would I keep it?' asked Ruby. 'I just got socked in the nose. I wasn't exactly in the mood to bring home somebody else's trash. Plus I was being escorted away by Sheriff Bridges. What was I going to say? "Excuse me while I take this empty bottle out of the garbage"?'

'Yeah, and I guess your folks woulda hated that, on top of all the other delinquent stuff you'd just done,' said Clancy. 'My dad would probably have made me join the foreign legion or something. He would not have taken well to the embarrassment of a son getting arrested.'

'How many times do I have to say I wasn't arrested?'

The bus came and Ruby and Archie boarded and headed back to the Lemon house, while Clancy went in search of Mrs Redfort's lost property.

❋ ❋ ❋

Forty minutes later, Clancy was breathless and ringing on the Redfort's front door. He handed over a plastic carrier bag containing Mrs Redfort's evening gown belt.

'Good going Clance, I owe you one,' said Ruby.

'No sweat,' said Clancy. 'I gotta split, let me know if you're right, OK?'

'You'll be the first to know,' said Ruby, 'and if not then at least the second or possibly third.'

Chapter 26.
Take a minute

HITCH WAS IN HIS APARTMENT FIXING SOMETHING TOO
SMALL TO SEE. Ruby thought it was probably some piece of
Spectrum gadgetry, and that reminded her about the camera
and Clancy's behavioural science project. She had promised to
at least try and acquire a small video camera from the Spectrum
gadget room for Clancy, but exactly when was she going to get
around to doing that?

It was hardly top of her agenda, though she hated to let
Clancy down.

Hitch took off his magnifying eyewear when Ruby entered
the room, and sat back in his chair.

'What is it kid, something happen?'

'I've been sorta wondering if perhaps it wasn't an oyster.'

Hitch took a second or two and then his brain caught up.

'...That poisoned your mother?'

'Yes.'

'Why not?'

'Because of the mucus – oysters are basically all mouth, gills and mucus – anyway, I told her how bivalves eat, and that put her right off. You know about how oysters eat?'

'No, but I think I might be coming around to your mom's point of view.'

'So I think it's highly probable she didn't eat one like she said from the beginning, and if I'm right then something else must have poisoned her.'

'So what are you suggesting? Another food stuff caused her to wind up in the ER?'

'I think it might have been her dress.'

'Her dress?'

'Yes, her dress.'

'Kid, I am actually not following.'

'Something toxic could have been on her dress, soaked into the fabric, an accident probably, but, I mean, I think that could be what happened.'

She repeated what she had explained to Clancy, and Hitch took his time before asking, 'Kid, you know how unlikely this sounds?'

'Yes,' agreed Ruby.

'Where is this dress?' asked Hitch.

'It's gone,' said Ruby.

'So we can't prove your theory?'

'Maybe we can,' said Ruby. She explained about the lost property, the belt, the chance that it might be able to prove her hypothesis.

'And you have this belt?'

Ruby held up the bag containing the red belt.

'OK,' said Hitch, 'if you feel there's a chance you're right, let's ask SJ to check it out.'

'You're taking me seriously?'

'Don't I always?' said Hitch.

'Not always,' said Ruby.

'Well, kid, I'm taking you seriously now.'

'If my parents find out I'm out and about without the Lemon they are going to give me major grief. That kid's my cover.'

'Redfort, *I'm* your cover,' replied Hitch.

They drove at some speed to the Dime a Dozen in Hitch's silver convertible. As they drove, Hitch called SJ, the Spectrum lab technician, and filled her in.

They reached the Dime a Dozen convenience store, stepped through the flyspray shelves and into HQ.

SJ was waiting for them, protective gloves on.

First of all she sniffed the red silk belt and then she carried out various tests in her lab.

Once she was satisfied, she took off her gloves. 'Yep,' she said, 'that's methanol all right. It's largely evaporated of course, but if your mother's dress was soaked in this stuff too then I would guess she is lucky she drank so many cocktails.'

'Was it deliberate?' asked Ruby. 'The methanol, I mean.'

'I'd say so,' replied SJ. 'It would be a pretty weird accident, wouldn't you think?'

Hitch, who was standing behind Ruby, was trying to silently mouth something to SJ and making a sort of cutting motion with his hand as if to say 'stop talking', but SJ wasn't reading this and instead was making it abundantly clear that she was marking this incident up as attempted murder. 'So now we know *how* your mother was poisoned,' she said, 'though it won't answer the bigger question of *why* someone might want to poison her.'

Ruby was feeling a little weak at that particular moment: sometimes being right about a thing did not lead you to a place of tranquil satisfaction. Why would someone want her mother dead?

Hitch looked at his watch. 'Look kid, you need to get going. I have you covered until six but your parents are going to think you have gone AWOL if you don't make it home by dinner.'

'I'm going,' nodded Ruby as she turned to leave, 'but what if someone isn't satisfied with *almost* poisoning my mother to death? What if they try again?'

'Kid, don't you worry about your mother, I got that covered. I have someone watching her, just a precaution.'

'I hadn't noticed,' said Ruby.

Hitch looked heavenwards. 'He's a professional, you're not meant to notice.'

'Oh right,' said Ruby.

'So scram,' said Hitch.

Ruby called Clancy as soon as she made it home and it didn't take Clancy long before he was ringing the Redforts' doorbell. Ruby could hear the exchange between her father and her best friend.

'How nice to see you Clancy.'

'Thank you?'

'So I see the wind is still raging out there.'

'Yes.'

'Do you think it will ever stop?'

'Yes.'

'So your father must be excited about the trip to Washington?'

'Yes, he is.'

'Are you excited?'

Pause.

'I guess.'

'How's your mother?'

'OK, she's had a new haircut.'

'Hair is important if you're married to an ambassador.'

'I guess.'

'How's school these days?'

'OK.'

'That's swell to hear Clancy, a kid's school days are the best of one's life, you should enjoy them.'

A pause and then, 'I'm depressed to hear that sir.'

'So I guess you're here to see Ruby.'

'Yes.'

'Well, don't let me keep you.'

'Thank you.'

Sound of footsteps racing up the stairs.

Door flinging open.

'Boy, do you *not* know how to sidestep my dad.'

'He's a tricky customer,' said Clancy. 'He actually kind of hypnotises me.'

'Just don't look into his eyes,' said Ruby, 'or listen. You gotta imagine you are very busy and you just smile and say something like "great to see you" and keep moving, never stop, that's the secret.'

'Got it,' said Clancy. 'So were you right?'

'Yeah,' said Ruby, 'my mom was poisoned and I know by what.'

'What?'

'Her dress was soaked with methanol. Just like I thought.'

'I don't get it, how did poison get in her dress?'

'Someone put it there.'

'Why is everyone always trying to kill your mom?' said Clancy.

'Everyone isn't always trying to kill her, it's only happened twice before.'

'That's quite a lot you know,' said Clancy.

'Yes, but that first time really had nothing to do with her, not really, it was only because Nine Lives Capaldi mistook her for some kind of security genius.'

'Wouldn't have made her any less dead if Nine Lives had been a more successful assassin.'

'That, my friend, is certainly true,' sighed Ruby.

'So do you think whoever tried it on this time is going to have another go?'

Ruby pondered this dark thought for a minute before replying, 'I really don't know.'

'This isn't good,' said Clancy. 'I mean what does Hitch think?'

'I think at this exact nanosecond he doesn't consider she is in too much danger. She's sitting downstairs eating nachos and watching *Take A Minute* with my dad.'

'What is it with *Take A Minute*?' said Clancy. *Take A Minute* was a dilemma show where celebrity guests had to make tricky decisions. '*This? Or this?*' is what the compere would ask, and then he would say, 'Take a minute.'

'I know,' agreed Ruby, 'pretty lame show, huh?'

'So why would they target your mom?' said Clancy. 'These poison-dress assassins?'

'I don't know,' said Ruby. 'I guess I'm going to have to take a minute.'

He opened the door...

...to find the woman from City Nurseries on the stoop. She was holding a large green box.

'That's it?' he asked.

She looked at her clipboard. 'You ordered a wolfsbane specimen?'

'That's right,' said the man.

'You do know how dangerous these plants are?' said the woman. 'You must wear gloves at all times. If the poison from the leaves gets onto your hands, you'll need to call 911. It works transdermally, and it's quick.'

'Oh don't worry,' he said, 'no one will be calling 911.'

Chapter 27.
The ill-fitting dress

CLANCY WAS OUT OF BREATH WHEN HE ARRIVED AT SCHOOL – he was cutting it fine, the bell about to go.

'What's got you all animated?' said Ruby, stuffing her gym bag into her locker.

'So you know how your hunch was correct about your mom's dress being saturated in poison?'

'You think I'm likely to forget?' said Ruby.

'And it worries you, right?' said Clancy.

'Sure it worries me, someone is trying to kill my mom, bozo.'

'But *why* would anyone want to kill your mom?' said Clancy. He had a weird look on his face like he was trying to get her to see something *he* could see already.

'I don't know,' said Ruby, 'because she wears nice clothes, runs the Twinford charity committee... I mean, why would *anyone* want my mom dead?'

'So maybe they didn't,' said Clancy. 'Maybe it was an accident.'

'You're saying someone *accidentally* got a poison substance into the fibres of her dress?'

Now Clancy was looking at her like she had lost a marble or two. 'No, duh brain, what I'm saying is *that* part was not the accident, the *accident* was your mom putting on the dress in the first place.'

'I hate to admit this, but I have no idea what you are saying.'

Clancy unzipped his backpack and pulled out a large brown envelope. He slid out a colour photograph: it was of him, his father, the mayor and a tall woman in a red dress with a yellow snake coiled around her arm. The tall woman was Amarjargel Oidov, and the dress she was wearing was exactly the same as the one her mother had worn, only it was a good deal shorter and a good deal tighter.

'This was taken that night after Amarjargel Oidov had won the Explorer Award.'

Clancy looked at her.

Ruby's face went from complete bafflement to total understanding. The photo in the newspaper! She had known there was something about it, but it had been in black and white, and had also only shown the people from the waist up – which was why Ruby hadn't made the connection. Now she saw the scene in full colour – it was staring her right in the face.

'Amarjargel Oidov is wearing the same red dress,' she said.

'Exactly,' said Clancy.

'But it's shorter than my mom's dress,' said Ruby. 'It doesn't fit right.'

'Exactly,' said Clancy.

'Because it's not her dress,' said Ruby.

'Exactly,' said Clancy.

Ruby remembered her mother complaining about the *cocktail crime scene* – how she and one of the honoured guests had been wearing the same gown.

'So no one wanted my mother dead. They wanted Amarjargel Oidov dead.'

'I would guess so.'

'Clance, for the second time, you're a genius.'

'Or maybe you're a numbskull,' said Clancy.

'Whatever,' said Ruby, 'the big question is: where is Amarjargel Oidov?'

**There was a knock
at the door of room 21...**

...Amarjargel Oidov supposed it would be room service. She was looking forward to her cup of English Breakfast tea. However, when she opened the door, instead of a person with a teapot on a tray she was greeted by a pleasant-looking man holding a bunch of flowers. He was smartly dressed in a green florist's apron and was wearing white gloves. The gloves seemed odd somehow; they didn't go with the gardener's apron.

'Amarjargel Oidov?' he asked.

'Yes, that's me,' she said smiling.

'Flowers for you,' he said.

'How beautiful,' she said touching the unusual purple blooms.

'You should smell them,' said the florist, 'really breathe in that scent.'

She smiled at him. He had a nice face, sweet looking.

'Who sent them? I had no idea anyone knew where I was staying.'

'The card's in there somewhere,' said the man. 'It might have slipped down between the stems. If you feel around for it, I'm sure you'll find it.' He turned to go. 'Enjoy!' he called as he walked back along the corridor.

Chapter 28.
Touch and go

RUBY PRESSED THE EMERGENCY CONTACT DEVICE ON HER WATCH and waited for Hitch to pick up the distress call.

HITCH: *'Kid? You in trouble?'*

RUBY: *'You gotta find the snake woman.'*

HITCH: *'Sorry?'*

RUBY: *'Amarjargel Oidov, she's the one.'*

HITCH: *'The one what?'*

RUBY: *'The one they were trying to kill.'*

HITCH: *'You know this?'*

RUBY: *'If I'm wrong, I'll eat my sneakers.'*

She could hear Hitch feeding the information back to Froghorn and then Froghorn's reply, distant but clear: 'She was staying at the Twinford Grand but she checked out yesterday morning.'

'So call every single hotel in this city until you find her,' said Hitch.

There was the sound of phones being dialled and agents' voices as the whole Spectrum 8 team was mobilised.

'Nice work kid,' said Hitch.

The line went dead.

An hour later, while Ruby sat in her biology class watching caterpillars inch around a large glass jar, a team of agents and police, medics among them, were running down corridors and jumping in cars.

'Ruby you seem distracted?' said Mrs Greg.

'Sorry ma'am, I'm just wrestling with the big question,' she said.

'The meaning of life?' asked the teacher.

'That kind of thing,' said Ruby.

One car pulled up in front of the boutique hotel just across from the zoo.

One man and one woman jumped out and ran into the building.

'Could you contact the guest in room 21?' said the man to the concierge.

The phone rang but there was no reply.

'Could you unlock her room for me?' said the man.

'I'm afraid not,' said the concierge.

The woman flashed a police badge and the concierge nodded.

'Right away.'

* * *

Ruby pretended to watch the caterpillar chomp through a small green leaf, but though her eyes were trained on it, her thoughts were elsewhere.

The lock turned and the man, the policewoman and the concierge entered the hotel room.

What they found was a dark-haired woman lying on the floor. Grasped in her hand was a flower. She appeared to be unconscious.

'Be careful,' said the man, 'it's highly likely she has been poisoned.'

The policewoman spoke into her radio device.

The medical team arrived on the scene, but the woman could not be brought round.

Amarjargel Oidov was carried out.

Ruby stared at the creature in the jar.

A message flashed up on her watch.

>> AO ALIVE.

And then,

>> CONDITION CRITICAL.

And finally:

>> POISONED.

Chapter 29.
A pig's tie

BEYOND THOSE FEW WORDS THERE WAS NO NEWS, not a bleep from her watch, not a crackle from her fly barrette. It was full-on radio silence. She sent a message but what came back from Spectrum was a ***wait for briefing*** symbol, i.e. don't call us, we'll call you.

When the school bell rang, Ruby grabbed her coat and caught the first bus home, not even a minute of locker-side chat. She was anxious to know what was happening with the snake woman. Had Spectrum made any progress figuring out who the poisoner was, and in a way more importantly, *why* this conservationist had been the victim of attempted murder? Just what was it that made her a target? Were the snakes with their fluorescent skin valuable to someone?

When Ruby arrived home the first thing she did was check to see if Hitch was in his apartment: he wasn't. She was not surprised. There was a poisoning maniac loose in the city – it would be strange if Hitch was sitting at home twiddling his thumbs.

She walked back upstairs. She could hear the radio playing in the kitchen. It was tuned to Chime Melody. The music stopped and the top-of-the-hour news broke in:

NEWS TODAY ON THE HOUR EVERY HOUR, THIS IS JUDD JERRAD TELLING IT LIKE IT IS. TODAY, THE PRESIDENT GETS BEHIND THE MARS SPACE PROGRAM. WILL WE SOON BE WELCOMING LITTLE GREEN MEN TO OUR PLANET? ARE TEMPERATURES RISING IN THE ARCTIC AND WHAT WILL IT MEAN FOR PENGUINS?

It's polar bears, you dufus. Jeepers where do they find these clowns? thought Ruby.

A JAILHOUSE FOOD FIGHT PROVIDES COVER FOR A BOLD ESCAPE, AND THE WARDEN IS LEFT WITH EGG ON HIS FACE.

Really, this is the best you can come up with Judd?

EXPLORER-AWARD-WINNER AND SNAKE PROTECTOR, AMARJARGEL OIDOV, FOUND POISONED IN A HOTEL ROOM. WE ASK, WAS SHE BITTEN BY HER OWN DISCOVERY? AND FINALLY, A FIRE AT A TWINFORD HAIR SALON. DID SOMEONE FORGET TO UNPLUG THE HEATED ROLLERS?

The Chime Melody news was light when it came to information – and *facts*, come to that.

'Hey Ruby, is that you?'

'Yeah Mom, I'm home,' she replied, but kept walking, 'just going up to my room, I have a ton of homework.'

'I don't know how you fit all that learning into your brain,' called her mother. 'I swear I don't remember a thing from my school days.'

Ruby walked into her room and closed the door behind her. There was a post-it note stuck to the top of her desk, obvious enough for her to find but not so obvious that anyone would know what it meant.

There was a drawing of a fly buzzing around an apple, and on the apple, making up the stalk and leaf, was the number 155.

The message was from Hitch, and Ruby knew exactly what he was trying to say. She pulled *Pick Your Poison* from the shelf and turned to page 155.

'**Wolfsbane, also known as monkshood** {aconitum} *is a flowering plant found mostly in mountainous regions of the northern hemisphere. The roots and leaves contain the alkaloid pseudaconitine, a deadly poison. Once swallowed or absorbed through the skin, this substance can kill within hours, or instantaneously in the case of large doses. Cases have been recorded of fatalities due to handling the plant without gloves, as the pseudaconitine is very easily absorbed through the skin. The risk of death increases with the amount of the poison ingested or absorbed – milder cases can be treated with drugs or electrical stimulus to counteract the heart arrhythmias caused by the toxin.'*

6.

1.

3.

2.

a.

6.

WOLFSBANE
(MONKSHOOD).

Aconitum

So Amarjargel Oidov had been lucky once, but this time the poisoner had got his victim. Whether she made it through depended on how much wolfsbane had made it into her system.

In the kitchen Ruby found Mrs Digby chatting to her mother, who was sitting at the counter reading the newspaper, looking almost like her usual self.

'I hope I'm going to feel fit enough to take that trip next week.'

'What trip?' said Ruby.

'Oh, hey Ruby,' said her mother. 'I was just talking about that trip to Washington, you know the Crews are going and those Explorer Awarders.'

'You mean the environmentalists?' said Ruby. 'They're going too?'

'Yes, those guys,' said Sabina. 'I'm actually pretty thrilled to be asked, it's such a surprise.' Ruby wasn't surprised; her parents were invited to everything, why not to the White House?

'Hanging out with the president,' said Ruby. 'I'll guess you'll be getting all dressed up for that.'

'Well, I should think so,' said Sabina. 'It's a reception at his house. Although I'm going to avoid the canapés and I certainly won't be buying my dress from Bergwend-Nyle not after the mess they made of those alterations, boy was that ever a pig's tie.'

'Pig's ear,' corrected Ruby.

'That too,' said her mother.

Hitch called an hour later. He spoke to Sabina and she listened carefully before saying, 'You know what, I'm going to trust you on this. If you think it's a good idea then so do I.'

She put the phone down and turned to Ruby.

'Hitch wants you to meet him.'

'Where?' asked Ruby.

'The Dime a Dozen,' said her mother.

Hitch wasn't actually waiting for Ruby in the Dime a Dozen, but then she hadn't expected him to be. She stepped in behind the flyspray and walked down to Spectrum HQ.

He was there in the atrium talking to Buzz – when he saw Ruby he pointed to the elevator.

'So what did you say to my mom?' she asked as they headed to level 4.

'I told her I was going to take you to a self defence class.'

'In the Dime a Dozen?'

'I told her I was picking up some groceries en route.'

'And where are we actually going?'

'To a self defence class, aikido actually, but it's the same general ballpark. I figure you could use some defence skills, with Baby Face still out there.'

'Thanks,' said Ruby.

They stepped out of the elevator. As they walked they talked.

'So any word on the poisoner?' asked Ruby.

'We think our florist was Baby Face Marshall,' he said. 'The bellhop at the hotel gave a pretty good description.'

'But why Marshall?' asked Ruby. 'Why would he want to poison a conservationist who's just looking to protect some rare snakes?'

'As yet we have no idea.' He sighed. 'Baby Face, we can be pretty sure, is just some hired hand. He has experience using toxic substances and we can be fairly sure he is also the poisoner who laced your mother's gown with methanol. But when it comes to why, we are just left guessing. The snakes *are* valuable of course and their skins alone would fetch large sums of money on the black market, and then there's the venom,' he said.

'But killing Amarjargel Oidov isn't going to get you to the snakes,' said Ruby. 'I thought she'd kept their location a secret?'

'She has,' said Hitch, 'but we can't dismiss the possibility that Marshall has somehow got his hands on this information – with her gone, it could be open season on these reptiles.'

'So who do you think Baby Face could be working for?' said Ruby.

'The sender of the muffins,' said Hitch. He smiled because it sounded sort of funny, though the situation was far from being any kind of laughing matter. 'Someone wanted to use his services and they took great pains to get him here, smuggled in some pretty state-of-the-art equipment to bust him out.'

'Yeah, about that,' said Ruby. 'Who would Baby Face have

to know to get hold of a gadget like that? I mean, we know he's worked for the Count but even the Count can't lay his hands on this kind of hardware, can he? I mean, it's not the basic file in a cake, is it.'

'That, kid, is undoubtedly true,' replied Hitch.

They walked in silence for a minute until Ruby asked, 'Is she gonna be OK, the snake lady?'

'Her chances are 50/50,' said Hitch. 'Not such great odds.'

They were now at the end of a corridor. Hitch opened the door and they walked into a dojo. The walls of the double-height room were Japanese screens which gave the space both light and a certain tranquility. In the centre of the floor was a large mat. There was a small notice on the wall and Ruby had to get close to see what it said.

> ### *Rules of Aikido:*
>
> **1.** *Proper aikido can never be mastered unless one strictly follows the master's teaching.*

'So who's the aikido master?'

'That would be me,' said Hitch.

Chapter 30.
Soft defeats hard

'THOUGH I SHOULD MAKE CLEAR,' Hitch continued, 'I didn't write these rules.'

'That I know,' said Ruby. 'They were written by the Aikido Doshu.' Though she had never actually studied aikido, the rules posted on the wall were familiar to her. Martial arts were just another subject Ruby knew a whole lot about.

> **2. *Aikido*** *as a martial art is perfected by being alert to everything going on around us and leaving no vulnerable opening (suki).*

> **3. *Practice*** *becomes joyful and pleasant once one has trained enough not to be bothered by pain.*

> **4. *Do not be satisfied*** *by what is taught at the dojo. One must constantly digest, experiment and develop what one has learned.*

5. ***One should never force things*** *unnaturally*
or unreasonably in practice. One should undertake
training suited to one's body, physical condition
and age.

6. ***The aim of aikido*** *is to develop the truly*
human self. It should not be used to display ego.

'That last rule, rule six, might be a good one for you to try
and master,' said Hitch. 'Go suit up.'

Ten minutes later they were standing facing each other,
each now wearing the traditional martial arts uniform of the *gi*,
white cotton belted jackets with loose pyjama-style bottoms and
the hakama sort of skirt-like trousers worn over the top of the
gi. Ruby was unsurprised to see that Hitch's belt was black.

'Aikido,' began Hitch, 'is a Japanese martial art created in
the 1920s by—'

'Morihei Ueshiba,' said Ruby.

'Very impressive,' said Hitch. 'So you will also know that
'Morihei Ueshiba believed that in fighting you should harmonise
with your opponent rather than try to defeat them through force
or power.'

'I'm not sure Vapona Begwell is much into harmony,' said
Ruby.

Hitch said, 'Yes, well, that's kind of the point of the lesson.
People sub-divide martial arts into hard and soft. Some believe

that striking the first blow is all-important, some that you must continue to strike until you are in no doubt that you have overcome your opponent.'

'If you think someone's gonna kill you, isn't that the sane thing to do?' said Ruby.

'What I am going to teach you, kid, is how to beat your opponent by avoiding their strikes. In aikido, we are working with the idea that only soft can overpower hard. The example is often used of water and rock – water yields to rock and flows around it, but over time it will shape it. You can defeat your aggressor by blending with the motion of the attacker and redirecting the force of their attack rather than opposing it head-on. You can learn how to deal with several attackers all coming at you at once, and train yourself to be alert, not just to what's happening in front of you, but on all sides, even behind you. Aikido as a martial art is perfected by being alert to everything going on around you so you don't leave youself vulnerable. Which is basically vital if you are an agent working in the field.'

And so they began, Ruby learning the key movements that she would practise again and again, until they became instinctual – the various ways to trip and throw and spin people to the ground when they came at you. Half the work was memorising the Japanese names for each move.

After they had practised for three hours Hitch said, 'Kid, I think you're a natural.'

Shomen uchi

Yokomen uchi

Chudan uchi

Jodan tsuki

Mae geri

Irimi nage

Kotegaeshi

Tenchi nage

Kaiten nage

Shiho nage

Kokyu ho

Chapter 31.
The Lemon

RUBY HAD BEGUN THE DAY BY LYING IN BED VISUALISING HER AIKIDO MOVES. She already knew them by heart, but what she was striving to do was to think herself into them so they became second nature, part of her.

Ruby hadn't really been in the mood for school and the day had dragged, though it had to be said she wasn't exactly relishing the prospect of what was to come once the school bell rang.

'So look, since you're grounded and we can't hang out *after* class then maybe we can hang out before?' said Clancy.

'You mean early?' said Ruby. 'Super early?'

'I mean when people get up,' said Clancy.

'But I get up a half hour before school,' said Ruby. 'Why would I waste perfectly good sleeping time?'

'I thought you were turning over a new leaf?' said Clancy.

Ruby thought about this. 'OK, that's true. So where do you want to meet?'

'At the Donut Diner, that way you only have to walk seven minutes around the corner.'

'OK,' said Ruby.

'Early?' said Clancy.

'How early?' asked Ruby.

'6.30?' said Clancy.

'Too early, make it 6.45,' said Ruby.

Clancy looked her in the eye. 'Who are we kidding? You're never gonna be there.'

'I will – have a little faith would you,' said Ruby.

'I'll try but I doubt it will make any difference.'

'OK, look, here's what I'll do,' said Ruby. 'If when I'm out taking the Lemon home tonight—'

'What, you're babysitting *again*?'

'Yeah, my folks signed me up for ongoing baby duty; they figured it's the best way to make me suffer, and they're right,' said Ruby. 'So if when I'm out I think there's a chance I might not make it in time for 6.45, I'll leave a note in the tree and tell you what time I'll be there.'

'Why don't you pick up the telephone?' said Clancy.

'Because it's more fun,' said Ruby, 'plus you're doubting me so you deserve to climb a tree.'

'You're not normal, you know that?'

'And proud of it. Look, I gotta split, but I'm telling you to be there 6.45 and don't be late unless I write otherwise!'

Ruby took the bus to Cedarwood Drive and instead of going home walked up the Lemon drive and rang the doorbell.

Elaine looked very pleased to see her; she was covered in

baby food, most of it in her hair.

'I'm having such trouble getting him to eat, Ruby, he's so picky. I keep making these super-flavoursome meals, but he spits them right out.'

'That's because little kids can't handle too much flavour. They have way more taste buds then adults and so the flavours can be too intense for them,' said Ruby. 'You have to think bland.'

'Wow Ruby, how do you know so much about babies?' said Elaine.

'I don't,' said Ruby. 'I know stuff about stuff and this is just something I read about to do with the human tongue. So is he ready to go?'

'Almost,' said Elaine, who then began pointing out all the various equipment that the baby would need for his two-hour excursion with Ruby.

'Now this is his milky and this is his muslin.'

'What's it for?' asked Ruby.

'Oh, that's for sucking,' explained Elaine.

'What, that rag? Kinda gross,' said Ruby. She caught Elaine's puzzled expression. 'I mean cute. Super cute.'

'I know,' Elaine smiled. 'And this is his cuddly, and this is his baby food and this—'

'You know what Elaine, don't worry, I'll figure it out, or he'll tell me. Let's go, Lemon.' And before Elaine could fuss about another thing, Ruby and the stroller rolled out.

Ruby pushed Archie Lemon up Flaubert Street. He was

making strange gurgling sounds and was occupied with the task of trying to stick his foot in his mouth. Ruby peered down at him. 'Is that a happy sound?' she asked. He smiled a gap-tooth smile and tried to grab Ruby's hair. 'Boy are you ugly Archie.'

He gurgle-giggled and Ruby resumed her stroller pushing.

Ruby was finding the minding of baby Lemon boring to say the least and she felt *anyone* who could string some kind of a sentence together – better still, actually say something interesting – would be preferable company. She considered calling Mouse or Red, but with a baby in tow how much fun was it going to be? If she took him to the Diner he was bound to grizzle and she would most likely end up standing outside on the sidewalk jiggling him. So instead she struck out in the opposite direction.

Flaubert took her north of her immediate neighbourhood, and if she kept walking she was unlikely to bump into anyone she knew. There was something about pushing a small kid around that made her feel not quite herself and for this reason she didn't especially want to see anyone from Junior High. She had narrowly missed bumping into Elliot and Del, but they had been so busy chatting they hadn't seen her.

It was as Ruby was pushing the stroller across the street that Archie let go his squirrel bean toy for the sixth time.

'Jeepers Archie, you can't do that in the middle of a street,' Ruby chided, 'you're gonna get us flattened into pancakes.'

She reached for the toy and a car honked its horn at her. 'What do you expect me to do, man?' she shouted. 'I have to grab this squirrel, don't I?'

She scooped it up and stuffed it in her pocket and was about to continue on her way when something made her freeze right where she was in the middle of the road.

What she saw was a young man in a bright red woollen hat looking up at the giant billboard attached to the old piano factory. Ruby followed his gaze. The billboard was an advertisment for Taste Twisters, widely advertised but not so easy to get a hold of it seemed. In fact, apart from the one empty bottle she'd seen roll out of the garbage can, not available *anywhere* as far as Ruby could tell. But today it wasn't the ad that Ruby was struck by – it was the way the man was gazing at it. Not just reading it, but searching it, like he was trying to figure something out. A horn tooted, and the driver shouted, 'Hey, kid! Are you crossing or what?'

Ruby began hurriedly pushing the stroller across the street and bumped it back onto the sidewalk, all the while keeping the man in her sights. He didn't notice her; he was just staring up at the billboard. Ruby yanked at the hood on her parka, pulling it close around her face, and zipped the coat so only her eyes and nose were visible. The man in the hat was still stood there staring intently.

Ruby bent down and pretended to adjust the straps that held Archie in his seat.

'*What is he seeing?*' she whispered. Archie blinked.

Ruby watched as this man pulled a small book – a notebook

or diary perhaps – from his jacket pocket, took out a pen, wrote something, looked at it, wrote something else and then took out another book and began flicking through it. If the book had a title then Ruby couldn't read it – her eyesight was not up to that. Quite suddenly, the man stuffed the book back into his jacket, turned and began walking at speed in the other direction.

'Come on Archie, I think we should tail him.'

It was easy tailing a person when you had a baby in tow; no one expected to be followed by someone pushing a pram. 'You know what Archie, I suddenly get the point of you.'

They had been walking for around fifteen minutes when the man stopped, turned around, took maybe ten steps and walked into the Little Seven Grocers store.

What is he doing?

Ruby quickened her pace, almost to a run. Archie liked that and was making those gurgly happy noises babies make. When she reached the store, she peered in through the window. She saw the man's red hat; the guy seemed to be looking for something. Soon enough he found it and, bottle in hand, walked to the counter. The boy at the till looked at the price, rung it up, then the man handed him some coins and headed for the door.

Ruby squatted down next to the stroller and pretended to be securing the rain cover over baby Archie.

From this vantage point Ruby was able to clearly see what happened next.

The man prised the metal cap from the bottle and sniffed the contents, as if he wanted to know exactly what was in the drink – *as if reading it* – then once he was done, he raised the bottle to his mouth and sipped the contents. Again, not like a person who was thirsty but like someone who needed to understand something.

He placed the bottle on the wall, scribbled something in his book and then – just like that – hailed a cab, stepped inside and was moving off into the traffic.

There was no way Ruby was going to get Archie, stroller and all, into a taxi in time to tail him.

Darn it!

Now what?

What she did was walk into the store and search the refrigerator, but they were all out of Taste Twisters.

'To be honest, I didn't even know we stocked it,' said the young man behind the counter, 'but then I only usually work Saturdays so there's a lot I don't know.'

'OK, well thanks,' said Ruby.

'We have Fruitzees, have you tried them? They come in lots of flavours and aren't bad, not too sweet.'

'Thanks but no thanks.'

Ruby pushed Archie back out of the store and eyed the Taste Twister drink still sitting there on the wall.

She walked over to it and picked it up. Then, with great caution, she brought it to her nose and sniffed. It smelled of lemons, perhaps a hint of mint, but mainly lemons. She considered tasting it but stopped short.

What if it's poisoned, she thought. *But how could it be? The man drank some, didn't he? Well, you thought he drank some but what if he was bluffing? What if it was all an elaborate trick to get people drinking some deadly drink and next thing you know you drop to the floor like some swatted fly?*

She examined the bottle. Same twisty shape she had dimly seen when Sheriff Bridges was picking her up. The label with that same picture of the kid and the winding words coming out of its mouth like a twisty straw and the name, TASTE TWISTERS. And in smaller type below: LOOK OUT FOR THE WHOLE RANGE OF TASTE TWISTER DRINKS!

She looked through the bottle at the reverse of the label. There was no company information, no address, just a strange logo. It was like something from the wall of the dojo Hitch had taken her to – a mandala, or a prayer wheel.

Under this were the words: FOUR GREAT TASTES SINCE 1922.

That was peculiar phrasing, Ruby thought. You'd expect it to say four *flavours*, not four *tastes*.

Ruby reached for the little metal bottle top, but just as she did so, Archie sneezed, Ruby jumped and the lid went spinning across the street and rolled inconveniently down a drain grate.

'Thanks, buster.'

So instead Ruby took the bottle and stuffed one of Archie's clean sucking rags into the neck of the bottle to stop the drink

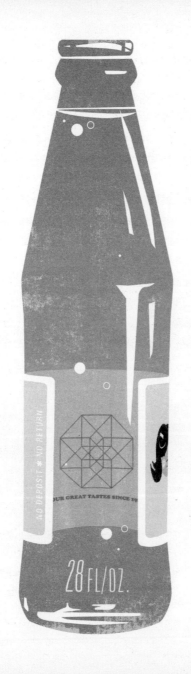

NO DEPOSIT ✷ NO RETURN

...OUR GREAT TASTES SINCE 19...

28 FL/OZ.

spilling out.

'Why do you suck these things anyway, Lemon? It's kinda gross, you know that?'

Archie just stared back at her. 'And didn't anyone ever tell you it's rude to dribble?' said Ruby. 'You do that a lot, you know?'

She began walking fast, heading for the subway station.

'Should I dump you back? No, you're not due home for a while yet. You're gonna have to come with. You're not authorised, but I don't see you blabbing.'

The baby smiled, like he understood.

'You gonna keep that tiny little mouth shut?'

Archie gurgled.

'I'll take that as a "yes".'

Chapter 32.
The littlest recruit

RUBY BUMPED THE STROLLER DOWN THE SUBWAY STEPS, through the turnstile, onto the train, seven stops to Crossways, and off again, up the steps into the brightly lit Dime a Dozen supermarket, and headed to aisle 17.

Buzz's usually blank expression gave way to one approaching mild alarm.

'Is Blacker in?' asked Ruby.

'No,' said Buzz.

'Can you get a message to him?'

'No,' said Buzz. 'Agent Redfort, you can't bring that in here.'

'Are you referring to the baby or the stroller?' replied Ruby.

'Both, neither are permitted, it's against protocol,' said Buzz.

'So it's come up in the past? Agents asking if they can bring a stroller in?'

'No,' said Buzz.

Ruby rolled her eyes. 'What do you want me to do, abandon a baby in a supermarket?'

Just then the elevator doors drew open and out stepped Hitch. He looked at Buzz, at Ruby, at the baby, and said, 'There you are kid, I wondered where you had got to, we're going to need to get the small guy's prints, just so we can eliminate him from our suspect list,' he turned to Buzz. 'Sorry for the inconvenience, if you wouldn't mind printing a pass for our tiny guest, Buzz, I will escort Ruby, baby and all, to my office.'

Buzz nodded, and three minutes later a pass was printed and handed to Hitch. Once the pass was firmly in Archie's small grasp, Hitch ushered them both into the elevator.

'Kid, just what do you think you are doing?' asked Hitch.

'I got something to show SJ,' said Ruby.

'You think she hasn't seen a dribbling baby before?'

'Not him, this,' said Ruby holding up the bottle of Taste Twister.

'OK,' said Hitch slowly, 'but what is it?'

'Lemonade I think,' said Ruby, holding it up to the light.

'Lemonade?'

'I think it is, but I can't be sure.'

'You are asking one of our laboratory experts to take a look at what you think is a bottle of lemonade?'

'I just want her to make sure that it *is* lemonade, no funny business I mean.'

'What would the funny business be?'

'I don't know, poison maybe.'

'I'm not sure I'm seeing the big picture here so why don't you save it for SJ and I'll go and see if we can find someone to watch the small person. I have to stop by the gadget room first.'

'So you are authorising me to seek assistance from the lab technician?'

'I'm giving you clearance. Now hand over the little guy.'

Ruby looked concerned. 'You're gonna need to make sure he doesn't get his teeth into anything that can't stand chewing, 'cause believe me everything ends up in his mouth and I don't want to be held responsible.'

Ruby walked on down to the laboratory, knocked on the purple door and entered the shiny white lab. SJ was looking down a microscope at a small something in a glass Petri dish.

'Hey,' said Ruby, 'do you have a minute?'

'You have something for me?' called SJ, not looking up.

'I'm not sure,' said Ruby holding up the bottle.

'Is that lemonade?' asked SJ.

'Could be?' said Ruby.

'OK, I'll take a look and you can explain why I should be interested,' she said.

So Ruby explained about the man in the scarlet hat and the billboard and SJ went about her tests.

'I still don't exactly see why this is of interest to Spectrum,' said SJ.

'Call it a hunch,' said Ruby.

'I think LB would call it a waste of resources,' said SJ, 'but I won't mention it.'

'I appreciate your discretion,' said Ruby.

An hour later and Ruby had her answer. 'Nothing in this but some sugar, some lemon juice and a little carbonated water.'

'And no poison?'

'No poison,' nodded SJ, 'unless you count the sugar.'

'You sound like my mom,' said Ruby. 'She's got it in for sugar.'

'Well, she has a point,' said SJ. 'Sugar has a profound effect on the brain, the whole body actually. You should see what it does to the liver. I can show you pictures?'

'No thanks,' said Ruby.

'Do you want me to store this?' asked SJ, pointing to the bottle.

'I'll take it,' said Ruby. 'Maybe it's nothing but I might wanna have another look at the label, just to be sure, thanks anyway.'

'My pleasure,' said SJ, turning back to her Petri dish. 'See you next time.'

And Ruby went off in search of her charge. He wasn't difficult to find. There was a lot of noise coming from the gadget room and it seemed Hitch had decided to leave Archie with Hal, the innovations man. What Ruby saw when she walked in were a lot of agents of varying ranks all gathered and peering at baby Lemon who was now wearing someone's hat.

Everyone was so distracted that no one spotted her walking between the glass gadget drawers, peering in at the high-tech hardware. She stopped when she noticed a tiny video camera.

The label said it was motion activated, had a long battery life, was easy to operate and very reliable. Ruby could think of someone who would most certainly appreciate it.

This is a dumb thing to do, Redfort. She knew it, but then she thought about Clancy's face and how happy he would be; she could already see his arms flapping. Quickly she palmed the little surveillance device, then slipped it into her pocket.

Ruby collected the baby, much to Hal's disappointment. 'He's kinda entertaining, you know,' he said.

'Are you for real?' said Ruby.

As she was wheeling Archie back towards the elevator bank, she saw a familiar figure coming towards her. 'Is this the latest recruit?' said Kip Holbrook.

'Could be,' said Ruby. 'I don't think he would do too well on foraging though, boy is he ever a fussy eater.'

'I don't think you exactly excel at that either,' said Holbrook.

Holbrook was a fellow field agent trainee and he and Ruby had first met when on dive camp. Since then they had teamed up for survival training, working well together building shelters, canoes, camp fires, rescue fires, and cooked up plenty of roots and berries. They had shared some pretty unappealing undergrowth, whether it be to sleep in or to chew on.

'Hey,' said Ruby. 'You working on anything?'

Holbrook shook his head. 'Nope. I just had my interview with Agent Delaware.'

Ruby pulled a face. 'I sympathise.'

'Yeah, it was pretty brutal. He gave me a super hard time for using the emergency function on my Spectrum contact device when, as he put it, "it was not strictly an emergency". Believe me, I won't make that mistake again. So where are you headed?' he asked.

'Gotta return the Lemon,' said Ruby.

'I hope you have a dingy, it's pouring down out there,' he said. 'You should see Froghorn – he just stepped in and looks like a rat that drowned.'

'He always looks like a rat,' said Ruby, pressing the elevator button.

'See you around,' said Holbrook.

When the elevator doors opened, there was the rat himself, soaking wet and dripping everywhere.

'Hey, there Froghorn,' said Ruby, 'is it raining out there or did you shower in your clothes?'

Froghorn gave her a thin smile and stepped out of the elevator. He glanced at the baby. 'I see you finally brought one of your kindergarten friends in to meet us. Must be nice to have someone on your own intellectual level to talk to,' he said.

Ruby stepped into the elevator. 'Yeah,' she yawned, 'I was missing good conversation.' The doors closed, opening again two floors up on atrium level where she was surprised to see Blacker standing talking to another agent Ruby had never seen before. He had thick black eyebrows that met in the middle. When he noticed her, he neither smiled nor said hello, but instead gestured a goodbye to Blacker and hurried off.

'Hey, I was told you weren't in today – you just get here?' Ruby asked Blacker.

'Just this minute,' said Blacker. 'Who's the little guy?'

'Archie Lemon,' said Ruby. 'It's stopped raining?' His coat was bone dry.

'I got lucky for once, just missed it,' said Blacker. 'So you wanted to see me?'

'Yeah, I thought I had something but I was wrong,' said Ruby. She held up the bottle. 'It's not a mystery drink after all – turns out it's just lemonade.'

He looked at her like he had no idea what she was talking about and said, 'OK, so call me if you *do* get something, any time at all, you know where I am.'

'I will,' said Ruby. 'I better go, gotta get the Lemon home before bedtime.'

It was as Ruby was crossing the vast atrium that baby Lemon decided to screw up his eyes, open his lungs and howl. The sound rang out loud and alien in this usually quiet hive of agents, and LB's voice could just about be heard from behind the white walls of her office saying, 'Is that a baby I'm hearing?' but Ruby pushed the stroller through the heavy steel door and up and out of Spectrum HQ before there was a chance she might have to explain what in tarnation a baby was doing in HQ.

'Jeepers, Lemon, could you not have waited ten more seconds?'

Ruby took the subway to Flaubert Street and stopped by the billboard. She wanted to take another look, to try and see what the man had seen. But it seemed it was just a billboard.

Are you going completely crazy Redfort?

She walked back up Flaubert, crossed Bleaker and turned into Amster, almost walking on past the little green before she remembered her meeting with Clancy.

I'm never gonna make it for 6.45am, who was I kidding? She parked Archie's stroller, found a piece of paper in her satchel, wrote a note using the code she and Clancy always used for notes like this. It said:

```
W vvza mzcm psln rsiwl oyfy jvgy zdzv.*
```

She folded it into an origami butterfly shape. Then she climbed the tree and pushed the paper butterfly into one of the knots in the bark. It was while she was clambering down that she found another note tucked into the bark, it was of course from Clancy and said:

```
Apmo qs lb ols Owiyh. Xifi we azzsy ndjhpmi.
```

'You think you're so smart Crew,' she muttered.

* AS EVER THIS IS A VIGENÈRE CIPHER. THE KEY WORD IS: A PERSON; FROM PUGLIA.

Chapter 33.
Doubt

RUBY SLEPT BADLY AS USUAL. She woke several times in the night: the wind was almost hurricane force and it sounded like every dog in the neighbourhood was going crazy. The howling of the wind combined with the howling of the hounds forced her to pull her pillow over her ears.

Almost as soon as she finally fell asleep, her alarm woke her up.

She was brushing her teeth, bleary-eyed, when the soap phone rang.

She grabbed it in her left hand and continued to brush her teeth with her right.

'Mmeah,' she said.

'What?' said a voice.

'Rornin Wrancy.'

'Where are you?' demanded Clancy.

He sounded angry. Ruby removed the brush from her mouth.

'What do you mean, where am I? Where do you think I am?

I'm in the bathroom.'

'So why aren't you here, bozo?' said Clancy.

'Watch who you are calling bozo, bozo.'

'OK, so why aren't you here, pal?' said Clancy.

'As in now?' said Ruby.

'Yes, as in *now*,' said Clancy.

'I left you a note,' said Ruby.

'I didn't get any note,' said Clancy.

'Well, I left you one,' said Ruby.

'In the tree?' said Clancy.

'Yes, in the tree,' said Ruby.

'There was no note,' said Clancy.

'Well, I left you one,' said Ruby.

'But I looked,' said Clancy.

'I don't doubt it,' said Ruby.

'So why didn't I see it?' said Clancy.

'Clancy, did you take a look at the weather recently? It's kinda windy out there, a wild guess, my note ended up in some other tree.'

'Oh,' said Clancy.

'I found yours by the way.'

'What did you think?' said Clancy.

'Ha ha,' said Ruby flatly.

'So what did it say? Your note, I mean?'

'Meet me at the Donut.'

'When?' asked Clancy.

'7.15,' said Ruby.

'That's now,' said Clancy.

'So I'm late,' said Ruby. 'Where are *you?*'

'At the Donut,' said Clancy.

'So what are you complaining about?' said Ruby. 'You're already there and nice and cosy, I'll be with you in ten minutes, weather permitting.'

When Ruby arrived she had to scour the room for a minute or two before she spotted Clancy. He was in one of the booths by the far window and he was wearing a large hat with earflaps.

'What exactly are you wearing?' asked Ruby as she slid into the booth.

'I found it on the street,' said Clancy. 'I asked in a few shops but no one was claiming it.'

'I wonder why,' said Ruby.

'What's that supposed to mean?'

'Did you take a look in the mirror yet?' said Ruby.

Clancy ignored her. 'This wind is giving me earache so this headgear's gonna be a total life-saver.'

'And possibly a red flag to any bullying types hanging around out there.'

'They don't get style and individuality, that's the problem with bullying types,' said Clancy. 'They're social sheep. Simple behavioural science.'

'Yeah, well it really sets you apart,' said Ruby, 'but as I always say, if anyone can carry off a giant hat with earflaps, it's you.'

She paused. 'And by the way, speaking of behavioural science, here's your order.'

She slid the little camera she'd stolen from the innovations room at Spectrum over to him.

He marvelled at its small size for a moment.

'Put it away!' she hissed.

Clancy slipped it into his pocket. 'Thanks Ruby. I owe you one.'

'You already owe me more than you could ever repay,' she said, good-naturedly.

'So how's the babysitting going? You must be about at the end of your punishment duty?' said Clancy.

'Only a day of it left,' said Ruby.

'I bet you can't wait to hand the little guy back, huh?' said Clancy.

'Well, I'm thinking of keeping him,' said Ruby.

'What?' said Clancy.

'He's turning out to be kinda handy.'

'You're not serious,' said Clancy.

'Well, I was tailing someone yesterday afternoon,' said Ruby.

'You were what?' said Clancy.

'I was pushing Archie down Flaubert Street when I saw something which struck me as strange,' said Ruby.

'What kind of strange, interesting or weird?' asked Clancy.

'I guess he would fall into both categories,' said Ruby.

Clancy looked intrigued. 'Who was he?'

'A guy in a red hat who seemed very interested in getting his hands on a Taste Twister,' said Ruby. She went on to explain just what she had seen and Clancy looked like he was going to pop.

'I knew it!' he said. 'I said it was some clever advertising campaign and I was right. Wait till I tell Elliot Finch.'

'Before you get all ahead of yourself, you might want to consider some alternatives, i.e. it might not be a clever advertising campaign.'

Clancy looked at her blankly. 'Meaning?'

Ruby adopted a creepy voice. 'Meaning the whole Taste Twister thing could be an elaborate riddle which seeks to draw people in, gets the public of Twinford following clues to an end which will bring about their end.'

'Yeah right,' said Clancy. 'Well, if that is true then I'm not sure what pushing around a twenty-four-pound baby could do for you, not unless Lemon's some kind of karate genius.'

'Turns out it's a great cover to push a pram about the place. I mean, no one looks at you twice. Del and Elliot walked straight past me.'

'That's because you're the last person anyone would expect to see pushing a baby around.'

'Exactly,' said Ruby, 'hence it's great cover.'

'Might I just remind you that you should be steering clear of trouble, not seeking it out,' he said.

'Well don't get your underwear in a bunch, Clance, because

I haven't been assigned any new cases, dangerous or otherwise.'

'Good,' said Clancy.

'But all I'm pointing out to you,' said Ruby, 'is that it's better to know where trouble is coming from than to close your eyes to it, right? I mean I think we would all sleep better at night if we knew what a super-psycho was planning.'

'Correction,' said Clancy, 'I don't think that knowing what a super-psycho is planning is going to make me sleep any better.'

'Oh really? So how do you expect bad guys to be caught if I were just to ignore the signs?' said Ruby. 'You want me to just head off in the other direction if I happen to see trouble?'

'Exactly,' said Clancy. 'Just hand it over to Blacker, don't get involved.'

Ruby didn't say anything.

'What?' said Clancy.

'I just don't think that's such a good idea,' said Ruby.

'Why not?' said Clancy. 'Sounds like a great idea to me.'

'I just got a funny feeling,' said Ruby.

'What about?' asked Clancy.

'One of my fellow agents,' said Ruby.

'Not Blacker, don't tell me it's got to do with Blacker?' said Clancy.

'Yeah, Blacker,' said Ruby. 'I have this funny feeling, something's not right.'

'What kind of funny?' asked Clancy. 'Funny he won't believe you, or funny he's gonna stab you in the back?'

'More like that's funny I thought it was raining out there,' said Ruby.

'I don't follow?' said Clancy.

'So did you happen to notice the rain yesterday afternoon?'

'Sure, I noticed, I nearly drowned,' said Clancy. 'It wasn't an umbrella sort of rain, more like inflate your life raft.'

'That's what Holbrook said,' remembered Ruby. 'So Blacker supposedly steps into HQ from out of this rainstorm without a drop of water on him.'

'And this makes him untrustworthy?'

'It makes him a liar,' said Ruby. 'Froghorn comes in soaked to his undershorts, I leave the place and it's a total washout, but in the intervening ten minutes Blacker manages to dodge every raindrop and come into HQ dry as a bone? Not a drip, not a splash.'

'Weird things happen with the weather. I mean it can rain frogs, you know that?'

'Yeah, I know that, and talking of frogs, if I'm right about Blacker being up to something then Froghorn's most likely involved too.'

'Why?'

'It just stands to reason.'

'How so?' said Clancy.

'Because they work together. It would be hard to keep the truth from Froghorn.'

Clancy shook his head. 'I can't agree with you there. You

remember that episode of *Crazy Cops* where information was being fed back to the mob and when it was discovered Lucas was the leak, they just assumed his partner, Synco, must be in on it too? Couldn't see how he wouldn't know, since they worked so closely together.'

Ruby nodded.

'But it turned out Synco knew nothing about it, even though he sorta shoulda.'

'Yeah, well that's true, he really shoulda,' said Ruby.

'But why *didn't* he figure Lucas was betraying the cops?' said Clancy.

'Because he trusted Lucas,' she said.

'Like a brother,' added Clancy.

'Do your sisters trust you like a brother?' asked Ruby.

'Minny doesn't trust anyone,' said Clancy. 'Anyway, that's not my point, my point is it is perfectly possible for a close colleague not to know.'

'Yeah, but this is Froghorn we're talking about – he isn't the trusting, trustworthy type.'

'You just want him to be a villain because you don't like him.'

'OK, I admit it, I don't, but that is not clouding my judgment.'

'That's baloney buster, and you know it,' said Clancy.

'Oh yeah and why's that?' said Ruby.

'Because *you* know that in any good thriller the one who betrays the hero is always the person you least expect it to be.

It's the biggest let down.'

'That is true,' said Ruby, 'but what does that have to do with—'

'The least likeable person,' interrupted Clancy, 'the one you hope is going to be the traitor or the murderer, that person always turns out to be on the side of good.'

'Agreed,' said Ruby.

'Which would make Froghorn the least likely traitor in the whole darned HQ,' said Clancy. 'You know it, but because you think he's a potatohead—'

'I *know* he's a potatohead,' said Ruby.

'OK, because you *know* he's a potatohead, you are willing Froghorn to be a bad apple.'

'But the thing you are forgetting here is that this *isn't* a thriller – this is real life.'

'But if it was a thriller, who would you suspect?' He was looking at her seriously.

'You mean if I was watching the film or reading the book?' asked Ruby.

'Yeah,' said Clancy. 'Not if *you* were a character *in* the thriller, obviously, then you would be as blind to the truth as anyone else.'

'So what's the question again?'

'If this *was* a book, who would you most suspect of being the master criminal?'

'You,' said Ruby.

'My money would be on Mrs Digby,' said Clancy.

'I think we can rule her out,' said Ruby.

'Yeah,' said Clancy, 'and if it *is* her, I'm switching sides.'

Chapter 34.
Crazy weather

ON THE WAY INTO SCHOOL, Ruby and Clancy bumped into Red, Elliot and Del. They were laughing about something, Elliot unsurprisingly doubled over, tears streaming down his cheeks, barely able to speak.

'Hey, what's so funny?' shouted Ruby.

'Red was just telling me about what happened yesterday afternoon,' said Del.

'What about it?' asked Ruby.

'You must have seen the rain,' said Red. 'It was crazy rain.'

'I saw it,' said Ruby.

'So me and Mouse got caught in it and were like wet to our skin in the time it takes us to step off the bus and cross the road, and we go into Cherry's 'cause we are waiting for Elliot, he has his ukulele lesson one block away, you see?'

'You play the ukulele?' said Clancy.

Elliot couldn't respond – he was still crumpled in two.

'And anyway, he walks in and he is bone dry,' said Red. 'I mean, not a drip or a drop on him.'

Ruby by now was really listening.

'He walks in and he says, "What happened to you? Did you fall in a lake or something?" and we look out the window and guess what, it's pouring with rain again.'

Clancy looked at Ruby. 'Like I said, the weather can do some freaky things.'

Ruby shot him a look back as if to say, *yeah, yeah, so you were right and I was wrong.*

By the time Ruby walked into class, she was feeling both relieved and just ever so slightly stupid.

Blacker was no liar. Blacker was the one person who she could 100% count on, aside from Hitch. *If you start doubting your allies Rube, you're gonna end up mighty lonely.*

It was like she had read in one of her psychology books – '*We are all capable of poisoning our own minds, we need little help with that.*'

Rube my old friend, you seem to be suffering from a touch of paranoia. She thought back to the six-second pause book that Dr Selgood had given her. It seemed she should have taken six seconds to think before she walked out on Blacker.

Mouse and Ruby trailed out of English class and into the school yard.

'Did I see you pushing a baby round town yesterday afternoon?' asked Mouse.

'Possibly,' said Ruby.

'Possibly yes or possibly no? I mean, I have to say if you said you had an identical twin right now who had taken up babysitting it would sound *more plausible*.'

'I know what you mean,' said Ruby.

'Where did it come from?' asked Mouse.

'Mars I think,' said Ruby, 'judging by the weird stuff that comes out of him. Sometimes I swear it could be ectoplasm.'

Mouse wrinkled her nose. 'What does he eat?'

'Gloop,' said Ruby, 'though most of the time he just spits it back up. Boy is that kid fussy.'

'So why are you wheeling him around?' asked Mouse.

'I sorta struck a deal with my folks, although they don't know I struck a deal exactly, they think it was all their idea.'

'Pardon me?' said Mouse.

'I mean, they grounded me, which is a drag because it means being in all the time, but then Mrs Lemon wanted someone to mind Archie and my folks, knowing how allergic I am to babies, volunteered me. They thought it would be a good punishment, which by the way it is, but on the upside it means I get to go out, and out with a baby is better than in without a baby, right?'

'Kinda, I guess,' said Mouse. 'And this is all because...'

'On account of the whole thing with the sheriff and the garbage and another thing to do with Mr Parker and his yard and a bunch of similar smaller things that have made my folks not like me so much – they're not too happy about the writing on my arm either,' said Ruby, pushing up her sleeve to reveal the marker-pen words.

'Yeah, but that's all 'cause of Del.'

'Well, I can't tell 'em that, they'll just get mad at her, and in any case I don't think they would see it as her fault. I mean, they would just say, "Well you were born with a brain Ruby, maybe you should use it".'

'Well, I guess they have a point,' said Mouse.

'Thanks for your support.'

'Yeah, well I just don't see the point in getting punched on the nose just to prevent Del from getting punched on the nose,' said Mouse. 'I mean, she wants to get punched on the nose, so let her.'

There was a certain logic to this argument, Ruby could see it.

They spotted the others and went to join them. Red had that look on her face, the one she got when she had been told something truly awe-inspiring.

'You know Clancy is going to meet the president,' said Red. 'That's true, right Clance?'

'Well, yes, no and maybe,' said Clancy. 'My family and I are off to Washington for a reception at the White House, but I don't know if the president will be attending. I mean, who knows if he will make it, stuff happens when you're the president.'

'But he could be there?' said Red.

'Yeah he could be there,' agreed Clancy, 'but it's not a definite.'

'So who *will* be there?' asked Red. 'For definite.'

'The Environmental Explorers and Ruby's mom and dad,' said Clancy, 'which to me is more exciting than the president.'

'But you see Ruby's mom and dad all the time,' said Red.

'I'm talking about the Explorers, Red,' said Clancy. '*They* are what's interesting about this trip. My dad's always meeting the president, so I mean, big deal.'

'I heard that the snake woman is in a coma and basically clinging on to life,' said Mouse.

'Is that true?' said Red.

'It's what I heard,' said Clancy.

'She was bitten by one of her own snakes,' said Elliot.

'That's actually garbage,' said Ruby, 'you are just making this stuff up.'

'Making what stuff up?' asked Del – she was walking towards them, a huge sandwich in her right hand, a soda sort of tucked in the crook of her left arm.

'Elliot's talking baloney,' said Ruby.

'Hey, and I'm eating it!' said Del, holding up her sandwich.

'I was only saying how deadly those snakes are, the ones just discovered by that Mongolian conservationist,' said Elliot.

'They live on toadstools is what I heard,' said Del.

'What?' said Elliot.

'They eat toadstools,' said Del.

'Really?' said Red.

'And you know right before you die, your tongue turns green,' said Del, 'you get this terrible ringing in your ears like church bells or something, and your tongue turns green and then you're dead. You know for a certainty you're gonna be dead because of the colour of your tongue. Luminous green I heard.'

'Where do you get this stuff from, Del?' Ruby was looking at her wide-eyed. 'I mean, this is just stuff that comes into your head and out of your mouth bypassing the brain.'

'I'm sure I read it,' said Del.

Red was now looking at Del like she might have read it too. Red was highly suggestible and it was easy to convince her of most things. 'It sounds sorta possible,' she said.

'Well, whatever colour her tongue might turn, one thing's for sure,' said Clancy, 'she won't be at the White House so I won't get to meet her.'

'I just hope you make it and don't get yourself caught up in that tornado the news is talking about,' said Elliot.

'Thanks for suggesting I might,' said Clancy.

'I didn't say you would,' said Elliot. 'You should just be prepared.'

'How can he be prepared?' said Mouse. 'I mean, if he's in a plane when a tornado hits then what's he gonna do, head to the basement?'

'Look guys, do you mind talking about something else?' said Clancy.

Basketball had been cancelled and Ruby was faced with a dilemma: she was grounded so therefore, strictly speaking, no basketball meant she should return home, but on the other hand, her mom and dad did *not know* there was no basketball and so wouldn't be expecting her home for a couple of hours.

She certainly didn't want to sit around waiting for no news to come through from Spectrum, so she decided to hang out with Del.

If she and Del got a move on, there was just enough time to grab a table at Back-Spin and play a few games.

There was a new girl working at the counter when they got there, allocating tables and hiring out bats and ping-pong balls. She had a cool street style and a lower eastside Twinford accent. 'Where's Nicky?' asked Ruby,

'She's off with laryngitis,' said the girl. 'I'm working her shifts 'cause I could really use the dough.'

Del flashed her membership card and pulled some coins from her jeans pocket.

'What tables you got free?' she asked. 'I prefer the ones by the window.'

The girl looked at the booking sheet. 'I only got the one near the door,' she said.

Reaching for a new tube of ping-pong balls, she added, 'And I can only let you have it for thirty minutes, OK? We're booked out today.'

'That's it?' said Del, making a face. 'I came all the way down here for thirty measly minutes?'

'Well, *I* shouldn't be here at all,' said Ruby, 'so maybe take what you can.'

'So dya want the table or not?' said the girl.

'Thirty minutes, that really it?' said Del.

'Ignore her,' said Ruby, 'she means, thank you.'

'Look, seeing as how you're regulars, I can probably stretch it to an hour,' said the girl, 'but don't go telling no one, OK?'

'Thanks,' said Ruby. 'So what's your name anyway?'

'Sal,' said the girl.

'I'm Ruby and this is Del, thanks for the hour.'

'You're welcome,' said the girl, giving them each a fist bump. 'Pleasure to meet you.'

'You too,' said Del.

'Enjoy,' Sal called, turning to walk away.

Ruby and Del played until their time was up, when they went back to the counter and handed the bats and balls over to Sal, who was sitting on top of it, chatting to the guy who had just taken over her shift.

'So are you still sore about missing the Explorer thing?' asked Del.

'I'm trying not to think about it,' said Ruby, 'so could you stop bringing it up?'

'But there were some really cool people there, right?'

'I guess if you consider a person who walked on the moon cool, and a person who happens to have swum with a polar bear cool, and a woman who has discovered the rarest snake known to humankind cool, then yes,' said Ruby, 'I missed a lot.'

'Sorry!' said Del.

'Would you stop saying sorry!' said Ruby.

Sal, who was busy lacing her purple Dash sneakers, was looking at them with an expression of amusement. 'Sounds like you guys have some issues,' she said.

'You have no idea,' said Ruby.

Ruby walked into the house exactly when she was expected to walk into the house. Her mother looked up from the paper she was reading, the headline: IS THERE A TORNADO ON THE WAY?

Ruby poured herself a glass of water, took out her schoolbooks and sat down to study, just like she was the model kid.

Sabina Redfort smiled. 'You know Ruby, forget this whole grounding thing, you've done your time.'

That was all very well, but it wasn't going to get her out of Lemon duty – Elaine had her down for at least three hours of it on Saturday.

Chapter 35.
Follow that cab

THAT SATURDAY, RUBY BEGAN HER DAY WITH SOME
AIKIDO PRACTICE. This was followed by a trip to the Diner;
she thought she might as well celebrate her newfound freedom,
as it wasn't going to last – she would be picking up baby Lemon
in an hour.

Del and Ruby were sitting in the Donut, two hot chocolates
in front of them and toes like ice blocks. They were discussing
the weather and what effect it might have on the Halloween
festivities.

'The tornado has been cancelled,' said Del.

'What do you mean cancelled?' said Ruby.

'There isn't going to be one,' said Del. 'It was on the news.'

'The news doesn't get to decide if there's going to be a tornado
or not,' said Ruby.

'Well, the weather office then,' said Del. 'Apparently the
conditions are all wrong for tornadoes so we are off the hook.'

'I would just like to remind you that tornadoes can strike
in any conditions – scientists are still struggling to understand

what triggers them.'

'Is that Begwell out there?' said Del looking out of the window. 'She better not come in here.'

'Why?' asked Ruby. 'Is this your private diner?'

'No, but it's my patch,' said Del.

'You sound like a gangster.'

The bell jangled and a few more people bundled in.

Del looked up. 'Hey, isn't that the new girl from the table tennis cafe?' Ruby turned to look. 'Yeah, you can't miss those purple Dash sneakers.'

'Boy, Back-Spin must pay its staff well, those sneakers cost a bunch,' said Del. 'Maybe she could get me a job.'

'Maybe she just has a rich mom and dad,' said Ruby.

'She doesn't,' said Del.

'How do you know?' said Ruby. 'Her accent and that whole "I could use the dough" thing she has going, I'll bet it's a cover.'

'A cover for what?' said Del.

'For the fact that she's some rich kid from uptown and she wants to be all, you know, downtown East Twinford.'

'You're full of it,' said Del, 'just envious because she's street cool.'

'What?' said Ruby.

'Hey, Sal,' called Del, 'you wanna join us?'

The girl turned, looked at them as if trying to figure how she knew them and then smiled a huge smile.

'Del and Ruby, right?' said Sal. 'What are you doing?'

'Arguing,' said Del.

Sal frowned.

'Don't worry, it's normal,' said Ruby.

Del nodded. 'Anyway, it's good to see you. I thought Vapona Begwell was going to walk through the door, which wouldn't have been pretty. She and I haven't been seeing eye to eye lately, if you know what I'm saying.'

'Is that how you got the busted hand?' said Sal, looking at Del's bandaged wrist.

'No,' said Ruby, 'but it's how I ended up with a flattened nose.'

'Bummer,' said Sal.

'She's OK,' said Del, 'just likes to whine.'

'Yeah?' said Ruby. 'I'm the one who's gonna wind up sweeping the streets of Twinford.'

'How's that?' asked Sal.

'It's what tends to happen when the cops pick you up for disorderly conduct,' said Ruby.

'Cool,' said Sal.

'Not really,' said Ruby.

'There was a fight,' said Del. 'A big one.' She was showing off now.

'So a lotta you guys in trouble?'

'No, just me,' said Ruby.

'How come no one else got squeezed?' said Sal.

'They ran,' said Ruby. 'I was not, strictly speaking, expecting to wind up in the middle of a fist fight, so I wasn't exactly dressed for the occasion, nor for running like stink in the other direction.' She directed this at Del.

'Doesn't that kinda tick you off,' asked Sal, 'you taking the rap for something you never did?'

'All part and parcel of being a friend of Lasco's,' said Ruby, thumping her friend on the arm.

'She's a good pal,' said Del, returning the punch.

'I guess she must be,' said Sal, looking at Ruby.

Ruby was just pushing Archie Lemon on the swing for about the five-hundredth time – that's what her arm felt like, anyway – when something scarlet red caught her eye. She turned to see a red hat bobbing across Harker Park towards the east gate. From that distance it was hard to tell if it was the same guy who she had seen the other day, but then again men in scarlet woollen hats weren't exactly commonplace, and if it *was* him then Ruby wanted to ask him some questions. So she pulled the surprised baby from the swing and snapped him into his sling, pulled on her backpack, zipped up her parker and began to fast walk down the parallel path.

The man was just far enough ahead to tail without difficulty. However, once he reached the street he stuck out his hand to hail a taxi, which meant Ruby had to break into a run.

'Boy, Lemon, what have you been eating? You seem heavier than you did last week.'

As the man stepped into a car, so Ruby got lucky.

'Where to?' said the driver.

'Follow that cab,' said Ruby.

'If I had a dime for the number of times I've heard that line,' said the driver.

The cab in front was driving northeast towards College Town, which was part of old Twinford – an area designed some seventy years ago by one of the university professors, a mathematician called Hugo Hennessey who had worked with an architect to create the university campus. At its centre was a park called Star Park, on account of its symmetrical eight-pointed-star shape, and nearly all the streets were named after numbers or mathematical theories.

The car finally pulled up in front of an old gothic building. Ruby didn't spend much time in this part of town, but she had attended the occasional lecture so knew this to be one of the many ivy-clad buildings which made up the University of Twinford. Ruby stepped out, paid her fare and kept a close eye on the red hat. The man was climbing the well-worn steps to the university's Erskine building. Ruby picked up the pace.

The man's shoes clicked loudly on the granite floors, up stairways, down stairways and along what seemed like miles of corridors. He exited the Erskine building through the south door, crossed the courtyard planted with lime trees and entered the music school, a newly built structure and one which had caused a great deal of controversy, since it had meant the destruction of the old comb building. Twinford was once famed for its comb industry, making both plain, inexpensive combs and combs for the luxury market, in tortoise-shell and mother-of-pearl for those who could afford it. John Micklebacker III, the great comb magnate, had bequeathed the grand building to the university in his will.

Once inside, the man strode towards the cafeteria, looked around, and having spied the chiller cabinet, reached behind the rows of canned drinks and pulled out a familiar-looking bottle.

Ruby's eyesight was by no means good, in fact it was lousy, but even she could make out the vague shape of the cartoon kid with black hair, and white-toothed smile.

Taste Twister.

The man didn't bother waiting in line to pay for the drink, instead he casually popped it up his sleeve and threaded his way back through the crowded cafeteria before exiting unnoticed by all but Ruby.

Why didn't he pay? thought Ruby. This intrigued her; it didn't fit with what she thought might happen. He wasn't even bothering to taste this drink, and where was he headed now?

This guy most definitely knew where he was going. He was moving at speed, up more stairs and along a corridor of practice rooms. Ruby heard sounds of cello, trumpet, flute, piano, as she passed. The man's footfall was less easy to follow now, since the building was designed to absorb sound and Ruby, who was keeping a safe distance, very nearly lost him when stairways split and corridors became other corridors.

But she was lucky – just as she was about to concede defeat, Ruby caught a flash of scarlet as the man disappeared through the concert theatre's swing doors. She wasn't so sure if she wanted to follow him into the theatre, her mood about the adventure had changed. It didn't seem like so much fun any more, but then again, if she didn't go in then she might never know.

And look, she told herself, *the baby's asleep and you're a trainee field agent and this is what field agents do.*

So she crept through the doors, crouching low behind the rows of steep raked seating, Archie Lemon still peacefully sleeping in his sling on her chest. To her surprise she heard voices – the man was not alone, he was talking to someone, another man. She couldn't see him from where she crouched, but he sounded like a bit of a meathead as far as she could tell. The acoustics were very good as one would expect in a music theatre and each word rang out clearly.

'I'm Leo...' said the meathead she couldn't see.

'Names are for amateurs, Leo,' said the man in the red hat. His accent: Australian.

'I just thought...'

'I have no interest in sending you a postcard, so why would I need to know your pathetic name?'

'Forget about it.'

'I plan to.'

'So I heard there might be a job for me – what is it?'

'My boss is looking for someone – here.' There was the sound of paper being torn as a piece was ripped from a spiral-bound notebook. 'He's gone AWOL you see.'

Ruby peeped over the seatback. She had a good vantage point, the room was in darkness and the stage lit by just one spotlight.

'So who is this Marshall guy?' asked the meathead.

'It doesn't matter who he is,' said the Australian guy. 'All you have to do is track him down, and when you find him, well, eliminate him.' He flipped the top off the bottle. He did exactly what he had done last time, breathed in the aroma and took a swig. He said nothing for a few seconds before jotting something in his notebook.

'Is that drink speaking to you?' said the meathead.

'Now how would it do that?' sneered the man. As he walked down the steps he placed the bottle under the spotlight centre stage, like it was a prop in some performance. 'I have to get going,' he said moving back through the audience seating. 'Places to be, you know.'

'No other message or nothing?' said Leo. 'From your boss, I mean.'

The guy in the red hat paused, stopping at the end of the row where Ruby crouched.

'Oh yeah, she did say one thing, I seem to remember her exact words were, *"Sweetie, if this chump messes up then feel free to take him out."* I don't think she was suggesting a dinner date by the way, Leo, and you should be in no doubt that she never makes idle threats.' His footsteps resumed; there was a swish of swing doors, and he was gone.

Ruby had turned very cold, the word *sweetie* had reminded her of one person, one very deadly person. Like most people, Ruby had a whole string of individuals she would prefer not to have to see again, but this person was not on that list, this person was on one very short list, a list comprising people she never *ever* wanted to see again, nor even hear about in passing. This was because the previous time Ruby had encountered her, this person had tried to kill her. On that occasion Ruby had stared into her steel blue eyes and been sure that she was about to die. Now it seemed she was back.

The Australian woman.

Who, it seemed, had an Australian henchman in a red hat doing her dirty work for her.

It was time to get out of there. Ruby began to crawl towards the door and then she remembered the Taste Twister drink. It meant something – he'd noted something down after tasting it – and she needed to know what. She sighed. She was going to have to wait until the meathead called Leo left the stage. He was taking his time about it, reading whatever was written on that scrap of paper.

Come on, thought Ruby, *split why don't you, then we can all go home.*

She realised why he was hanging around when she heard a second man.

'Hey, Leo, you get your orders?'

'Yeah, he thought he was some kinda hard nut, British I think.'

Ruby figured Leo didn't watch enough international TV: if he had, that Australian accent would have been unmissable.

Goon number two sat down.

I don't believe it, she thought, *now they're gonna have a little heart to heart about some murder plan?*

'So, Leo, the money's good?'

'Yeah, and what she wants us to do, it's a piece of cake.'

There was no way of grabbing that bottle, not while these two creeps were hanging around, so she waited and hoped that Archie was as patient as she was.

At last Ruby heard the creaking of wood as the men stood.

'Come on Bruno, let's get outta here.'

They walked down the stage steps and were just making their way back up through the tiered seating, in fact had almost reached the large swing doors, when the worst thing happened – Archie woke up.

Chapter 36.
Baby talk

'DID I JUST HEAR A BABY?' said the first guy.

'Couldna been,' said the second.

Now they were both listening.

Ruby was feeling around for Archie's pacifier: *where is it, darn it?* She pulled it from her pocket and was just fumbling to pop it in the baby's little mouth when it slipped from her fingers and bounced under one of the seats.

Archie began to wail. No mistaking that.

'So it seems we have an audience,' said the first guy. 'Are you a baby all on your lonesome or do you have company?' As he talked they moved, Goon One seemed to be trying to distract Ruby while Goon Two was trying to figure out exactly where she was hiding – for a man so hulking he was very light on his feet.

'Come out, come out, wherever you are!' called Goon One.

Jeepers Archie, now see what you've done... Her urge was to run, to sprint to the door. *Six seconds Ruby, take six seconds and breathe.* Keeping her cool, she reached far under the seat, patted the floor with her hand, found the pacifier, placed it in Archie's angry mouth – instant quiet. *Better*, now she could think. If she stayed put, it was just a matter of time before this second light-footed goon found her and dragged her out – by her hair, no doubt.

Ruby could hear the guy feeling around for something, the lights most probably. She had no idea where the other one had got to since he was keeping quiet.

'Let's get outta here Archie,' whispered Ruby. She moved stealthily and speedily towards the front. She flew up the steps to the stage, grabbing the Taste Twister bottle as she went.

Then *vwoom* – dazzling white as every spotlight in the theatre came on.

For a few seconds she was blinded, shielding her face with her arm and Archie with her coat. Where to go? She was staring at the floor since it was the only place she could look. A small brass ring lay there glinting on the wooden boards. Not a ring but a handle – a handle to the trapdoor!

Holding the Taste Twister bottle in one hand, she lifted the trapdoor back and slipped down under the stage, quietly pulling it shut after her. She heard footsteps on the stage above, one of the goons was running this way and that trying to figure out where she could have gone. The other was shouting.

Ruby thought about **RULE 19: PANIC WILL FREEZE YOUR BRAIN**. So she stood very still and counted.

1.

2.

3.

4.

5.

6.

Now she felt calmer.

First: put that drink in your backpack. Second: contact Hitch.

She depressed the button on the fly barrette and hoped that Hitch would hear her.

'Where did she go?' said Goon One.

'Beats me, just disappeared,' said Goon Two.

He stopped when he saw the door.

He's figured it out, she whispered in baby Lemon's ear. '*I'm beginning to wish we'd stayed home watching* A is for Ant.' The baby looked at her; he was still sucking on the pacifier and looked unduly calm.

Ruby felt around for the other door out of there, the door in the wall that would lead to the back-stage steps. *Don't panic*, she told herself, *take it easy*. It was pitch black down there and they were not alone; the goon had dropped through the boards and was now down there with them.

'I know you're here,' he whispered.

Ruby's fingers found a catch, she yanked and the door opened and she slipped through, pulling it closed behind her.

'I hear you,' called the goon.

Ruby ran up the steps as fast as she could. To the side in the wings was a fixed metal ladder – this she climbed. Now she was high above the stage with the cables and lights and wires, all hitched this way and that to scaffolding. Ruby tiptoed across one of the poles that held the lights. A tiny voice issued from the fly barrette. 'You in trouble?'

Ruby tapped the transmit button on the fly: long-short-long-short, the Morse code for C, the universal shorthand for "yes".

The tiny voice came back.

'I have you on my radar kid. I'm maybe a half mile away, hang tight, I'm almost with you.'

OK, thought Ruby, *all we gotta do is inch our way over here into that dark space and wait for Hitch.* She began crawling across the steel framework, but Archie, now asleep, let the pacifier slip from his mouth and go spinning through the air. It hit the deck and the goon looked up.

'Ah, there you are. You wanna come down or do you wanna make me climb? I should probably tell you, too much exertion always puts me in a bad mood.'

'*Uh oh, he's spotted us,*' hissed Ruby.

'What do you mean, *us*?' asked Hitch.

'Uh *me*, I mean me.'

'Can you get out of there?'

'I think so.'

'Well, get out of there.'

'I'm going to have to fly.'

'So fly.'

'I'll probably have to sort of jump.'

'Kid, if you're about to confess that you've suddenly developed a fear of heights then this isn't a good time.'

'That's not what I'm saying, it's just the thing is I have—'

'Would you get outta there!'

The words came out as an order, albeit a very quiet and tinny one.

Parkour with a baby was one thing – probably not a very good one thing – but parkour with a baby and a couple of, no doubt violent, goons on your tail was another.

'You know what,' shouted Goon One, 'I think I'll wait down here, see if my pal Bruno can't shake the tree a bit. I'll try and catch you, but I gotta warn you, everyone says I'm a bit of a butter-fingers.'

Ruby held her breath and waited until Goon Two had reached the lights, then she leapt, catching hold of a rope in her right hand, swinging across the stage, catching a second rope in her left, her body low enough that as she flew towards Goon One she could bend her legs and kick, *DOOF*, he was down – and, it looked like, out.

She let go of the rope, dropped to the floor and ran, leaping from the stage and sprinting over the seat backs. Goon Two had no idea why his pal, Leo, was lying spread-eagled on the stage, but he wasn't losing time thinking about it and he was a lot more agile than he looked. At this precise moment, Ruby could have done without the extra weight that was Archie. He didn't weigh a ton, but when you were quietly trying to escape from a pair of murderous villains then it was better to be free of all burdens, babies especially.

Gotta lose the Lemon, she thought. She climbed up to the balcony seating and vaulted over in one easy move. Then, crouching low so she was hidden from view, she undid the sling and looked around her for a safe place to deposit the baby. There was a high-sided box full of concert programmes, tall enough that he couldn't get out or be seen. She clicked off the fly barrette just for a minute.

'Sorry to do this to you Lemon,' she said as she emptied out the box and placed him in it. He didn't look like he minded, just smiled up at her. 'Now look, I gotta leave you for a few minutes.' He looked like he was going to start grizzling. 'Don't start that up again Archie, you're gonna get us both into some serious horse manure if you open that tiny mouth of yours.' The baby was looking at her watch, reaching one small hand towards it.

'You have to be kidding,' she hissed. 'You know this is a serious piece of gadgetry – belonged to Bradley Baker, agent of agents – and all you're gonna do is stick it in your mouth. Am I right or am I right?' But what choice did she have? 'Darn it, Lemon!' She took the watch off and handed it to him and he put it in his mouth. Ruby rolled her eyes. 'OK, so suck on that while I go trip up the mean guy.'

She switched the fly barrette back on. 'Kid, what happened? I thought I'd lost you there.'

'No, still right here,' hissed Ruby.

'Come out, little girl,' threatened the heavy, 'or I'll huff and

I'll puff and I'll tear this place apart.'

Ruby had to draw him away from Archie so she ran as fast as she could along the balcony rail and jumped right down in front of him. She was facing him now. He was approximately six foot five in stocking feet, and she was, well, she was a whole lot shorter. Maybe a foot and a half shorter. He smirked an ugly smirk when he saw her there. 'Oh please, this is too easy,' he said.

He went to grab her but she dodged him. He laughed and lunged at her, but still she avoided his reach. Less pleased, he lashed out; she ducked. He pitched forward, grabbed her arm, but she knew just what to do – using his own momentum she executed a perfect *kotegaeshi*, twisting on the spot while using her other hand to push on his neck, flipping him in the air to land heavily on his back.

The man's expression went from puzzlement to fury. He sprang to his feet, spun round to deliver a karate kick, but Ruby turned her body sideways and tilted backwards, and his attack made no contact. He ran at her, swinging his fist, and this time she caught his hand, pushed her leading knee forward and somersaulted him over in a textbook *tenchi nage*.

He hit the ground with his back, even harder this time. He lay there gasping for breath. He couldn't get up or stagger, let alone run.

The other goon was still out cold. She wasn't going to wait for him to come round. *Don't push your luck Redfort, get out while the going's good* – so she did. She climbed up to the balcony, picked baby Lemon out of the box, strapped him back into the sling and ran for the exit. As she did so, she tapped the fly barrette. 'I'm safe,' she said.

'And the bad guys?'

'Out for the count.'

'Nice going kid. Now get out of there. You can tell me the story once I've got them safely tucked up in jail.'

Out in the fresh air, she breathed deep. The adrenaline was still coursing through her and her heart still beating so fast that she needed to steady herself, her hand reaching out for the trunk of one of the sturdy old lime trees which had stood in the university courtyard for a reassuringly long time. When at last she regained her breath, she looked down at the baby.

'Are you OK Lemon?' she asked. Her heart was racing. She touched his face. He was sleeping so soundly that he barely stirred. He looked utterly serene, the rescue watch still clutched in his fat hand. 'I guess goons and murderers don't exactly bother you.'

At the women's correctional facility...

...they tossed the escaped prisoner's cell, as they always did after a breakout.

There was nothing in the little cupboard.

Nothing under the bed.

But there was something hidden inside the mattress.

A book.

A book filled with colourful descriptions of what the prisoner intended to do to some un-named enemy, if she ever caught her.

'This makes for some pretty unpleasant reading,' said the prison warden.

'Who do you think she had it in for?'

'I don't know. Could be her mother, her sister, her childhood friend, perhaps it's some poor sap who simply had the grand misfortune to bump into her one day. But I'll say this – whoever it might be, I wouldn't want to be in her shoes.'

'Should we contact the cops?'

'I think this might be a job for the FBI,' said the warden. He picked up the book and shook his head. 'Honest to goodness, what's written here is enough to give me sleepless nights for the rest of time.'

Chapter 37.
Limes are not the same as lemons

RUBY STAYED UP LONG AFTER HER PARENTS HAD GONE TO BED. She sat there in the dim light of the kitchen, waiting for the sound of Hitch's car in the driveway. Bug kept her company, his nose resting on her feet. When Hitch finally walked in, he poured himself a drink and joined her there in the semi-darkness.

'You OK kid?'

'Yeah, but my arm kinda aches, that creep twisted it practically in two.'

'Looks like you got the better of him.'

'You got him?' said Ruby.

'Got them both... impressive for such a small kid.'

'Yeah, well, they underestimated me.'

'Maybe they got distracted by the baby.'

'What baby?'

'One of them kept mumbling something about a baby.'

'Probably suffering from concussion; he did hit the deck

real hard.'

'That's probably it,' said Hitch. 'So do you mind filling me in a little, I think I'm missing something.'

'I saw the red hat guy again in Harker Park, the one I spotted looking at the billboard.'

'The Taste Twister thing?'

'Yeah,' said Ruby, 'so I followed him. I was just curious, I wanted to know if Clancy was right.'

'About what?' asked Hitch.

'Well, see, he has this theory that the Taste Twister billboards are some sophisticated advertising ploy to get all of Twinford desperately searching for Taste Twister drinks.'

Hitch raised an eyebrow. 'Why would they do that?'

'To make the brand seem cool or something,' said Ruby. 'But anyway, I thought I'd follow this guy in the red hat, see if he located another bottle and then ask him straight out.'

'So what happened?'

'Well he *did* find another bottle, it was in the music school canteen,' said Ruby, 'but he didn't taste it then and there, he carried it off, which is why I followed and we both ended up in the concert hall. He took a slurp, wrote something down and headed off.'

'So where's the bottle?' asked Hitch.

'Oh, I got it,' she patted her backpack. 'I just hope it's worth it because it wasn't easy to come by, you know.'

'Bring it in to Spectrum and let's see what SJ and Blacker make of it.'

'There's more,' she said she paused, took a breath. 'It *also* turns out he is some kind of assassin.'

'What?' said Hitch.

'Those goons you arrested, they're after Baby Face Marshall.'

'You heard them say that?'

'Yeah. The red hat guy just hired them to rub him out.'

Hitch rolled his eyes. 'Rub him out?'

'OK, end his life,' said Ruby, dramatically. 'But the point is, the orders didn't come directly from him. The orders came from his boss.'

'And who's his boss?'

'The Australian,' said Ruby.

'He *said* so?' asked Hitch, suddenly sitting up very straight.

'Well, not exactly,' said Ruby, 'but he quoted her and the words sounded exactly like words she would use. You know how I told you she called me "sweetie" in this really creepy *"I'm going to kill you yet I'm talking to you in this really soft mom voice"* voice? Plus the red hat guy, he was Australian.'

Hitch was looking less convinced. 'This isn't exactly overwhelming evidence you have here.'

'I swear, I'm sure it's gotta be her.'

'Well, whoever this guy's boss is, she doesn't sound like someone you'd want to run into, so I'm going to go in and see if I can get some more information from your two meathead friends, and then maybe we'll have something to go on. And kid, get some sleep would you, you look kind of beat.'

'I'm sure I'll sleep like a baby,' she said.

Blacker was waiting for her when Ruby arrived at Spectrum the next morning.

'Hitch filled me in,' he said as they walked to the lab. 'Are you finding trouble or is trouble finding you?'

SJ looked a little fraught.

Blacker sniffed the air. 'What's that smell?'

'That'll be my hair,' said SJ. 'Some dufus somehow mixed the labels on my test samples and my shampoo.' She caught sight of the bottle in Ruby's hand. 'More *possibly poisoned* beverages?'

'Yeah,' said Ruby. 'I mean, I doubt it is. Actually I think the bottle contains some kind of code.'

SJ looked puzzled.

'I think it's contained in the taste? Or rather the flavours,' she said. 'When the guy sipped it he seemed to be analysing it, trying to decipher what was in it, and once he figured it out, he wrote it down.' She paused before remembering, 'Oh yeah, and there's what's printed on the reverse of the label, you can see it through the liquid – FOUR GREAT TASTES SINCE 1922. I'm sure it means more than what it seems to mean, if you know what I mean?'

Blacker and SJ were just looking at her; it was disconcerting.

'Am I rambling?' she asked.

'Only a little,' said Blacker, 'but I follow you.'

'That's good,' said Ruby. 'So anyway, before I taste it for myself, I'd like to know for certain that one of the ingredients isn't toxic.'

'Always wise,' said SJ. 'You'd only have yourself to blame if you woke up dead.'

SJ took no time in getting on with the tests, the same procedure as before.

When she was satisfied she said, 'Well, like last time, there's no poison. There are various trace metals in there etcetera, but mostly it's just water, salt and sugar.'

'*Salt* and sugar?' said Ruby.

'Uh huh.'

SJ pushed her goggles on top of her head, which gave her the appearance of a fly. Then she held the bottle up to the light. 'Where can a taste take you?' she muttered. 'Well, let's see.' She poured a little of the liquid into tiny beakers and they all sampled the drink. 'The taste is... what do you think?'

'Kinda gross,' said Ruby.

'As a drink, I'm not sure,' said Blacker.

'No,' said SJ. 'It's like seawater. But sweet too.'

'So you agree,' said Ruby, 'there's something else to it?'

Blacker nodded and peered through the bottle at the label's reverse. '"Four great tastes since 1922." What do you think that's trying to tell us?' he mused.

'I have no idea,' said Ruby.

Was the intention to convey a message? A location maybe? If the taste was a code, pointing to something, someone or somewhere, then they were not seeing it.

There were a lot of unknowns, but at least now they knew that these elusive drinks were in some way connected to the dealings of some unsavoury people, even if they didn't have a clue as to how or why.

'What was in the first bottle?' said Blacker. 'The one purchased at the store?'

'Water, lemon and sugar,' said SJ.

'No salt?'

'Not in that one.'

Blacker scratched his head. 'So the guy tastes the first drink, the sugary lemony one, and then a few days later arrives at the university music school,' he said.

'But I mean, what's sugar and lemon got to do with the music school?' said Ruby. 'Is there any connection?'

'There are lime trees in the courtyard,' said Blacker.

'Limes are not the same as lemons,' said Ruby. She paused – she was thinking about the sleek new music school with its state-of-the-art concert hall. 'So what used to be there, before the music building got built?'

'The old comb factory,' said Blacker.

Her face fell. 'So nothing lemony about the place?'

'Nope,' said Blacker, 'and no, it was never ever painted yellow.'

'Nothing's coming up lemons,' said Ruby.

Blacker's watch bleeped. He looked at the message and his relaxed expression faded.

'I have to be somewhere,' he said, jumping to his feet. He looked anxious, worried even, Ruby thought.

'Everything OK?' asked Ruby.

'Sure, it's nothing,' he said, 'just a routine briefing thing.' But his face told another story. 'Are you able to work on this alone, or do you want to team up with Froghorn?'

She gave him a look as if to say, *you serious?*

'I guess not,' he said, as he attempted to twist himself into his raincoat.

'You got the sleeves all inside out,' said Ruby, taking the coat from him and untangling it, 'here.'

'Thanks,' said Blacker, 'I'd be lost without you.' He put the coat on. 'So look, call me as soon as you get something, OK?'

'Assuming I do,' said Ruby. 'So far I've been lucky – just happened to see strangers doing strange things.'

'So keep your peepers peeled and you might just get lucky again,' said Blacker, exiting the room.

Ruby thought about what Blacker had said, how she should keep her eyes peeled, so instead of going home she headed to Flaubert Street.

She found a bench on the far side of the road from the old piano factory and stared across at the huge Taste Twister billboard. Ruby took out her notebook and pencil and made a sketch of what she saw, making sure to get the details just right. The billboard, the image, the words and all.

She zipped her parker and sat watching for a while. Would the guy in the red hat come back? She sat like that for two whole hours in fact, before figuring that this was probably the dumbest thing she had ever done. The odds that anyone would just happen along were remote – she couldn't rely on getting lucky – so instead she would have to use her brain. She thought back, visualising the guy in the red hat, staring up at the billboard.

What had he seen to make him go to the Little Seven Grocers store to buy the bottle?

The billboard told him to go. Either the name of the store was written somewhere on that advertisement or...

The billboard somehow gave the *location* of the store!

She stood up, waited for a gap in the traffic and crossed to the other side. She walked to the billboard and peered up at it, like the Australian man had done. A few minutes later, she saw it. At the bottom, in small numerals, was a set of numbers.

32.7410, -117.1705

To a casual passer-by, it might just seem like this was a serial number for the poster. But Ruby had a hunch those numbers were not just any numbers – they had to be coordinates.

And if she wasn't much mistaken, they were *California* coordinates.

In fact – she would put money on it – they were most probably the exact coordinates of the Little Seven store where the man had picked up the first Taste Twister bottle.

Was she right about this? Only one way to find out.

She began to run.

Chapter 38.
The Yellow Wind-Dragon

RUBY SAT AT HER DESK IN HER BEDROOM AND FLICKED
THROUGH HER ATLAS. It was a sizeable volume and the most
complete atlas available on the market. She had put it on her
Christmas list when she was just four, and Santa didn't disappoint.
In fact, he made sure he delivered an updated volume every
other year.

At the back of the atlas was a section on longitudes and
latitudes.

Different regions of the world were shown on each spread,
with the vertical and horizontal lines marked and numbered.

She turned the pages till she got to western America. Then
she traced her finger down the page.

Longitude 32...

Latitude -117...

Her finger stopped.

It was over Twinford.

She nodded to herself. The atlas didn't give enough detail –
she'd have to check the precise location with Blacker, or someone

else at Spectrum – but she knew what the other numbers would give: the address of the store where the man bought the first bottle.

OK, she thought. *So if the billboard gave a location, then maybe the bottle gives a location too.*

She picked it up and peered through the glass at the reverse of the label. FOUR GREAT TASTES SINCE 1922. And that weird mandala shape. She frowned. It reminded her of something. Something—

There was a knock at the door. Ruby put the bottle aside.

'Yeah?' she said.

The door opened and there was Hitch. He looked... not himself. A little drawn. A little pale.

HITCH: *'You ever study kung fu, kid?'*

Ruby almost fell off her chair.

RUBY: *'What makes you ask that?'*

HITCH: *'OK, let's say for the sake of speed, I know you did. Let's say I know you were a black belt.'*

Ruby said nothing – and then:

RUBY: *'How do you know, anyway?'*

HITCH: *'I read it in your file.'*

RUBY: *'What file?'*

HITCH: *'The one Spectrum holds; don't make like you didn't think there was one.'*

RUBY: *'Of course I know there's a file, LB's mentioned it enough times, I just didn't think this would be in there is all.'*

HITCH: *'Everything's in there.'*

RUBY: *'I doubt that.'*

Hitch raised an eyebrow.

HITCH: *'You want a bet?'*

RUBY: *'My dad told me not to gamble.'*

HITCH: *'Very wise.'*

RUBY: *'But I happen to know Mrs Digby plays poker at least every week and does pretty well on it.'*

HITCH: *'That's gambling for you; you never can tell.'*

She looked him dead in the eye.

RUBY: *'So you know what happened?'*

HITCH: *'I know you broke a kid's arm once.'*

Ruby said nothing.

HITCH: *'I know you pretty much smooshed his nose too.'*

RUBY: *'Yeah, well, it wasn't much of a nose.'*

HITCH: *'I bet he was pretty attached to it.'*

RUBY: *'Yeah, and in all the usual places.'*

HITCH: *'So why did you feel the need to flatten his nice little snout?'*

RUBY: *'He wasn't such a nice little kid.'*

HITCH: *'True, he wasn't little, and he wasn't much of a kid either – what was he, 6' 1" and ten years older than you? You were seven, is that right?'*

RUBY: *'I was trying to stop him from hurting someone. Someone who didn't stand a chance.'*

HITCH: *'So it was all on you?'*

RUBY: *'Someone had to do something. He was dangerous.'*
HITCH: *'You were pretty dangerous too; this guy could have wound up with more than just a broken nose.'*
RUBY: *'I didn't intend to break his nose.'*
HITCH: *'But you went too far?'*
RUBY: *'It's hard to know what's too far.'*
HITCH: *'And this is why your parents hate you fighting?'*
RUBY: *'It's the one thing they're pretty serious about – that and good manners.'*
HITCH: *'No more kung fu.'*
RUBY: *'No more kung fu.'*
HITCH: *'Maybe you just needed the right teacher.'*

Ruby frowned. 'Why do I get the feeling you want me to take up kung fu again?'

'Because I do,' said Hitch.

'But you've already got me learning aikido,' said Ruby. 'I took care of those goons, didn't I?'

'Yes,' said Hitch, 'but they were amateurs. Aikido is a smart way to defeat a gorilla using his own gorilla strength against him. But for taking on someone smart and trained? Someone who doesn't play it by the rules? No good at all.'

'You think I'm going to have to take on a smart, trained cheat some time soon?'

He looked her square in the eye. 'I hope not kid, but I wouldn't bet against it.'

'So you want me to study kung fu again... just in case?'

'Yes.'

'You think I might be in danger?'

'Kid, when you're in our line of work things can happen, unexpected things.'

'We're talking life-threatening things?'

'Maybe.'

'But you can't guard against every eventuality.'

'You might as well have the odds stacked in your favour.'

'And this sudden desire for me to become the kung fu kid has nothing to do with the Australian woman making a reappearance? Or the Spectrum mole? I mean, if there is a Spectrum mole.'

'I can't say.'

Ruby sighed. 'Are you trying to give me sleepless nights?'

'Quite the contrary,' said Hitch. 'If I'm honest with you, I for one might sleep a whole lot better if I thought you were ready for anything – think like a girl scout and be prepared.'

'I don't think most girl scouts are expecting to run into psychopaths.'

'Put the murderers to one side for a while and just think of it as an assignment,' said Hitch. 'Here. I got something for you.' He took a small white business card from his inside jacket pocket, handed it to Ruby and said, 'Your problem was never kung fu itself, kid, it was about discipline.'

The card was embossed with an origami pattern. Ruby turned it over and saw printed in red a name: Jen Yu, Yellow Wind-Dragon kung fu master.

'She can teach you what you don't know,' said Hitch.

'Why do I get the feeling I'm in the dark here?' said Ruby.

Hitch shrugged. 'It's a secret agency,' he said. 'The clue is in the name.'

He turned to head back down the stairs but he stopped when Ruby called, 'Hey, can you find out what these coordinates relate to?' She handed him a piece of paper on which she had written the numbers from the billboard.

'Why?' said Hitch.

'Ah, I'll tell you if I'm right. It might all be seawater and lemon juice.'

Chapter 39.
So who blabbed?

NOT LONG AFTER RUBY ARRIVED AT SCHOOL THE FOLLOWING DAY, she was summoned to the principal's office. He had a very particular subject he wanted to discuss and he took no time at all bringing it up.

'The fight outside Sunny's Diner, what can you tell me?'

Ruby shrugged.

He asked her a whole lot of questions and she gave him not many answers, at least none of the answers he was hoping for.

'No, I can't remember.'

'No, I didn't see.'

'The whole incident's a blur on account of my getting clonked on the head.'

He sighed. 'So you can't tell me who else was involved in this mindless act of vandalism?'

'I wish I could sir.'

'How about Del Lasco?'

'Del? I don't know why you would bring her name up,' said Ruby.

'Let's just say a little bird told me.'

Ruby blinked. Who had told him that?

'Maybe your little bird heard wrong.'

He sighed again. 'Very well, Redfort. Dismissed.'

By the time she had returned to class, Del Lasco was in the hot seat.

'What's going on?' hissed Red. 'Are you in more trouble?'

'I'm not sure that's possible,' said Ruby.

But as it turned out, she was very wrong. She knew this for a fact when she saw Del Lasco marching towards her at some speed. For a second, a split second, Ruby thought Del was going to punch her, but once Del got up close and Ruby was able to see her expression more clearly it became obvious that Del appeared injured rather than angry.

'If you felt you had to rat on me then I understand. What I don't understand is why you couldn't have warned me,' said Del. She looked truly injured. 'I mean, I just need to know when to stop bluffing.'

'I didn't rat on you,' said Ruby.

'Really? So you just *happen* to leave the principal's office and then I just *happen* to get called in and he *knows* I was there?'

'I spoke to him, yeah. But I didn't *say* anything.'

'Sure. I can deal with anything, but not standing there like a total bozo lying my head off when they know the truth anyways,' said Del.

'But I didn't rat on you,' repeated Ruby. 'I don't rat, and if I did rat then I would tell you my reasons, which in any case I wouldn't *have*, because I DON'T rat.'

'So how do they know?' said Del.

'My guess would be some big mouth busybody like Mr Chester told them.'

Del's expression turned from indignant to puzzled. 'You think? But why now?'

'Maybe he only just figured it out, perhaps he only just found out your name? I don't know, maybe it was someone else entirely. Let's face it, there are hundreds of mean-minded folks queuing up to give teenagers a bad rap.'

'You really think that's it?'

'Yes, I do,' said Ruby,

'Oh,' said Del.

'Principal Levine asked me all about it and I said I had no recollection of what transpired due to a bump on the old noodle and smashed up glasses.'

'What did *he* say?' asked Del.

'He didn't like it, but there wasn't much he could do. So could you just get it through your blockhead skull, I didn't squeal?'

'Got it,' said Del. She stuck her hand out and Ruby shook it. 'Thanks Rube, I appreciate it and sorry for doubting, you know.'

'That's OK, doubt is an important part of belief.'

After school, Mouse and Ruby started walking on over to Back-Spin to see if they could get a table. If Sal was on, their chances were good. Soon after they arrived, Elliot walked in.

'How come you got a table?' he asked. 'I thought it was all booked out.'

'Ruby's got in with Sal, the bookings girl, they're real tight.'

'Nah, it's Del who's got all in with her,' said Ruby. 'She's all, "Sal this and Sal that".'

'You think she thinks Sal's cooler than you?' said Elliot.

Ruby rolled her eyes. 'What is this, third grade?'

'You envious of her purple Dash sneakers, is that it?'

'My mistake, we seem to be back in kindergarten.'

'He's trying to wind you up,' said Mouse.

'Well he's succeeding,' said Ruby.

'So did you rat?' asked Elliot.

'What are you talking about?' said Ruby.

'Del,' said Elliot, 'did you rat on her?'

'Not this again! Have I ever ratted on anyone?' said Ruby.

Elliot didn't need to think about it. 'No, but did you?'

'Course she didn't bozo,' said Mouse. 'If it were *you* being interrogated then it's a probable certainty, but Ruby would never give up an ally.'

'But someone did, right?' said Elliot.

'Why would she take the punishment, miss the Explorer event, and then rat on Del?' asked Mouse.

'I was just testing,' said Elliot. 'It's what the cops do; they just ask the same question over and over until the suspect is so worn down that they just admit the truth.'

Mouse clapped her hand to her forehead. 'Jeepers Elliot.'

'He's right,' said Ruby, 'get 'em mad, get 'em confused, if they *are* lying then they get caught in their own tangled web. It's easy to trip people up this way.'

'It will be Vapona,' said Mouse. 'She wants to set you two against each other so she's spreading this rumour that you told Principal Levine on Del when of course it was her.'

Ruby thought this highly unlikely.

'Vapona would never do that. It's a dangerous game to point the finger at an enemy when they can turn around and point the finger back. If Del goes down then Bugwart gets dragged down with her. Vapona's a lot of things, but stupid ain't one.'

'I wonder who it was then,' said Elliot.

As it turned out, they didn't need to wait for an answer because Del walked in through the door of the table tennis cafe and told them straight out.

She was in no doubt as to who had got her in the dog house. It was not Vapona 'Bugwart' Begwell, it was not Mr Chester. 'It's Brenda Skelton,' declared Del.

Actually there was no way of *proving* it was Brenda Skelton, since the call had been anonymous. It had been made to the principal himself, from someone who claimed to have seen Del fighting outside Sunny's Diner. Actually, Principal Levine had told Mrs Lasco that the voice had sounded like it belonged to a young person, a teenager perhaps, but there was no way to confirm this either.

Mrs Lasco was no pushover and she knew exactly what was going on here.

'You don't want to cross my mom,' said Del proudly, 'she doesn't suffer fools.' Her mother, it seemed, had picked up the phone to Principal Levine and told him a thing or two about anonymous callers: *'Either this person comes out of the woodwork and accuses my daughter to her face or they can mind their own darned beeswax.'*

Principal Levine, on reflection, decided to drop the whole thing since he agreed he had: *'no solid evidence other than one person's word against another's'* and he didn't *'make a habit of playing fast and loose with justice'.*

Ruby had her own problems; unlike Del's, there were no anonymous accusations, but she *did* have a feeling somewhere deep in her gut that someone, somewhere, wanted to see her fall. Why else would Hitch urge her to brush up on her kung fu kicks?

Wake up and smell the banana milk, Redfort, someone's out to get you.

As a result, though her curfew had been lifted, she wasn't exactly feeling in the right state of mind for freedom. More than anything, she needed to get home. She made her excuses and left Del chatting happily to Sal about the injustice which had almost befallen her.

As Ruby walked back down Amster, she felt increasingly

uneasy. Was it simply paranoia brought on by the day's events, or was someone watching her? She looked around but could see no one. Even so she broke into a run when she reached the green, and then a sprint, arriving on her doorstep out of breath, adrenaline pumping.

Slamming the door behind her, she went straight on up to her room – no snack, no chat with Mrs Digby – and picked up the bottle from her desk. As she did so she saw a note from Hitch. It said:

That thing you asked me? It's a convenience store
called the Little Seven, in downtown Twinford.
That mean anything to you?

So she'd been right about the coordinates.

She hoped she was going to be right about this next bit too.

Carefully she peeled off the label and turned it over to properly examine the back. She'd *known* it reminded her of something... and now suddenly she knew what that was.

'Where's a road map?' She was looking at Bug, but he had no idea what she was on about. 'Mom's car!' She leapt to her feet, ready to sprint downstairs before realising her mother would have taken it to work. She tapped her fingers on the desk. 'The downstairs bathroom!' she shouted.

Bug began to wag his tail; he didn't know what was going on, but Ruby seemed excited about something. She raced down the two flights of stairs. Bug followed close behind. When they arrived in the hall, he picked up his leash in his mouth and was confused when, rather than open the front door again, Ruby dodged into the small guest bathroom. Her mother had had it wallpapered with a scaled-up map of Twinford, showing all the road junctions. The tasteful of Twinford might doubt its success as a piece of interior decorating, but many a guest had found it a very practical way of planning their journey home.

Ruby scanned the walls, trying to find the part of the map she needed. It turned out it was above the toilet and Ruby had to stand on the seat to reach it. She studied the map, tracing the roads until she reached the concert hall where she'd encountered the goons.

It was when she held up the label printed with the strange logo that she saw it. The shape almost exactly mirrored the layout of the roads in the College Town district. The eight-pointed star at the logo's centre was the exact same shape as that of Star Park.

This wasn't simply a logo: this was a road map.

Chapter 40.
Tesseract

RUBY SPRINTED TO HER DAD'S STUDY AND GRABBED A
PENCIL AND A PIECE OF PAPER. Then she headed back to
the bathroom. Working quickly, she redrew the shape and then
circled the concert hall.

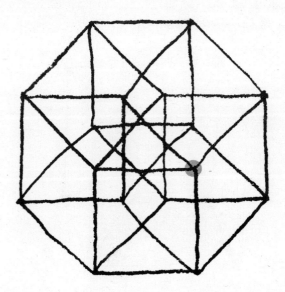

There it was, at the intersection of four roads.

OK Redfort, think. If the logo is a map then what does it use for coordinates? She let her mind go empty, and just gazed at the label.

At the logo.

At the caption: FOUR GREAT TASTES SINCE 1922.

Four.

Tastes.

Four.

Four!

How could she have been so blind? For the final answer she'd drawn a tesseract – a 4-dimensional cube. To fake it, she'd had to draw its shadow in 3D. Actually a 2D picture of the 3D shadow! Now she sketched it again.

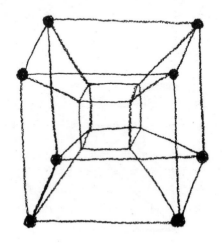

But if you turn a shape then its shadow changes. So what if she drew the shadow from a different angle? As she turned the shape in her mind she suddenly saw that by twisting the perspective you would end up with... the logo on the bottle.

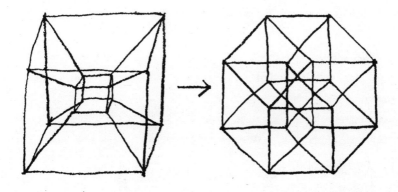

It was the same thing. The same shape, rendered in different ways. The logo was a road map: but it was also a 4-dimensional cube.

Four dimensions meant four coordinates for each point. She drew the logo again – the 2-dimensional projection of the 4-dimensional cube – and sketched in the coordinates for each point.

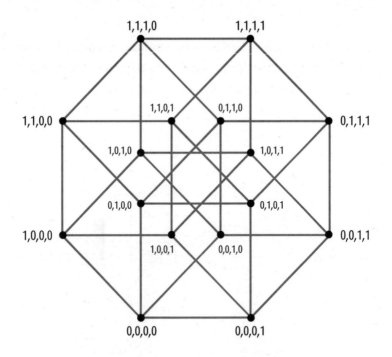

She stared at the label again.

FOUR GREAT TASTES.

'Four, great, tastes,' she muttered. 'Four, great, tastes.'

'Taste!' she shouted. Bug yelped.

Of *course!* thought Ruby. Because there *were* four tastes, weren't there? Salt, bitter, sour, sweet. So if you wanted to lead someone to a point on the map... all you needed to do was put the right combination of tastes into the bottle – a 1 if the taste was there and a 0 if the taste wasn't – and you could pinpoint a location.

She kept scribbling. What taste would correspond to what coordinate? The natural thing would be to order the tastes as they appeared on the tongue map. She sketched it out.

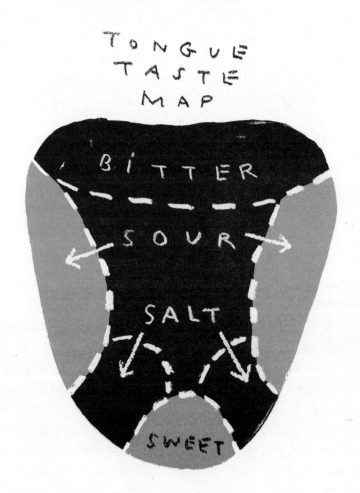

TONGUE TASTE MAP

BITTER

SOUR

SALT

SWEET

{0,0,0,0}	TASTELESS

{1,0,0,0}	**BITTER**
{0,1,0,0}	**SOUR**
{0,0,1,0}	**SALT**
{0,0,0,1}	**SWEET**

{1,1,0,0}	BITTER SOUR
{1,0,1,0}	BITTER SALT
{1,0,0,1}	BITTER SWEET
{0,1,1,0}	SOUR SALT
{0,1,0,1}	SOUR SWEET
{0,0,1,1}	SALT SWEET

{1,1,1,0}	**BITTER SOUR SALT**
{1,1,0,1}	**BITTER SOUR SWEET**
{1,0,1,1}	**BITTER SALT SWEET**
{0,1,1,1}	**SOUR SALT SWEET**

{1,1,1,1}	BITTER SOUR SALT SWEET

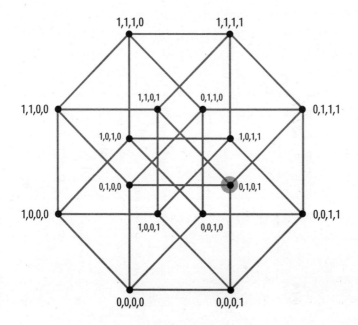

Then she circled the music school again, this time on the drawing with the coordinates.

(0,1,0,1) would correspond to... SOUR SWEET.

Bingo.

The first bottle had been sugar and lemon in water. Sweet and sour. Sour and sweet. Or, if you mapped it using binary, in four dimensions of taste...

(0,1,0,1)

It was clever. Fiendishly clever.

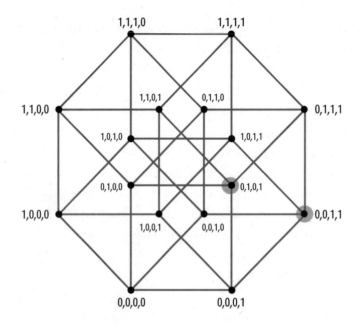

So where was the second bottle pointing to? Ruby cast her mind back to the lab, with SJ. *Salt and sugar* – that's what the second bottle had contained. Salt and sweet. She circled the matching point on the shape.

Then she held it up next to the map of Twinford, looking for the corresponding place on the College Town district road map.

'The Mirror,' said Ruby. Bug looked up, ears alert, but 'Mirror' meant nothing to him.

'That's the Twinford Mirror building,' she said. This time

Bug didn't lift his head. He was bored of this game. No treats, no walks.

The billboard had given her the first location, which was the Little Seven Grocers on Little Seven Street. The bottle bought from the Little Seven Grocers had announced where the next bottle could be found: the university music school, as it turned out. The *third* bottle would be located somewhere in the Twinford Mirror building on Gödel Avenue.

She was about to grab her coat and run right down there when a thought occurred to her. Who was to say the bottle would even be there right now? After all, the guy in the red hat hadn't immediately scooted off to the music school the second he had tasted the contents of the bottle he had got from the Little Seven Grocers. In fact he hadn't shown up there until four days later. So the question to ask was, how did he know *when* it would be there?

She wondered if she was too late already. It could be that if there was a bottle at the Twinford Mirror building and it hadn't already been taken away by the man in the red hat, then it had been found by someone else – maybe a janitor had disposed of its partly drunk contents and it was sitting at the bottom of a garbage can.

How to know?

She picked up the bottle, turning it round and round, reading every word on the label before finally twisting the lid back on top and then...

Click.

She saw what she hadn't seen before.

No! No, it would not be there, not now, not yet. She knew this for a certainty now. OK, not a certainty, but she would have staked the contents of her piggy bank on it. The drink she had tasted was just salt and sugar and water – it would last almost forever when the bottle was closed. So it was strange that the best before date stamped on the lid was tomorrow's date.

There was something else unusual about the lid. Around its edge were twelve little dashes, all slanting in, reminding her of a clock face. One of the dashes was coloured red. What if it represented a time, in this case eleven? But did this mean eleven in the morning or eleven in the evening? She could see nothing else that might tell her. She flipped out the magnification glass from the Escape Watch and held it over the lid and there it was, very faint but just possible to see: the letters PM.

This was a breakthrough – this was something to tell Blacker.

She was about to radio him when there was a buzz from her watch. The message read:

>> MEET ME IN LUCELLO'S.

Chapter 41.
Best before

SHE LOCATED LUCELLO'S DELI EASILY ENOUGH. It was in the heart of the Village, sometimes referred to as Little Italy, a part of town known for its bohemian cafes, Italian shops and interesting residents. People travelled across town to purchase their squash tortellini and twenty-year-aged pecorino; during the Christmas season queues could be seen circling the block. It had become very up-market.

One of those interesting residents Ruby was surprised to see while walking to the deli was Sal from the Back-Spin. As Ruby crossed Constanza, she saw Sal walk up to an exclusive apartment building – formerly a tea warehouse – carrying bags of expensive-looking groceries. The doorman opened the door for her and she went in.

Huh, Ruby thought. *Either Back-Spin pays ten times the minimum wage or Sal does have a rich ma and pa after all.* She couldn't wait to tell Del. *I knew she was a phoney!* A moment later – about the time it would take to go up in an elevator – a light came on in a topfloor window.

Penthouse, thought Ruby. *Scratch that – filthy rich ma and pa; super phoney.*

She continued on her way to Lucello's.

Hitch was standing at the counter sipping espresso.

He spotted Ruby's arrival in the mirror. 'You eaten kid?'

'A snack,' said Ruby, 'but the apple donuts look good.'

'We'll take a donut, Paulie,' said Hitch, handing the man a few bills, 'better make that two.'

Ruby looked around her. 'So where's the door?'

'Same place,' said Hitch. 'I only told you Lucello's because the coffee's good.' He pulled on his raincoat, turning up the collar against the cold, and they headed out into the wind and drizzle. Newly fallen leaves and hotdog wrappers chased each other along the sidewalk and into the shadows. Ruby and Hitch crossed the street, turning left until they reached Broker Avenue.

'So you had a breakthrough kid?'

'How dya know?' said Ruby. 'You got me bugged or something?'

'No,' said Hitch, 'I've just got confidence in you.'

'That's good,' said Ruby. 'I get the feeling you might be alone in that.'

'If that was a fact then you wouldn't be working here,' he said. 'So you finally cracked something?'

'I have no idea what any of it means, but I've cracked the code,' said Ruby.

Hitch raised an eyebrow. 'Sounds complicated.'

'So who wants to see me?' she looked at him. 'Oh, don't tell me, Dr Selgood wants a chat?'

'Worse than that kid, your boss wants to see you – alone,' he added.

'Why?' said Ruby.

Hitch shrugged. 'Maybe she wants to tell you how great you are, how should I know?'

When they arrived, they shook of the rain and walked over to where Buzz sat.

'Agent Redfort, you can go right on in,' said Buzz.

Ruby turned to Hitch. 'You sure you're not coming?' she asked.

'You're on your own kid.'

Perfect, muttered Ruby.

Chapter 42.
The truth but not the whole truth

RUBY KNOCKED AND WAITED FOR LB'S 'COME IN' before she opened the door and stepped inside.

'Sit,' said LB.

Ruby sat and LB opened the file that lay on her desk.

'I regret I couldn't meet with you when you were last in.' She looked down at the file. 'Hitch has brought me up to speed on what you *say* you witnessed at the music school.'

Ruby noted LB's use of words – like she was not 100% sure Ruby was telling the truth.

'He informed me that you believe there may be a connection back to the *Australian*.' Again LB read from the file. 'So this man you followed in Harker Square. The man in the red hat. You say he works for her?'

'Yes, he was on the way to meet a couple of beefcakes at the university music school.'

LB looked at her, one eyebrow raised.

'Goons for hire, you know, leg breakers?' said Ruby.

Her boss's expression morphed into one of irritation.

'Assassins?' said Ruby.

LB nodded. 'Yes, the assassins, they are both locked up downtown and undergoing police questioning.'

'Has either one of them squealed?' asked Ruby.

LB looked at her impatiently. 'This is not an episode of *Crazy Cops*, Redfort. Could you please refrain from using this appalling TV slang.'

'Sorry, I mean, are they talking? Did they say anything? Anything we don't already know?'

'I'm afraid not,' said LB, 'though it's not unusual for hard nuts...' LB corrected herself, 'criminals for hire, to keep their silence. No doubt talking to *us* would bring about "consequences" – none of them very pleasant, I'm sure.'

'So we don't know who this Aussie woman... I mean Australian woman is and who she is working for?'

'No, not yet,' said LB, 'though what interests me is that *you* are the only one to have seen her.'

'You're beginning to sound like Agent Delaware.'

'Well, at the risk of sounding like him again, do you have any thoughts on why this might be?'

'Just lucky I guess.'

'Spectrum has never picked up on her, there has never been any sighting of any woman fitting the description you gave us, what was it –' she read from the file – 'a "comfortably dressed middle-aged woman, floral dress, blonde hair, blue eyes, shoulder purse, gun".'

'What do you want me to say – maybe I just bring out the psychopathic tendencies in people?'

'That sounds totally plausible,' said LB.

'What exactly are you asking me?' said Ruby.

'What I am asking *myself*,' said LB, giving her a stern stare, 'is why Spectrum, with all its agents, all its intelligence and high-tech search-and-find equipment, can't even begin to find a match for the woman you describe.'

'You think I invented her?' said Ruby. 'Who do you think persuaded me to walk backwards off that cliff edge on Wolf Paw Mountain?'

'Could you have slipped, hallucinated, maybe? You were under a lot of stress.'

'Now you're sounding like Dr Selgood,' said Ruby.

'I'm trying to get to the cold unemotional heart of things – that's my job,' said LB.

'Well, this woman you don't think exists is back in Twinford and planning murder,' said Ruby.

'Oh, yes,' said LB peering down at her file, 'you overheard a man with an Australian accent quote his boss and use the word "sweetie" – so you're saying this boss would be her?'

Ruby nodded.

LB was about to quiz her again on the subject when she paused and said, 'Redfort, why do you have the words WAKE UP AND SMELL THE BANANA MILK inked on your arm?'

As it transpired, Ruby didn't have to answer that question

because LB's telephone began to ring. She picked up the receiver. 'I'll be there in two minutes.' She pointed to the door and without another word, Ruby exited the room.

When Ruby arrived back in the atrium, she found Hitch gone and not an agent soul to be seen. Only the mushroom was left. She walked over to where Buzz sat, her coloured telephones beeping and blinking.

'So where is everybody?' asked Ruby.

'In a briefing,' replied Buzz.

'What briefing?' said Ruby.

'It's classified,' said Buzz.

'Shouldn't I be in there?'

'No.'

'Why not?'

'You're not on the list.'

'What list?'

Buzz pointed up at the names projected on the huge white wall of the atrium.

'That list, you're not on it.'

And it was true, she wasn't, just about everyone else was, but she wasn't.

'Everyone else seems to be on it,' she said.

'Well, they're not,' said Buzz. 'Not everyone is on the list.'

It was a very 'Buzz' reply, annoying yet accurate, and there was little point arguing about it.

'Blacker,' said Ruby.

'Pardon?'

'Blacker, he's not on the list.'

'No.'

'So I think I might just go down to his office and pay him a visit.'

'He's not in.'

'Where is he?'

'He's not in.'

'Jeepers Buzz, could you be a little less helpful.'

'I'm not here to be helpful.'

'Well, congratulations on not straying from your employment brief.'

Buzz made no wisecrack smart reply, it wasn't her style, which was because she wouldn't know a wisecrack smart reply if it bonked her on the nose.

'Could you perhaps do me a big favour and contact Blacker and tell him I have solved the Taste Twister conundrum – it's a code, by the way,' said Ruby. 'Here, this is the bottle and these are my workings, tells him everything he needs to know, including the time. I'm sure he'll be super interested when he finally makes it in.'

Buzz was clearly not interested. 'Leave it on the table in the administration room, I will schedule a contact call,' she said.

Jeepers, thought Ruby, *do you ever feel a desire to be impulsive?*

But what she actually said was, 'I appreciate your help. Look, is it OK if I go to the canteen and eat my apple donut while I wait for Hitch?'

The telephone operator looked at her without expression and said, 'Yes.'

So Ruby picked up the little brown bag containing the two donuts from Lucello's and headed down the corridor to the Spectrum canteen. She'd reached the bank of elevators when it occurred to her it might be a nice touch to leave one of these delicious marvels on Blacker's desk. He was no small fan of the donut.

She was nearing the coding room when she saw a man coming out. He didn't look in her direction, but she recognised him as the agent Blacker had been speaking with the other day, the one whose eyebrows met in the middle. He didn't see her and she didn't do anything to attract his attention. The guy gave her the creeps. He had left the door slightly ajar and she was about to push on in when she heard a voice.

Blacker's voice. He was talking to someone on the phone.

'Yes, I'm on to it...'

She listened.

'It's strictly classified... my job is to lock this thing down... it's only by luck and happenstance that she hasn't heard.'

Who hasn't heard? thought Ruby. *And what hasn't she heard?*

'She's struck out on her own – so until we find out what's occurring, say nothing... yes, that's correct.'

He must be talking about someone outside of coding? But why would he need to say this? It was entirely understood that information would be released when the coding team deemed it useful.

'I know it's irregular but I'm telling you, it's important that it doesn't reach her... she mustn't suspect. Just keep watching.'

Or was it someone higher up the food chain? Not LB, surely not LB...

Her mind was beginning to spin. But as it happened she was right, he wasn't talking about LB.

'I repeat,' he said, 'she's a loose cannon, who knows what she'll do, she's a danger to all concerned... Look, how many ways have I got to say this, she's dangerously unhinged.'

And then:

'So whatever you do, don't let Redfort in on this.'

Ruby felt the breath knocked out of her, though she hadn't been struck.

As quietly as she could she backed away from the door, and when it was safe to, she ran.

She managed to make it back to the exit without anyone noticing her, and while Buzz was engaged on a call, she slipped past her into the administration room.

The admin team showed no sign of interest as Ruby walked over to the package still sitting on the desk.

She was aware that she couldn't do anything about the information she had already passed onto Blacker, too late to change that, too late to unsolve the code. Once he knew the Taste Twister puzzle was cracked, he would pick up the third clue and maybe she needed this clue herself – if she didn't crack this case then she couldn't prove that she wasn't some unreliable loose cannon, or worse: dangerously unhinged.

She couldn't stop him knowing about it but she could take back one small piece of information.

'What are you doing?'

Ruby spun around to see Miles Froghorn not two feet away from her.

'That's Spectrum property,' he said, his eyes fixed on the bottle.

She counted to six.

'I am aware of that, I was the one who brought it in to HQ and *made* it Spectrum property,' said Ruby, trying to keep her voice calm and even and resist the urge to call this potatohead a potatohead.

'It's evidence,' said Froghorn.

'I know, Froghorn,' this time she observed the silent G, 'which is why I am putting it in the refrigerator – it needs to be kept chilled.'

Agent Froghorn seemed grudgingly satisfied with this and watched her place the bottle in the chiller. He did *not* notice her unscrew the lid and let it fall inside her sleeve. Nor did he notice how she replaced it with another lid, taken from another random bottle in the chiller – one with today's date on it.

Blacker might know where the next location was, but only *she* knew the right time to be there.

Chapter 43.
Ride the wind

RUBY MADE HER WAY BACK UP TO THE SUPERMARKET
and found herself once again in canned goods, which was exactly
how she felt.

As she walked out into the dark of the evening, she pushed
her hands deep into her pockets, wishing she had remembered
her gloves. She felt something and pulled out the white card
embossed with the Yellow Wind-Dragon.

She stopped still there on the sidewalk. She turned the card
over and over in her hand as she turned the possibilities over
and over in her mind.

1) **Blacker was the mole**
2) **Blacker thought _she_ was the mole**
3) **Blacker thought she was dangerously unhinged**
4) *...something else.*

Whatever it was, it wasn't going to be good. People were being
left off lists. She was being left off lists. Blacker was warning

people about her behind her back. The Australian woman was out there somewhere... Her mind was running away with itself now. **RULE 8: DON'T LET YOUR IMAGINATION RUN AWAY WITH YOU OR YOU MIGHT WELL LOSE THE PLOT.** Maybe this was a good time to visit the Yellow Wind-Dragon dojo.

She drew her hood down firmly over her head, walked to the Crossways subway and took the College Town line to Cathedral where she changed trains and took the Red Line to Chinatown.

It would have been easy enough to walk past the building – it showed no sign of what it might be, just plain brick with an unwelcoming metal door set to one side. Spray painted onto the door were the same Chinese characters as on the card.

She tried the door, not expecting it to give, but it did and in she went. The interior bore no relation to the outside. It was a tranquil space, no harsh lighting, carved wooden pillars, practice mats, sliding opaque screens and much bigger than the Spectrum dojo.

She was greeted by a man in a white *gi* who, once she had explained who she was, led her to Jen Yu.

'Ruby Redfort?'

'That's me.'

'Hitch told me you would come.'

'Yeah, well he was right.'

'Who taught you?'

'Li Mu Bai.'

'So you studied White Leopard kung fu?'

Ruby nodded.

'Very aggressive.'

Again Ruby nodded.

'Strikes many times and aims to kill.'

Ruby said nothing.

'So I will teach you something different – a style of kung fu suited to someone of your slight build. It uses momentum, fluidity and speed at its heart.'

The lesson began and it was all about dragons.

'You can create more power in your strike when the movement originates from the feet,' said Jen Yu. 'Use your waist to guide it and let it flow through your body and exit through your fist. I will demonstrate. Stand in a neutral stance.'

Ruby frowned. 'You're going to punch me?'

'Well, yes. How do you expect to improve your kung fu without getting punched?'

Ruby nodded; she understood. She settled into a ready stance. But she wasn't ready at all. With amazing power and speed, Jen Yu suddenly moved her hands forwards and up, sending Ruby reeling.

Ruby picked herself up from the mat, a little winded.

'Back into your stance,' said Jen Yu.

Ruby did as she was told – Jen Yu was not a teacher to be argued with.

'Dragon leg work is characterised by a zigzag motion,' continued the teacher. 'This mimics the movement of the dragon.

This also enables one to use floating and sinking movements – these are very important in generating power and stability, making one's body calm and relaxed. But they are also important because you will learn to ride the wind. In dragon-style kung fu, this means to follow rather than lead. But in Yellow Wind-Dragon kung fu, this also means to fly.'

Ruby liked the sound of that.

'Yellow Wind-Dragon uses the momentum of the body to carry oneself high into the air, the feet only touching the ground in order to propel you up. Use this momentum to rotate over the head of your opponent; much of your fighting will be airborne. Like this.'

Ruby was even less ready this time. Jen Yu jumped into the air and seemed to float there, then turned into a kick that knocked Ruby flat on her back on the mat again. Ruby got up. 'How do I learn how to do that?' she said, when her breath was back.

Jen Yu smiled, and bowed. 'Simple,' she said. 'You practise over and over until you can do it.'

Ruby arrived home late to find Hitch in the kitchen; he looked like he might have been waiting for her.

HITCH: *'So how did your meeting with the boss go?'*
RUBY: *'Usual thing.'*
HITCH: *'Did you let her in on your big discovery?'*
RUBY: *'I didn't see the point.'*

HITCH: *'Something bothering you kid?'*

RUBY: *'Why would there be?'*

HITCH: *'Well you look like your pet hamster just died, so I'm figuring something's up.'*

RUBY: *'Yeah, well, now you mention it, there is actually.'*

HITCH: *'Are you planning on telling me, or do you want me to guess?'*

RUBY: *'The briefing tonight – how come I wasn't on the list?'*

HITCH: *'You weren't required to be there, nothing personal.'*

RUBY: *'It's not personal that I was the only agent not required?'*

HITCH: *'Not true, Alonso wasn't there.'*

RUBY: *'I happen to know that Alonso is in the hospital having his appendix removed, so that really doesn't count.'*

HITCH: *'Look kid, what you need to understand is that there are a whole lot of things you don't know about. Let's be honest here, there are a whole lot of things I don't know about. Let's take your meeting with LB – I have no idea what that little tête-à-tête was about, but what I figure is, LB has her reasons.'*

Ruby was getting the message loud and clear: focus on your own stuff and stop whining about everyone else's.

She noted that Hitch didn't bring up Blacker. Why not? It would have been the obvious thing to do. Blacker would be the one agent's name that would have prevented her feeling sore about being left off the list.

So Hitch knows he was in the building.

But did Hitch know what Blacker was playing at? Did he know Blacker was making phone calls, warning people not to talk to her, not to trust her? Spreading rumours and poisoning the mind of every agent in Spectrum? And if he did, then was he standing up for her or was he just standing back waiting to see how it all played out?

She tried to banish the thoughts as she lay on her bed that night, but they kept creeping back, staving off sleep and twisting her mind into a knot of dead ends. Unable to fight it, she lay back on her pillow and let her paranoia lead her to dark places.

Chapter 44.
Shaking hands with the enemy

RUBY LEFT THE HOUSE EARLY THE NEXT MORNING, partly because of the previous evening's uncomfortable conversation with Hitch, and partly because she couldn't sleep. She'd managed perhaps two hours between 2am and 4am, and seeing how she was awake, she thought she might as well try and earn herself a punctuality point from Mrs Drisco.

She arrived well before the bell was due to sound. None of her friends were there so she sat down on a bench and took out her comic and decided to read until one of them tapped her on the shoulder. To her surprise it was *Vapona Begwell* who did the tapping.

'Look Redfort, I don't like you but I gotta say, I appreciate what you did, you're no snitch. You coulda blabbed to Levine, but you didn't.'

Then, the weirdest thing of all, Vapona Begwell stuck out her arm and shook Ruby's hand, a firm, almost crushing handshake, the sort that might break a finger or two, but a handshake nonetheless.

'I guess I owe you,' she said. 'I don't like owing people.' Then she turned on her heel and walked off down the corridor.

Had the world gone mad? What was going on here? Her fellow agents didn't trust her but her sworn enemy was shaking her by the hand.

Ruby didn't want company that day; she needed to collect her thoughts, understand what was going on here and figure out how she was going to deal with it. She particularly wanted to avoid Clancy, not because this was something she couldn't talk about with him but because this was something she didn't want him getting in a stew about – it was one thing him fearing the bad guys might take a pop at his best friend, it was another fearing that the so-called good guys were also on her tail. No, best not tell Clancy.

For once it was pretty easy to dodge him as he was completely immersed in his behavioural science project, setting up his little camera in the corridor, adjusting the angle, loading the tape, and for this reason his usually highly sensitive antennae was tuned to low. He barely seemed to notice that she was absent at recess, choosing to spend the breaks in the school library. In fact the truth was, none of her friends noticed.

She was in math class when a message flashed up on the Bradley Baker watch.

She stared at it, the words vivid, spelled out in green light.

>> COME IN WHEN YOU CAN. BLACKER.

She left school five minutes before the bell sounded; she wanted to get out ahead of the others, didn't want to get caught up in any tricky lies and explanations as she headed to the subway rather than the bus stop.

She thought about what she was going to say to Blacker and she thought about **RULE 51: WHEN YOU DON'T TRUST THE OTHER PLAYERS, ALWAYS PLAY YOUR CARDS CLOSE TO YOUR CHEST.**

She went right on down to the coding room and as she walked through the door she gave Blacker her usual good-natured smirk.

'You wanted to see me?' she said, like butter wouldn't melt.

'Hey Ruby, sorry I missed you yesterday,' said Blacker.

'Yeah, you should be because you lost out on a pretty nice donut.'

'That's too bad,' said Blacker.

'Yeah, I nearly came down to your office and left it on your desk.' She waited for a flicker of unease, but there was none. 'I was halfway down there and then I decided to eat it myself.'

'You probably did me a favour, Rube, I need to clean up my act as far as my diet goes,' said Blacker.

'Yeah, maybe you should,' said Ruby. *Boy, this guy,* she thought, *cool as a cucumber.* She was trying to gauge what might be going on behind the eyes, but she could see nothing. He was talking the talk. Smiling the smile.

'Good going on the Taste Twister decode. Froghorn passed it on. You know, he actually looked impressed – a rare sight, wish I'd had a camera.'

Ruby smiled back. 'Woulda been a waste of film,' she said.

'Smart of you to figure out the lid of the bottle gave us the date of the pick up. It's simple, but it's the simple things which are so easy to overlook,' said Blacker. 'Just a shame we didn't make it to the Twinford Mirror building in time. I went down there myself, but came back with nothing.' He sighed heavily and then looked at her. 'You were sure that was the original bottle top?'

Was he seeing through her or was he swallowing her deception in one easy bite?

Ruby shrugged. 'There wasn't another one if that's what you're asking. I mean the red hat guy could have swapped it I guess, but why? Why leave the bottle if he thought there was a chance it would be found?' Not a flicker, not a blink. She wasn't a bad liar either.

Two can play at this game, she thought.

'That's that then,' sighed Blacker. 'We had the location but we missed the pick-up.'

Ruby did a good job of pulling her face into an expression which conjured extreme frustration combined with downright disappointment.

Blacker's watch beeped: he checked it, sighed again and said, 'Look, I have to go, but keep me updated on this, OK? You see anything strange, I mean *anything*, and you contact me.'

Ruby nodded. She wasn't going to feel bad about this. He didn't trust her, so she didn't trust him. But what she really wanted to know was just how deep this went, how many other agents had been warned off talking to her? She thought for a moment and decided that the best place to start might be the coding office and, more specifically, Froghorn's desk. Froghorn's office door would be locked, his files would be password protected, but neither of these two issues were exactly problems.

Getting into the room was a cinch, the number he had chosen for his door code, I mean please... who picked the Catalan numbers series and actually expected to get away with it? She keyed in 12514.

Once she was in she began by looking in his desk, and when this search threw up nothing useful she set to work figuring out his file safe code. Again, a no-brainer. The lazy caterer's sequence? Jeepers. This was sophomore stuff. She turned the dial on the safe: 1 click left, 2 right, 4 left, 7 right, 11 left.

With a clunk, it opened.

Rummaging through someone else's desk at Spectrum was, of course, strictly a no-no, and sneaking information out of the file room no doubt a firing offence, but as she would have told anyone had she been caught: *if it was such a big deal then the keeper of those files should have thought up a better password for his file drawer.* Or as her T-shirt so aptly put it: ***you snooze, you loose, sucker***.

Ruby let her fingers walk across the files until they reached R, Rabin, Railey, Reads, Redfort.

Slowly she pulled her file from its slot and laid it on the table. She didn't have to do much looking, she opened the cover and her blood froze.

Chapter 45.
Going it alone

AS SHE STEPPED OUT OF THE SUBWAY, UTTER DARKNESS SEEMED TO ENVELOP HER. There were no streetlights, no store lights and no house lights to guide her way home. The pitch black was all there was, no buildings, no trees, no road ahead. It would be easy to lose oneself in this nothing land. Someone was trying to destroy her – was it Blacker alone who wanted her gone?

In her pocket was a photo, taken with a polaroid camera she'd found on Froghorn's desk.

But what should she do with it? Who could she show?

Her problem now was if *she* couldn't trust Blacker, then how could she rely on anyone who did? How could she trust anyone who trusted *him*?

Blacker was a likeable guy, always steady, always even, never rattled, at least not by people – soda, yes; jelly donuts, always; but when it came to people he was steady as they came.

She thought about this as she let herself in and made her way upstairs to her room. Could it be that his whole clumsiness thing was an act, a cover, was it just a way of distracting people? The smiling likeable fool, like that TV cop, the one in the raincoat with the uncombed hair... The guy looked a mess, like he had just rolled out of bed or spent the night sleeping in his tin can of a car, but this was a ruse to throw folk off the scent. His brain was razor sharp and when criminals let down their guard, he took them apart. Was that what Blacker was?

Had he been put there to observe her, lull her into a false sense of security so he could assess her strengths, her weaknesses, and report back? Did he think she was incompetent? Or was it worse than that – she felt a stab of panic – was *she* the suspect? Did Blacker actually think it could be *her* – Spectrum's mole, the double agent? She was beginning to feel like she had been dropped into some seventy-five-cent thriller, where the tables had turned and suddenly the good guys were all pointing their fingers at her; the bad guys too.

There was a knock at the window and Ruby nearly jumped out of her sneakers.

'Let me in would you,' came a muffled voice.

Ruby peered into the dark. 'Clancy, what are you doing out there?'

'Checking up on you bozo, now let me in, it's creepy out here, all the power lines are down.'

She unlatched the window and he climbed through.

'So what happened?' asked Clancy. 'One minute you were there, the next you were nowhere.'

'I've had a lot on my mind.'

'School, home or Spectrum?' asked Clancy.

'All three, as it happens, but right now my biggest headache is Blacker.'

'You're being paranoid Rube.'

'Am I? So why would he get Buzz to tell me he was out of HQ when I happen to know he was there?'

'You're sure?'

'I saw him with my own two eyes. Not only that but he was busy on the phone warning someone not to talk to me, does that sound like a guy who's on the same side?'

'OK,' said Clancy, 'but maybe he had his reasons.'

'I'd like to hear them,' said Ruby.

'It's just I'm not sure Rube, I mean you were wrong about the rain.'

'I *might* have been wrong about the rain, but how do I even know?'

'Because of what happened to Elliot?' suggested Clancy.

'Doesn't prove anything,' she said. 'You can argue all you like Clancy, but I got 100% proof.'

'OK, so show me the evidence,' said Clancy.

Ruby took out the polaroids and laid them on the table so the message could be read.

'What is this?' asked Clancy.

'I broke into the file room and this is what I found,' said Ruby.

FOR THE ATTENTION OF ALL AGENTS:
CLASSIFIED, DO NOT SPEAK TO REDFORT,
DO NOT CONVEY LATEST INFORMATION, DENY ALL.
SIGNED: BLACKER.

'He might come over as Mr Apple-pie-down-the-tie, Clancy, but he sure as darn it speaks with a forked tongue.'

Clancy was all out of arguments. He just looked at her, looked right into her eyes and said, 'I didn't see this coming, and I'm usually good with my hunches.'

'Well, he's not a secret agent for nothing,' said Ruby. 'He's got one heck of a poker face. The whole time we've been working together he's been keeping his beedy eyes on me and it turns out he doesn't trust me one iota.'

'So what are you gonna do?' said Clancy.

'I'm going to have to go it alone,' said Ruby, 'nothing else for it.'

'That sounds like a truly bad idea,' said Clancy.

'Well, it seems I don't have a whole lotta choice, Clance.'

'What do you mean? You have a whole team of agents down there, under the supermarket – talk to one of *them*.'

'You don't get it Clancy. I mean, if Blacker doesn't trust me, then who does? Not Froghorn, that's for darned sure. Agent Gill thinks I'm a hot head, Dr Selgood thinks I have a God complex, so I can't see him exactly backing me up.'

'And Hitch?' said Clancy.

'It doesn't matter what Hitch says. Once Blacker makes his case, I'll be canned.'

'But what evidence does he have? I mean, there isn't any,' said Clancy.

'LB's been trying to find any reason she can to fire me. She never wanted me in Spectrum in the first place.'

'She hired you, didn't she?'

'Only because there was no one else.'

'You're saying you don't trust *anyone* to back you?' said Clancy.

Ruby looked down at her arm, the words written by Del in that most permanent of permanent markers were still there and she sort of half smiled, half sighed. 'I guess I need to wake up and smell the banana milk. I'm all alone in this and no one's gonna get me out of it but me.'

She stared into the darkness, there was nothing to see, no moon, no streetlights... It was hard to believe a city existed beyond her room.

What Ruby hadn't told anyone, not even Clancy, was that she was going to the Twinford Mirror building that night, following the location and date on the last bottle.

RULE 11: BE PREPARED, she told herself.

Ruby hoped it would be an in and out sort of job, but she couldn't count on it. She thought she knew where the bottle would be and there shouldn't be too much trouble getting into the Twinford Mirror building since newspapers worked through the night. Being spotted was going to be the problem.

She got changed into the jumpsuit Hitch had given her, the one that was not only super warm, should one decide to scale a two-hundred-foot wall, but also had glider wings concealed inside the back zip. It was thanks to these glider wings that she hadn't gone splat when Lorelei von Leyden dropped her off the hotel roof.

She glanced in the mirror and saw she looked not unlike some kind of schoolgirl superhero. The jumpsuit was cooler than the usual stretchy stuff they made superheroes wear – one thing you could say for Spectrum: they knew style.

She pulled her coat on over the jumpsuit and grabbed her backpack, opened the window and slipped out into the night.

She ran most of the way through the city, her parkour skills coming in handy for propelling her over walls and onto roofs, leaping alleyways and stairways, taking shortcuts, her feet barely touching the ground.

She arrived at Gödel Avenue, snuck down a side alley and slipped into the Twinford Mirror building through a restroom window, her small frame easily wriggling through the tiny opening. She hadn't gone more then a few yards down the corridor when she saw it.

The bottle stood on top of a vending machine just to the left of the doors that led to the canteen. She reached up, checked the lid was on securely and popped the Taste Twister in her backpack.

Nothing to it. No grizzling baby, no giveaway tell-tale beepers or squeakers or bouncing pacifiers – piece of cake.

She went straight home and once inside the door climbed the stairs to her room.

She twisted the lid off the bottle and sniffed the liquid: acidic.

She tasted it: and spat it out immediately.

Geez. Cabbagey. It reminded her of something, a drink she had smelled before. She could almost hear Consuela's voice urging her to drink it. This was the unmistakeable bitter flavour of kale. Mixed with... something salty? And maple syrup?

So: kale, salt and maple syrup.

In other words:

Bitter, salt, sweet.

In digits:

(1,0,1,1)

She ran back down to the guest bathroom, stepped up on the toilet and searched the map on the wall. She traced her fingers along the grid until she identified the location.

It was the city's movie museum on Fibonacci Street. Twinfordites often referred to it affectionately as The Bodice Ripper Museum on account of the Twinford motion picture industry, which was famed for making a huge number of romantic costume dramas back in the day. The museum had a lot of monster costumes as well, zombies, vampires, mummies and the like – the thriller genre had been big business too.

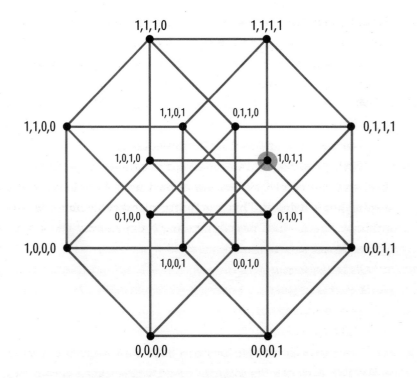

She checked the date on the bottle top. The date was three days away.

The time for collection: 1am.

She just needed to hold her nerve.

Chapter 46.
How to suck eggs

THE NEXT MORNING RUBY LEFT FOR SCHOOL JUST LIKE ALWAYS, but when she made it to the bus stop she just kept on walking. There was a payphone next to the subway steps, she pushed in her quarter and dialled the school secretary.

'Oh Hello, is that Mrs Bexenheath? It's Sabina Redfort here, proud mother of Ruby... I wonder if you could advise, I do so value your experience with all things disease... I may be wrong, but Ruby is exhibiting all the signs of possible pink eye and I don't wish to teach you how to suck eggs since I am sure, given your daily interaction with children, you could write a book on conjunctivitis, but I believe pink eye is highly contagious... I want to keep her home today and see what transpires, but you know Ruby, she's all about the learning and is just insisting on making her classes today despite the doctor warning me that she might be a walking bacteria bomb, so I guess what I am asking is, should she come to school and perhaps start an epidemic or should I keep her at home?... I quite agree... thank you, Mrs Bexenheath, I will... and if we're wrong you will see her tomorrow, bright-eyed and bushy tailed... thank you! You have put my mind at

ease... what would we parents do without your knowledge on these gruesome matters!'

Then she skipped down the subway steps and rode the train to Chinatown and the Yellow Wind-Dragon dojo.

She practised until 2pm.

At 2.30pm she arrived at the Twinford council offices, changed into some orange overalls (much too large) and was issued with a roll of plastic sacks, a pair of thick gloves and a trash grabber.

'OK Redfort,' said the guy doling out the community service tasks, 'you got your first three hours today, you got your instructions, you know what do.'

She headed off to Oakwood and the place where the whole sorry event had taken place.

She had been working for about two hours, sweeping up trash and shovelling it into sacks, and had just begun her next task, which was to plant a sapling – a replacement for the one that had been damaged in the fight – when she heard a voice behind her.

'Rube, is that you?'

Ruby looked up to see Elliot. 'Does it look like me?' she asked.

'Kind of,' said Elliot. 'What are you doing?'

'What does it look like I'm doing?' said Ruby.

Elliot shrugged. 'Shovelling dirt around a tree?'

'Or as we gardeners like to call it, planting stuff,' said Ruby.

'Looks like hard work,' said Elliot.

'Beats picking up garbage,' said Ruby.

'So what do you have to do once you've planted the tree?' asked Elliot.

'Pick up more garbage,' said Ruby.

Elliot made a face. 'Can I help?'

Ruby smiled up at him. 'That's really nice of you Elliot, but unless you happen to be assigned one of these orange jumpsuits then I'm afraid you're out of luck.'

Elliot peered into the huge bag of trash. 'Did you find anything interesting?' he asked.

'A lot of lone sneakers,' said Ruby. 'Who are these people who go about losing single shoes?'

'Beats me,' said Elliot, 'but let me know if you find anything interesting, OK?'

'I'll keep it for you,' said Ruby.

It was when she was nearing the end of her final half hour on trash collection that she did find something interesting. Not that it would be possible to hand it to Elliot; it wasn't something you could take home. It was lying under a pile of junk in the small paved seating area to the side of Sunny's Diner. As she was levering up an old car tyre, she discovered a brass plaque set into the paving. On it were the words:

SITE OF THE FIRST
TWINFORD LAW COURTS.

Amazing what you discover when you pick through the garbage, she thought.

When she got home, she showered and had another go at trying to scrub away the permanent, permanent marker pen words, but the scrubbing made her arm sore. It would go eventually, she thought. *By the time I'm sixteen it will probably be almost invisible.*

The phone was ringing when she stepped out of the bathroom.

'Twinford garbage control, you drop it, we pick it up.'

'Hey Ruby, it's Del. How about I buy you table time at Back-Spin, throw in a milkshake?'

'Why would you wanna do that?' asked Ruby.

'Just to, you know, show my appreciation. I bumped into Elliot; he said you were picking up trash on account of the whole community service thing.'

'It was easy,' said Ruby.

'Still,' said Del, 'tomorrow after school?'

'You got yourself a deal.'

Chapter 47.
The locked locker

THE NEXT DAY AT SCHOOL BEGAN IN THE USUAL WAY FOR EVERYONE BUT RUBY. She had decided to devote another day to Yellow Wind-Dragon kung fu.

While Ruby was perfecting her movements, Del Lasco was sitting in the hot seat again. In fact, she had been in Principal Levine's office for almost an hour and, although Del Lasco often found her way into the principal's office and so this alone wasn't unusual, what was strange was that she had no idea what had brought her here.

'I'm truly sorry sir, but I have no idea what you are talking about.'

The principal gave her one of his hard stares.

'Vapona Begwell's behavioural science project was found in your locker. What can you tell me about that?' he said.

But Del had nothing to say. What could she say? She was as surprised as anyone to find Vapona Bugwart's behavioural science project in her locker.

'You're telling me that you have absolutely no clue as to how another student's work came to be inside your locked locker?' said Principal Levine.

Del shrugged. 'Beats me, I mean why would I even *want* Bugwar— I mean, Vapona's project? I'm not judging or anything, but I mean, Vapona's work isn't exactly Nobel Prize material.'

Principal Levine took out a file and dropped it onto his desk. 'Del, I'm not suggesting that you have any interest in Vapona's *work*. What I am putting to you is that you have an interest in messing with her life.'

Del tried to look outraged, thought about it and decided it wasn't really going to fly. The file Principal Levine had in front of him told the whole story. Vapona and Del had a long-running feud – a feud that had brought them both to this room more times than a few.

'OK, sir, you're right, Bug— Vapona and I don't always see eye to eye.'

The principal raised an eyebrow.

'OK, Vapona and I aren't friends.'

Again, the principal's eyebrow got mobile.

'OK, it's no secret, we hate each other's guts. The Atlantic Ocean will probably freeze over before she stops being a royal pain in the butt.'

Del caught Principal Levine's expression. 'Sorry, anyway, I might not like her, but I wouldn't touch her stupid project and I wouldn't stuff it in my own locker so I would get caught. If I was gonna take it then I would most probably throw it in the Twinford River...' Principal Levine coughed. 'I mean, but I never would.'

'So how are we to explain that the project was in your locker?'

Del shrugged. 'How should I know, man— I mean, sir. I guess someone is trying to set me up... Maybe Bugwart put it there herself?'

'And why would she do that?'

'Like I said, to get me in trouble.'

'But with no behavioural science project, wouldn't she be the one to find herself in trouble?'

'She tipped you off, she told you to break into my locker, this way she causes me a whole lotta grief *and* gets to hand her project in.'

'I think that's unlikely somehow.'

'Why?'

'Because Vapona's been off school for the last couple of days.'

'Oh.'

'I regret that until I have some solid answers from you, I have no alternative but to send you home. As of now (he looked at his watch) you are suspended.'

'You are totally not serious.'

'I regret, Ms Lasco, that I am – totally serious.'

Del rolled her eyes and exhaled. 'Man!' And as she walked through the school secretary's office she continued to mutter, 'This is totally not fair and totally not in the interest of truth and freedom.'

❀ ❀ ❀

Ruby, who had missed the day's drama, was waiting patiently at Back-Spin.

While she waited, she used the time to fill in the blanks in Clancy's French homework. *Most* of it was blanks, but the essay she wrote was really pretty good, though not too good – she made sure there were plenty of mistakes.

'You doing your homework?' asked Sal.

'Clancy's homework, actually – just killing time until Del shows.'

'You're some friend,' said Sal admiringly. 'There's no way I'd do another kid's homework.'

Ruby waited a little longer, looked at her watch more than a few times and eventually realised that perhaps Del Lasco was not going to show.

She went over to the counter where Sal was chatting to Danny Jupiter. Del would be annoyed to miss him, she had a thing about Danny Jupiter. Ruby couldn't see it herself.

'Hey Sal, if Del comes in could you tell her I got better things to do than wait around for her?'

'Sure Ruby, I'll tell her,' said Sal.

'See you around,' said Ruby.

When Ruby got home she realised what she'd forgotten. *Darn it, Clancy's homework!* It was still sitting on the table in Back-Spin.

She called the table tennis cafe.

'Sal, could you do me a total favour and give Clancy's book to Danny and ask him to put it on Madame Loup's desk tomorrow?'

'No problem,' said Sal.

That taken care of, Ruby made herself a sandwich, poured a glass of banana milk and went up to her room. She found Bug waiting for her. He looked pleased to see her and got to his feet, tail wagging.

Ruby flumped down on the beanbag, reached for a yellow plastic chicken and dialled Del's number.

'Yeah?' came Del's reply.

'Hey, Lasco, where were you? I thought you wanted to play table tennis?'

'You haven't heard?'

'Heard what?'

'I got busted, is what. Levine sent me home – suspended for the duration, I guess, and now majorly grounded too.'

'How come? What have you done?'

'It's a mystery to me. Apparently I stole Bugwart's behavioural science project and stashed it in my locker.'

'Why would you do that?' asked Ruby.

'Because I'm a duh brain,' said Del.

'What?'

'I didn't do it, dope!'

'So what happened?' asked Ruby.

'Someone framed me, that's what happened.'

'But why?' said Ruby. 'Why would anyone do that?'

'You don't believe me?' said Del.

'Of course I believe you,' said Ruby. 'What I'm saying is, if you want to find out who set you up then you need to think why.'

'I don't need to know why,' said Del. 'I just want to find out who it is, and when I do, I'm going to punch their lights out.'

'It's weird though, isn't it?' said Ruby. 'I mean apart from Bugwart, who's got a problem with you?'

Del was silent.

'OK stupid question,' said Ruby.

'Look Rube, I appreciate your concern here, but if you don't mind, right now all I wanna do is turn my stereo up real loud and eat my corn dippers.'

Chapter 48.
Locker 237

THE NEXT DAY TWINFORD JUNIOR HIGH WAS ABUZZ WITH THE DEL LASCO PROJECT THEFT. Turn any corner that Friday morning and someone was talking about it.

'I don't get it,' said Ruby. 'I mean why does anyone think Del would do something that means she's bound to get caught? Sure, she can be dumb sometimes, but this is *off* the idiot scale.'

'Yeah,' said Clancy, 'it's not her style. She's a lot of things, but she's not a planner.'

'It's not a very good plan,' said Mouse.

'Good plan, bad plan, that's not the point,' continued Clancy. 'What I'm saying is, she hasn't got the patience for a plan.'

'No,' agreed Elliot, 'she's strictly sock you in the nose and ask questions later.'

It was during that morning that the whole sorry incident was explained. It didn't make the least bit more sense than it had yesterday, but it did get Del Lasco off the hook. Fortunate for Del, less fortunate for the poor schmuck who was about to take the blame.

Ruby had gone off to the City Library; she needed a particular translation of a book she was studying for music class, *Sounds and Furies in E Minor*, and she had been granted a couple of hours off campus.

Clancy, meanwhile, was in his behavioural science class, standing up front explaining why and how he had come up with the idea for his project and the lengths he had gone to collecting the evidence.

'I set this camera up in the main corridor that leads to the lockers. I wanted to prove that the locker areas are invaluable to students.'

Vapona yawned.

Mr Cornsworth said, 'Put a sock in it, Miss Begwell.'

Clancy continued. 'My theory is that it is important for students to gather, talk, hang out, and the lockers are instrumental in strengthening bonds between individuals. Students migrate to the lockers not only for practical reasons but also because it helps bring about natural collisions and allows people to engineer social interaction without fear of losing face.'

Vapona was cleaning her ears with a pencil and generally making a big display to her friends about how bored she was. Gemma Melamare was checking her nose in the mirror of her compact.

Mr Cornsworth was trying to look encouraging. Not every student put so much effort into the projects he set, so he was appreciative of Clancy's hard work.

'OK,' said Clancy, 'you can run the tape.' Mr Cornsworth switched out the lights and everyone stared at the screen. The film flickered on and students began walking up and down the school corridor. Clancy had sped up the playback so several days' observation could be covered in just a few minutes.

It was during the very last section, the final frames of the film, that something peculiar happened.

A slight girl with long dark hair walked down the corridor to the bank of lockers. She was wearing a pair of jeans, Yellow Stripe sneakers and a short sleeved T-shirt with the word **Bozo** printed across the front.

As she walked, she looked around her like she was watching to see if anyone was coming, then out of her satchel she took a file. On the file was written, clear as day: Vapona Begwell. The quality of the picture captured by Clancy's camera was really very good.

The girl could then be seen reaching for something in her back pocket. Her hair was kept in place by a fly barrette; the barrette kept her hair from falling too far over her right eye.

The girl pushed the key into the lock of locker 237, Del's locker, and looking around her again, just checking the coast was clear, she yanked open the door and quickly but deliberately stuffed everything in. When she was done, she could be seen hurrying off in the opposite direction.

She looked shifty, sure, she looked satisfied, and most of all she looked like Ruby Redfort.

Chapter 49.
Always better to know

IT WAS NOT A HALF HOUR AFTER THIS REVELATION
THAT MRS LASCO GOT A PHONE CALL. It was from the school
secretary, Mrs Bexenheath.

'Mrs Lasco, could you please bring Del back to school.
Principal Levine would like to have a chat with her.'

Mrs Lasco replied, 'I don't see how she can have got in any
more trouble, she's been sitting right here in my study – I'm
watching her.'

Ruby Redfort was blissfully unaware of what had just
transpired. She had been deep in a movement in E minor when
at 11am the behavioural science group was being given an inside
track into her true nature. She didn't actually leave the library
and arrive back at school until noon and by then everyone in
Twinford Junior High knew what kind of kid Ruby Redfort
really was. By now, Del Lasco also knew.

As Ruby walked her way down the main corridor she got a
weird feeling like a tsunami might be about to hit. People weren't
quite looking her in the eye, they were muttering. It all seemed

eerily quiet.

'Is it me who's the zombie? Or is it everyone else?'

No answer.

'Hey, Del,' she called.

Del didn't answer.

'Del!' she shouted. 'Is all forgiven? Did they catch the true culprit?'

Del Lasco merely turned her head, pausing for just a few seconds, barely giving her the time of day. 'Redfort, I just thought you were cooler than this,' she said.

'What?' said Ruby. 'I have no idea what you are talking about.'

'Yeah right, you get in a bit of trouble with your mom and dad, your crabby neighbour and the local law enforcement, and it's payback time, is that it?'

'What...?'

But Del had already turned on her heel and was walking off down the corridor, her hand raised in the internationally understood *'Save it for someone who gives a darn'* gesture.

Ruby was sort of frozen, unsure what she was meant to do. What exactly had just happened and why was Del so mad at her? She didn't need to wait long to find out – five minutes later and she too was sitting in front of Principal Levine trying to figure out what on earth was going on.

She was then sent straight home. Neither of her parents could be contacted and it was Mrs Digby who picked up the happy news.

'Child, what in tarnation is going on?'

'Beats me, Mrs Digby, but I swear someone is out to ruin my life.'

Mrs Digby put her hands on her hips. 'Something is strange, that's for darn sure. I might have to start reading your horoscope, see if I can't figure it out.'

Ruby glanced at the kitchen clock.

'So when are mom and dad getting back?' she asked. 'I don't think I'm in the mood for a grilling.'

'You're in luck,' said Mrs Digby. 'They decided to leave for Washington this morning. They won't have to hear about this little fiasco until Monday night.'

Ruby spent the next couple of hours reading a book on psychological training. It was all about how to develop strength of mind and character. With Blacker out to get her and someone framing her at junior high – not to mention some threat out there that had got Hitch worried enough to send her to kung fu school – Ruby figured her mind could use some strengthening.

She read until her stomach reminded her she hadn't eaten since breakfast, and decided it was time to head down to the kitchen.

Hitch was there, eating a Digby club sandwich (a Mrs Digby special) and he raised a hand in greeting when she walked in.

She returned the gesture, took some juice from the refrigerator and picked up the evening paper that was lying on the counter top.

Drip, drip, drip.

'What's that sound?' she said.

'Leaking tap,' said Hitch. 'The plumber is on his way.'

'You couldn't fix it yourself?'

'Sure I could,' said Hitch. 'It's a simple case of replacing the valve, which if I'm looking at it correctly is a 3/4 inch ceramic. But I've got bigger fish to fry.'

'Some butler you are.'

'House manager,' corrected Hitch, 'and nowhere in my job description does it say I have to fix taps.'

'You don't have a job description,' said Ruby, 'you're not actually a house manager.'

'Exactly, so let's wait for the plumber.'

Ruby spread out the paper. There was a piece titled TELL US YOUR WORST FEARS. Several interviewees had told the *Twinford Hound* about the things they most dreaded. One woman, Julia from Apple Oak County, had claimed dry hands were right up there in the nightmare department. Greg from Mountain View had claimed meeting a brown bear as his greatest fear and this Ruby felt was a little more on the scale.

'One of my worst fears, I guess, would be having the whole of my junior high school think I'm a lowdown lying sneak.'

'I'm sorry to hear *that* worst fear came true,' said Hitch.

'Oh it's OK,' said Ruby. 'I'm sure it's character building – I've been reading up on psychological strength and training.' She took a big swig of juice. 'Mrs Digby told you what happened, huh?'

'Yep,' said Hitch, 'she thinks there is something wrongly aligned in your stars.'

'Maybe's she's right,' said Ruby. 'Something somewhere is out of whack, that's for sure, not that my parents are going to see it that way.' She made a face. 'Nope, when they find out about this I'll be right back in the dog house.'

'You've got a couple of days until they get home, you might as well enjoy your freedom because by Monday evening I reckon you'll be back on Lemon duty.'

'You're right,' said Ruby. 'I think I might go out, breathe the air as a free person while I still can.'

She took Bug with her and she was glad of his company. She rode the subway to Chinatown, and left the dog sitting outside the dojo while she trained. There was no chance of Bug walking off: he would wait for her no matter what. There was no chance of him being dog-napped either: he knew how to defend himself.

It was after her training, as she stepped off the train at Greenstreet, that she was particularly grateful to have him at her side. The feeling of being watched, observed, followed, was perhaps heightened by the day's dramatic events, but however much she wanted to, she didn't think she was imagining it.

It was a relief to slam the door behind her, turn all three locks and sit in the cosy light of the kitchen, drinking her drink and listening to the drip, drip of the tap.

The plumber had obviously not made it after all. The drip of the tap was not so different from the drip drip beyond the window; the rain seemed to have set in for the duration and Ruby stared at the droplets running down the huge expanse of glass.

She sat there for a long time just thinking, until the kitchen sounds were interrupted by the perky ping of the doorbell. Ruby didn't answer. Mrs Digby was out at her blackjack class, and Hitch... she had no idea where he was.

She didn't stir from her seat until she became aware of the knocking on the back door and then a familiar...

'It's me, Clancy – are you there?'

Only then did Ruby finally get up and open the door.

He sat down next to her and without any preamble came straight to the point.

'I know it wasn't you in the video footage, and don't worry because I am going to prove it, though I feel kinda bad that it's because of me that you are in this mess.'

'It's not *your* fault,' said Ruby.

'I know, but I still feel bad,' said Clancy.

'Well don't,' said Ruby. 'Do you remember how you were telling me about that magician guy a month back?'

'The one with the stupid name?'

'Yeah, Darnley Rex.'

'Yeah, boy, I mean, who calls their son Darnley?' said Clancy. 'So what about him?'

'Well, I was thinking about the way he gets people doing stuff by planting an idea in their head and he manages to make them believe that they are seeing something or experiencing something and even if you were to try and convince them otherwise they would just carry on believing.'

'Until he brings them out of their trance,' said Clancy, 'then they stop believing right away.'

'Exactly, and it's kind of like what's happening here to me. Someone is out there undermining me by planting ideas in people's minds, but I don't think this person has any intention of letting anyone believe anything other than that I am a total phoney.'

'You have any theory about who it could be?'

'That's the weird thing. I mean there's no one, no one I know, who would do this,' said Ruby, 'but if I had to guess, I'd say I don't think it's got a whole lot to do with school.'

'I agree,' said Clancy, 'this is beyond anything Vapona would do, or even that guy Beetle, plus I mean, Rube, when it comes down to it, everyone likes you – even the ones that don't like you, like you.'

Ruby smiled. 'That's nice of you to say, Clance.' She paused before adding, 'So if this isn't a school thing then where exactly is it coming from?'

'I have no idea,' he said. He looked at his watch. 'I'm afraid I gotta go. We are flying to Washington at 6am so I need to get home before my folks start flipping out.'

'Don't forget to pack your elasticated bow tie,' said Ruby.

Clancy gave a flat sounding, 'Ha ha.' He wasn't laughing

because he knew that he might well be required to wear an elasticated bow tie.

Just before he disappeared into the dark he said, 'You need to talk to Blacker. Just ask him straight. Better to know, it's always better to know – isn't that what you are constantly telling me?'

But there was no way Ruby was going to do that.

Chapter 50.
More like a ninja

RUBY WAITED UNTIL MIDNIGHT BEFORE ZIPPING HERSELF INTO THE SPECTRUM-ISSUE JUMPSUIT, grabbing her backpack and heading for the subway. She arrived at the Movie Museum on Fibonacci just before 1am, and having walked around the building once, decided that she would enter by the old side door; she could pick the lock easy enough and it would be far less effort than scaling the wall.

The pick up went exactly as it had done at the Twinford Mirror building – no goons, no guy in a red hat. She was just on her way out when she walked smack bang into a large metal trashcan, which toppled over and began rolling loudly down a flight of stairs, gathering speed as it went.

Unsurprisingly, this alerted the two security guards.

'What was that, Charlie?'

'I don't know, Dale, but it sounded like something.'

They ran into the foyer and Ruby's only option was to sprint up the stairs to the floor above. The trashcan had finished its descent to basement level, but the guards were not heading down to check it out; they wanted to know just who had sent it tumbling.

'I think they went up the stairs,' said Dale.

Charlie was on his walkie-talkie; it sounded like he might be calling for back up.

Get out of there Redfort.

She could hear them coming, their feet on the marble steps, slow at first but then picking up speed.

She broke into a sprint, ran to the floor above, kept running. They were fit these guys, close behind. She made it into the upper gallery, its display cases filled with historical costumes from movies – mannequins dressed in 18th century clothes, huge dresses with wasp waists, bodices laced up tight.

No doors, no exits.

She ran back into the stairway. There was a window, she stood on the ledge and pulled at the latch – it wouldn't budge.

'Come on,' pleaded Ruby.

She was beginning to panic.

Six seconds, she counted.

1.

2.

3.

4.

5.

6.

What popped into her mind was the laser tool. It was one

of the functions of the Escape Watch and she had used it before. She depressed the operate button and directed the beam at the catch. The catch gave and the window swung open.

'Is that a kid?' said Charlie.

'More like a ninja,' said Dale.

Get out of here, thought Ruby.

And she jumped.

The glider wings deployed exactly as they should and Ruby sailed clear over rooftops, but the wind was strong and she had no choice but to let it take her, and where it took her was to a narrow alleyway secured by a chain-link fence.

She landed just fine and though it was gonna be a drag to have to climb the fence, she wasn't going to whine about it. She was lucky to have escaped arrest for breaking and entering, she could so easily be sitting in a squad car heading down town...

However, feelings of relief weren't to last, for the sound she heard next was blood-curdling.

With great caution, she turned to face this new enemy – dogs, two of them, closing in. They were snarling, teeth bared and dribbling drool.

Oh jeepers! What are the chances? I jump out of a window and land up with the Hound of the Baskervilles and his less friendly brother.

Ruby made sure not to look them in the eye, but began moving very calmly towards them. If she could get enough of a run up she could make it; if not, then she would most probably be ripped arm from leg.

Seven paces, eight paces, nine... then she turned and ran at the wall as fast as her feet would carry her.

The dogs sprang at her heels and their growls became barks as she flew, tick-tacking herself up the narrow alley walls, reaching for the top and pulling herself over, and onwards, across the rooftops, higher and higher, the dogs still leaping at the wall, their barks echoing into the night.

When she was perhaps seventy feet above the alley she looked down. The dogs were losing interest, only barking intermittently. Their quarry gone, they slunk off into the shadows.

Ruby took the fire escape and dropped down to the safety of the street.

Chapter 51.
Back to square one

IN THE QUIET OF HER ROOM, Ruby sipped from the bottle she had found at the Movie Museum.

She was cautious, after the unpleasant kale incident; she didn't want to take any chances and slurp.

The overriding taste was of tamarind. There was also salt and honey running through it.

Salt, sweet, sour.

(0,1,1,1)

She marked it up...

...then went to check the bathroom map, and was surprised to see that the point she had circled was: the Little Seven Grocers store, where the first bottle had been found. It was a loop.

She was, quite literally, back where she had started. Back at square one.

She examined the lid of the bottle. This time there was no date, so she figured there was no next bottle to find. What there *was*, instead, was a shallow impression of an X, nothing more.

She had no idea what it meant and how it might link to any

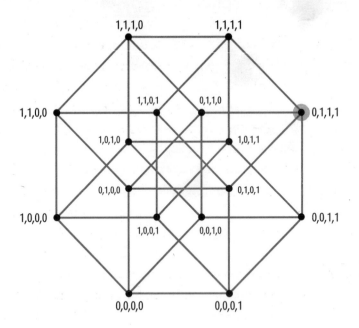

of the previous clues. Was someone playing a game here? Was this actually about anything at all?

She looked at the locations and tried to see a connection.

They were all more or less in the College Town district.

She wrote down the four locations in her notebook:

```
The Little Seven Grocers on Little Seven Street.
The music school on the university campus, Algebra
    Street.
The Twinford Mirror building on Gödel Avenue.
The Movie Museum on Fibonacci Street.
```

If there was a connection, she couldn't see it.

Her brain ached, her legs ached, her arms ached. Too tired to do much else but stumble from her chair to her bed, she kicked off her shoes, pulled the covers over her and fell asleep.

When she woke, the rain was falling. It had been falling through the night and had been the white noise of her dreams. When she hauled herself from her bed, she found a note taped to the outside of her window. It said:

You can count on me.

She unlatched the window and pivoted it towards her – water poured in onto the floor and as she peeled the paper from the glass, so it split into tiny fragments and was washed away.

She wasn't sure when he had left it, but there was no doubt who had written it. Suddenly she didn't feel so alone.

She had Clancy Crew on her side and that was a lot.

Chapter 52.
Watch your back

RUBY PEELED OFF THE JUMPSUIT, showered, pulled on her jeans and a T-shirt (the T-shirt, appropriately, had the word **Framed** printed across the front) and went to the hall to fetch her coat. She put it on, zipped it up and felt in the pockets for her gloves.

An envelope fell out onto the floor. She picked it up, tore it open and found two things. One was a note. It said:

> *I thought you might find this useful – you never can tell when you might need to tie things up.*

She looked at the second thing. It was a red leather wristband, and at its middle it had a yellow dragon that looked to be made from enamel. Its eye was raised a little and glittered red.

She turned the note over.

> *Kid, if you ever find kung fu isn't enough – then cheat.*

```
INSTRUCTIONS:
Aim dragon mouth at enemy and press the red
eye to release vapour. Vapour will solidify on
contact and create a temporary binding, which
will render your enemy incapable of movement for
approximately twenty-four minutes. The binding
will also become as heavy as lead within seconds:
do not attempt to lift the captive. Be aware that
due to temporary muteness – experienced three
minutes after vapour is released – captive will
not be able to respond to questioning.
To release, press dragon tail.

WARNING: never aim at self.
WARNING 2: you only get one shot of vapour.
```

There was a P.S.:

Watch your back kid, it's a dangerous world out there.

'You're telling me,' she muttered, as she pushed the envelope back into her pocket and headed out into the rain. She walked without purpose, striking off down Amster for no other reason than that it was there, turning left, turning right, no thought of a destination. Half-considered dreads filled her mind.

Her world suddenly seemed a great deal more hostile.

Her fellow Junior High students eyed her suspiciously, Del Lasco wasn't even speaking to her, and *trusted* colleague Blacker no longer trusted her, to say nothing of the rest of Spectrum. Who even knew what they were saying. Hitch clearly feared for her safety, though he gave no indication as to where the threat might come from.

The Taste Twister code had led full circle, and brought her right back to the beginning. A bottle top marked with an X was all she had going for her, and it wasn't enough.

She was drawn out of her sorry feelings by another feeling, a creeping unease that seemed to shadow her steps.

The thoughts of lost reputation and nowhere to turn might feel threatening, but right now not half as threatening as the feeling Ruby was getting of being watched.

And she *was* being watched.

Spectrum had taught her a few things about dealing with a tail; it was part of basic training. So she did as she had been instructed. She did *not* pick up the pace. Instead she slowed it right down, even stopped to tie her shoelace. She pretended she had dropped a coin so she might have an opportunity to look back, but this guy was good, a real pro; she couldn't see him though she was sure he was seeing her. She walked on, every now and again lingering to peer in a store front window, like she was looking to see someone or something when really she was hoping for a face reflected in the glass, but her tail was not going to give himself away so easily.

It was when she reached a stall selling cheap fun sunglasses that she finally saw his image. It was twice reflected back at her in the lenses of a pair of outsized star-shaped frames. She faked an interest in the shades, turning them this way and that. All the time she was looking at *him*, a guy she recognised – a guy with eyebrows that met in the middle. She had seen him twice only, and on both occasions he had been talking to Blacker. *Both* times he had exited the scene as soon as she had arrived. Now she knew for sure.

He was Spectrum.

And more than that: he was an associate of Blacker's.

She put the sunglasses back in the rack and walked on towards the subway. She knew exactly what she was going to do now.

When she reached Spectrum, Ruby did not bother to announce her arrival to Buzz, nor did she stop by the canteen to pick up a donut, instead she marched right along to the coding office.

If Blacker wanted to destroy her reputation, plant bad seeds in her colleagues' heads, mess with her mind, then she wanted to hear his reasons to her face. *No more lurking in the shadows, let's get everything out there in the open.*

She walked right into the coding office, didn't knock, didn't close the door quietly behind her.

'Why don't you just say it out loud?' said Ruby.

Blacker looked up. 'Huh, what?'

RUBY: *'That you don't trust me.'*

BLACKER: *'Why wouldn't I trust you?'*

RUBY: *'I don't know, you tell me.'*

BLACKER: *'You must have some idea?'*

RUBY: *'OK, since you're asking, I think it might be to do with the key.'*

BLACKER: *'The 8 key?'*

RUBY: *'Yeah, the 8 key, I think you think I took it.'*

BLACKER: *'Why would I think that?'*

RUBY: *'Because of those other things I took.'*

BLACKER: *'What other things you took?'*

Oops, she could tell just by the way he asked that he really *didn't* know. She was referring to the various gadgets she had sort of 'accidentally borrowed' from the gadget department over the past eight months. Now she found herself breaking her own **RULE 22: IF YOU THINK YOU MIGHT TALK YOURSELF INTO A TRAP, KEEP YOUR TRAP SHUT.**

'Never mind,' said Ruby.

'Well, now you mention it, I kinda do mind, Ruby. You're saying I don't trust you and that I'm falsely accusing you of taking LB's code key, and I guess I'm wondering two things here,' said Blacker, 'one is, what makes you think I would carry on working with you in any capacity if I thought you were involved in this? I mean, if this is true, don't you think I should report it?'

Ruby said nothing because she couldn't think of any good answer.

'And the second is: it occurs to me that if you are saying I don't trust you then it is also fair to assume you don't trust me, am I right about that?'

He was, and she didn't see the point in denying it.

'But I overheard you,' she said. 'I heard you talking about me, you were on the phone telling someone I was a loose cannon, dangerously unhinged.' Her voice was rising and a little unsteady; she sounded like someone dangerously unhinged.

'What you overheard was *one half* of a conversation, you've put two and two together and you think you're making four but you're way off.' His phone was buzzing. 'Look, I have to go, but you are going to need to make up your mind here, Ruby, about what it's gonna be.'

'Maybe I will once you explain why you've been having me tailed.'

'I'm not at liberty to say,' said Blacker.

'So you admit it?' said Ruby, surprised that he wasn't dancing around it. 'Straight up, no denials, you admit it?'

'Why wouldn't I admit it?' he replied. 'You're right, I had someone watch you.'

'I knew it,' she said. 'You don't trust me and you never did.'

'Do you think there could be any *other* reason for my having you watched – one which doesn't involve a lack of faith in *you?*' He picked up his coat. 'Think about it Ruby, use that smart brain of yours for six seconds.'

And he walked from the room.

※ ※ ※

Ruby sat completely still until she could no longer hear his footsteps. She was surprised by his reaction. He had looked her dead in the eye. He had neither smiled in a reassuring way, nor had he become flustered or angry. He had exhibited none of the behaviour of a person caught in a web of lies.

Did she really believe this colleague of hers had it in for her? This guy who had talked her through cases and backed her up no matter who might disagree? Could he really be the one who was trying to bring her down?

Could he?

Chapter 53.
Back on the map

AS JEN YU WAS FOND OF REPEATING, sometimes the answer is only found by completely emptying the mind.

Ruby decided that this might be best achieved by giving herself a little kung fu time. At the dojo she tried to banish all thoughts and become formless, shapeless, like water, like the wind...

It was only after several hours' practice that her mind at last became clear and she found her answer. She knew immediately what she must do.

Ruby, you have to talk to Blacker.

Clancy had been right.

And she had been wrong.

Ruby changed, gathered her things and wasted no time, practically running from the dojo and tearing off towards the subway, and on to Spectrum.

She found Blacker sitting at his desk. He was reading, his brow furrowed. When he saw her standing in the doorway, he closed the file and looked her square in the eye.

'Look, I think I might have got the wrong end of the stick somewhere along the way...' said Ruby. 'The wrong end of something anyway.'

'It happens,' said Blacker. 'Working in this field tends to bring on the paranoia.'

'It's just I seem to be on the outside of everything lately and it's making it hard to see which way is up.' She paused. 'Does that make sense?'

Blacker nodded. 'Maybe it's time to level with you about a few things.' He picked up the phone, had a brief exchange with the person on the other end, before replacing the receiver and pointing to the door.

'Come with me,' he said.

Ruby followed him through the Spectrum corridors until they reached the boss's office.

Agent Delaware was already there, sitting legs crossed, file on lap. LB was behind her desk.

'Take a seat,' she said.

Ruby looked to Blacker, but it was LB who broke the silence.

'Look Redfort, I understand from Blacker that you have been struggling with the whole idea that information here is imparted – 'on a need-to-know basis'.

We secret agencies tend to use this as a general way of rationalising information. You seem to be taking it personally, and I regret to say that there is no room for personal feelings –

hurt or otherwise – in the area of secret intelligence.' She stared hard at Ruby.

Ruby shifted uncomfortably in her chair.

'There *is* a point in keeping information contained and in this particular case a very good one.'

LB looked over at Delaware, who looked at Ruby, cleared his throat and began, 'What you may have read in your file when you made an unauthorised visit to the file room was there to protect you.'

Ruby froze: *how did they know she had been in the files?*

She opened her mouth, but LB raised her hand to silence her. 'How did we know?' she said second-guessing Ruby's question. 'You should know by now, Redfort, nothing gets past me. Maybe it's time you took that on board as fact.'

Agent Delaware continued. 'Let's put that disciplinary incident to one side for a while.' He cleared his throat. 'Two weeks ago a prisoner escaped from a maximum security government facility where said prisoner was being held pending trial. This individual is highly dangerous and extremely smart and happens to have you in her sights.' He held up a small black book. 'Scrawled on the pages of this journal are thoughts and ambitions that should you read them might have you sleeping with the light on for the rest of your days.'

Ruby's eyes widened.

'It was Spectrum's decision to withhold this information from you; you are, after all, a minor and it was considered best not to inform you of any danger you might be in.'

'But why?' asked Ruby. 'Isn't it better to be forewarned? If I knew then I might be able to...'

'You think you can defend yourself against someone like this?' Agent Delaware shook his head. 'You are a child playing at being an agent. This woman is a killer.'

'It's Lorelei?' said Ruby.

Delaware nodded. 'Von Leyden was within a hair's breadth of ending your life not one month ago – you survived by chance, not design.'

'So much of life and death is chance,' said Ruby.

'I don't argue with that, Agent Redfort,' said LB, 'but I do like the odds to be stacked in our agents' favour. To continue the gambling analogy – when the chips are down, you, Agent Redfort, are playing with a weak hand.'

Again Ruby started to speak, but LB interrupted.

'I asked Blacker to have you tailed, in part for your own protection and in part to see if von Leyden might be drawn out. If she was watching you, we would find her.'

'You're using me as bait?' said Ruby.

'Now you *object* to your life being put in danger?' said LB. 'I thought you were all about the risk.'

'It would just be nice to be informed,' Ruby replied. 'You know, *by the way Redfort, do you mind if we pop you on a hook and see if we catch a shark?*'

'How many ways do I have to say it? There is no nice in this line of work.' LB was glaring now. 'Plus, by the way, if it helps to reassure you, *no one* is interested in seeing an agent brought down. Everyone at Spectrum is committed to seeing you survive this threat to your life, even if there are times, Redfort, when I would personally like to strangle you.'

This wasn't quite the last word spoken, but near enough.

When Ruby was dismissed she and Blacker returned to the coding room, where it was Ruby's turn to come clean.

'There's something you need to know,' said Ruby.

'Does it have to do with the Taste Twister mystery?' asked Blacker.

'How did you know?'

'A wild guess,' he said. 'So spill the beans, why don't you.'

And she did.

When she had divulged everything she knew, Blacker picked up a marker and wrote the four locations on four cards and stuck them on the wall.

```
The Little Seven Grocers on Little Seven Street.
The music school on the university campus,
   Algebra Street.
The Twinford Mirror building on Gödel Avenue.
The Movie Museum on Fibonacci Street.
```

Then he made a sketch of the tesseract map.

'OK,' he said. 'So let's circle the four points revealed by the bottles.' He checked Ruby's notes and then drew four circles.

They stood back and looked at it.

'There are lots more points of course,' he said. 'Maybe the idea is to collect bottles for each one?'

'You're not serious?' said Ruby. 'That could take weeks. Months.'

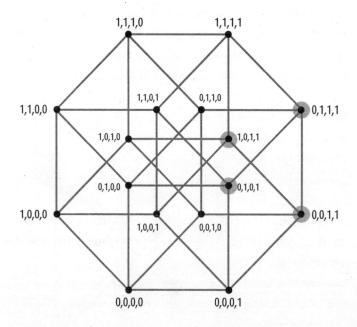

'Or maybe we're missing something,' said Blacker. 'Something on the bottle, or...'

Ruby lifted a hand. 'The lid.'

'What?'

'"X marks the spot".'

'I'm not with you,' said Blacker.

She picked up the final bottle top. 'No time, no date, just an X, see? X marks the spot. Like a treasure map.'

'So where's the X?'

For a moment, Blacker looked at the map blankly... then he got it. He stepped forward and circled the spot where the lines between the four locations crossed.

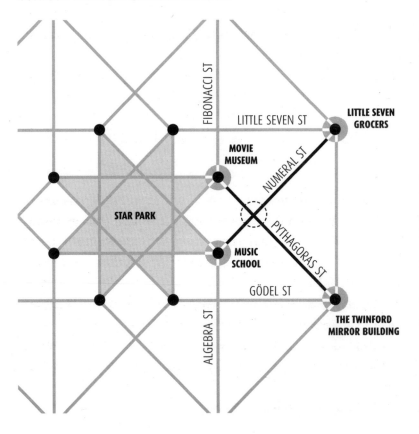

'OK,' said Blacker, 'let's see where that takes us.'

He pushed a button on the huge display board which covered one wall of the code room and punched in a few numbers until a map of Twinford's College Town came up. He transferred the information from the tesseract to the map.

Ruby frowned. 'There?' she said, pointing to where the lines intersected. 'But that's the elevated subway.'

'So,' said Blacker, 'maybe the X is marking the location *underneath* the elevated subway line.'

'But isn't that just the intersection where Numeral Street crosses Pythagoras?' said Ruby. 'There's no building or anything.'

'Only one way to know for sure,' said Blacker, pulling on his raincoat. 'Let's go.'

Blacker and Ruby took the subway to Cathedral. It was one of the few stations on the short section of elevated subway taking the trains up and over that part of town. Why the planners hadn't simply run it underground Ruby didn't know since it wasn't too pretty to look at.

To reach the exact point where the lines on the tesseract crossed meant negotiating heavy traffic, as the X-marks-the-spot was indeed in the middle of the busy intersection where Pythagoras and Numeral streets met. And when they got there...

Nothing to be seen.

Just trucks, buses and cars crossing an empty square of concrete. The elevated subway clickety-clacking overhead. And in one corner of the intersection, an abandoned lot.

One could be forgiven for thinking the lot was part of the city dump. It was covered in broken TVs, furniture, a shopping cart, about a hundred cardboard boxes and other bits of random junk. The two of them stood there trying to make sense of it, but nothing was adding up.

'I guess X doesn't always mark the spot,' said Ruby, kicking an old soda can.

They made their separate journeys back, Blacker to Spectrum, Ruby to Cedarwood Drive. As far as this case went, it seemed they had reached the end of the road.

**He heard the
lock turn...**

...no one had a key but him, no one knew where he was hiding out, no one was expected, so who was this?

He sprang to his feet, grabbed the baseball bat, killed the lights and stationed himself just to the right of the door. It swung open and in walked someone... He swung at the figure, but to his surprise the bat was knocked from his grasp. He felt a kick to the back of his knees and the feeling of cold floor against his cheek. He tried to heave himself up but a voice said, 'Stay there alive or stay there dead, makes no odds to me.'

He didn't move. The lights flicked on.

'Baby Face Marshall... So this is where you've been lurking.' She walked around surveying the room. 'If you're planning on staying here a whole lot longer, you might want to open a window or two, let in a little air.'

'Who are you?'

She pulled the mask from her face.

His expression went from alarm to terror.

'Lorelei?' he gasped. 'I heard you were out.'

'You heard correct.'

'So I guess you must be here to do his dirty work?' His voice trembled.

She looked at him blankly, before replying, 'Oh, the Count you mean? Yes, I did pick up that your some-time employer wasn't too happy with how things went. You really messed up there with that snake lady. How did you confuse a Twinford socialite with a Mongolian explorer? Too funny for words.'

'Who was to know two dumb party people were going to wear exactly the same dumb dress to that same dumb event?'

'Not you dumbo, that's for sure.'

'So you're saying you would have known better?'

'I'm saying I would have made it my business to know, because it would have been my business to know. What kind of rank amateur are you? Boy, no wonder he wants to kill you – he does want to kill you, yes?'

'I didn't stick around. You know what I'm saying?'

'Sounds like the first smart move you've made since breaking out of jail.'

 She circled the room.

'So what does he want from that Oidov woman anyway?' said Lorelei. Is it all about the snakes?'

'How should I know? I tend not to ask questions, questions aggravate him.'

'Yes, he can get rather tetchy, that's something I don't miss,' she said.

'So you're telling me you're not working for him?'

'No, I'm no longer on the payroll. I'm going it alone. I'm more of a freelancer, I hate taking orders, don't you?' She laughed. 'Well of course orders are all you've ever known.'

'So you're not here to...' He drew a finger across his throat.

'Kill you?' She laughed. 'No, not at all.'

'So what do you want?'

'Nothing Boyd... I have a business proposition for you. Call it an *opportunity – you look out for me, I look out for you.'*

'And who are you looking to avoid?' asked Baby Face.

'The same Australian as you,' said Lorelei. 'She's looking to kill you, yes?'

He said nothing.

'Well, I'm looking to kill her, so you might want to stick close and do exactly as I say.'

'OK,' he said. 'What do you want?'

'I need a snake or two, or seven, all kinds – poisonous ones. And the antivenoms too, just in case.'

'You want them to bite her?'

'Not just her,' she said.

'Who else?' he asked.

'I thought you didn't ask questions,' she said.

'You're planning an accident?'

'Sort of.'

'Who's the victim?'

'A child, it should be easy enough.'

'The thing is, these snakes, the ones I have, they're already promised to someone and if I give them to you... Well, let's just say, she isn't a very understanding client?'

'Neither am I.'

'So if I refuse?'

'Goodbye Boyd.'

Chapter 54.
Who's messing with Ruby Redfort?

WHEN CLANCY RETURNED TO TWINFORD JUNIOR HIGH THE FOLLOWING MONDAY he was immediately called into Principal Levine's office.

Clancy of course had no idea why. The principal motioned for him to sit down, and Clancy sat.

'Do you know why I have called you in?'

Clancy shook his head. There were about thirty possibilities that came to mind, but he wasn't going to start throwing them about. He had learnt this from watching *Crazy Cops*: never incriminate yourself by offering up indiscretions.

'It has come to my attention...' started Principal Levine, (*never a good opener*, thought Clancy) 'that you have been getting assistance with your French homework.'

Clancy said nothing.

'Is this true?' asked the principal.

'I am not sure what you're getting at sir,' said Clancy.

'I'm trying to discover the truth of the matter. Someone has accused you of deception and I want to hear what you have to say about it.'

'Who?' said Clancy. 'Who has?'

Principal Levine steepled his fingers. 'Ruby Redfort,' he said. He was staring hard at Clancy watching for the reaction.

'Really?' said Clancy.

'Yes, really,' said Levine. 'What do you say?'

'If Ruby told you that then she must have had her reasons.'

'She didn't say it to me, but a note was found. The handwriting is unmistakably hers and the tone of the note undeniably Redfortesque.' He took a small folded piece of paper from his desk drawer and handed it to Clancy.

Clancy examined the paper – it looked to be from one of Ruby's schoolbooks, her French textbook to be precise, torn from a page listing the vocabulary that might be required when one embarked on a boating trip. In the top right-hand corner was a drawing, which Clancy recognised as the sketch he himself had done of Madame Loup. Underneath it was a message:

```
Look mon ami, I can't keep doing your homework
   for you, it's not fair and in any case you're
not exactly gonna faire des progrès if you keep
   cheating. I accept that it's sort of my fault
           for offering, but really Clance,
                  ressaisis-toi!
```

'Where did you find this?' asked Clancy.

'It was tucked in your homework; you must have missed it when you handed it in on Friday.'

'I didn't hand it in on Friday,' said Clancy.

'Well, someone did. I imagine Ms Redfort was expecting you to take a look at her efforts before Madame Loup graded your test.'

Silence.

'Do you have anything to say?'

'No sir.'

'Well, if you really have nothing to add, you may go. I will of course be writing to your parents.'

Clancy exited the office, walked past Mrs Bexenheath and on down the corridor and out of the front gates. When he got to the payphone on the corner, he dialled Ruby's number. The phone rang and rang until the answerphone clicked in.

'Rube, it's me, it's happened again... Someone or a whole bunch of someone's are trying to bring you down. Watch your back.'

Then he walked back into school. All the time he was thinking:

Who's messing with Ruby Redfort?

When the school bell rang, Clancy went to his locker, retrieved the tiny video camera and went right on home. His parents were out and Principal Levine's letter would not reach them until the following day – he had perhaps twenty-four hours before that little bomb went off. He studied the film very carefully. He watched Ruby walk down that corridor over and over until he knew her every step by heart. He scrutinised her clothing, her sneakers and her satchel. It was all as it should be. Her hair, her fly barrette, her T-shirt, nothing out of the ordinary. Except... He leant in closer. Something was missing. And slowly a smile spread across his face.

The light was blinking on the family answer machine when Ruby walked into the house. She hadn't felt like school that morning – I mean, what had it done for her lately? Instead, she had been at the dojo all day and was now feeling like she could do with a little R&R. She pressed play and began to peel off her wet coat – this rain was something else.

Beep. 'This is Mrs Bexenheath, secretary at Twinford Junior High. I wonder if you could call me to arrange a meeting with the principal. I am afraid there is evidence to suggest that your daughter has been involved in some highly reprehensible behaviour. Since this follows hot on the heels of some previous reprehensible behaviour, you understand we are very concerned.'

Ruby pressed the delete button, walked into the kitchen and poured herself a glass of water. She drank the whole thing down and was about to pour herself another when the doorbell rang.

When she opened the front door she was met by the sight of Elaine Lemon, who was standing on the Green-Wood house doorstep with Archie.

This day is on the slide, thought Ruby.

'Look Ruby, I hate to do this to you,' began Elaine, 'it's just my mother's been taken into hospital and I need to be there and I can't take Archie. Niles is away on business and I have no one else to ask.' She didn't actually stop there, she went into some detail about her mother's condition and how it might be treated and the likely convalescence period. 'Six weeks! I mean how will I ever manage?'

Ruby sighed, she had no real reason not to mind Archie, and Elaine Lemon looked like she might actually dissolve into tears and Ruby didn't think she could handle that, so she said yes – well, her actual words were, 'OK, hand him over Elaine.'

Maybe she could palm him off on Mrs Digby. She took Archie into the living room, popped him on the floor and was about to run down to find the housekeeper when she saw a large note stuck to the TV set:

Gone to bingo.

Beneath that was a clipping from the *Twinford Echo*.

YOUR TWINFORD ECHO HOROSCOPE: STAY INDOORS
AND AVOID TROUBLE.

Below that was another note from Mrs Digby:

My advice would be stay in doors and
avoid trouble.

Ruby glanced back at Archie. 'Just as well,' she said, 'because looks like I don't have a whole lotta choice.' She took him up to her room, switched on the TV, and up popped *A is for Ant*.

She turned to the baby and said, 'And B is for Bored, bozo.'

Chapter 55.
The look in her eye

CLANCY WAS ON HIS WAY TO THE TABLE TENNIS CAFE.
He knew Del was going to be there, she was probably hanging
out with her new friend Sal, the girl she kept talking about. No
doubt playing table tennis with that guy Danny Jupiter. Boy, did
he think he was the bee's knees.

He saw Del as soon as he walked in. There she was, bat in
hand, just playing a warm-up game with Danny and two other
kids who Clancy didn't recognise.

'Can I have a word with you?' asked Clancy.

'Oh, hi Clance.' She signalled to her teammate and stepped
out of the game. 'Sure thing, what's it about?'

Clancy didn't waste time getting around to the point. 'I like
you Del, you're cool, a good friend, but I gotta say, you're being
a total duh brain about this.'

Del's eyes narrowed. '*Excuse* me?'

'You honestly think Ruby would sell you out?' said Clancy.
'I mean, honestly?'

'I don't think so, I know so,' said Del, jutting out her jaw.

'You're not using your noodle,' said Clancy. 'What possible reason would Ruby have for ratting on you?'

Del crossed her arms. 'Revenge.'

'Oh yeah, that sounds a lot like Ruby, she really lives for revenge,' said Clancy.

Del said nothing but her face was set like stone.

'Remember that time when Mouse accidentally let slip to Mrs Drisco that Ruby was *not* at the dentist but had actually gone ice-skating? Or when *you* gave away her ticket to the Gloom gig because you were mad at her for skipping a basketball match, do you remember that? Do you remember *her* taking revenge on you?'

Actually what had happened was Ruby had apologised to Del for letting her down with the match, and given her an earful about the ticket. But the important thing was, she had born no grudge.

'If Ruby was mad at you, she would tell you to your face. If she didn't feel like being your friend any more, she just wouldn't talk to you. What she *wouldn't* do is go and let your tyres down or waste her time ratting you out to Principal Levine.' Clancy was talking kind of loud now; he was pretty angry. Sal and the kids at the counter were looking at them, no doubt wondering what was occurring here.

'So how come I can see her on *your* film footage breaking into my locker?' asked Del.

'You remember what happened the day we met at the Donut

to talk about Halloween?'

'I remember all right,' said Del irritably. 'Redfort fell asleep at the table.'

'So you remember how you picked up that permanent marker of mine and you wrote REDFORT WAKE UP AND SMELL THE BANANA MILK all up her left arm?'

Del nodded. 'Yeah, you were right about that marker pen, boy does it never come off.'

'Exactly,' said Clancy, 'it's still there. You can take a look next time you see her. It's the most permanent permanent marker there is.'

'OK, so I shouldn't have done that,' said Del. 'But what's any of that got to do with the price of potatoes?'

Clancy reached into his bag and pulled out the tiny video camera and set it down on the table. 'This is the film I took that shows "*Ruby*" putting Vapona's project in your locker. Maybe you should watch it, really watch it.' He walked towards the exit, and when he reached the counter, he called back, 'Pay special attention to that left arm.'

Clancy went up to Sal at the front counter. He'd never met her before, only heard Del going on about how cool she was. She was getting ready to leave, her shift over for the day.

She called out, 'Jeez, will I be glad to get home and out of these sneakers.'

The guy who worked the food counter laughed loudly. 'I hear you Sal.'

'Could I get some change for the payphone?' asked Clancy.

'Sure,' said Sal, she took the bill and handed him the quarters.

'I don't suppose you've seen Rube, have you?' said Clancy.

'Who?' said Sal.

'Ruby,' said Clancy. 'I've been trying to get hold of her.'

'No, but hey, look any friend of Ruby's is a friend of mine, so you're welcome to use the counter phone, save your quarters, just don't tell the manager, OK?' said Sal.

Clancy smiled at her. 'Thanks, I appreciate it.'

'Any time,' said Sal. She was looking for her apartment keys. 'Where did I put 'em?'

'There,' said Clancy, pointing to the keys.

'Thanks,' said Sal.

He dialled Ruby's number and she picked up.

'Hey Rube, you *are* there, did you get my message?'

'No,' said Ruby.

'Why not?'

'I do *do* stuff you know. I've been busy trying to solve a crime – or at least *something* I think might be connected to a crime, anyway, I haven't had the energy to check my answerphone, especially not after listening to the family one, which I can tell you did *not* make for happy listening.'

'Meet me in the tree,' said Clancy.

'I can't, I got the Lemon with me,' said Ruby.

'What, again?

'It's a long story, at least the way Elaine Lemon tells it,' said Ruby.

'So meet me at the Donut, you can bring the Lemon.' Clancy turned to see Bailey Roach and his friends walk through the door; they were making a lot of noise.

'OK, I'll be with you in an hour,' said Ruby.

'An *hour*?' said Clancy.

'Do you have any idea how long it takes to get a baby into its zippy coat bag thingy?' said Ruby.

'No, actually I don't. Just be there sooner.'

'I'll try,' said Ruby.

'Right,' said Clancy. He didn't sound convinced.

'A half hour OK? ...Boy it's loud where you are,' said Ruby.

'I know, that guy Beetle and the bozos just arrived and they're making trouble...'

'He's such a haircut,' said Ruby. 'So anyway, why did you call?'

'The first time, to tell you that you're in trouble again.'

'Yeah, Mrs Bexenheath left my folks a message. What did I do this time?'

'Aided and abetted,' said Clancy, 'basically did some kid's homework for him.'

Ruby whistled. 'That's got be worth a week of detentions.' She paused. 'Wait a minute, I totally forgot to give you your homework. I left it at Back-Spin. Sorry about that, by the way.'

'That's OK. The point is, how did it wind up in Madame

Loup's stack of marking?'

'I asked Sal to give it to Danny Jupiter – got *him* to hand it in for you.'

'So did *he* write the note or did someone else?'

'What note?'

'The note from you?'

'What?' said Ruby.

'Never mind, I'll explain when I see you. The good news is, I got proof that you weren't the one who stole Vapona's project.' Clancy was now having to practically shout. 'I've given it to Del...'

'Let go of the phone...'

'What?'

'Lemon, I'm telling you, let go of the phone...'

Click.

The line went dead.

'Geez!' exclaimed Clancy. There was a sudden rise in the noise level and then ping-pong balls started flying around the place, and the poor new girl was having a hard time taking control. She came out from behind the counter. 'Look, please guys,' she pleaded, 'could you maybe not do that?'

But they weren't listening. Worse than that, they started giving her a hard time and Clancy wasn't going to stand by and watch. He might be fond of his teeth, but he had to help her. And that's when something happened that Clancy couldn't quite explain. It wasn't that Sal got mad. Not *really* mad. She didn't

shout or scream or anything – even though she had every right
to be angry. It was hard to put your finger on exactly what she
did – it was just when she did it, the boys froze. Suddenly they
were afraid, and they weren't the only ones. Clancy felt it too.
Just for a split second, a fraction of a split second, Sal seemed to
change into someone else.

And as she swished calmly past him, peace now restored,
Clancy could have sworn he could smell something. Something
that made his blood stop pumping.

The unmistakeable smell of... Turkish delight.

Lorelei von Leyden. It had to be.

Very calmly and without any sign of alarm, he replaced the
receiver and walked towards the exit like nothing had happened
– he was just a kid heading home.

'You leaving so soon?' said Sal.

'Er, yeah, I... um, I forgot something at home. I'll be back in
a half hour.'

She made a sad face. 'I'm clocking off in ten,' she said.
'Heading home myself.' Another smile. But now Clancy saw how
it didn't reach her eyes. 'I'll be back tomorrow though, maybe
I'll see you! It would be cool to get to know you... any friend of
Ruby's is a friend of mine!'

'Thanks,' said Clancy, as brightly as he could manage.

When he reached the payphone just outside, he paused as
if he had thought of something, remembered someone he was
supposed to call. He redialled Ruby's number.

The phone rang six times, seven, eight and then...

'I'm sorry to inform you that Ruby Redfort is not here. Leave your words after the beep, and better make them interesting buster, or I won't call you back.'

'Look Rube, maybe you're on your way, but if you aren't just get to the Donut fast... I think I just worked out who your double is.'

Even as he spoke, something else clicked. The French homework – Sal – she wrote the note, before handing it to Danny Jupiter. No doubt she snitched on Del too.

He replaced the receiver just as Sal walked out. She saw him standing at the payphone.

'See you around,' she called.

And Clancy shivered.

Chapter 56.
Cousin Nerris

RUBY HADN'T BEEN ABLE TO ANSWER THAT SECOND CALL
FROM CLANCY because she had been on another call which
had come through to the family phone.

'Hello Ruby, how are you? It's Quent!'

'Oh, hey Quent, I'm fine, what gives?'

'I'm just around the corner.'

'Oh Quent, that's a real shame because you know, well the
thing is... I'm out.'

Long pause.

'But I just phoned you on your home phone and you are
talking to me, how can you be out?'

'Ah well, what I meant by "out" was I'm about to be out, as
in, I have my coat on and I'm headed to the door.'

'Oh that's great, I was going to ask you if you wanted to come
out – I'll meet you there.'

'Where?'

'At your door.'

'Quent, where are you exactly?'

'I'm at the phone booth across from your house.'

Oh brother.

'See you in a minute Ruby.'

'It looks likely Quent.'

She hung up. 'It would seem we're going out, Lemon.' She manoeuvred the baby into his snuggle suit, which wasn't easy because he grabbed a fist full of her hair and wouldn't let go.

'You know that really hurts Lemon!' It took her a minute to free herself, and when she had, she popped him in his stroller.

She opened the door and there was Quent Humbert, waiting for her.

'Hey Ruby, how are you?'

'Since one minute ago, I'm still fine,' said Ruby. 'Now look, you can walk with me as far as the Double Donut, but then I'm gonna have to lose you, I have a meeting, you see.'

'Sure,' said Quent. 'I don't mind.'

Quent talked non-stop the whole way there.

QUENT: *'So Del has asked me if I would join in with your Halloween idea.'*

RUBY: *'She did?'*

QUENT: *'She didn't tell you?'*

RUBY: *'No, she did not.'*

QUENT: *'That's funny.'*

RUBY: *'Ha ha.'*

QUENT: *'No, I meant funny peculiar.'*

RUBY: *'It's peculiar all right.'*

QUENT: *'Can you guess what she had in mind?'*

RUBY: *'Revenge?'*

QUENT: *'I mean what costume – for me, I mean?'*

RUBY: *'I reckon she's gonna have your head tucked under her arm.'*

QUENT: *'Hey, how did you guess?'*

RUBY: *'She likes to get people in headlocks.'*

Quent looked slightly baffled.

QUENT: *'So who are you gonna be?'*

RUBY: *'The ghost of friendship past.'*

QUENT: *'Is there a ghost of friendship past living in Mortis Square?'*

RUBY: *'No.'*

QUENT: *'So where do you come in?'*

RUBY: *'Exactly.'*

Quent was looking puzzled again. By now they were almost opposite the Double Donut.

'Don't worry about it,' said Ruby, parking the stroller. 'Look, could you mind the baby for a minute while I go in search of some Hubble-Yum, I'm feeling the need. It helps with stress.'

'What if he cries?' asked Quent.

'Here,' said Ruby, taking off the Escape Watch, 'this timepiece has a function for that.' She handed the Bradley Baker heirloom to the Lemon and he put it in his mouth.

'I won't be a minute,' she said.

Clancy was sitting in the Diner in one of the window booths.

Rain had just begun to drizzle down and those who had umbrellas were flipping them open and those who didn't were quickening their pace. Heavy rain was predicted and now anyone who had been lucky enough to hear the forecast was taking cover. Clancy heard the jangle of the bell as the Diner door opened and closed, opened and closed. But still no Ruby.

Clancy looked at his watch – it had been thirty-eight minutes and he was beginning to worry.

'Hey,' said a voice behind him.

Clancy turned. It was Elliot; in one hand was his ukulele and in the other his skateboard.

'Oh hey, Elliot.'

'What are you doing?'

'Looking out of the window,' said Clancy.

'Yeah, that I can see, *what* are you looking out *for*?'

'Ruby,' said Clancy. 'You seen her?'

'No,' said Elliot. He placed his skateboard on the table, ukulele on the bench and slid into the seat next to Clancy. 'I'll keep you company until my dad comes. I've got the jitters because I got my ukulele exam in an hour.'

Clancy wasn't listening.

Marla shouted from across the Diner. 'Get that piece of wood and wheels off my table, or else go stand out in the rain, makes no difference to me, cookie.'

'Boy, she never misses a thing, huh?' said Elliot, setting the board on the floor.

'So Del's really mad at old Ruby, I wouldn't be surprised if she never speaks to her again.'

'Yeah, well, if that's so then Del's an idiot,' said Clancy.

'You don't think Ruby did it?' said Elliot.

'Do you?'

Elliot shook his head. 'No way in ever,' he said.

Clancy was still staring out of the window.

'Why you so desperate to see her anyway?' said Elliot picking up the menu like he needed reminding of what might be on it. He really didn't; he knew that menu back to front and upside down.

'I might have the eggs,' he said.

Clancy was busy thinking. *If only she had picked up, if only I knew she had actually listened to my message, if only she could be punctual for once... why can she never be on time?*

He looked out of the window. Still no Ruby.

If he went in search of her, he was bound to miss her. It was a classic mistake that people made in movie thrillers – they always gave up waiting and this always led to trouble. So instead he just checked his watch and stared out to the street.

All the time drumming his fingers on the windowsill.

'Probably that baby,' said Elliot.

'What?' said Clancy.

'That baby Orange holding her up.'

'Baby *Lemon*,' corrected Clancy. *Elliot is right, baby Lemon probably needed a diaper change or something.*

'There she is!' said Elliot.

Clancy exhaled as he saw Ruby walking towards the pedestrian crossing on the other side of the street, parka zipped, hands in pockets (no umbrella). There was no sign of the baby.

'She musta left the Lemon at home,' said Clancy. 'That's good.'

'Maybe she left him on the bus,' said Elliot. 'It happened to my aunt once. She left my cousin Nerris on the bus, and walked two blocks before she realised.'

A huge red truck drew up, windshield wipers going like crazy, its arrival masked Clancy's view of Ruby and he waited for her to appear from behind it, only she was taking her time about it.

'So what happened?' asked Clancy.

'She basically panicked,' said Elliot.

'How did she find Nerris?'

'She called the bus depot and there he was,' said Elliot.

Clancy watched as the truck finally pulled away. There were plenty of people hurrying by, only thing was, there was no Ruby.

'Where's she gone?' said Clancy. 'What just happened?' He was standing now, his arms beginning to flap. 'I gotta go.' He started towards the door. 'Actually I gotta borrow this,' he said running back to the table, grabbing Elliot's skateboard and dashing out into the rain.

'If it means so much to you,' called Elliot. 'YOU KNOW YOU'RE ACTING WEIRD!' was the last thing Clancy heard Elliot shout as the door closed behind him.

Chapter 57.
Your old friendly maniac

RUBY SAUNTERED OUT OF THE CONVENIENCE STORE and over to where Quent was sheltering with baby Archie.

'He's really cute,' said Quent.

'That's debatable, but thanks for watching him,' said Ruby.

'By the way, I just saw your friend Clancy. He was on a skateboard, going real fast too.'

'You have to be kidding, which way did he go?' said Ruby, looking in every direction.

'North,' said Quent.

'Darn it! He's probably mad at me because I'm late. He's a stickler for punctuality. I gotta split,' said Ruby and she ran, stroller and all, north up Amster.

She spotted him as he was about to step onto a bus.

'Clancy!' she screamed. 'Where the Sam Hill are you going?'

He was a good way ahead, but he heard her and turned, his expression changing from high anxiety, to extreme relief and then sort of to full-on fury. He began striding back towards her.

'Where were you?' he shouted. 'Why can you never be

anywhere when you say you will?'

'What's the big deal here?' said Ruby.

'What's the big deal? What's the big deal! The big deal here, bozo, is I'm trying to save your life!'

'Be careful who you call bozo, bozo!' shouted Ruby. 'And what do you mean "save my life"? Forty-seven minutes ago you were going to tell me how you knew it wasn't me who stole Bugwart's stupid school project. Did I miss something?'

'Yeah a lot actually!' shouted Clancy, his voice even louder. Passers-by were giving them both a wide berth, some of them even choosing to cross the road. 'Turns out the person who set you up for that little crime is your pal Sal.'

'Sal isn't my pal!' shouted Ruby. 'Sal is Del's pal, and why would a pal of Del's want to set me up?'

'Because Sal isn't Sal!' shouted Clancy.

'OH YEAH?' shouted Ruby. 'And if Sal isn't Sal, then who is Sal?'

'Sal...' said Clancy, stalling for a moment, aware of how crazy it was going to sound, 'I mean, call it a hunch, but I'd stake my life on it... Sal,' he repeated, 'is your old friendly maniac, Lorelei von Leyden!'

Silence.

'Ruby?'

Ruby couldn't say anything; her throat had gone very dry.

'Ruby,' said Clancy, his voice almost whispering now, 'are you OK?'

'It's just I know you're right. It all fits. Lorelei von Leyden escaped from a maxium security facility two weeks ago, Sal arrived a week later, and if that isn't enough, I happen to know she's not too crazy about me.'

'What do you mean?'

'I'm number one on her list of least likely to live.'

'She has a list?' said Clancy.

'Actually I get the sense she mostly spent her whole time in the can writing stuff about the various awful ways she was going to kill me. Spectrum wouldn't even let me read it. What made you suspect Sal?' said Ruby.

'It was when the phone line cut out,' said Clancy, his voice a little creaky. 'Something happened, that duh brain Beetle was being a bozo and Sal lost it. I saw this look in her eye and I just knew, just like before...' Clancy paused; the memory of his incarceration on the top of Wolf Paw Mountain was vivid. 'I've been face to face with that psycho before and it doesn't matter what disguise she puts on – once I look into her eyes, she can't fool me. Plus, I smelled that smell she wears. Turkish delight.'

'Why didn't you call me right back?' said Ruby.

'I did, but you didn't pick up,' said Clancy.

Ruby looked at him straight. 'I have to go to Back-Spin, I have to find Del.'

'Sal's not there,' said Clancy. 'She finished her shift.'

'Where was she going, Clance? Did she say?'

'Home,' said Clancy, 'and who knows where that is?'

Ruby smiled. 'Me!' she said, and she began walking. She knew exactly where Sal lived. She'd seen her walking into an apartment right near Lucello's, an apartment way too up-market for a girl who worked a few shifts at the table tennis cafe. But it all made sense now.

'Where are you going?' called Clancy.

'To find Sal,' Ruby replied.

'What, are you insane?' shrieked Clancy. 'You can't go marching up to her front door on your own.'

Ruby stopped and turned to look at him. 'I'm not a total idiot, Clancy. I'm going to call for backup. The last thing I want to do is take on a murder-minded individual alone. I mean what am I, crazy?'

'Only occasionally,' said Clancy but he looked relieved.

Ruby peered into the stroller. 'So you gotta give the watch back now, Lemon.' She prised the Escape Watch out of his baby grip. 'Jeepers Lemon, it's totally covered in dribble.' Archie was not pleased about having to give it up and looked like he was going to cry. Clancy lent in to try and soothe him and Archie took the chance to reach for Clancy's pocket, where he could hear the jingle of house keys.

'You better give 'em to him, Clance, or we'll never hear the end of it.'

'What?!' said Clancy. Reluctantly he handed over his keys.

Ruby was trying to radio Blacker, but it wasn't going through. 'Darn it,' she said.

She reached for the fly barrette to call Hitch instead, but it wasn't there.

'I don't believe this!' she said. 'How could I have lost it?'

So instead she typed a message to them both on the Escape Watch:

```
>> URGENT.
HAVE LOCATED LORELEI.
SHE IS AT 479 CONSTANZA, TOP FLOOR.
>> BRING PLENTY OF BACKUP.
>> BE CAREFUL.
```

'Right,' said Ruby, 'we better run or we're gonna miss all the action.'

'Haven't you forgotten something?' said Clancy.

Ruby looked blank. 'What?'

Clancy pointed at the stroller.

'Oh darn it,' she said looking at Archie. 'Where are we gonna park you?'

And that's when fortune struck.

Vapona Begwell was heading towards them, weaving her way through the pedestrians on her brand-new yellow skateboard.

'Hey – Begwell!' shouted Ruby.

Vapona looked around and came to an abrupt halt when she saw who it was.

'Redfort,' she nodded. There was no insult today.

'So remember how you said you owe me one?'

'I remember,' said Vapona.

'And remember how you said you hate owing people?'

'Yeah, what of it?'

'So I got a solution to your problem, a way of clearing your debt.'

'What is it?'

Ruby pointed to the stroller. 'Take care of him for a couple of hours and we're quits.'

'You have to be kidding,' said Vapona.

'I'm afraid this is going to be your only opportunity to make things even, otherwise you'll be forever in my debt,' said Ruby.

Vapona gave Ruby a look – it was the sort of look which said, 'I want to sock you on the nose,' but what she actually said was, 'If you tell anyone that I babysat your little squirt friend here then you better be prepared to run like you never ran before.'

'Relax, Vapona, I know how to keep my mouth shut. Give me your address and I'll pick him up in a while.'

'What's its name anyway?' asked Vapona looking into the stroller.

'Archie,' said Ruby, 'and a word of warning: he likes to chew things.'

While Vapona was scribbling her home details on a piece of paper, Clancy was looking at the traffic, which due to the torrential rain was pretty much gridlocked.

Clancy looked at Vapona's board and said, 'Oh and we need your skateboard.'

'What?' said Vapona.

Clancy shrugged. 'Well, it's not like *you* can use it.'

'Good thinking Clance,' said Ruby. 'We definitely need the board.'

Vapona gave him a very hard stare before handing it over.

'Anything happens to it, Crew, and you're dead meat.'

And off she went with Archie.

'You know Clance, you can be quite the genius when you want to be.'

'I know,' said Clancy.

Chapter 58.
A total phoney

NEITHER OF THEM EXPECTED TO ARRIVE AT 479 CONSTANZA AS QUICKLY AS THEY DID. They zigzagged through the stationary traffic and cut across the park, down back streets and side streets, until they reached the Village. They stashed the skateboards behind a pretentious little lemon tree to the side of the door and snuck into the building while the doorman was busy chatting to an elderly resident. Then, rather than take the elevator, just to be safe they climbed the back stairs.

'What makes you think she lives on the eighth floor?' wheezed Clancy.

'Because that time I saw her, I watched, for the lights to switch on. I was curious, no reason to know – curiosity is what makes for a good spy,' said Ruby.

'Curiosity... can also... make for... a dead spy,' said Clancy, finding it hard to get the words out – seven flights of stairs was a lot of steps. 'How come... you're... not out of... breath?' he asked.

'It's the kung fu training,' said Ruby.

'The what?' said Clancy.

But Ruby wasn't listening; she was looking at her watch.

The fly that circled the dial was flashing red – the signal that meant backup had arrived. 'They're here!' whispered Ruby.

'One would hope!' hissed Clancy.

'You need to stay out of sight in the stairwell... Don't move, and whatever you do, don't come in.'

'Are you sure it's safe?' asked Clancy.

'Are you kidding? Half the Spectrum SWAT team will be there by now... It's probably the *safest* place *to* be.'

'So what am I doing in the stairwell?' complained Clancy.

'Because,' Ruby explained, 'if anyone at Spectrum sees you, they'll know I've been blabbing about classified Spectrum stuff and trouble won't even begin to describe what I'll be in.'

'OK,' said Clancy, 'but be careful, that woman's dangerously unhinged.'

She rolled her eyes. 'Like I need reminding,' she said as she slipped through the door into the hallway.

She tiptoed over to the apartment entrance and listened at the keyhole.

She could hear shouts and orders, and a woman's voice full of fury... Lorelei was not taking this lying down.

Ruby picked the lock – it was easy when you knew how – and, making no sound to announce herself, she pushed her way in.

She saw the purple Dash sneakers lying – one here, one there – in the hall, Sal's coat thrown onto a chair, her sweatshirt strewn on the floor. Ruby followed the trail that led her steadily towards the noise.

These warehouse apartments were huge, rooms leading off rooms, but Ruby just followed the clamour.

The noise became shouts.

'Put your hands on your head!'

The next room, she thought.

'You'll never take *me!*' A woman's voice, angry and sharp.

Ruby's heart quickened, this was a volatile situation, a dangerous situation, let the SWAT team do their thing...

'I repeat, put your hands on your head,' a man ordered.

The door was ajar and there was a flickering light. And all of a sudden – there was gunfire!

Ruby threw herself to the ground, hardly daring to breathe... until she realised she was also hearing sirens and screeching tyres and slamming car doors...

All coming from the room.

She got to her feet and peered through the doorway to see a completely empty room, lit only by a TV screen. The voices of arresting officers and resisting criminals had become the soothing voice of a woman.

'LET YOUR BABY KNOW JUST HOW MUCH HE MEANS TO YOU BY FEEDING HIM BABY YUM-YUMS, DELICIOUS FOOD FOR THE LITTLE GUYS IN YOUR LIFE. BABY YUM-YUMS, NO SALT, NO ADDED SUGAR, JUST THE NATURAL FLAVOUR OF PURE GOODNESS.'

Ruby slowly pushed at the door and stepped into the room.

The commercial playing now was for deodorant and Ruby for one was beginning to sweat.

She could see very little so she stepped like someone trying to avoid imaginary snakes. Slowly, slowly, across the floor towards another doorway.

And then she screamed.

Something grabbed her ankle.

Lorelei laughed.

She was crouching low on the floor like she was ready to spring. 'How nice of you to visit, bubblegum girl. I wasn't in the least expecting you.' Her voice became conspiratorial. 'Did your little friend tip you off?'

Ruby twisted her foot free and stepped back and Lorelei sank down onto the floor and laughed some more.

She looked strange, caught as she was between two faces, half Sal, half Lorelei. The amazing mask, a work of art in its way, was only partially removed, the mouth was Sal's, but the eyes belonged to Lorelei.

'Must take a lot of work being someone else,' said Ruby.

'I'm very dedicated,' Lorelei replied.

'So how do you do it?' asked Ruby.

Lorelei put a finger to her lips. 'Trade secret,' she whispered. She stared up at Ruby. 'You know, I enjoyed being you, but I wonder, is it a burden to be Twinford Junior High's most loved?' She frowned, and corrected herself: '*Was it a burden*, I should say, 'cause they all despise you now, don't they? How fickle fans can be, they love you, they hate you. You must be wondering where it all went wrong...'

But what Ruby was wondering was, *where has Hitch got to? Where is the backup? How am I going to get out of here?*

She wasn't going to say any of that to Lorelei though.

'What I am wondering,' said Ruby, 'is why you are wasting your precious villain-time messing with the life of a school kid?'

''Cause it's, like, *super* fun,' said Lorelei, adopting a valley-girl voice. 'All that stuff with Del, that was a total blast. It took a while, but now she *really loathes* you. Clancy, he's a tough nut to crack, I thought the note in the homework would do it, but I was wrong.'

'Clancy isn't fooled so easily,' said Ruby.

Lorelei sighed. 'But I went to so much effort.'

'Yeah but your *Sal* character,' said Ruby, rolling her eyes, 'I mean, please... she's a total phoney.'

Lorelei's eyes flashed fury and she sprang to her feet, her face contorted into an ugly snarl.

'Oh, sorry, did I touch a nerve?' said Ruby. 'I just thought she was a little two-dimensional – no street-smart lower-eastside girl would wear purple Dash sneakers and no kid handing out table tennis bats could *afford* them.'

Meanwhile, Clancy was wondering what was taking so long.

Ruby had told him the action would be over in minutes.

He was getting a bad feeling about this. A little voice in his head told him things were not as they should be. A little voice was telling him something was wrong... A little voice... was coming from his jacket pocket – a tiny tinny little voice.

Cautiously he pulled his coat to his ear – yes, a voice – he peered into the pocket half expecting a pixie to jump out.

Get a grip Clance!

He pushed his hand deep inside and felt around until his fingers closed on something small and metal. What he pulled out was Ruby's fly barrette.

For just a moment he looked at it blankly, wondering how it came to be there, and then it came to him – Archie Lemon.

'Ruby, do you read me?'

Clancy held the barrette to his mouth and said, 'Hitch?'

Silence.

'It's Clancy, are you here? Is Blacker with you? The backup? The SWAT team?'

'Where's here?' said Hitch. 'I see your location, but where are you?'

'Lorelei's,' said Clancy. 'The apartment of Lorelei von Leyden. You didn't get the message?'

Hitch told him to stay right where he was and that they were on their way and it would be OK and *I repeat, STAY RIGHT WHERE YOU ARE!* because *that was an order!*

Meanwhile, Ruby and Lorelei were getting better acquainted.

All the time they spoke, they were circling each other, round and round the room, slowly, like two tigers.

'And so what brings you to Twinford?' asked Ruby, never taking her eyes from Lorelei's.

'I felt like catching up with some old faces,' she said, staring right back.

'Would they be business acquaintances?' asked Ruby.

'Curses, no.' Lorelei's voice was sharp. 'I don't work *with* or for anyone, not any more, I'm not really what you would call a "team player".' She shot Ruby a vicious look. 'Not like you, Miss Goody Two-shoes.'

Ruby wasn't feeling much like a team player either. Where *was* her team anyway? 'So whose face were you looking to see?' she asked, pacing two steps left.

'Why yours, of course,' replied Lorelei.

'I'm flattered, and now you have, what do you want?' said Ruby, her feet settling into position below her, ready for the zigzag movements of Yellow Wind-Dragon kung fu, designed to evade an opponent's blows.

'Apart from to see you dead?' said Lorelei.

'You're going to have to join the queue,' said Ruby.

'I hate queuing,' said Lorelei.

'I hear you,' said Ruby. 'Who doesn't?' She moved two steps

right.

'I don't wait in line for anyone. But in any case,' she added, with an evil smile, 'why see you dead when I can see you suffer?'

'And how do you propose to do that?' said Ruby.

And then Lorelei lashed out, and Ruby zigzagged and dodged the blow.

'Is that all you got because I got something else for you.'

'And what's that?' asked Lorelei.

'This!' screamed Ruby and she threw her head backwards and flew into a somersault and kicked Lorelei off her feet and flat on her back.

Surprised, but only for a moment, Lorelei, did not stay down long. She propelled herself up and forward, her hands clawed, tiger-style, her kung fu every bit as rehearsed as Ruby's, the moves flowing every bit as smoothly.

Hitch's words rang in Clancy's ear, but what he asked was impossible. He could not cower in a stairway while Ruby Redfort faced terror all alone.

He crept out of his hiding place and along the hallway, and through the open door. He heard the grunts and thuds and thwacks, cries and curses of this fight of girl versus killer.

The element of surprise was what was needed, so he began to creep through rooms, trying to find an advantage.

Boyd Marshall was a heavy sleeper and he was unnaturally tired, but even he wasn't going to sleep through the battle that had just broken out in the huge living room.

He stumbled to his feet and lurched into the hall... and came face to face with a scrawny-looking boy whose face was most familiar.

'How nice of you to stop by,' he said with a smile.

And he grabbed Clancy by the throat.

The furniture was a casualty of battle – the chairs, the coffee table, the huge TV set, all sticks and broken glass. The fighters barely noticed as the floor crunched beneath their accurate steps.

Lorelei came at Ruby, striking her hard with slicing moves. Ruby countered with a plum flower punch that knocked Lorelei back for a second, but she came forwards again in a flurry of punches, and followed by planting her hand on the floor and executing a tiger tail kick that sent Ruby sprawling backwards across the debris.

'Ready to die, Redfort?'

'Not yet,' she hissed.

Ruby used her legs to propel her back to her feet. Then she ran, striking the wall with both feet, and flipped backwards, high over Lorelei's head.

As she descended, so she kicked, but Lorelei anticipated the move and plucked her downwards, with one powerful arm and Ruby was flat on her back, the breath knocked from her.

Lorelei stood, legs firmly planted and hands on hips, a wicked look of satisfaction playing upon her face.

'I take it you give up?' she asked.

But Ruby had one more move yet to play.

The red band was a tiny detail on her wrist, easy to ignore, but when Ruby stretched out her arm and directed the dragon's mouth at her foe, Lorelei von Leyden's face fell.

The vapour engulfed her.

A blood-curdling scream as the translucent bindings formed.

And in the blink of an eye things were all tied up.

'You're a cheat,' she spat.

'Why lose when you can win?' said Ruby.

'You think this is the end, bubblegum girl?' snarled Lorelei.

'I really couldn't say,' said Ruby. 'I keep hoping I'll never see your face again, and then here you are! And by the way, those bindings get heavier by the minute, give it five and Mr Universe himself will struggle to lift you.'

'I loathe you,' Lorelei snarled.

'And that's the other thing – you'll find your voice goes too.'

'You'll pay with your life,' screamed Lorelei.

'You're not exactly in a great position to make threats.'

Lorelei paused. 'Oh I wouldn't say that,' she said, her voice suddenly much calmer.

'You think you're not going back to that cosy little cell of yours?' said Ruby.

'Maybe, and maybe not,' said Lorelei. She was really smiling now, and Ruby noticed how Lorelei's gaze was not directed at her but at some point beyond.

Slowly Ruby turned so she could see what Lorelei was seeing.

Chapter 59.
All the aces

'OH HI, BABY FACE,' said Ruby, 'not dead yet I see.'

Baby Face Marshall smiled his cute smile.

'You looking for a fight?' said Ruby. She was ready. If he was, though, he would probably kill her.

But he surprised her.

'I'm here to offer you a deal.'

'From where I'm standing, you don't look like you have many cards to play.'

Boyd Marshall cocked his head. 'Funny, 'cause I reckon I have all the aces here.'

'Yeah?'

He nodded. 'I think so, unless of course I judged you wrong and your head rules your heart, but somehow I don't think that's you. No, I think little Ruby is a soft touch.' He was smiling again. 'I think you're going to let this nice lady go on her way.'

'Are you her protector, or is it the other way around?'

'A little of both,' said Marshall.

'How cosy,' said Ruby.

'So I think you're going to do what I ask,' he said.

'Oh, and why's that?' said Ruby.

'Because if you don't then you're never going to get the chance to say bye-bye to your little pal.' Marshall made a sad face. 'He's so loyal, isn't he?'

Ruby's expression became puzzlement. 'You're bluffing.'

'Bluffing is for people who don't hold all the cards.' He crooked his finger and beckoned her into a room and she followed, already knowing what she would find...

In the gloom she could see the figure of a boy, lying crumpled on the floor.

She gasped.

'How touching,' said Baby Face.

She could see Clancy's arm, see two scarlet red drops, blood beading on his skin, the width of snake teeth apart.

'Looks like something got him, doesn't it?' said Baby Face. 'Something like some kind of snake maybe. I wonder how long he's got?'

Chapter 60.
Australian trouble

LOOKING DOWN AT CLANCY'S PAINED FACE THE ANSWER SEEMED CLEAR. Not long, not long at all.

He read her expression. 'No, not long,' he said. He seemed to be fading.

Ruby felt utterly defeated.

'What do you want?' she asked Baby Face.

'What would you say if I told you we had a way out of this little cul-de-sac we find ourselves in?' said Baby Face Marshall. 'To be or cease to be? That is the question?' He held a little brown bottle in front of Ruby's eyes. 'The antivenom or no antivenom? You decide, but if you want to save a life? I'll need something in exchange.'

Clancy shook his head. 'Don't Rube, don't.' His voice was weak.

Slowly, very slowly Ruby nodded her head. 'What do you want me to do?' she asked.

'Release Lorelei from those bonds and I'll give you this little brown bottle,' said Baby Face.

Ruby shook her head. 'I'll release Lorelei when you hand me the antivenom.'

'OK, I see you have trust issues, so let's compromise,' he said, placing the small brown bottle on the table. 'I'll leave this here while you do what you need to do.' He paused. 'Wait a minute, what's this?' And he smiled as he drew out another bottle, and another, from his pocket until there were three. Three identical little brown bottles.

'I can't for the life of me remember which is which.' He smiled the cutest smile. 'Choices choices, but you're a smart girl, you figure it out.'

She moved towards the table, but Boyd Marshall put out an arm. 'Release Lorelei or I'll snap your neck in two.'

There was no time to fight it out and, even if there had been, she had little fight left in her, so she did as he ordered and walked to the room where Lorelei lay trussed in leaden ropes. As she passed the huge window, she glanced out, hoping to goodness she might see Hitch and his faithful SWAT team – but no.

Instead what she saw was a whole lot more trouble for all of them. For not so far away, walking purposefully along Constanza, was the woman she feared even more than Lorelei.

'Looks like you've got trouble of your own sweetie,' said Ruby. 'Australian trouble.'

Marshall followed her gaze and his face turned grey. 'Step it up!' he screamed. 'Or you and your friend die now!'

Ruby, who also had no desire to bump into this cold-blooded

killer, did just that. She ran over to Lorelei whose expression had morphed from one of rage to one of terror. It was clear Ms von Leyden wanted to get out of there as fast as anyone. Ruby released her with the reverse vapour action, spraying the strange mist over her until the bonds had dissolved.

'Her limbs will take a while to regain feeling, so looks like you'll be carrying her out,' said Ruby, 'though on the upside, she'll be mute for a lot longer.'

But Boyd Marshall wasn't listening – he already had Lorelei's slight body slumped in his arms and he was losing no time in making his exit.

Ruby ran to the room where Clancy lay.

Chapter 61.
Give me a break

'HOW ARE YOU DOING, CLANCY?'

'Ah, you know Rube, I'm not gonna make it to swim club.'

'Big deal,' said Ruby, 'you were never gonna go anyway.'

'No fooling you huh?'

'You know me Clance, I'm foolproof. Tell me you saw the snake that bit you?'

Clancy slowly shook his head.

All the while she was talking, she was checking his breathing, looking into his eyes, examining his arm, pulling his jacket from him, trying to see what could be done.

She looked at the bottles, picked up the first and turned it in her hand. Then the second. Then the third. Though the bottles were identical, each bottle's label was patterned like snakeskin, and each pattern was different. Ruby knew them all.

One was a king cobra. One was a black mamba. And the other was a Russell's viper.

So which one had bitten Clancy? She thought quickly, pulling up the symptoms of each snake's bite in her mind, running through the different types of venom and their different effects: neurotoxins, haemotoxins, crototoxins, cardiotoxins...

'Are you feeling dizzy?' she asked.

'What?'

'Are you feeling dizzy?'

'What do you think?' whispered Clancy. 'I've just been bitten by a reptile.'

She put her fingers on his wrist, felt his heart rate. Steady. So it wasn't a cardiotoxin, which meant she could rule out the black mamba. No real surprise, since if Clancy had had the misfortune to be bitten by a black mamba, he would most probably be dead already.

Focus Ruby, focus.

'OK Clance, I need to check you for swelling.' She felt his ankles, his wrists, his arms, examined his skin, looking for bruising. 'Are you paralysed anywhere?' If it was a Russell's viper that had bitten Clancy, then his system would be full of hemotoxin, making his blood clot, cutting off circulation to his extremities.

'I don't know! How would I know?'

'So move your hands and your feet.'

He did; no problem there.

'You're *drooling*,' she said.

'I'm dying here Rube, give me a break, would you?'

'No, I mean you're drooling, as opposed to puking, which means the venom in your bloodstream is most likely a neurotoxin, causing numbness and paralysis, and of the three snakes depicted on the bottles, only the king cobra fits your symptoms. It blocks receptors in your brain, that's why you're dribbling all over the place.'

'Sorry,' said Clancy.

She took the stopper from the bottle, filled the syringe with king cobra antivenom and lost not a second injecting it into Clancy's arm.

'I hope I'm right about this,' she said.

'You're not the only one,' said Clancy.

There was a pause.

Then: 'Clance, don't hate me,' said Ruby.

'Why would I hate you?' whispered Clancy.

'Because you have to stand up.'

'I hate you,' moaned Clancy.

'It's just I think we gotta get out of here.'

'I like lying down,' said Clancy, 'and I like this floor.'

'I know,' said Ruby, 'but if I told you that the Australian woman is walking towards the building what would you say?'

'I'd say let's take the stairs.'

Ruby grabbed him around the waist and hoisted him up over her shoulder, much like a firefighter might carry a person from a burning building, and began tottering towards the door.

'Have you... been eating... spinach or something?' croaked Clancy.

'I told you, it's the kung fu.'

They had not got far before they heard a shout.

'Ruby, you in there?'

It was Hitch, and following hot on his heels a SWAT team, all trampling down the stairs from the roof, weapons at the ready.

Hitch looked relieved when he heard her call out to him, but less so when he saw Clancy's frail body.

She explained about the antivenom and Hitch explained that, fearing the worst (although he was expecting the worst to be an injured Ruby as opposed to a poisoned Clancy), he had a paramedic team waiting outside.

Soon they were on the sidewalk and Clancy was in an ambulance. There was no sign of the Australian woman, nor of Lorelei or Baby Face. It was as if they had melted into the night.

In the blink of an eye and a flash of blue and red lights, Clancy was driven at great speed to the St Angelina Hospital.

Ruby made a call to Mr and Mrs Crew to let them know that their son *would be* OK and that he was doing just fine but that he had stepped on a nest of vipers while walking across some wasteland. *'There's a lot of it going around,'* she said.

Hitch had Ruby checked out too for good measure, but apart from an unpleasant bruise round the eye and a cut to her arm she was just fine.

'What took you so long anyway?' demanded Ruby.

'What do you mean, what took me? I arrived in ten minutes flat, which considering the traffic is pretty remarkable.'

'You didn't *have* any *traffic*,' said Ruby, angrily, 'you came by *helicopter*, and by the way I radioed for assistance more than *forty* minutes back.'

'Well, that seems unlikely since we *got* no call.' They were almost shouting at each other now.

'Well perhaps you should blame this *dumb spy watch* Spectrum is so proud of,' said Ruby, pulling it from her wrist, 'BECAUSE IT DOESN'T WORK!' she slapped it in his hand.

He didn't look too happy about it.

'What is this?' he said holding it by its strap. He was referring to the drool that was dribbling out of the watch.

Ruby fell silent.

'In your own time,' said Hitch.

'That's dribble,' she said. 'It's from a baby.'

Hitch raised an eyebrow.

'I was babysitting Archie Lemon. He... likes to suck on the watch.'

'You let a *baby* suck a piece of highly sophisticated Spectrum equipment?'

'Talking of which,' said Ruby, 'we really need to go fetch the Lemon, I promised to have him home by seven.'

Chapter 62.
Beep

VAPONA WAS SURPRISED WHEN SHE OPENED THE DOOR to see a battered-looking Ruby, her clothes a little torn, her left cheek and eye swollen and her hair a tangled mess.

'Boy, Redfort, what happened to you during the past couple of hours?'

'We were skateboarding,' said Ruby.

'You're obviously not doing it right,' said Vapona.

'Also, we got into a fight with some snakes.'

Vapona looked impressed.

'Cool,' she said.

The skateboard was swapped for the baby, and Hitch and Ruby drove back to Cedarwood Drive.

Ruby zipped her parker hood tight to prevent Mrs Lemon from seeing the state of her face – a freaked out Elaine Lemon was more than she could handle right now. Then she deposited the Lemon and returned home.

Mrs Digby was in the kitchen and when Ruby walked in she simply shook her head and said, 'I won't even ask.'

'Just as well,' said Ruby, 'because it's a long story and I could use a bath.'

'You won't get any argument from me,' said the housekeeper.

Ruby climbed the stairs to her room and while she waited for the tub to fill she began easing off her battered sneakers and tattered clothing.

The light on her answerphone was blinking like crazy.

Every single message was from Del and every single one started the same way.

'Rube, it's Del, I made a mistake, a huge mistake, I'm super sorry, I got things all up the wrong way and I guess you hate me now but please don't because I know you're one in a million.'

Beep.

'Ruby, I figured it out, the person who set you up was Dakota Lyme, she's mean enough to do it, plus she kinda looks like you, only not cool and she's super unattractive – I can't prove it, of course, but I told the principal how it wasn't you, so you're off the hook.

Beep.

'Rube, I even confessed to the whole homework scandal, I told Levine that I had written the note because I was mad at you, he believed me right off the bat, means a lot of detentions but I don't mind about that.'

Beep.

'Rube, I 100% admit I was a total duh, look I'll let you have my new sneakers, you can have my bike too if you want.'

Beep.

'Look Rube, I got a big mouth and a short temper and sometimes I wonder if I even have a brain.'

Beep.

The messages got shorter and shorter as they went, until finally:

'Rube, I'm sorry, please call, even if you hate me.'

Beep beep beep.

She would have liked to have called Del there and then so she could tell her not to sweat it, but at this exact instant all she wanted to do was climb into a nice warm tub and stay there a while.

Chapter 63.
It's cryptic

RUBY WAS ON HER WAY UP TO CLANCY'S HOSPITAL ROOM.
She had slept long and late, and by the time she woke, the day
was already the afternoon.

Flustered, she had quickly pulled on her clothes – no time to
eat breakfast; she had promised to be with him just as soon as
she could. She'd cast around for some kind of get-well gift, had
grabbed a carton of banana milk, which she'd tied to a bouquet
of peach-coloured roses (roses she had taken from her mother's
dressing table, but she guessed her mom would understand). The
note attached said:

```
Crew wake up and smell the banana milk.
```

Then she had run all the way to the Greenstreet subway.

Having finally arrived at St Angelina's, she stepped into
the large hospital elevator to join an assortment of other people
on their way to wish loved ones well. The doors closed and the
elevator began travelling upwards. Ruby's finger hovered over

the buttons... she couldn't remember which floor, was it fourth or fifth?

Clancy had been moved from intensive care, but where had they taken him? Well, happily not to the LLG – the lower-lower-ground floor level – because that was the morgue. She shivered, for had it not been for her careful study of deadly snakes then the morgue was where Clancy Crew might certainly have wound up. The lower-lower-ground floor was the place to avoid – a place for the dead, for crypts and catacombs.

Crypts.

Catacombs.

And just like that it struck her.

What if the location she and Blacker had been looking for was *under the ground*?

What if she was actually trying to find a building that was no longer there?

Or at least a building that one could no longer see...

She thought about the map of old Twinford her father had found for Mrs Digby, now framed and up on the housekeeper's wall. Ruby remembered her words... *'Seems every day now they go knocking an old building down, or running a road through it... If it weren't for the place names, you wouldn't have a blind clue what used to be there.'*

She thought about the slogan on the back of the Taste Twister labels. FOUR GREAT TASTES SINCE 1922. The **four** had been significant – a 4-dimensional cube was used to encode the locations. The **tastes** had been significant – that was how the coordinates were communicated.

So why shouldn't the **1922** be important too?

She remembered on her community service duty lifting up that tyre and discovering the plaque to mark the site of the old law courts.

She thought of the road running under the subway line, the vacant lot just next to the intersection, the lot that had become a trash heap... She and Blacker had concluded there was nothing there. But what if they hadn't looked hard enough? What if they had needed to dig?

What if we were looking at the wrong map? thought Ruby.

'Which floor?'

Ruby looked up at the woman, and was pulled out of her thoughts.

'Getting out,' she said, as she dodged through the closing doors. She needed to get home fast. She grabbed a passing nurse.

'Excuse me,' she asked, 'would you be able to give this to Clancy Crew? He's the kid recovering from the snake bite.'

'We have several boys recovering from snake bites,' said the nurse. 'There's an epidemic in Twinford.'

'Is that so?' said Ruby. 'Well, this kid has an ambassador for a dad, and if you'll pardon me for saying it, this dad likes everyone to know it.'

The nurse gave her a look of weary recognition. 'Sure, I know the one.' She took Ruby's gift. 'Who shall I say it's from?'

'He'll know,' said Ruby, 'just tell him I had to be somewhere, but I'll be back before you can say "painkillers".'

Ruby arrived home to find the house empty – even Bug was absent. There was an envelope lying on the kitchen table and inside it was the watch. The note that came with it simply said:

Fixed. P.S. keep clear of dribbling infants.

She ran down to Mrs Digby's apartment, half expecting to find the old lady sitting on the settee watching one of her early evening shows, but the apartment was quiet.

But no matter, it was the map she wanted to see. It was freshly framed and newly fixed to the kitchenette wall just by the table. Ruby stood right up close and searched for the spot where Numeral Street crossed Pythagoras, and there she saw no vacant lot, no elevated subway line but instead the Sacred Heart Cathedral. Where the trash was now piled was where the church steps had once been.

Bingo.

So the cathedral had been knocked down when they extended the subway line, which was maybe in the late 1940s or early 50s... anyway, it was gone. It had been razed to the ground...

Or at least, thought Ruby, *from the ground's surface*.

She sprinted back upstairs to her father's study and located a book on Twinford history. She flipped through the pages looking for a photograph of anything that looked like a church, and after a few minutes, there it was. Sacred Heart Cathedral. Spanish revival style. Sure enough, it had been demolished in 1947 to make way for the elevated subway.

She glanced through the few paragraphs of text until something caught her eye:

'The cathedral was one of the few in America to possess an underground crypt in the medieval European style, where important Twinfordites were often buried in the early decades of the town's history. Notable residents interred here included...'

It went on, but nothing more that was relevant. *Still*, thought Ruby, *what if the crypt remains? What if they only destroyed the part* above *the ground?*

Those important Twinfordites might very possibly still be there. The crypt would be a good reason for not running a subway tunnel underground – it would have disturbed the dead. Instead the elevated track swooped over the roads, the roads beneath burying the crypt below.

Ruby pressed the radio transmitter on the watch, hoping for Blacker to pick up.

He didn't, either his transmitter was off or he was busy. Ruby's finger hovered over the emergency button, but she remembered how Holbrook had been scolded by Delaware for being a bit trigger happy with the emergency button and immediately thought better of it. *Don't use the emergency button unless there is a life-or-death situation in progress.*

So instead she called through to reception.

'Agent Redfort, convey your message,' said Buzz.

'I'm trying to contact Blacker, his transmitter is off,' said Ruby.

'He's in a briefing,' she said.

'It's important,' said Ruby.

'He's in a briefing,' repeated Buzz.

'It's urgent,' said Ruby.

'Please hold the line, I'll phone through to the briefing room,' said Buzz.

No more than fifteen seconds later and: 'I have Agent Blacker for you.'

BLACKER: *Is there a problem Ruby?*

Ruby could hear voices in the background; LB she thought, maybe Hitch.

RUBY: *Am I interrupting?*

BLACKER: *It's OK, how can I help?*

RUBY: *I think I have figured it out.*

BLACKER: *You have?*

RUBY: *It's exactly where we thought it was, only impossible to see.*

BLACKER: *How's that?*

RUBY: *It has to do with 1922.*

BLACKER: *Meaning?*

RUBY: *It's cryptic – that's a joke by the way.*

BLACKER: *I'm not sure I'm with you.*

RUBY: *You'll need an old map of Twinford... do you want me to explain over the airwaves?*

BLACKER: *No, come in to HQ.*

RUBY: *OK, I'll be in as soon as.*

Pause.

RUBY: *Do you mind if I grab a snack first? I'm actually starving.*

BLACKER: *Sure, take your time, I'll be in the coding room.*

RUBY: *I won't be long.*

Ruby felt better having spoken to Blacker. She poured herself a glass of banana milk, dropped some bread in the toaster and thought about what it was they might be about to discover.

When she heard the ping of the toaster, she reached around grabbed the toast and very nearly missed what it was trying to tell her.

```
Change of plan
Meet me at the
Sacred Heart Crypt
P.S. I got the joke!
```

She was surprised but happily so: this was a sign that things were looking up for her and her career at Spectrum. She was a trusted member of the team. In the past, Spectrum had gone out of their way to ensure she was kept out of the action (mostly unsuccessfully). She grabbed her raincoat and the map with the location area outlined in red, not that she needed a map, she knew exactly where she was going. She checked that her watch was on her wrist, even though she knew it was; she checked her hair for the fly barrette – she was taking no chances this time – and then she headed on out into the rain.

She took the subway downtown, changing at Acacia Park onto the College Town line and travelling on to Cathedral Avenue. She had never before considered why this station might be named 'Cathedral', but now of course she knew.

She took the steep steps down from the station to the sidewalk and then walked towards the section of busy road that crisscrossed underneath the elevated tracks. There, just to the left, was a paved area where the steps to the cathedral had once been – the traffic was heavy, it being late rush hour now, and it took a minute to get there. When she reached it there was still very little to see, just a whole lot of trash, mounded up, leaves blown in and trapped there, spinning in the wind. She set about lifting the garbage, searching under it until, beneath a Dime a Dozen shopping cart, was revealed a grate about the size of a very small door, and next to it a tarnished and grimy plaque which read: SITE OF THE SACRED HEART CATHEDRAL.

There was no sign of Blacker so she tried him via the watch, but the signal came back blocked.

So she continued to wait. The traffic was beginning to ease, rush hour almost over, she looked at her watch again. *Where are you Blacker?*

She had been there an hour now. What should she do? Continue to wait? She looked at the grate and bent down to see if it was secured. It had a padlock but when she held it in her hand it fell apart.

That was strange.

She looked at her watch and remembered the message her colleague had sent.

Meet me at the Sacred Heart Crypt

The penny dropped.

Ruby, you bozo, he's down there already!

She heaved the grate up, looked around her, saw no sign of anyone lurking in the shadows, could feel no eyes on her, no one watching, so she ducked down into the dark, pulling the grate closed after her.

She shivered. Not because it was cold, though it was. She shivered because although when she looked up through the bars she could still see light, she was aware that beyond her there would be nothing but black.

She steadied herself, calming her breathing, then stared ahead into the pitch darkness. Her worst fear in reality was *not* being ostracised by all her friends and fellow pupils as she had claimed to Hitch. It was in fact a fear of being trapped and lost in the darkness of what lay underground.

To be buried alive was Ruby's worst fear.

She called out Blacker's name, her voice a dull echo in the dank chamber.

No one was down here – well, no one except for the long-dead, and she wasn't a bit scared of them.

But where was Blacker?

Where Blacker was, was back in the coding room waiting for Ruby.

He'd told her to take her time but still, I mean, how long did it take to grab a snack?

He kept looking at his wrist but he'd mislaid his watch somewhere between here and the canteen. He'd put an announcement out, but so far no one had handed it in. He looked at the huge map of Twinford displayed on the light-board and the notes taped next to it.

The Little Seven Grocers, the Bodice Ripper movie museum, the music school, and... the fourth one had slipped from the wall, it was lying on top of Ruby's book, *Pick Your Poison*, with the big red apple shiny on the cover. He took the note in his hand and looked up at the wall clock.

Rube, he thought, *you're a great kid, but do you ever look at a watch?*

Ruby crept through the passageways, past unseen marble plaques carved with the names of the dead.

As she wound her way through, so the passageways widened,

the arched ceilings became higher, and soon she thought she could see light.

She had almost reached what she assumed must be the centre, the main part of the crypt where all the passageways met and the great and good of Twinford would be lying in their solid stone tombs. The light she could see came from beyond one of the arches and, curious, she walked towards it.

Blacker was flicking through the book. He stopped when he arrived at the well-thumbed chapter on transdermal poisoning, then he leafed past the frogs and the plants until he reached the bride's dress. *Smart of Ruby to have figured that out,* he thought. He turned the page, to an illustration of Snow White.

'A fairy tale in which three objects are laced with poison in order that they might kill a young girl,' said the text underneath the illustration.

'A comb, a bodice, an apple.'

There was a second illustration of the wicked queen looking into her magic mirror, her face aghast as Snow White's reflection stared back at her. The text underneath read, *'Mirror, mirror, on the wall, who's the fairest of them all?'*

He paused.

The fourth note was in his hand, written on it were the words:

```
The Twinford Mirror building...
```

He looked to the wall:

The Little Seven Grocers, the Bodice Ripper
        movie museum, the music school…

Before it was a music school it was a factory, the comb factory. A bodice, a comb, a mirror and the Little Seven… like the seven dwarves… was it just a coincidence?

His eyes flicked back to the book, the illustration of Snow White with her black hair and neat white teeth. She looked a lot like the kid on the Taste Twister bottle, who looked a little bit like another kid he knew.

His heart was beginning to quicken – what had she said, something about 1922, some joke about it being cryptic? How what they had been looking for had been there *all the time*. He picked up the phone and dialled through to the records department.

'Agent Blacker here, I wonder if you could look something up for me. Back in 1922, before the elevated subway was built, what building stood on the Numeral Street–Pythagoras intersection?'

He waited while the researcher went off to find the answer. It didn't take long.

'The Sacred Heart Cathedral,' was her reply.

'And did this Cathedral have a crypt?' asked Blacker.

'Yes,' said the woman, 'and the crypt remains. The entrance

is beneath the vacant lot. Anything else you need?'

He thanked her and ended the call. He tried putting a message through to Ruby's transmitter, but she wasn't picking up. He sent her an URGENT GET IN TOUCH IMMEDIATELY symbol, but she did not respond. So without further hesitation, he grabbed his weapon, and ran up to the atrium and on out of the building.

Chapter 64.
One bad apple

THERE WAS AN APPLE SITTING ON THE STONE TOMB IN THE CENTRE OF THE CRYPT. A perfect, rosy-red apple. Ruby walked over to where it sat. *What is it doing here?* she wondered. *Is it even real?* She picked it up – it was real all right. So how did it come to be down here in this long-locked space? More importantly, *who* had brought it here?

The sound of footsteps.

'Blacker?' she called.

The tap tap of shoes continued, and a faint whistling and then a voice, a soft rich voice.

'Mirror, mirror, on the wall, who must hate you worst of all?'

She felt the tiny hairs rise on the back of her neck.

He laughed as he appeared from the shadows, elegant in a suit and Italian shoes, as always. 'It's a riddle, my dear Snow White.'

Still she could not speak.

'You have been following my clues, no?' he asked. 'And all

the time wondering, *what do they mean? Where could they lead?* Tick, tick, tick, tick in that little head of yours until finally you figured it out.' He waved his arm with a flourish. 'And here you are.'

Ruby slowly surveyed the scene: she was in a crypt with a madman; she could see nothing else.

'All the clues were just there to lead us to you?' she asked.

'To lead *you* to me, dear Ms Redfort,' said the Count. This small but important correction was not something she wanted to hear. 'I know how you love puzzles, so I designed this one especially for you.' He frowned. 'I thought you would be quicker to solve it, I almost tired of waiting.'

She didn't reply.

He looked at her, his expression full of concern. 'You're wondering what I want with you; it's a reasonable thought given our history. I must confess, you have angered me in the past. How I loathed you when you stole the Jade Buddha from my grasp, snatched back the Sisters' treasure, the invisibility skin and that wolf.' His voice filled with such regret. 'Oh, how I wanted that Blue Alaskan wolf.'

'The stealing of the wolf *was* your doing – I wasn't sure, but...'

'Oh, I was busy with other things, I outsourced help, in retrospect a bad decision, but there we are.'

'But for what?' said Ruby. 'So much effort for what...? Just *things.*'

'Yes, I collect *things*,' said the Count coldly. 'Trinkets, souvenirs. Have you never been to Hawaii or Disneyland and felt you wanted to mark the occasion by bringing back a little something for yourself?'

'An eighth-century Jade Buddha counts as a little something?' said Ruby. 'I usually find a keyring or a pin badge does the trick.'

He waved his hand in a dismissive gesture. 'It's all the same, just there to remind you of your holiday fun or, in my case, a job well done.'

A job well done... did that mean she was right? That all along these cases had been about something else? Not the jade, or the gems, the wolf or the invisibility skin, but something much bigger and much less obvious... Something the Count had been... *hired* for?

'I see that little brain of yours whirring. You almost have it, don't you Ms Redfort?'

'There's someone else...' she said. 'Someone you work for... and they have a plan?'

'Bravo.' He clapped his hands.

'And the snake woman... that was part of the plan? To kill Amarjargel Oidov?'

'Yes. My employer needed her out of the way. So I made arrangements.'

She nodded. 'So it *was* you who ordered Baby Face to murder her?'

'Oh yes, poor Mr Marshall, blundering idiot, may he rest in pieces.'

'He's dead?' said Ruby.

'My associate caught up with him.'

'The Australian?' whispered Ruby, like her name was too much to say.

He looked amused. 'Oh, is that what you call her? I must be sure to pass that on. Yes, she's not a forgiving woman, so I'm afraid Mr Marshall... well, I won't spell it out.'

'And Lorelei von Leyden?'

He sighed. 'Dear meddling Lorelei. I'm afraid she's quite out of control. I hear she tried to kill you and that little friend of yours. She's not a forgiver and I'm sorry to say once you've crossed her she'll never give up.' He shook his head sadly. 'If only prison walls could hold her.' He looked at her with interest. 'But enough about what is past. You must be wondering why you're here, right now.'

'You plan to murder me?' said Ruby – she said this as casually as she was able.

'Bravo again.' The Count clapped.

'What I don't understand is, why you went to so much trouble? Why the bottles, the clues, the trail? Why go to such pains to bring me here if you simply plan to...?'

'Because that is what I was hired to do. I needed to make it look like I was making an effort, my employer is... not easily fooled. Besides, I like the fun of it, the drama. Don't you? Life is short, one must take pleasure where one can.'

'Your employer?' said Ruby. 'It isn't *you* who wants me dead?'

'No. Did I not explain? This is all work for me, a job, a task, and one has to earn a living.'

So this was it, her number up, her fate to die alone, her demise witnessed only by the dead.

'But what if,' he began, 'I told you I had changed my mind? That I did not want to undertake this particular... task.'

She swallowed. 'I think I'd have a hard time believing you.'

'But have I ever lied to you in this matter?'

No, the Count had never lied to her about his murderous intent – when he said he intended to kill, he meant it. Just because so far he had been thwarted in his efforts didn't mean his intentions weren't bad – they undoubtedly were.

He had wanted to kill her before, and now he didn't.

He had changed his mind, but why?

'You want me to say,' he said, 'that the world's a better place with you in it?'

'Not really – coming from you, I'm not sure what that would say about me.'

'Well, don't worry, my reasons are far from sentimental –' he stared deep into her eyes – 'I need you, that's the only reason I choose to keep you alive.'

Now that was creepy. A murderous psychopath needed her – for what?

'My employer wants you dead, but I don't think *you* dead is in my best interests – not at this precise moment anyway.'

This was not very reassuring news.

'So I have lured you here, and kept my employer happy thus far. But now I intend to let you go. Not that it will do you much good.'

'Why do you say that?'

He leaned down closer to her. 'It's true what they say,' he said, his voice sympathetic, 'every secret agent's career ends in failure.'

'Do they say that?'

'Probably not, but they should – it's inevitable, isn't it?'

'What is?' said Ruby.

'Failure. You strive to identify the bad apples hidden in a barrel of good ones, but as we all know, good apples can't cure the bad, yet the bad do contaminate the good. Isn't that so? When you return to your little agency, do you really think you will be safe there?'

'You're saying that you have contaminated Spectrum?'

'Oh no, not me, the apple has been there for a long time. Look no further than your own colleagues, Ms Redfort.'

'That's garbage.'

'You're sure about that? Is there not as we speak an investigation to seek out a mole?'

Ruby was silent.

'Is that a little maggot of mistrust eating away at your apple?'

He smiled. 'You see what happens when you linger too long with the bad folk.'

'Who are you working for?'

The Count put his elegant finger to his lips.

'Information is power, Ms Redfort, that is for me to know and you to find out, but don't leave it too long... Just as for the fly caught in a web, the spider will come – so just because your predator is not yet upon you, it doesn't mean your fate is not sealed.'

'So I'll make sure I don't get caught in any webs,' said Ruby.

'Too late dear Ms Redfort, you already are.'

He turned as if to leave, and then: 'One final clue for you, little Ruby, did you ever wonder why Bradley Baker had to die?'

'You told me he was killed in a plane crash.'

'So Ms Redfort, you believe everything you're told?'

'Not when you put it like that,' she said, 'but you said you didn't have anything to do with it.'

'I told you his death was not my undertaking, but an accident? Maybe not. There are many ways for a plane to crash.'

'You're suggesting someone sabotaged his plane?'

'It would seem likely, wouldn't it?' said the Count. 'Though shooting it from the sky would be simpler. Yes, let's say it was shot down. A spy as clever as he has many enemies. But the question is: who pulled the trigger?' Suddenly he plucked the apple from the tombstone and threw it into the air. 'An apple for the teacher,' he called.

She stooped to pick up the fallen fruit, turning it in her hand, and saw that far from being perfect, there was a hole where a maggot had burrowed.

She looked up to face him, to stare deep into those shark-black eyes, to see if she might search out the answer to this complicated game, but he was no longer there.

The debriefing

Ruby was sitting in LB's office. She had told her boss and fellow agents most of what had happened in the crypt of the Sacred Heart, and the mood was sombre.

The Spectrum 8 boss was looking unusually unsettled – talk of Bradley Baker's death had opened an old wound.

LB: *'So we are in no doubt now, the Count is* not *working alone.'*

RUBY: *'No, and whoever he's working for has been working on this plan since this whole case began, seven months back.'*

LB: *'Yet we have no idea what or why?'*

RUBY: *'No.'*

DELAWARE: *'Did the Count give any reason as to why this employer of his might have targeted you?'*

RUBY: *'No.'*

DELAWARE: *'And he gave no reason as to why he then decided not to follow the instructions he had been given?'*

RUBY: *'To kill me you mean?'*

There was no point dancing around the subject: *someone*

wanted her dead.

RUBY: *'He just said it was in his best interests that I live – though he made it kinda clear that this interest in my continuing to breathe would one day wane.'*

DELAWARE: *'But there was no explanation for Amarjargel Oidov's poisoning? What their motivation might be for wanting her dead?'*

RUBY: *'No.'*

HITCH: *'And Lorelei? Where does she fit in?'*

RUBY: *'Nowhere, as far as the higher purpose goes. She used to be on the Count's payroll, was an assassin for hire, but now as far as I can tell, she's gone "rogue".'*

DELAWARE: *'So what is her backstory?'*

RUBY: *'The Australian told me that Lorelei was her kid; they obviously don't have such a great mother–daughter relationship since Lorelei looked like she was going to puke when I mentioned her mom was about to pay a visit. The first time I saw Lorelei she was working for her mom, the second time I saw her she was working for the Count, but she double-crossed them both.'*

DELAWARE: *'So coming back to the Australian – is she working with the Count?'*

Ruby made a face; the expression said, *oh so* now *you all believe she exists?*

LB, who was no slouch in reading faces, read her expression correctly.

LB: *'Stop being a child, Redfort, and answer the question: is the Australian working with the Count?'*

RUBY: *'She and the Count seem pretty cosy, but he seems to call the shots.'*

Ruby was silent for a moment.

RUBY: *'You know she's a dangerous woman?'*

HITCH: *'You don't have to convince me, you should see the state she left Baby Face in – or rather I should say, states.'*

DELAWARE: *'How do you mean? Where is he now?'*

HITCH: *'Well, he left his heart in San Francisco.'*

BLACKER: *'His head was found in Monterrey.'*

HITCH: *'And his legs have yet to show.'*

LB: *'Excuse me?'*

BLACKER: *'He's a goner.'*

LB took a gulp of water.

LB: *'So getting back to the issue in hand, where does this leave us?'*

BLACKER: *'My concern is for Ruby.'*

Ruby gave Blacker an appreciative look.

LB: *'That's very touching Blacker, but my concern is for Spectrum. I'm sorry Redfort, but this is much bigger than you.'*

RUBY: *'That's OK, I won't take it personally.'*

LB: *'You say the toast message came through to you as if from Blacker, yet we know Blacker could never have sent it since he was in a briefing with myself and Hitch.'*

DELAWARE: *'So not only do we know Spectrum has a double agent...'*

HITCH: *'...We now know this agent is feeding information to the Count.'*

His face looked grave.

HITCH: *'It's a great deal worse than we'd first thought.'*

LB: *'I agree. Given the reference made to Baker's death, the premeditated attempt on Redfort's life and the recent security breach, we have to assume that Spectrum has not only been infiltrated in order to leak information out but is also under attack from within.'*

LB looked at them all in turn.

LB: *'And what we need to ask ourselves is, can we survive this?'*

Halloween with a twist

In many ways, Mayor Abraham's Halloween pageant of 1973 was a success – it really put him on the map. He had ignored all meteorologists' advice and insisted that Twinford get this show on the road.

'*Don't let me down Twinford!*' he had rallied on the radio airways. '*Let's make this Halloween a Halloween to remember!*'

And as darkness fell, it looked like the whole city had lined the lantern-lit streets to watch the parade wend its ghoulish way.

The rains had ceased, the winds had stilled. It was a perfect night.

The Redfort household were all there, all except Bug, who had been behaving oddly all day, barking loudly when anyone tried to venture out. At the very last minute before they were all due to leave, he had crawled under Mrs Digby's bed and refused to move. Not even a cut of prime Texan steak was enough to tempt him out, and in the end the family had departed dogless.

Mrs Digby, Sabina and Brant were gathered on the sidewalk

of Twinford Square along with Marjorie and Freddie Humbert, and Elaine and Niles Lemon.

All were eagerly waiting for their children's float to appear.

'I'd so wanted her to go as Snow White,' said Sabina. 'Don't you think she'd make a heavenly Snow White, Marjorie? I mean, I hadn't really pictured her going as a severed head.'

'She'll look cute whatever she's wearing,' said Brant.

'What *she's* wearing is Del Lasco,' said Mrs Digby, 'and that child is no portrait of cute.'

'Kids,' said Marjorie, 'you just gotta love 'em.'

'Is your boy in the pageant?' asked Freddie.

'He is,' said Niles Lemon, loud and proud. 'I wasn't sure he could handle the excitement since the biggest thrill he has ever had is taking the *bus* into town.' He laughed and shook his head. 'He's such a timid kid.'

'Archie really should be tucked up in his crib,' said Elaine, 'but Ruby insisted he would love it. I didn't think it was such a good idea, but I trust her 100%.' She shrugged. 'After all, she was right about the baby food.'

A few blocks away, Ruby and her friends were about to take their places on their Rigors of Mortis Square float. Red Monroe's mother, Sadie, had finished making final adjustments to their costumes and everyone was ready to go.

Red, who was having the best birthday of *her entire actual life* was particularly thrilled with everything, and even the fact that there were three other Rigors of Mortis Square floats didn't tone down her delight.

'*We* got the original costumes,' she said as she hopped from foot to foot in her shiny black Cordelia Rigor tap shoes.

'And we got a real baby,' said Elliot. 'No one else has a *real* Baby Grim.' He glanced at Ruby. 'How did you even get him?'

'Just used my powers of persuasion,' said Ruby.

They all looked down at Archie Lemon.

And he peered back at them from his large Victorian bonnet and gurgled.

'He's kinda cute, *isn't* he?' said Del. 'Especially with that little moustache.'

'Yes,' said Ruby, 'the moustache is an improvement.'

'Thanks for showing up,' said Del, giving Ruby a friendly pinch to her cheek.

'How could I pass up the chance to have my head stuck under your armpit?'

'You know your make-up is super realistic,' said Red. 'How did you achieve such a perfect black eye?'

'I got someone to punch me,' said Ruby.

'You're very dedicated,' said Clancy.

'So are you,' said Mouse, 'I mean, you really got into character.' She was referring to the fact that Clancy was playing the part of Edgar Mortis who tragically died when bitten by a snake.

'What can I say,' said Clancy, 'I'm a method actor.'

'Too bad about Bug,' said Elliot. 'What are we going to do

now we don't have a dog to play Toadstool?'

But that was about to change.

'Hey Ruby, it's me, I'm here.' A ghost was waving at her and it was holding a leash. 'And look, I got Dorothy with me!' Quent Humbert was impossible to recognise, covered as he was in a bedsheet, but his little black pug dog Dorothy was very clearly dressed to play Toadstool.

Ruby found herself giving Quent Humbert, if not a hug exactly, then a head-butt; it wasn't easy to hug when you no longer had a body, and in any case, she probably wouldn't actually have *hugged* Quent. Ruby reserved her hugs for the rare few.

'You know Quent, I have to say, sometimes you're not such a bedsheet.'

'Yeah,' said Clancy, 'and who else could rustle up a levitating pug?'

There was a loud bang and a flurry of fireworks to signal the start of the parade and slowly the float began to move.

The parade had been going for no more than forty minutes when something dramatic happened: the wind suddenly picked up, catching bunting and orange lanterns, pulling them from their fixings and sailing them into the sky. And as the parade rolled on, the gusts grew stronger and pieces of costume were snatched and whirled into the night. It was only when someone shouted 'tornado!' that people began diving for cover.

A funnel of wind appeared and twisted across the skyline. It moved at such speed that there was little time to do much but run this way and that.

Pageant-goers watched from a distance as it tore through West Twinford making matchwood of houses before losing its power and disappearing altogether.

A few houses in the Cedarwood Drive area were victims of the storm and one of these was the Lemons' place, though the only part of their home that had been truly destroyed was the room where Archie Lemon slept.

Had he not been playing the part of Baby Grim, the ghostly infant, at 7.23pm on the 31st of October, then he would have been sucked into the wind funnel and taken high into the dark sky, never to be seen again.

The Lemon was a lucky kid.

From the
Twinford Mirror

BABY GRIM SAVED FROM GRIM END
Last night's tornado could have claimed
a tiny victim. 'Had it not been for our
babysitter, our nine-month-old son would
have been abducted by a twister,' said
thirty-two-year-old mother of one, Elaine
Lemon. She went on to say, 'Ruby is like
his guardian angel. If she had not insisted
on taking him to the Halloween pageant last
night, we would never have seen Archie
again.'

ENDANGERED-SNAKE PROTECTOR OUT OF DANGER
Amarjargel Oidov finally came out of her coma
last night. She has only a sketchy memory
of the events that led to her poisoning and
says she has no light to shed on the question
of why anyone might wish her dead. She has
requested that well-wishers kindly do not
send her flowers.

SNAKE BITE EPIDEMIC

There have been an unusual number of snake-bite incidents in Twinford this past October and herpetologists can only put it down to changing weather patterns. 'Nests of vipers have been turning up here, there and everywhere,' said snake wrangler, Ralf Erwin. 'If you see one, back away,' was his advice. The public has been warned to keep off wasteland after Ambassador Crew's son Clancy (thirteen) suffered a severe bite to his arm.

DOG PREDICTS TORNADO

Ten-year-old Old English Sheepdog, Bessie, saved her owner's life when she prevented him from leaving the house. Seventy-four-year-old Al Budget was planning to drive to the supermarket, but his dog Bessie had other ideas. 'When I picked up my car keys, she started growling at me in this real spooky type of way, and as I approached the door, she tripped me up, took me clean off my feet, then she just plum came and sat on top of me. There was nothing I could do, she's a big dog, weighs about sixty to sixty-five pounds.'

MATHLYMPICS MAYHEM

Mathematics prodigy Dakota Lyme has been requested to partake in anger management classes after she attacked another contestant at the Yuleton Mathlympics quarterfinals. Dakota Lyme became so enraged when she lost out to eleven-year-old Ward Partial that she began hurling protractors, set squares and other geometry-based tools at him. Ward, though shaken, did not sustain any critical injuries.

STOP PRESS: MIRROR READERS PRAISE NEW LOOK

The Twinford Mirror launched its exciting new-look format to rave reviews. 'I've never seen anything like it in Twinford before,' exclaimed one regular reader, adding, 'Come to think of it, it's identical to the *Twinford Echo*.'

Shopping cart

Despite being back in everyone's good books, Ruby Redfort still had one last task to complete. She had requested that her final stint of community service should be spent clearing the trash from the vacant lot where the Sacred Heart Cathedral had once stood.

Sabina for one applauded her daughter's efforts to keep Twinford tidy and thought it might be nice if the Twinford Garden Committee planted some roses. 'Red ones, like hearts,' said Sabina.

Brant Redfort said he would speak to the Twinford Historical Society to see if it might be possible to open the crypt to the public. 'I'm sure Dora Shoering would enjoy taking tour groups down there.'

Mrs Digby said she was happy for the Sacred Heart's dead to be remembered, but there was no way in a month of Sundays that anyone was getting her to visit them.

Ruby shivered at the very thought, but didn't say anything.

It was after she had completed her task, eight and a half

hours later, and was wondering what should be done with the Dime a Dozen shopping cart she had found, that an idea hit her.

She walked it all the way from College Town back to Amster, stopping only to buy a tin of cat food. This done, she continued on her way to Cedarwood Drive. When she reached Mrs Beesman's house, she parked the cart in front of her gate and placed the cat food in the basket. Then she went on home to Green-Wood house, where she was looking forward to taking a long, hot soak in the tub.

The apple

The apple was sitting on Ruby's desk, the bruise deepening and the rot spreading. She looked at it for a long while, wondering what it meant, if indeed it meant anything.

Finally she took her penknife and plunged it deep into the fruit. And a strange thing happened: the knife sliced the apple in two, and out fell a piece of folded white paper.

Taking it up in her hand she opened it and read it.

There was only one word, a name.

She thought about the very last thing the Count had said: *the question is: who pulled the trigger?*

She looked back down at the paper and read the name out loud.

What it said was:

LB.

THINGS I KNOW:
....

The Australian is working for the Count.
The Count is working for someone.
The Count has betrayed this someone.
This someone has a grand plan.
This someone wants to kill me.
Lorelei wants to kill me.
LB killed Bradley Baker.

THINGS I DON'T KNOW:
....

WHY to all of the above.
Where my mom's snake earrings are.

Ruby Redfort.

How to see in four dimensions

by Marcus du Sautoy, supergeek
consultant to Ruby Redfort

Ruby discovers that the key to decoding the Taste Twister code
is the geometry of a 4-dimensional cube. But what on earth is
a 4-dimensional cube? We live in a 3-dimensional universe
– seeing the objects around us in terms of their height, width
and depth – so it's impossible to see something that lives in four
dimensions. Instead we must use some mathematics to conjure
up this shape in our mind.

The key to creating a 4-dimensional cube is the discovery
that you can change geometry into numbers, and numbers into
geometry. For example, every position on the surface of the earth
can be located by two numbers. Ruby uses this fact to find out
that the Taste Twister poster points to the Little Seven Grocers.
She takes the two numbers written on the Taste Twister billboard
and changes these numbers into a location.

Called latitude and longitude, these two numbers are like a
code to locate any place on the earth. For example, the Little Seven
Grocers is located at the position given by the two numbers:

(32.7410, -117.1705)

These are known as the GPS coordinates of this location. The first number tells you how many units north or south you must go from the equator. The second number tells you how many units east or west you should travel from the line of longitude running through Greenwich in London. (From the equator to each pole consists of 90 units, corresponding to the 90 degree angle between the equator, the centre of the earth and each pole.)

So, for example, the coordinates of my college in Oxford, New College, are (51.7542, -1.2520). So you can get to New College by going 51.7542 units north of the equator and 1.2520 steps west. If you want to find out the coordinates of your house then try putting your address into: **http://www.gps-coordinates.net/**

It was the great French mathematician and philosopher René Descartes, born in 1596, who came up with this clever way of changing a geometrical location into numbers. Called Cartesian coordinates, they can be used to plot all kinds of things – not just locations on earth. You can describe any geometric shape using these coordinates. If you take a piece of graph paper with a shape drawn on it then we can change the shape into the numbers that tell us the location of the points making up that shape.

For example, how can I change a square into numbers? What I do is tell you the location of all four corners of the square.

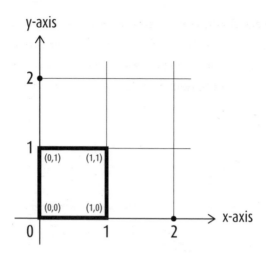

The corners of the 2D square are located at the positions (0,0), (1,0), (0,1) and (1,1). The geometry of the square has been translated into these four pairs of numbers. (When describing shapes using Cartesian coordinates, the first number, called the x-coordinate, tells you how many units to move left or right, the second coordinate, called the y-coordinate, tells you how many units to move up or down. Beware: it is the opposite order to GPS coordinates.)

But we don't just have to stick to using two numbers. Ruby could also have added a third coordinate to the location of the Little Seven Grocers, telling us how high up from sea level the shop is. Using these three coordinates we can then describe the location of any point in our 3-dimensional universe.

We can also use the same idea to change 3D shapes into numbers. If we want to describe a 3-dimensional cube in coordinates, instead of a square, then we can add a third direction which describes the height of the point above the 2-dimensional graph paper.

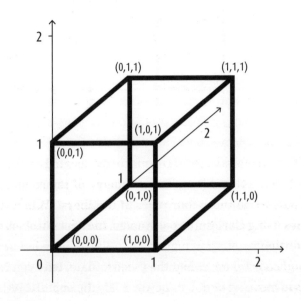

The corners of the 3D cube are located at the positions (0, 0, 0), (1, 0, 0), (0, 1, 0), (0, 0, 1), (1, 1, 0), (1, 0, 1), (0, 1, 1) and finally the point furthest from the first corner, located at (1, 1, 1). So the geometry of the cube has been translated into these eight triples of numbers.

Descartes' idea of changing geometry into coordinates is a bit like a dictionary changing words from English into French. But this dictionary changes shapes into numbers. On the shapes side of the dictionary, we have seen 2D shapes and 3D shapes, but then the dictionary runs out because we can't draw a shape in 4D. But the exciting thing is that the numbers side of the dictionary doesn't run out. It was the great German mathematician Bernhard Riemann, born in 1826, who discovered that you could carry on building shapes out of numbers, even if you couldn't see them.

What Riemann realised is that you could use the numbers to describe what a shape was made of, despite being unable to physically build it. All you needed to do was add more coordinates. So to describe a 4-dimensional object, we just add a fourth coordinate that will keep track of how far we are moving in this new imaginary direction. So although I can never physically build a 4-dimensional cube, by using numbers I can still describe it precisely.

It has 16 vertices, starting at (0,0,0,0), with edges extending to 4 points at (1,0,0,0), (0,1,0,0) , (0,0,1,0) and (0,0,0,1) and then continuing along the edges we hit points at (1,1,0,0), (1,0,1,0), (1,0,0,1), (0,1,1,0), (0,1,0,1), (0,0,1,1), (1,1,1,0), (1,1,0,1), (1,0,1,1), (0,1,1,1) until we reach the farthest point, at (1,1,1,1). This 4D cube is sometimes known as a Tesseract.

The numbers are a code to describe the shape, and we can use this code to explore the shape without ever having to physically see it. So, using the numbers, we can actually work out that, in addition to the 16 corners, this 4D cube has 32 edges, 24 square faces, and is made by putting together 8 cubes.

Sometimes people talk about time being the fourth dimension, but actually these dimensions can be used to keep track of anything. For example, suppose you wanted to keep track of the temperature at every location on the earth. You could use three coordinates to locate the position and the fourth coordinate to tell you the temperature at that point.

In the Taste Twister code, the four different directions keep track of the four different tastes we can detect with our tongues: BITTER, SOUR, SALT, SWEET. Every taste turns into a point located somewhere on this 4-dimensional cube.

Although we can never actually see a 4D cube, there are ways to fake a view, as Ruby showed in her mathlympics competition. For example, the picture I drew of the cube isn't actually a cube. It's a 2D picture of the 3D cube. The great breakthrough by artists like Leonardo da Vinci in the fifteenth century was the idea of perspective – a way to draw 3D shapes on a 2D canvas to give you the illusion of seeing a scene in 3D. So for example, one way to draw a 3D cube on a 2D canvas might be to draw a large square with a smaller square inside, then join up the corners. This gives you the illusion of 'seeing' a 3D cube.

Shadows work the same way. If I took a cube made out of wire and shone a light on the shape, then the 2D shadow I would see on the floor might look like the square inside a square.

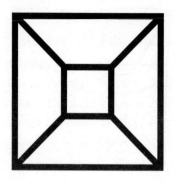

Just as you can paint a 3D shape on a 2D canvas or shine a light on a 3D shape and create a 2D shadow, there is a way to create a shadow or picture of a 4D shape in 3 dimensions. A 3D cube when squashed into 2D became a square inside a square. It turns out that the shadow of a 4D cube in 3 dimensions is a small cube inside a larger cube where there are extra edges inserted to join the points of the large cube to the points of the smaller cube. This is the picture that Ruby draws in the final round of the mathlympics competition.

If you ever go to Paris then you can actually see an example of this 3D shadow of a 4D cube. At La Défense in Paris there is a huge structure called La Grande Arche built by Danish architect Johann Otto von Spreckelsen. It is essentially a large cube with a smaller cube inside with the corners of the cubes joined up. If you visit La Grande Arche and count carefully, you can see the 32 edges that can be described using Descartes' coordinates.

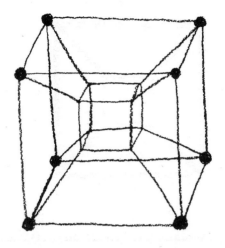

But every shape has many different shadows. If I take my 3D wire cube and I alter the position of the torch, I can get different 2D shadows or perspectives. This is the breakthrough Ruby makes with the mandala shape on the back of the labels on the Taste Twister bottles.

By taking different perspectives on a 4D cube, you can get different 3D viewpoints. (An animation showing these changing shadows of the Tesseract can be seen here: **https://commons. wikipedia.org/wiki/File:8-cell.gif**.) The mandala shape that is the key to decoding the locations of the taste code is arrived at by turning the 4D shape and getting a new perspective. You can actually see the two cubes still in the mandala shape. One is highlighted in the figure overleaf. The other is obtained by shifting this cube down and right.

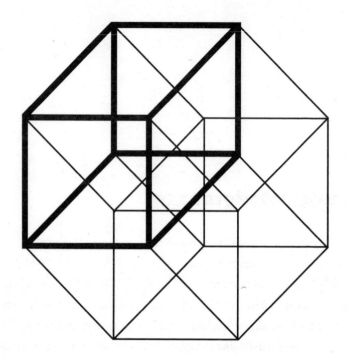

The mandala image is actually a 2D picture of a 3D shape which is itself a shadow of a shape in four dimensions.

And if your brain isn't smoking by now then maybe you could be the next Ruby Redfort or Bernhard Riemann.

Acknowledgments

Without the following three people, I am not sure this book would have been finished before Christmas. Nick Lake, for his superb editing and inspired additions, Lily Morgan, a fabulous copy-editor who knows Twinford like the back of her hand, and David Mackintosh, for his impeccable design taste and perfect illustrations. I would like to thank them for being so generous with their time and so incredibly nice to boot.

Thank you to Marcus du Sautoy for creating not only a sophisticated code, but also one that I can actually understand. Thank you to Derek Landy for taking my call (even though he was mid-deadline), and chatting me through kung fu and aikido, at breakneck speed.

Thank you to AD and TC for their support, Folder for inspired ideas, George for facts, Marcia for creating time, Wendy for trouble-shooting, and Phil for making most things possible.

Special thanks as always to AJM.

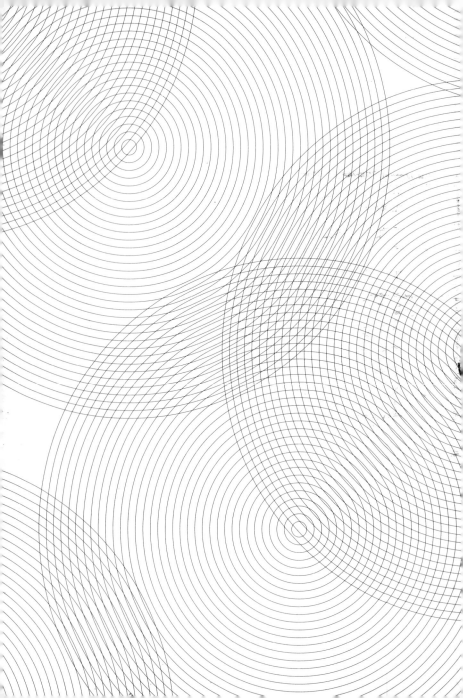